VIRAGO
MODERN CLASSICS

Sarah Waters

Sarah Waters was born in Wales and lives in London. She is the author of five novels. She has won a Betty Trask Award and the Somerset Maugham Award, and *Fingersmith* and *The Night Watch* were both shortlisted for the Orange Prize and the Man Booker Prize. *The Little Stranger*, a *Sunday Times* bestseller, was also shortlisted for the Man Booker Prize. *Affinity, Tipping the Velvet, Fingersmith* and *The Night Watch* have all been adapted for television. Sarah Waters has been named Author of the Year four times: by the British Book Awards, the Booksellers Association, Waterstones and the Stonewall Awards.

By Sarah Waters

Tipping the Velvet
Affinity
Fingersmith
The Night Watch
The Little Stranger

TIPPING THE VELVET

Sarah Waters

VIRAGO

First published by Virago Press in 1998
This hardback edition published in 2012 by Virago Press

Copyright © Sarah Waters 1998

The song 'If I Ever Cease to Love' copyright © IMP

The moral right of the author has been asserted.

A CIP catalogue record for this book
is available from the British Library.

ISBN 978-1-84408-819-5

Printed and bound in Great Britain by
Clays Ltd, St Ives plc

Papers used by Virago are from well-managed forests
and other responsible sources.

MIX
Paper from
responsible sources
FSC
www.fsc.org   FSC® C104740

Virago Press
An imprint of
Little, Brown Book Group
100 Victoria Embankment
London EC4Y 0DY

An Hachette UK Company
www.hachette.co.uk

www.virago.co.uk

PART ONE

Chapter 1

Have you ever tasted a Whitstable oyster? If you have, you will remember it. Some quirk of the Kentish coastline makes Whitstable natives – as they are properly called – the largest and the juiciest, the savouriest yet the subtlest, oysters in the whole of England. Whitstable oysters are, quite rightly, famous. The French, who are known for their sensitive palates, regularly cross the Channel for them; they are shipped, in barrels of ice, to the dining-tables of Hamburg and Berlin. Why, the King himself, I heard, makes special trips to Whitstable with Mrs Keppel, to eat oyster suppers in a private hotel; and as for the old Queen – she dined on a native a day (or so they say) till the day she died.

Did you ever go to Whitstable, and see the oyster-parlours there? My father kept one; I was born in it – do you recall a narrow, weather-boarded house, painted a flaking blue, halfway between the High Street and the harbour? Do you remember the bulging sign that hung above the door, that said that *Astley's Oysters, the Best in Kent* were to be had within? Did you, perhaps, push at that door, and step into the dim, low-ceilinged, fragrant room beyond it? Can you recall the tables with their chequered cloths – the bill of fare chalked on a board – the spirit-lamps, the sweating slabs of butter?

Were you served by a girl with a rosy cheek, and a saucy manner, and curls? That was my sister, Alice. Or was it a man, rather tall and stooping, with a snowy apron falling from the knot in his necktie to the bow in his boots? That was my father. Did you see, as the kitchen door swung to and fro, a lady stand frowning into the clouds of steam that rose from a pan of bubbling oyster soup, or a sizzling gridiron? That was my mother.

And was there at her side a slender, white-faced, unremarkable-looking girl, with the sleeves of her dress rolled up to her elbows, and a lock of lank and colourless hair forever falling into her eye, and her lips continually moving to the words of some street-singer's or music-hall song?

That was me.

Like Molly Malone in the old ballad, I was a fishmonger, because my parents were. They kept the restaurant, and the rooms above it: I was raised an oyster-girl, and steeped in all the flavours of the trade. My first few childish steps I took around vats of sleeping natives and barrels of ice; before I was ever given a piece of chalk and a slate, I was handed an oyster-knife and instructed in its use; while I was still lisping out my alphabet at the schoolmaster's knee, I could name you the contents of an oyster-cook's kitchen – could sample fish with a blindfold on, and tell you their variety. Whitstable was all the world to me, Astley's Parlour my own particular country, oyster-juice my medium. Although I didn't long believe the story told to me by Mother – that they had found me as a baby in an oyster-shell, and a greedy customer had almost eaten me for lunch – for eighteen years I never doubted my own oyster-ish sympathies, never looked far beyond my father's kitchen for occupation, or for love.

It was a curious kind of life, mine, even by Whitstable standards; but it was not a disagreeable or even a terribly hard one. Our working day began at seven, and ended twelve hours later; and through all those hours my duties were the same. While Mother cooked, and Alice and my father served, I sat upon a high stool at the side of a vat of natives, and scrubbed, and rinsed, and plied the oyster-knife. Some people like their oysters raw; and for them your job is easiest, for you have merely to pick out a dozen natives from the barrel, swill the brine from them, and place them, with a piece of parsley or cress, upon a plate. But for those who took their oysters stewed, or fried – or baked, or scalloped, or put in a pie – my labours were more delicate. Then I must open each oyster, and beard it, and transfer it to Mother's cooking-pot with all of its savoury flesh intact, and none of its liquor spilled or tainted. Since a supper-plate will hold a dozen fish; since oyster-teas are cheap; and since our Parlour was a busy one, with room for fifty customers at once – well, you may calculate for yourself the vast numbers of oysters which passed, each day, beneath my prising knife; and you might imagine, too, the redness and the soreness and the sheer salty soddenness of my fingers at the close of every afternoon. Even now, two decades and more since I put aside my oyster-knife and quit my father's kitchen for ever, I feel a ghostly, sympathetic twinge in my wrist and finger-joints at the sight of a fishmonger's barrel, or the sound of an oyster-man's cry; and still, sometimes, I believe I can catch the scent of liquor and brine beneath my thumb-nail, and in the creases of my palm.

I have said that there was nothing in my life, when I was young, but oysters; but that is not quite true. I had friends and cousins, as any girl must have who grows up in a small town in a large, old family. I had my sister Alice – my dearest friend of all – with whom I shared a bedroom and a bed, and who heard all my secrets, and told me all of hers. I even had a kind of beau: a boy named Freddy, who worked a dredging smack beside my brother Davy and my Uncle Joe on Whitstable Bay.

And last of all I had a fondness – you might say, a kind of passion – for the music hall; and more particularly for music-hall songs and the singing of them. If you have visited Whitstable you will know that this was a rather inconvenient passion, for the town has neither music hall nor theatre – only a solitary lamp-post before the Duke of Cumberland Hotel, where minstrel troupes occasionally sing, and the Punch-and-Judy man, in August, sets his booth. But Whitstable is only fifteen minutes away by train from Canterbury; and here there was a music hall – the Canterbury Palace of Varieties – where the shows were three hours long, and the tickets cost sixpence, and the acts were the best to be seen, they said, in all of Kent.

The Palace was a small and, I suspect, a rather shabby theatre; but when I see it in my memories I see it still with my oyster-girl's eyes – I see the mirror-glass which lined the walls, the crimson plush upon the seats, the plaster cupids, painted gold, which swooped above the curtain. Like our oyster-house, it had its own particular scent – the scent, I know now, of music halls everywhere – the scent of wood and grease-paint and spilling beer, of gas and of tobacco and of hair-oil, all combined. It was a scent which as a girl I loved uncritically; later I heard it described, by theatre managers and artistes, as the smell of laughter, the very odour of applause. Later still I came to know it as the essence not of pleasure, but of grief.

That, however, is to get ahead of my story.

I was more intimate than most girls with the colours and scents of the Canterbury Palace – in the period, at least, of which I am thinking, that final summer in my father's house, when I became eighteen – because Alice had a beau who worked there, a boy named Tony Reeves, who got us seats at knock-down prices or for free. Tony was the nephew of the Palace's manager, the celebrated Tricky Reeves, and therefore something of a catch for our Alice. My parents mistrusted him at first, thinking him 'rapid' because he worked in a theatre, and wore cigars behind his ears, and talked glibly of contracts, London and champagne. But no one could dislike Tony for long, he was so large-hearted and easy and good; and like every other boy who courted her, he adored my sister, and was ready to be kind to us all on her account.

Thus it was that Alice and I were so frequently to be found

on a Saturday night, tucking our skirts beneath our seats and
calling out the choruses to the gayest songs, in the best and
most popular shows, at the Canterbury Palace. Like the rest of
the audience, we were discriminating. We had our favourite
turns – artistes we watched and shouted for; songs we begged
to have sung and re-sung again and again until the singer's
throat was dry, and she – for more often than not it was the
lady singers whom Alice and I loved best – could sing no
more, but only smile and curtsey.

And when the show was over, and we had paid our respects
to Tony in his stuffy little office behind the ticket-seller's
booth, we would carry the tunes away with us. We would sing
them on the train to Whitstable – and sometimes others,
returning home from the same show as merry as we, would
sing them with us. We would whisper them into the darkness
as we lay in bed, we would dream our dreams to the beat of
their verses; and we would wake next morning humming them
still. We'd serve a bit of music-hall glamour, then, with our fish
suppers – Alice whistling as she carried platters, and making
the customers smile to hear her; me, perched on my high stool
beside my bowl of brine, singing to the oysters that I scrubbed
and prised and bearded. Mother said I should be on the stage
myself.

When she said it, however, she laughed; and so did I. The
girls I saw in the glow of the footlights, the girls whose songs
I loved to learn and sing, they weren't like me. They were
more like my sister: they had cherry lips, and curls that danced
about their shoulders; they had bosoms that jutted, and elbows
that dimpled, and ankles – when they showed them – as slim
and as shapely as beer-bottles. I was tall, and rather lean. My
chest was flat, my hair dull, my eyes a drab and an uncertain
blue. My complexion, to be sure, was perfectly smooth and
clear, and my teeth were very white; but these – in our family,
at least – were counted unremarkable, for since we all passed
our days in a miasma of simmering brine, we were all as
bleached and blemishless as cuttlefish.

No, girls like Alice were meant to dance upon a gilded stage, skirted in satin, hailed by cupids; and girls like me were made to sit in the gallery, dark and anonymous, and watch them.

Or so, anyway, I thought then.

The routine I have described – the routine of prising and bearding and cooking and serving, and Saturday-night visits to the music hall – is the one that I remember most from my girlhood; but it was, of course, only a winter one. From May to August, when British natives must be left to spawn, the dredging smacks pull down their sails or put to sea in search of other quarry; and oyster-parlours all over England are obliged, in consequence, to change their menus or close their doors. The business that my father did between autumn and spring, though excellent enough, was not so good that he could afford to shut his shop throughout the summer and take a holiday; but, like many Whitstable families whose fortunes depended upon the sea and its bounty, there was a noticeable easing of our labours in the warmer months, a kind of shifting into a slower, looser, gayer key. The restaurant grew less busy. We served crab and plaice and turbot and herrings, rather than oysters, and the filleting was kinder work than the endless scrubbing and shelling of the winter months. We kept our windows raised, and the kitchen door thrown open; we were neither boiled alive by the steam of the cooking-pots nor numbed and frozen by barrels of oyster-ice, as we were in winter, but gently cooled by the breezes, and soothed by the sound of fluttering canvas and ringing pulleys that drifted into our kitchen from Whitstable Bay.

The summer in which I turned eighteen was a warm one, and grew warmer as the weeks advanced. For days at a time Father left the shop for Mother to run, and set up a cockle-and-whelk stall on the beach. Alice and I were free to visit the Canterbury Palace every night if we cared to; but just as no one that July wanted to eat fried fish and lobster soup in our stuffy

Parlour, so the very thought of passing an hour or two in gloves and bonnet, beneath the flaring gasoliers of Tricky Reeves's airless music hall, made us gasp and droop and prickle.

There are more similarities between a fishmonger's trade and a music-hall manager's than you might think. When Father changed his stock to suit his patrons' dulled and over-heated palates, so did Tricky. He paid half of his performers off, and brought in a host of new artistes from the music halls of Chatham, Margate and Dover; most cleverly of all, he secured a one-week contract with a real celebrity, from London: Gully Sutherland – one of the best comic singers in the business, and a guaranteed hall-filler even in the hottest of hot Kentish summers.

Alice and I visited the Palace on the very first night of Gully Sutherland's week. By this time we had an arrangement with the lady in the ticket-booth: we gave her a nod and a smile as we arrived, then sauntered past her window and chose any seat in the hall beyond that we fancied. Usually, this was somewhere in the gallery. I could never understand the attraction of the stalls ticket; it seemed unnatural to me to seat oneself below the stage, and have to peer up at the artistes from a level somewhere near their ankles, through the faint, shimmering haze of heat that rose above the footlights. The circle gave a better view, but the gallery, though further away, to my mind gave the best of all; and there were two seats in the front row, at the very centre of the gallery, that Alice and I particularly favoured. Here you knew yourself to be not just at a show but in a *theatre*: you caught the shape of the stage and the sweep of the seats; and you marvelled to see your neighbours' faces, and to know your own to be like theirs – all queerly lit by the glow of the footlights, and damp at the lip, and with a grin upon it, like that of a demon at some hellish revue.

It was certainly as hot as hell in the Canterbury Palace on Gully Sutherland's opening night – so hot that, when Alice and I leaned over the gallery rail to gaze at the audience below,

we were met by a blast of tobacco- and sweat-scented air, that
made us reel and cough. The theatre, as Tony's uncle had cal-
culated, was almost full; yet it was strangely hushed. People
spoke in murmurs, or not at all. When one looked from the
gallery to the circle and the stalls, one saw only the flap of hats
and programmes. The flapping didn't stop when the orchestra
struck up its few bars of overture and the house lights dimmed;
but it slowed a little, and people sat up rather straighter in
their seats. The hush of fatigue became a silence of expectation.

The Palace was an old-fashioned music hall and, like many
such places in the 1880s, still employed a chairman. This, of
course, was Tricky himself: he sat at a table between the stalls
and the orchestra and introduced the acts, and called for order
if the crowd became too rowdy, and led us in toasts to the
Queen. He had a top hat and a gavel – I have never seen a
chairman without a gavel – and a mug of porter. On his table
stood a candle: this was kept lit for as long as there were
artistes upon the stage, but it was extinguished for the interval,
and at the show's close.

Tricky was a plain-faced man with a very handsome voice –
a voice like the sound of a clarinet, at once liquid and pene-
trating, and lovely to listen to. On the night of Sutherland's
first performance he welcomed us to his show and promised
us an evening's entertainment we would never forget. Had we
lungs? he asked. We must be prepared to use them! Had we
feet, and hands? We must make ready to stamp, and clap! Had
we sides? They would be split! Tears? We would shed buckets
of them! Eyes?

'Stretch 'em, now, in wonder! Orchestra, please. Limes-men,
if you will.' He struck the table with his gavel – *clack!* – so that
the candle-flame dipped. 'I give you the marvellous, the musical, the very, very merry, *Merry*' – he struck the table again –
'Randalls!'

The curtain quivered, then rose. There was a seaside back-
drop to the stage and, upon the boards themselves, real sand;

and over this strolled four gay figures in holiday gear: two ladies – one dark, one fair – with parasols; and two tall gents, one with a ukulele on a strap. They sang 'All the Girls are Lovely by the Seaside', very nicely; then the ukulele player did a solo, and the ladies lifted their skirts for a spot of soft-shoe dancing on the sand. For a first turn, they were good. We cheered them; and Tricky thanked us very graciously for our appreciation.

The next act was a comedian, the next a mentalist – a lady in evening dress and gloves, who stood blindfolded upon the stage while her husband moved among the audience with a slate, inviting people to write numbers and names upon it with a piece of chalk, for her to guess.

'Imagine the number floating through the air in flames of scarlet,' said the man impressively, 'and searing its way into my wife's brain, through her brow.' We frowned and squinted at the stage, and the lady staggered a little, and raised her hands to her temples.

'The Power,' she said, 'it is very strong tonight. Ah, I feel it burning!'

After this there was an acrobatic troupe – three men in spangles who turned somersaults through hoops, and stood on one another's shoulders. At the climax of their act they formed a kind of human loop, and rolled about the stage to a tune from the orchestra. We clapped at that; but it was too hot for acrobatics, and there was a general shuffling and whispering throughout this act, as boys were sent with orders to the bar, and returned with bottles and glasses and mugs that had to be handed, noisily, down the rows, past heads and laps and grasping fingers. I glanced at Alice: she had removed her hat and was fanning herself with it, and her cheeks were very red. I pushed my own little bonnet to the back of my head, leaned upon the rail before me with my chin upon my knuckles, and closed my eyes. I heard Tricky rise and call for silence with his gavel.

'Ladies and gentlemen,' he cried, 'a little *treat* for you now.

A little bit of *helegance* and top-drawer style. If you've champagne in your glasses' – there was an ironical cheering at this –
'raise them now. If you've beer – why, beer's got bubbles, don't
it? Raise that too! Above all, raise your voices, as I give to you,
direct from the Phoenix Theatre, Dover, our very own Kentish
swell, our diminutive Faversham masher . . . Miss Kitty' –
clack! – 'Butler!'

There was a burst of handclapping and a few damp
whoops. The orchestra struck up with some jolly number, and
I heard the creak and whisper of the rising curtain. All unwillingly I opened my eyes – then I opened them wider, and lifted
my head. The heat, my weariness, were quite forgotten.
Piercing the shadows of the naked stage was a single shaft of
rosy limelight, and in the centre of this there was a girl: the
most marvellous girl – I knew it at once! – that I had ever
seen.

Of course, we had had male impersonator turns at the
Palace before; but in 1888, in the provincial halls, the masher
acts were not the things they are today. When Nelly Power
had sung 'The Last of the Dandies' to us six months before she
had worn tights and bullion fringe, just like a ballet-girl – only
carried a cane and a billycock hat to make her boyish. Kitty
Butler did not wear tights or spangles. She was, as Tricky had
billed her, a kind of perfect West End swell. She wore a suit –
a handsome gentleman's suit, cut to her size, and lined at the
cuffs and the flaps with flashing silk. There was a rose in her
lapel, and lavender gloves at her pocket. From beneath her
waistcoat shone a stiff-fronted shirt of snowy white, with a
stand-up collar two inches high. Around the collar was a white
bow-tie; and on her head there was a topper. When she took
the topper off – as she did now to salute the audience with a
gay 'Hallo!' – one saw that her hair was perfectly cropped.

It was the hair, I think, which drew me most. If I had ever
seen women with hair as short as hers, it was because they had
spent time in hospital or prison; or because they were mad.
They could never have looked like Kitty Butler. Her hair fitted

her head like a little cap that had been sewn, just for her, by some nimble-fingered milliner. I would say it was brown; brown, however, is too dull a word for it. It was, rather, the kind of brown you might hear sung about – a nut-brown, or a russet. It was almost, perhaps, the colour of chocolate – but then chocolate has no lustre, and this hair shone in the blaze of the limes like taffeta. It curled at her temple, slightly, and over her ears; and when she turned her head a little to put her hat back on, I saw a strip of pale flesh at the nape of her neck where the collar ended and the hairline began that – for all the fire of the hot, hot hall – made me shiver.

She looked, I suppose, like a very pretty boy, for her face was a perfect oval, and her eyes were large and dark at the lashes, and her lips were rosy and full. Her figure, too, was boy-like and slender – yet rounded, vaguely but unmistakably, at the bosom, the stomach and the hips, in a way no real boy's ever was; and her shoes, I noticed after a moment, had two-inch heels to them. But she strode like a boy, and stood like one, with her feet far apart and her hands thrust carelessly into her trouser pockets, and her head at an arrogant angle, at the very front of the stage; and when she sang, her voice was a boy's voice – sweet and terribly true.

Her effect upon that over-heated hall was wonderful. Like me, my neighbours all sat up, and gazed at her with shining eyes. Her songs were all well-chosen ones – things like 'Drink Up, Boys!' and 'Sweethearts and Wives', which the likes of G. H. Macdermott had already made famous, and with which we could all, in consequence, join in – though it was peculiarly thrilling to have them sung to us, not by a gent, but by a girl, in necktie and trousers. In between each song she addressed herself, in a swaggering, confidential tone, to the audience, and exchanged little bits of nonsense with Tricky Reeves at his chairman's table. Her speaking voice was like her singing one – strong and healthy, and wonderfully warm upon the ear. Her accent was sometimes music-hall cockney, sometimes theatrical-genteel, sometimes pure broad Kent.

Her set lasted no longer than the customary fifteen minutes
or so, but she was cheered and shouted back on to the stage at
the end of that time twice over. Her final song was a gentle
one – a ballad about roses and a lost sweetheart. As she sang
she removed her hat and held it to her bosom; then she pulled
the flower from her lapel and placed it against her cheek, and
seemed to weep a little. The audience, in sympathy, let out one
huge collective sigh, and bit their lips to hear her boyish tones
grow suddenly so tender.

All at once, however, she raised her eyes and gazed at us
over her knuckles: we saw that she wasn't weeping at all, but
smiling – and then, suddenly, winking, hugely and roguishly.
Very swiftly she stepped once again to the front of the stage,
and gazed into the stalls for the prettiest girl. When she found
her, she raised her hand and the rose went flying over the
shimmer of the footlights, over the orchestra-pit, to land in
the pretty girl's lap.

We went wild for her then. We roared and stamped and she,
all gallant, raised her hat to us and, waving, took her leave. We
called for her, but there were no more encores. The curtain fell,
the orchestra played; Tricky struck his gavel upon his table,
blew out his candle, and it was the interval.

I peered, blinking, into the seats below, trying to catch sight
of the girl who had been thrown the flower. I could not think
of anything more wonderful, at that moment, than to receive a
rose from Kitty Butler's hand.

I had gone to the Palace, like everyone else that night, to see
Gully Sutherland; but when he made his appearance at last –
mopping his brow with a giant spotted handkerchief, complaining about the Canterbury heat and sending the audience
into fits of sweaty laughter with his comical songs and his
face-pulling – I found that, after all, I hadn't the heart for him.
I wished only that Miss Butler would stride upon the stage
again, to fix us with her elegant, arrogant gaze – to sing to us
about champagne, and shouting 'Hurrah!' at the races. The
thought made me restless. At last Alice – who was laughing at

Gully's grimaces as loudly as everybody else – put her mouth to my ear: 'What's up with you?'

'I'm hot,' I said; and then: 'I'm going downstairs.' And while she sat on for the rest of the turn, I went slowly down to the empty lobby – there to stand with my cheek against the cool glass of the door, and to sing again, to myself, Miss Butler's song, 'Sweethearts and Wives'.

Soon there came the roars and stamps that meant the end of Gully's set; and after a moment Alice appeared, still fanning herself with her bonnet, and blowing at the dampened curls which clung to her pink cheeks. She gave me a wink: 'Let's call on Tony.' I followed her to his little room, and sat and idly twisted in the chair behind his desk, while he stood with his arm about her waist. There was a bit of chat about Mr Sutherland and his spotted handkerchief; then, 'What about that Kitty Butler, eh?' said Tony. 'Ain't she a smasher? If she carries on tickling the crowd like she did tonight, I tell you, Uncle'll be extending her contract till Christmas.'

At that I stopped my twirling. 'She's the best turn I ever saw,' I said, 'here or anywhere! Tricky would be a fool to let her go: you tell him from me.' Tony laughed, and said he would be sure to; but as he said it I saw him wink at Alice, then let his gaze dally, rather spoonily, over her lovely face.

I looked away, and sighed, and said quite guilelessly: 'Oh, I do wish that I might see Miss Butler again!'

'And so you shall,' said Alice, 'on Saturday.' We had all planned to come to the Palace – Father, Mother, Davy, Fred, everyone – on Saturday night. I plucked at my glove.

'I know,' I said. 'But Saturday seems so very far away . . .'

Tony laughed again. 'Well, Nance, and who said you had to wait so long? You can come tomorrow night if you like – and any other night you please, so far as I'm concerned. And if there ain't a seat for you in the gallery, why, we'll put you in a box at the side of the stage, and you can gaze at Miss Butler to your heart's content from there!'

He spoke, I'm sure, to impress my sister; but my heart gave

a strange kind of twist at his words. I said, 'Oh, Tony, do you really mean it?'

'Of course.'

'And really in a box?'

'Why not? Between you and me, the only customers we ever get for those seats are the Wood family and the Plushes. You sit in a box, and make sure the audience gets a look at you: it might give them ideas above their station.'

'It might give Nancy ideas above her station,' said Alice. 'We couldn't have that.' Then she laughed, as Tony tightened his grip about her waist and leaned to kiss her.

It would not have been quite the thing, I suppose, for city girls to go to music halls unchaperoned; but people weren't so very prim about things like that in Whitstable. Mother only gave a frown and a mild *tut-tut* when I spoke, next day, of returning to the Palace; Alice laughed and declared that I was mad: *she* wouldn't come with me, she said, to sit all night in the smoke and the heat for the sake of a glimpse of a girl in trousers – a girl whose turn we had seen and songs we had listened to not four-and-twenty hours before.

I was shocked by her carelessness, but secretly rather glad at the thought of gazing again at Miss Butler, all alone. I was also more thrilled than I cared to let on by Tony's promise that I might sit in a box. For my trip to the theatre the night before I had worn a rather ordinary dress; now, however – it had been a slow day in the Parlour, and Father let us shut the shop at six – I put on my Sunday frock, the frock I usually wore to go out walking in with Freddy. Davy whistled when I came down all dressed up; and there were one or two boys who tried to catch my eye all through the ride to Canterbury. But I knew myself – for this one night, at least! – apart from them. When I reached the Palace I nodded to the ticket-girl, as usual; but then I left my favourite gallery seat for someone else to sweat in, and made my way to the side of the stage, to a chair of gilt and scarlet plush. And here – rather unnervingly exposed, as it turned out, before the idle, curious or envious gaze of the whole, restless hall – here I sat, while the Merry Randalls shuffled to the same songs as before, the comic told his jokes, the mentalist staggered, the acrobats dived.

Then Tricky bade us welcome, once again, our very own Kentish swell . . . and I held my breath.

This time, when she called 'Hallo!' the crowd replied with a great, genial roar: word must have spread, I think, of her success. My view of her now, of course, was side-on and rather queer; but when she strode, as before, to the front of the stage it seemed to me her step was lighter – as if the admiration of the audience lent her wings. I leaned towards her, my fingers hard upon the velvet of my unfamiliar seat. The boxes at the Palace were very close to the stage: all the time she sang, she was less than twenty feet away from me. I could make out all the lovely details of her costume – the watch-chain, looped across the buttons of her waistcoat, the silver links that fastened her cuffs – that I had missed from my old place up in the gallery.

I saw her features, too, more clearly. I saw her ears, which were rather small and unpierced. I saw her lips – saw, now, that they were not naturally rosy, but had of course been carmined for the footlights. I saw that her teeth were creamy-white; and that her eyes were brown as chocolate, like her hair.

Because I knew what to expect from her set – and because I spent so much time watching her, rather than listening to her songs – it seemed over in a moment. She was called back, once again, for two encores, and she finished, as before, with the sentimental ballad and the tossing of the rose. This time I saw who caught it: a girl in the third row, a girl in a straw hat with feathers on it, and a dress of yellow satin that was cut at the shoulders and showing her arms. A lovely girl I had never seen before but felt ready at that moment to despise!

I looked back to Kitty Butler. She had her topper raised and was making her final, sweeping salute. Notice me, I thought.

Notice me! I spelled the words in my head in scarlet letters, as the husband of the mentalist had advised, and sent them burning into her forehead like a brand. *Notice me!*

She turned. Her eyes flicked once my way, as if to note only that the box, empty last night, was occupied now; and then she ducked beneath the dropping crimson of the curtain and was gone.

Tricky blew out his candle.

'Well,' said Alice a little later, as I stepped into our parlour – our real parlour, not the oyster-house downstairs – 'and how was Kitty Butler tonight?'

'Just the same as last night, I should think,' said Father.

'Not at all,' I said, pulling off my gloves. 'She was even better.'

'Even better, my word! If she carries on like that, just think how good she'll be by Saturday!'

Alice gazed at me, her lip twitching. 'D'you think you can wait till then, Nancy?' she asked.

'I can,' I said with a show of carelessness, 'but I'm not sure that I shall.' I turned to my mother, who sat sewing by the empty grate. 'You won't mind, will you,' I said lightly, 'if I go back again tomorrow night?'

'Back again?' said everyone in amusement. I looked only at Mother. She had raised her head and now regarded me with a little puzzled frown.

'I don't see why not,' she said slowly. 'But really, Nancy, all that way, just for one turn . . . And all on your own, too. Can't you get Fred to take you along?'

Fred was the last person I wanted at my side, the next time I saw Kitty Butler. I said, 'Oh, *he* won't want to see an act like that! No, I shall go on my own.' I said it rather firmly, as if going to the Palace every night was some chore I had been set to do and I had generously decided to do it with the minimum of bother and complaint.

There was a second's almost awkward silence. Then Father

said, 'You are a funny little thing, Nancy. All the way to Canterbury in the sweltering heat – and not even to wait for a glimpse of Gully Sutherland when you get there!' And at that, everybody laughed, and the second's awkwardness passed, and the conversation turned to other things.

There were more cries of disbelief, however, and more smiles, when I came home from my third trip to the Palace and announced, shyly, my intention of returning there a fourth time, and a fifth. Uncle Joe was visiting us: he was pouring beer from a bottle, carefully, into a tilted glass, but looked up when he heard the laughter.

'What's all this?' he said.

'Nancy's mashed out on that Kitty Butler, at the Palace,' said Davy. 'Imagine that, Uncle Joe – being mashed on a masher!'

I said, 'You shut up.'

Mother looked sharp. '*You* shut up, please, madam.'

Uncle Joe took a sip of his beer, then licked the froth from his whiskers. 'Kitty Butler?' he said. 'She's the gal what dresses up as a feller, ain't she?' He pulled a face. 'Pooh, Nancy, the real thing not good enough for you any more?'

Father leaned towards him. 'Well, we are *told* it is Kitty Butler,' he said. 'If you ask me' – and here he winked and rubbed his nose – 'I think there's a young chap in the orchestra pit what she's got her eye on . . .'

'Ah,' said Joe, significantly. 'Let's hope poor Frederick don't catch on to it, then . . .'

At that, everybody looked my way, and I blushed – and so seemed, I suppose, to prove my father's words. Davy snorted; Mother, who had frowned before, now smiled. I let her – I let them all think just what they liked – and said nothing; and soon, as before, the talk turned to other matters.

I could deceive my parents and my brother with my silences; from my sister Alice, however, I could keep nothing.

'*Is* there a feller you've got your eye on, at the Palace?' she asked me later, when the rest of the house lay hushed and sleeping.

'Of course not,' I said quietly.

'It's just Miss Butler, then, that you go to see?'

'Yes.'

There was a silence, broken only by the distant rumble of wheels and faint thud of hooves, from the High Street, and the even fainter sucking *whoosh* of sea against shingle from the bay. We had put out our candle but left the window wide and unshuttered. I saw in the gleam of starlight that Alice's eyes were open. She was gazing at me with an ambiguous expression that seemed half amusement, half distaste.

'You're rather keen on her, ain't you?' she said then.

I looked away, and didn't answer her at once. When I spoke at last it was not to her at all, but to the darkness.

'When I see her,' I said, 'it's like – I don't know what it's like. It's like I never saw anything at all before. It's like I am filling up, like a wine-glass when it's filled with wine. I watch the acts before her and they are like nothing – they're like dust. Then she walks on the stage and – she is so pretty; and her suit is so nice; and her voice is so sweet . . . She makes me want to smile and weep, at once. She makes me sore, here.' I placed a hand upon my chest, upon the breast-bone. 'I never saw a girl like her before. I never knew that there were girls like her . . .' My voice became a trembling whisper then, and I found that I could say no more.

There was another silence. I opened my eyes and looked at Alice – and knew at once that I shouldn't have spoken; that I should have been as dumb and as cunning with her as with the rest of them. There was a look on her face – it was not ambiguous at all now – a look of mingled shock, and nervousness, and embarrassment or shame. I had said too much. I felt as if my admiration for Kitty Butler had lit a beacon inside me, and opening my unguarded mouth had sent a shaft of light into the darkened room, illuminating all.

I had said too much – but it was that, or say nothing.

Alice's eyes held my own for a moment longer, then her lashes fluttered and fell. She didn't speak; she only rolled away from me, and faced the wall.

The weather continued very fierce that week. The sun brought trippers to Whitstable and to our Parlour, but the heat jaded their appetites. They called as often, now, for tea and lemonade, as for plaice and mackerel, and for hours at a time I would leave Mother and Alice to work the shop, and run down to the beach to ladle out cockles and crab-meat and whelks, and bread-and-butter, at Father's stall. It was a novelty, serving teas upon the shingle; but it was also hard to stand in the sun, with the vinegar running from your wrists to your elbows, and your eyes smarting from the fumes of it. Father gave me an extra half-crown for every afternoon I worked there. I bought a hat, and a length of lavender ribbon with which to trim it, but the rest of the money I put aside: I would use it, when I had enough, to buy a season ticket for the Canterbury train.

For I made my nightly trips all through that week, and sat – as Tony put it – with the Plushes, and gazed at Kitty Butler as she sang; and I never once grew tired of her. It was only, always, marvellous to step again into my little scarlet box; to gaze at the bank of faces, and the golden arch above the stage, and the velvet drapes and tassels, and the stretch of dusty floor-board with its row of lights – like open cockle shells, I always thought them – before which I would soon see Kitty stride and swagger and wave her hat . . . Oh! And when she stepped on stage at last, there would be that rush of gladness so swift and sharp I would catch my breath to feel it, and grow faint.

That is how it was on my solitary visits; but on Saturday, of course, as we had planned, my family came – and that was rather different.

There were nearly twelve of us in all – more by the time we reached the theatre and took our seats, for we met friends and neighbours on the train and at the ticket-booth, and they attached themselves to our gay party, like barnacles. There wasn't room for us to sit in one long line: we spread ourselves about in groups of threes and fours, so that when one person asked *Did we care for a cherry?* or *Did Mother have her eau-de-cologne?* or *Why had Millicent not brought Jim?* the message must be passed, in a shriek or a whisper, all along the gallery, from cousin to cousin, from aunt to sister to uncle to friend, disturbing all the rows along the way.

So, anyway, it seemed to me. My seat was between Fred and Alice with Davy and his girl, Rhoda, on Alice's left, and Mother and Father behind. It was crowded in the hall and still very hot – though cooler than it had been on the previous, sweltering Monday night; but I, who had had a box to myself for a week, with the draught from the stage to chill me, seemed to feel the heat more than anyone. Fred's hand upon mine, or his lips at my cheek, I found unbearable, like blasts of steam rather than caresses; even the pressure of Alice's sleeve against my arm, and the warmth of Father's face against my neck as he leaned to ask us our opinion of the show, made me flinch, and sweat, and squirm in my seat.

It was as if I had been forced to pass the evening amongst strangers. Their pleasure in the details of the show – which I had sat through so often, so impatiently – struck me as incomprehensible, idiotic. When they sang out the chorus along with the maddening Merry Randalls, and shrieked with laughter at the comedian's jokes; when they gazed round-eyed at the staggering mentalist and called the human loop back on to the stage for another tumble, I chewed my nails. As Kitty Butler's appearance grew more imminent, I became ever more agitated and more wretched. I could not but long for her to step upon the stage again; but I wished, too, that I might be alone when she did so – alone in my little box with the door shut fast behind me – rather than seated in the midst of a crowd of people to whom she was nothing, and who thought my particular passion for her only queer, or quaint.

They had heard me sing 'Sweethearts and Wives' a thousand times; they had heard me tell the details of her costume,

of her hair and voice; I had burned all week to have them see
her, and pronounce her marvellous. Now that they were gathered here, however, gay and careless and hot and loud, I
despised them. I could hardly bear for them to look upon her
at all; worse still, I thought I couldn't endure to have them
look upon *me*, as I watched her. I had that sensation again,
that there had grown a lantern or a beacon inside me. I was
sure that when she stepped upon the stage it would be like
putting a match to the wick, and I would flare up, golden and
incandescent but somehow painfully and shamefully bright;
and my family and my beau would shrink away from me,
appalled.

Of course, when she strode before the footlights at last, no
such thing occurred. I saw Davy look my way and give a wink,
and heard Father's whisper: 'Here's the very gal, then, at last';
but when I glowed and sparkled it was evidently with a dark
and secret flame which no one – except Alice, perhaps –
looked for or saw.

As I had feared, however, I felt horribly far from Miss Butler
that night. Her voice was as strong, her face as lovely, as before;
but I had been used to hearing the breaths she drew between
the phrases, used to catching the glimmer of the limes upon
her lip, the shadow of her lashes on her powdered cheek. Now
I felt as though I was watching her through a pane of glass, or
with my ears stopped up with wax. When she finished her set
my family cheered, and Freddy stamped his feet and whistled.
Davy called, 'Stone me, if she ain't just as wonderful as Nancy
painted her!' – then he leaned across Alice's lap to wink and
add, 'Though not so wonderful that I'd spend a shilling a week
on train tickets to come and see her every night!' I didn't
answer him. Kitty Butler had come back for her encore, and
had already drawn the rose from her lapel; but it was no comfort to me at all to know my family liked her – indeed, it made
me more wretched still. I gazed again at the figure in the shaft
of limelight and thought quite bitterly, *You would be marvellous, if I were here or not. You would be marvellous, without*

*my admiration. I might as well be at home, putting crab-meat
in a paper cone, for all you know of me!*

But even as I thought it, something rather curious happened. She had reached the end of her song – there was the
business with the flower and the pretty girl; and when this was
done she wheeled into the wing. And as she did it I saw her
head go up – and she looked – *looked*, I swear it – towards the
empty chair in which I usually sat, then lowered her head and
moved on. If I had only been in my box tonight, I would have
had her eyes upon me! If I had only been in my box, instead of
here!

I glanced at Davy and Father: they were both on their feet
calling for more; but letting their calls die, and beginning to
stretch. Beside me Freddy was still smiling at the stage. His
hair was plastered to his forehead, his lip was dark where he
was letting whiskers grow; his cheek was red and had a pimple
on it. 'Ain't she a peach?' he said to me. Then he rubbed his
eyes, and shouted to Davy for a beer. Behind me I heard
Mother ask, How *did* the lady in the evening dress read all
those numbers with a blindfold on?

The cheers were fading, Tricky's candle was out; the
gasoliers flared, making us blink. Kitty Butler had looked for
me – had raised her head and looked for me; and I was lost and
sitting with strangers.

I spent the next day, Sunday, at the cockle-stall; and when
Freddy called that night to ask me out walking, I said I was too
tired. That day was cooler, and by Monday the weather seemed
really to have broken. Father came back to the Parlour full
time, and I spent the day in the kitchen, gutting and filleting.
We worked till almost seven: I had just enough time between
the closing of the shop and the leaving of the Canterbury train
to change my dress, to pull on a pair of elastic-sided boots
and to sit down with Father and Mother, Alice, Davy and
Rhoda for a hasty supper. They thought it more than strange, I
knew, that I should be returning to the Palace yet again; Rhoda,

in particular, seemed greatly tickled by the story of my 'mash'. 'Don't you mind her going, Mrs Astley?' she asked. 'My mother would never let me go so far alone; and I am two years older. But then, Nancy is such a steady sort of girl, I suppose.' I had been a steady girl; it was over Alice – saucy Alice – that my parents usually worried. But at Rhoda's words I saw Mother look me over and grow thoughtful. I had on my Sunday dress, and my new hat trimmed with lavender; and I had a lavender bow at the end of my plait of hair, and a bow of the same ribbon sewn on each of my white linen gloves. My boots were black with a wonderful shine. I had put a spot of Alice's perfume – *eau de rose* – behind each ear; and I had darkened my lashes with castor oil from the kitchen.

Mother said, 'Nancy, do you really think—?' But as she spoke the clock on the mantel gave a *ting!* It was a quarter-past seven, I should miss my train.

I said, 'Good-bye! Good-bye!' – and fled, before she could delay me.

I missed my train anyway, and had to wait at the station till the later one came. When I reached the Palace the show had begun: I took my seat to find the acrobats already on the stage forming their loop, their spangles gleaming, their white suits dusty at the knees. There was clapping; Tricky rose to say – what he said every night, so that half the audience smiled and said it with him – that *You couldn't get many of those to the pound!* Then – as if it were part of the overture to her routine and she could not work without it – I gripped my seat and held my breath, while he raised his gavel to beat out Kitty Butler's name.

She sang that night like – I cannot say like an angel, for her songs were all of champagne suppers and strolling in the Burlington Arcade; perhaps, then, like a fallen angel – or yet again like a *falling* one: she sang like a falling angel might sing with the bounds of heaven fresh burst behind him, and hell still distant and unguessed. And as she did so, I sang with her – not loudly and carelessly like the rest of the crowd, but softly, almost secretly, as if she might hear me the better if I whispered rather than bawled.

And perhaps, after all, she did. I had thought that, when she walked on to the stage, she had glanced my way – as much as to say, The box is filled again. Now, as she wheeled before the footlights, I thought I saw her look at me again. The idea was a fantastic one – and yet every time her gaze swept the crowded hall it seemed to brush my own, and dally with it a little longer than it should. I ceased my whispered singing and merely stared, and swallowed. I saw her leave the stage – again, her gaze met mine – and then return for her encore. She sang her ballad and plucked the flower from her lapel, and held it to her cheek, as we all expected. But when her song was finished she did not peer into the stalls for the handsomest girl, as she usually did. Instead, she took a step to her left, towards the box in which I sat. And then she took another. In a moment she had reached the corner of the stage, and stood facing me; she was so close I could see the glint of her collar-stud, the beat of the pulse in her throat, the pink at the corner of her eye. She stood there for what seemed to be a small eter-nity; then her arm came up, the flower flashed for a second in the beam of the lime – and my own hand, trembling, rose to catch it. The crowd gave a broad, indulgent cheer of pleasure, and a laugh. She held my flustered gaze with her own more certain one, and made me a little bow. Then she stepped back-wards suddenly, waved to the hall, and left us.

I sat for a moment as if stunned, my eyes upon the flower in my hand, which had been so near, so recently, to Kitty Butler's cheek. I wanted to raise it to my own face – and was about to, I think, when the clatter of the hall pierced my brain at last, and made me look about me and see the inquisitive, indulgent looks that were turned my way, and the nods and the chuckles and the winks that met my up-turned gaze. I reddened, and shrank back into the shadows of the box. With my back turned to the bank of prying eyes I slipped the rose into the belt of my dress, and pulled on my gloves. My heart, which had begun to pound when Miss Butler had stepped towards me across the stage, was still beating painfully hard; but as I left my box and made my way towards the crowded foyer and the street beyond, it began to feel light, and glad, and I began to want to smile. I had to place a hand before my lips so as not to appear an idiot, smiling to myself as if at nothing.

Just as I was about to step into the street, I heard my name called. I turned, and saw Tony, crossing the lobby with his arm raised to catch my eye. It was a relief to have a friend, at last, to smile at. I took the hand away, and grinned like a monkey.

'Hey, hey,' he said breathlessly when he reached my side, 'someone's merry, and I know why! How come girls never look so gay as that, when *I* give them roses?' I blushed again, and returned my fingers to my lips, but said nothing. Tony smirked.

'I've got a message for you,' he said then. 'Someone to see you.' I raised my eyebrows; I thought perhaps Alice or Freddy were here, come to meet me. Tony's smirk broadened. 'Miss Butler,' he said, 'would like a word.'

My own grin faded at once. 'A word?' I said. 'Miss Butler? With me?'

'That's right. She asked Ike, the fly-man, who was the girl that sat in the box every night, on her own, and Ike said you was a pal of mine, and to ask me. So she did. And I told her. And now she wants to see you.'

'What for? Oh, Tony, what on earth for? What did you tell her?' I caught hold of his arm and gripped it hard.

'Nothing, except the truth—' I gave his arm a twist. The truth was terrible. I didn't want her to know about the shivering and the whispering, the flame and the streaming light. Tony prised my fingers from his sleeve, and held my hand. 'Just that you like her,' he said simply. 'Now will you come along, or what?'

I did not know what to say. So I said nothing, but let him lead me away from the great glass doors with the blue, cool,

Chapter 2

I had been backstage at the Palace with Tony once or twice before, but only in the daytime, when the hall was dim and quite deserted. Now the corridors along which I walked with him were full of light and noise. We passed one doorway that led, I knew, to the stage itself: I caught a glimpse of ladders and ropes and trailing gas-pipes; of boys in caps and aprons, wheeling baskets, manœuvring lights. I had the sensation then – and I felt it again in the years that followed, every time I made a similar trip backstage – that I had stepped into the workings of a giant clock, stepped through the elegant casing to the dusty, greasy, restless machinery that lay, all hidden from the common eye, behind it.

Tony led me down a passageway that stopped at a metal staircase, and here he paused to let three men go by. They wore hats and carried overcoats and bags; they were sallow-faced and poor-looking, with a patina of flashness – I thought they might be salesmen carrying sample-cases. Only when they had moved on, and I heard them sharing a joke with the stage door-keeper, did I realise that they were the trio of tumblers taking their leave for the night, and that their bags contained their spangles. I had a sudden fear that Kitty Butler might after all be just like them: plain, unremarkable, almost

unrecognisable as the handsome girl I had seen swaggering in
the glow of the footlights. I very nearly called to Tony to take
me back; but he had descended the staircase, and when I
caught up with him in the passageway below he was at a door,
and had already turned its handle.

The door was one of a row of others, indistinguishable from
its neighbours but for a brass figure 7, very old and scratched,
that was screwed at eye level upon its centre panel, and a
hand-written card that had been tacked below. *Miss Kitty
Butler*, it said.

I found her seated at a little table before a looking-glass;
she had half-turned – to reply, I suppose, to Tony's knock – but
at my approach she rose, and reached to shake my hand. She
was a little shorter than me, even in her heels, and younger
than I had imagined – perhaps my sister's age, of one- or two-
and-twenty.

'Aha,' she said, when Tony had left us – there was a hint,
still, of her footlight manner in her voice – 'my mystery admirer!
I was sure it must be Gully you came to see; then someone said
you never stay beyond the interval. Is it really me you stay for?
I never had a fan before!' As she spoke she leaned quite
comfortably against the table – it was cluttered, I now saw, with
jars of cream and sticks of grease-paint, with playing cards and
half-smoked cigarettes and filthy tea-cups – and crossed her
legs at the ankle, and folded her arms. Her face was still thickly
powdered, and very red at the lip; her lashes and eyelids were
black with paint. She was dressed in the trousers and the shoes
that she had worn for her act, but she had removed the jacket,
the waistcoat and, of course, the hat. Her starched shirt was
held tight against the swell of her bosom by a pair of braces, but
gaped at the throat where she had unclipped her bow-tie.
Beyond the shirt I saw an edge of creamy lace.

I looked away. 'I do like your act,' I said.

'I should think you do, you come to it so often!'

I smiled. 'Well, Tony lets me in, you see, for nothing . . .'
That made her laugh: her tongue looked very pink, her teeth

extraordinarily white, against her painted lips. I felt myself blush. 'What I mean is,' I said, 'Tony lets me have the box. But I would pay if I had to, and sit in the gallery. For I do so like your act, Miss Butler, so very, very much.'

Now she did not laugh, but she tilted her head a little. 'Do you?' she answered gently.

'Oh, yes.'

'Tell me what it is you like then, so much.'

I hesitated. 'I like your costume,' I said at last. 'I like your songs, and the way you sing them. I like the way you talk to Tricky. I like your . . . hair.' Here I stumbled; and now *she* seemed to blush. There was a second's almost awkward silence – then, suddenly, as if from somewhere very near at hand, there came the sound of music – the blast of a horn and the pulse of a drum – and a cheer, like the roaring of the wind in some vast sea-shell. I gave a jump, and looked about me; and she laughed. 'The second half,' she said. After a moment the cheering stopped; the music, however, went on pulsing and thumping like a great heartbeat.

She left off leaning against the table, and asked, Did I mind if she smoked? I shook my head, and shook it again when she took up a packet of cigarettes from amongst the dirty cups and playing cards, and held it to me. Upon the wall there was a hissing gas-jet in a wire cage, and she put her face to it, to light the cigarette. With the fag at the side of her lip, her eyes screwed up against the flame, she looked like a boy again; when she took the cigarette away, however, the cork was smudged with crimson. Seeing that, she tutted: 'Look at me, with all my paint still on! Will you sit with me while I clean my face? It's not very polite, I know, but I must get ready rather quick; my room is needed later by another girl . . .'

I did as she asked, and sat and watched her smear her cheeks with cream, then take a cloth to them. She worked quickly and carefully, but distractedly; and as she rubbed at her face she held my gaze in the glass. She looked at my new hat and said, 'What a pretty bonnet!' Then she asked how I knew Tony – was he my beau? I was shocked at that and said, 'Oh, no! He is courting my sister'; and she laughed. Where did I live? she asked me then. What did I work at?

'I work in an oyster-house,' I said.

'An oyster-house!' The idea seemed to tickle her. Still rubbing at her cheeks, she began to hum, and then to sing very low beneath her breath.

> 'As I was going down Bishopgate Street,
> An oyster-girl I happened to meet –'

A swipe at the crimson of her lip, the black of her lashes.

> 'Into her basket I happened to peep,
> To see if she'd got any oysters . . .'

She sang on; then opened one eye very wide, and leaned close to the glass to remove a stubborn crumb of spit-black – her mouth stretching wide, out of a kind of sympathy with her eyelids, and her breath misting the mirror. For a second she seemed quite to have forgotten me. I studied the skin of her face and her throat. It had emerged from its mask of powder and grease the colour of cream – the colour of the lace on her chemise; but it was darkened at the nose and cheeks – and even, I saw, at the edge of her lip – by freckles, brown as her hair. I had not suspected the existence of the freckles. I found them wonderfully and inexplicably moving.

She wiped her breath from the glass, then, and gave me a wink, and asked me more about myself; and because it was somehow easier to talk to her reflection than to her face, I began at last to chat with her quite freely. At first she answered as I thought an actress should – comfortably, rather teasingly, laughing when I blushed or said a foolish thing. Gradually, however – as if she was stripping the paint from her voice, as well as from her face – her tone grew milder, less pert and pressing. At last – she gave a yawn, and rubbed her knuckles in her eyes – at last her voice was just a girl's: melodious and strong and clear, but just a Kentish girl's voice, like my own.

Like the freckles, it made her – not unremarkable, as I had feared to find her; but marvellously, achingly real. Hearing it, I understood at last my wildness of the past seven days. I thought, How queer it is! And yet, how very ordinary. *I am in love with you.*

Soon her face was wiped quite bare, and her cigarette smoked to the filter; and then she rose and put her fingers to her hair. 'I had better change,' she said, almost shyly. I took the hint, and said that I should go, and she walked the couple of steps with me to the door.

'Thank you, Miss Astley,' she said – she already had my name from Tony – 'for coming to see me.' She held out her hand to me, and I lifted my own in response – then remembered my glove – my glove with the lavender bows upon it, to match my pretty hat – and quickly drew it off and offered her my naked fingers. All at once she was the gallant boy of the footlights again. She straightened her back, made me a little bow, and raised my knuckles to her lips.

I flushed with pleasure – until I saw her nostrils quiver, and knew, suddenly, what she smelled: those rank sea-scents, of liquor and oyster-flesh, crab-meat and whelks, which had flavoured my fingers and those of my family for so many years we had all ceased, entirely, to notice them. Now I had thrust them beneath Kitty Butler's nose! I felt ready to die of shame.

I made, at once, to pull my hand away; but she held it fast in her own, still pressed to her lips, and laughed at me over the knuckles. There was a look in her eye I could not quite interpret.

'You smell,' she began, slowly and wonderingly, 'like—'

'Like a herring!' I said bitterly. My cheeks were hot now and very red; there were tears, almost, in my eyes. I think she saw my confusion and was sorry for it.

'Not at all like a herring,' she said gently. 'But perhaps, maybe, like a mermaid . . .' And she kissed my fingers properly, and this time I let her; and at last my blush faded, and I smiled.

I put my glove back on. My fingers seemed to tingle against the cloth. 'Will you come and see me again, Miss Mermaid?' she asked. Her tone was light; incredibly, however, she seemed to mean it. I said, Oh, yes, I should like that very much, and she nodded with something like satisfaction. Then she made me another little bow, and we said good-night; and she closed the door and was gone.

I stood quite still, facing the little 7, the hand-written card, *Miss Kitty Butler*. I found myself unable to move from in front of it – quite as unable as if I really were a mermaid and had no legs to walk on, but a tail. I blinked. I had been sweating, and the sweat, and the smoke of her cigarette, had worked upon the castor oil on my lashes to make my eye-lids very sore. I put my hand to them – the hand that she had kissed; then I held my fingers to my nose and smelled through the linen what she had smelled, and blushed again.

In the dressing-room all was silent. Then at last, very low, came the sound of her voice. She was singing again the song about the oyster-girl and the basket. But the song came rather fitfully now, and I realised of course that as she was singing she was stooping to unlace her boots, and straightening to shrug her braces off, and perhaps kicking free her trousers . . .

All this; and there was only the thickness of one slender door between her body and my own smarting eyes!

It was that thought which made me find my legs at last, and leave her.

Watching Miss Butler perform upon the stage after having spoken to her, and been smiled at by her, and had her lips upon my hand, was a strange experience, at once more and less thrilling than it had been before. Her lovely voice, her elegance, her swagger: I felt I had been given a kind of secret share in them, and pinked complacently every time the crowd roared their welcome or called her back on to the stage for an encore. She threw me no more roses; these all went, as before, to the pretty girls in the stalls. But I know she saw me in my box, for I felt her eyes upon me, sometimes, as she sang; and always, when she left the stage, there was that sweep of her hat for the hall, and a nod, or a wink, or the ghost of a smile, just for me.

But if I was complacent, I was also dissatisfied. I had seen beyond the powder and the strut; it was terribly hard to have to sit with common audiences as she sang, and have no more of her than they. I burned to visit her again – yet also feared to. She had invited me, but she hadn't named a time; and I, in those days, was terribly anxious and shy. So though I went as often as I was able to my box at the Palace, and watched and applauded her as she sang, and received those secret looks and tokens, it was a full week before I made my way again backstage, and presented myself, all pale, sweating and uncertain, at her dressing-room door.

But when I did so, she received me with such kindness, and chided me so sincerely for having left her unvisited so long; and we fell again to chatting so easily about her life in the theatre, and mine as an oyster-girl in Whitstable, that all my old qualms quite left me. Persuaded at last that she liked me, I visited her again – and then again, and again. I went nowhere else that month but to the Palace; saw no one else – not Freddy, not my cousins, not even Alice, hardly – but her. Mother had begun to frown about it; but when I went home and said that I had gone backstage at Miss Butler's invitation, and been treated by her like a friend, she was impressed. I worked harder than ever at my kitchen duties; I filleted fish, washed potatoes, chopped parsley, thrust crabs and lobsters into pans of steaming water – and all so briskly I barely had breath for a song to cover their shrieks with. Alice would say rather sullenly that my mania for a certain person at the Palace made me dull; but I didn't speak to Alice much these days. Now every working day ended, for me, with a lightning change, and a hasty supper, and a run to the station for the Canterbury train;

and every trip to Canterbury ended in Kitty Butler's dressing-room. I spent more time in her company than I did watching her perform upon the stage, and saw her more often without her make-up, and her suit, and her footlight manner, than with them.

For the friendlier we grew the freer she became, and the more confiding.

'You must call me "Kitty",' she said early on, 'and I shall call you – what? Not "Nancy", for that is what everyone calls you. What do they call you at home? "Nance", is it? Or "Nan"?'

'"Nance",' I said.

'Then I shall call you "Nan" – if I might?' If she might! I nodded and smiled like an idiot: for the thrill of being addressed by her I would gladly have lost all of my old name, and taken a new one, or gone nameless entirely.

So presently it was 'Well, Nan . . . !' this, and 'Lord, Nan . . . !' that; and, increasingly, it was 'Be a love, Nan, and fetch me my stockings . . .' She was still too shy to change her clothes before me, but one night when I arrived I found that she had had a little folding screen set up, and ever afterwards she used to step behind it while we talked, and hand me articles of her suit as she undressed, and have me pass her the pieces of her ladies' costume from the hook that she had hung them on before the show. I adored being able to serve her like this. I would brush and fold her suit with trembling fingers, and secretly press its various materials – the starched linen of the shirt, the silk of the waistcoat and the stockings, the wool of the jacket and trousers – to my cheek. Each item came to me warm from her body, and with its own particular scent; each seemed charged with a strange kind of power, and tingled or glowed (or so I imagined) beneath my hand.

Her petticoats and dresses were cold and did not tingle; but I still blushed to handle them, for I couldn't help but think of all the soft and secret places they would soon enclose, or brush against, or warm and make moist, once she had donned them. Every time she stepped from behind the screen, clad as a girl, small and slim and shapely, a false plait smothering the lovely, ragged edges of her crop, I had the same sensation: a pang of disappointment and regret that turned instantly to pleasure and to aching love; a desire to touch, to embrace and caress, so strong I had to turn aside or fold my arms for fear that they would fly about her and press her close.

At length I grew so handy with her costumes she suggested that I visit her *before* she went on stage, to help her ready herself for her act, like a proper dresser. She said it with a kind of studied carelessness, as if half-fearful that I might not wish to; she could not have known, I suppose, how dreary the hours were to me, that I must pass away from her . . . Soon I never stepped into the auditorium at all, but headed, every night, backstage, a half-hour before she was due before the footlights, to help her re-don the shirt and waistcoat and trousers that I had taken from her the night before; to hold the powder-box while she dusted out her freckles, to dampen the brushes with which she smoothed out the curl in her hair, to fasten the rose to her lapel.

The first time I did all this I walked with her to the stage afterwards, and stood in the wing while she went through her set, gazing in wonder at the limes-men who strode, nimble as acrobats, across the battens in the fly-gallery; seeing nothing of the hall, nothing of the stage except a stretch of dusty board with a boy at the other end of it, his arm upon the handle that turned the rope that brought the curtain down. She had been nervous, as all performers are, and her nervousness had infected me; but when she stepped into the wing at the end of her final number, pursued by stamping, by shouts and 'Hurrahs!', she was flushed and gay and triumphant. To tell the truth, I did not quite like her then. She seized my arm, but didn't see me. She was like a woman in the grip of a drug, or in the first flush of an embrace, and I felt a fool to be at her side, so still and sober, and jealous of the crowd that was her lover.

After that, I passed the twenty minutes or so that she was

gone each night alone, in her room, listening to the beat of her
songs through the ceiling and walls, happier to hear the cheers
of the audience from a distance. I would make tea for her – she
liked it brewed in the pan with condensed milk, dark as a
walnut and thick as syrup; I knew by the changing tempos of
her set just when to set the kettle on the hearth, so the cup
would be ready for her return. While the tea simmered I would
wipe her little table, and empty her ashtrays, and dust down
the glass; I would tidy the cracked and faded old cigar-box in
which she kept her sticks of grease-paint. They were acts of
love, these humble little ministrations, and of pleasure – even,
perhaps, of a kind of *self*-pleasure, for it made me feel strange
and hot and almost shameful to perform them. While she was
being ravished by the admiration of the crowd, I would pace
her dressing-room and gaze at her possessions, or caress them,
or *almost* caress them – holding my fingers an inch away from
them, as if they had an aura, as well as a surface, that might be
stroked. I loved everything that she left behind her – her petticoats and her perfumes, and the pearls that she clipped to the
lobes of her ears; but also the hairs on her combs, the eye-
lashes that clung to her sticks of spit-black, even the dent of
her fingers and lips on her cigarette-ends. The world, to me,
seemed utterly transformed since Kitty Butler had stepped
into it. It had been ordinary before she came; now it was full of
queer electric spaces, that she left ringing with music or glowing with light.

By the time she returned to her dressing-room I would have
everything tidy and still. Her tea, as I have said, would be
ready; sometimes, too, I would have a cigarette lit for her. She
would have lost her fierce, distracted look, and be simply
merry and kind. 'What a crowd!' she'd say. 'They wouldn't let
me leave!' Or, 'A slow one tonight, Nan; I believe I was
halfway through "Good Cheer, Boys, Good Cheer" before they
realised I was a girl!'

She would unclip her necktie and hang up her jacket and
hat, then she would sip her tea and smoke her fag and – since

performing made her garrulous – she would talk to me, and I would listen, hard. And so I learned a little of her history.

She had been born, she said, in Rochester, to a family of entertainers. Her mother (she did not mention a father) had died while she was still quite a baby, and she had been raised by her grandmother; she had no brothers, no sisters, and no cousins that she could recall. She had taken her first bows before the footlights at the age of twelve, as 'Kate Straw, the Little Singing Wonder', and had known a bit of success in penny-gaffs and public-houses, and the smaller kinds of halls and theatres. But it was a miserable sort of life, she said – 'and soon I wasn't even little any more. Every time a place came up there was a crush of girls queuing for it at the stage door, all just the same as me, or prettier, or perter – or hungrier, and so more willing to kiss the chairman for the promise of a season's work, or a week's, or even a night's.' Her grandmother had died; she had joined a dancing troupe and toured the seaside towns of Kent and the south coast, doing end-of-pier shows three times a night. She frowned when she spoke about these times, and her voice was bitter, or weary; she would place a hand beneath her chin, and rest her head upon it, and close her eyes.

'Oh, it was hard,' she'd say, 'so hard . . . And you never made a friend, because you were never in one place long enough. And all the stars thought themselves too grand to talk to you, or were afraid you would copy their routines. And the crowds were cruel, and made you cry . . .' The thought of Kitty weeping brought the tears to my own eyes; and seeing me so affected, she'd give a smile, and a wink, and a stretch, and say in her best swell accent: 'But those days are all behind me now, don't you know, and I am on the path to fame and fortune. Since I changed my name and became a masher the whole world loves me; and Tricky Reeves loves me most of all, and pays me like a prince, to prove it!' And then we would smile together, because we both knew that if she really were a masher Tricky's wages would barely keep her in champagne;

but my smile would be a little troubled for I knew, too, that her contract was due to expire at the end of August, and then she would have to move to another theatre – to Margate, perhaps, she said, or Broadstairs, if they would have her. I couldn't bear to think what I would do when she was gone.

What my family made of my trips backstage, my marvellous new status as Miss Butler's pal and unofficial dresser, I am not sure. They were, as I have said, impressed; but they were also troubled. It was reassuring for them that it was a real friendship, and not just a schoolgirl mash, that had me travelling so often to the Palace, and spending all my savings on the train fare; and yet, I thought I heard them ask themselves, what manner of friendship could there *be* between a handsome, clever music-hall artiste, and the girl in the crowd that admired her? When I said that Kitty had no young man (for I had found this out, early on, amongst the pieces of her history) Davy said that I should bring her home, and introduce her to my handsome brother – though he only said it when Rhoda was near, to tease her. When I spoke of brewing her pans of tea and tidying her table, Mother narrowed her eyes: 'She's doing all right out of you, by the sound of it. It's a little more help with the tea and the tables we could do with, from you, home here . . .'

It was true, I suppose, that I rather neglected my duties in the house for the sake of my trips to the Palace. They fell to my sister, though she rarely complained about it. I believe my parents thought her generous, allowing me my freedom at her own expense. The truth was, I think, that she was squeamish of mentioning Kitty now – and by that alone I knew that it was she, more than any of them, who was uneasy. I had said nothing more to her about my passion. I had said nothing of my new, strange, hot desire to anyone. But she saw me, of course, as I lay in my bed; and, as anyone will tell you who has been secretly in love, it is in bed that you do your dreaming – in bed, in the darkness, where you cannot see your own cheeks pink, that you ease back the mantle of restraint that keeps your passion dimmed throughout the day, and let it glow a little.

How Kitty would have blushed, to know the part she played in my fierce dreamings – to know how shamelessly I took my memories of her, and turned them to my own improper advantage! Each night at the Palace she kissed me farewell; in my dreams her lips stayed at my cheek – were hot, were tender – moved to my brow, my ear, my throat, my mouth . . I was used to standing close to her, to fasten her collar-studs or brush her lapels; now, in my reveries, I did what I longed to do then – I leaned to place my lips upon the edges of her hair; I slid my hands beneath her coat, to where her breasts pressed warm against her stiff gent's shirt and rose to meet my strokings . . .

And all this – which left me thick with bafflement and pleasure – with my sister at my side! All this with Alice's breath upon my cheek, or her hot limbs pressed against mine; or with her eyes shining cold and dull, with starlight and suspicion.

But she said nothing; she asked me nothing; and to the rest of the family, at least, my continuing friendship with Kitty became in time a source not of wonder, but of pride. 'Have you been to the Palace at Canterbury?' I would hear Father say to customers as he took their plates. 'Our youngest girl is very thick with Kitty Butler, the star of the show . . .' By the end of August, when the oyster season had started again and we were back in the shop full time, they began to press me to bring Kitty home with me, that they might meet her for themselves.

'You are always saying as how she is your pal,' said Father one morning at breakfast. 'And besides – what a crime it would be for her to come so near to Whitstable, and never taste a proper oyster-tea. You bring her over here, before she goes.' The idea of asking Kitty to sup with my family seemed a horrible one; and because my father spoke so carelessly about the fact that she would soon have left for a new hall, I made him a stinging reply. A little later Mother took me aside. Was my father's house not good enough for Miss Butler, she said, that I couldn't invite her here? Was I ashamed of my parents, and my parents' trade? Her words made me gloomy; I was quiet and sad with Kitty that night, and when after the show she asked me why, I bit my lip.

'My parents want me to ask you over,' I said, 'for tea tomorrow. You don't have to come, and I can say you're busy or sick. But I promised them I'd ask you; and now,' I finished miserably, 'I have.'

She took my hand. 'But, Nan,' she said in wonder, 'I should love to come! You know how dull it is for me in Canterbury, with no one but Mrs Pugh and Sandy to talk to!' Mrs Pugh was the landlady of Kitty's rooming-house; Sandy was the boy who shared her landing: he played in the band at the Palace, but drank, she said, and was sometimes silly and a bore. 'Oh, how nice it would be,' she continued, 'to sit in a proper parlour again, with a proper family – not just a room with a bed in it, and a dirty rug, and a bit of newspaper on the table for a cloth! And how nice to see where you live and work; and to catch your train; and to meet the people that love you, and have you with them all day . . .'

It made me fidget and swallow to hear her talk like this, all unself-consciously, of how she liked me; tonight, however, I had no time even to blush: for as she spoke there came a knock at her door – a sharp, cheerful, authoritative knock that made her blink and stiffen, and look up in surprise.

I, too, gave a start. In all the evenings I had spent with her, she had had no visitors but the call-boy – who came to tell her when she was wanted in the wing – and Tony, who sometimes put his head around the door to wish us both good-night. She had no beau, as I have said; she had no other 'fans' – no friends at all, it seemed, but me; and I had always been rather glad of it. Now I watched her step to the door, and bit my lip. I should like to say I felt a thrill of foreboding, but I did not. I only felt piqued, that our time alone together – which I thought little enough! – should be made shorter.

The visitor was a gentleman: a stranger, evidently, to Kitty, for she greeted him politely, but quite cautiously. He had a silk hat on his head which – seeing her, and then me lurking in the little room behind her – he removed, and held to his bosom. 'Miss Butler, I believe,' he said; and when she nodded, he gave a bow: 'Walter Bliss, ma'am. Your servant.' His voice was deep and pleasant and clear, like Tricky's. As he spoke he produced a card from his pocket and held it out. In the second or so it took Kitty to gaze at it and give a little 'Oh!' of surprise, I studied him. He was very tall, even without his hat, and was dressed rather fashionably in chequered trousers and a fancy waistcoat. Across his stomach there was a golden watch-chain as thick as the tail of a rat; and more gold, I noticed, flashed from his fingers. His head was large, his hair a dull ginger; gingerish, too – and somehow at once both impressive and rather comical – were the whiskers that swept from his top lip to his ears, and his eyebrows, and the hair in his nose. His skin was as clear and shiny as a boy's. His eyes were blue.

When Kitty returned his card to him, he asked if he might speak with her a moment, and at once she stood aside to let him pass. With him in it, the little room seemed very full and hot. I rose, reluctantly, and put on my gloves and my hat, and said that I should go; and then Kitty introduced me – 'My friend, Miss Astley,' she called me, which made me feel a little gayer – and Mr Bliss shook my hand.

'Tell your Mother,' said Kitty as she showed me to the door, 'that I shall come tomorrow, any time she likes.'

'Come at four,' I said.

'Four it is, then!' She briefly took my hand again, and kissed my cheek.

Over her shoulder I saw the flashy gentleman fingering his whiskers, but with his eyes turned, politely, away from us.

I can hardly say what a curious mix of feelings mine were, the Sunday afternoon when Kitty came to call on us in Whitstable. She was more to me than all the world; that she should be visiting me in my own home, and supping with my family, seemed both a delight too lovely to be borne and a great and dreadful burden. I loved her, and could not but long to have her come; but I loved her, and not a soul must know it – not even she. It would be a torture, I thought, to have to sit beside her at my father's table with that love within me, mute and restless as a gnawing worm. I would have to smile while Mother asked, Why didn't Kitty have a beau? And smile again when Davy held Rhoda's hand, or Tony pinched my sister's knee beneath the table – when all the while my darling would be at my side, untouchable.

Then again, there was the crampedness, and the dinginess – and the unmistakable fishiness – of our home to fret over. Would Kitty think it mean? Would she see the tears in the drugget, the smears on the walls; would she see that the arm-chairs sagged, that the rugs were faded, that the shawl which Mother had tacked to the mantel, so that it fluttered in the draught from the chimney, was dusty and torn, its fringes unravelling? I had grown up with these things, and for eight-een years had barely noticed them, but I saw them now, for what they really were, as if through her own eyes.

I saw my family, too, anew. I saw my father – a gentle man, but prone to dullness. Would Kitty think him dull? And Davy: he could be rather brash; and Rhoda – horrible Rhoda – would certainly be over-pert. What would Kitty make of them? What would she think of Alice – my dearest friend, until a month ago? Would she think her cold, and would her coldness puzzle her? Or would she – and this thought was a dreadful one – would she think her pretty, and like her more than me? Would she wish it had been Alice in the box for her to throw that rose to, and invite backstage, and call a mermaid . . . ?

Waiting for her that afternoon I was by turns anxious, gay and sullen – now fussing over the setting of the tea-table, now snapping at Davy and grumbling at Rhoda, now earning scolds from everyone for fretting and complaining, and generally turning what should have been a glad day for myself into a gloomy one, for us all. I had washed my hair and it had dried peculiarly; I had added a new frill to my best dress, but had

sewn it crooked and it wouldn't lie flat. I stood at the top of the
stairs, sweating over the silk with a safety-pin, ready to weep
because Kitty's train was due and I must run to meet her, when
Tony emerged from our little kitchen, carrying bottles of Bass
for the tea-table. He stood and watched me fumbling. I said,
'Go away', but he only looked smug.

'You won't want to hear my bit of news, then.'

'What news?' The frill was flat at last. I reached for my hat
on the peg on the wall. Tony smirked and said nothing. I
stamped my foot. 'Tony, what is it? I'm late and you're making
me later.'

'Well then, nothing at all, I expect. I dare say Miss Butler
will tell you herself . . .'

'Tell me what?' Now I stood with my hat in one hand, a hat-
pin in the other. 'Tell me *what*, Tony?'

He glanced over his shoulder and lowered his voice. 'Now,
don't let on about it yet, for it ain't been properly settled. But
your pal – Kitty – she's due to leave the Palace, ain't she, in a
week or so?' I nodded. 'Well, she won't be going – not for a
good while, anyway. Uncle has offered her a sparkling new
contract, till the New Year – said she was too good to lose to
Broadstairs.'

The New Year! That was months away, months and months
and weeks and weeks; I saw them all spread out before me,
each one full of nights in Kitty's dressing-room, and good-
night kisses, and dreams.

I gave a cry, I think; and Tony took a swig of Bass, complacently. Then Alice appeared, demanding to know what it was
that must be talked about in whispers, and shrieked over, on
the stairs . . . ? I didn't wait for Tony's answer, I thundered
down to the door and into the street, and ran to the station like
a hoyden, with my hat flapping about my ears – because I had
forgotten, after all, to pin it properly.

I had hardly expected Kitty to swagger to Whitstable in her
suit and her topper and her lavender gloves; but even so, when
she stepped from the train and I saw that she was clad as a girl,

and walked like a girl, with her plait fastened to the back of her head and a parasol over her arm, I felt a little pang of disappointment. This swiftly turned, however – as always – to desire, and then to pride, for she looked terribly smart and handsome on that dusty Whitstable platform. She kissed my cheek when I went up to her, and took my arm, and let me lead her from the station to our house, across the sea-front. She said, 'Well! And this is where you were born, and grew up?'

'Oh yes! Look there: that building, beside the church, is our old school. Over there – see that house with the bicycle by the gate? – that's where my cousins live. Here, look, on this step, I once fell down and cut my chin, and my sister held her handkerchief to it, the whole way home . . .' So I talked and pointed, and Kitty nodded, biting her lip. 'How lucky you are!' she said at last; and as she said it, she seemed to sigh.

I had feared that the afternoon would be dismal and hard; in fact, it was merry. Kitty shook hands with everyone, and had a word for them all, such as, 'You must be Davy, who works in the smack', and 'You must be Alice, who Nancy talks about so often, and is so proud of. Now I can see why' – which made Alice blush, and look to the floor in confusion.

With my father she was kind. 'Well, well, Miss Butler,' he said when he took her hand, nodding at her skirts, 'this is rather a change, ain't it, from your usual gear?' She smiled and said it was; and when he added, with a wink, 'And something of an improvement, too – *if* you don't mind a gentleman saying so', she laughed and said that, since gentlemen were usually of that opinion, she was quite used to it, and did not mind a bit.

All in all she made herself so pleasant, and answered their questions about herself, and the music hall, so sweetly and cleverly, that no one – not even Alice, or spiteful Rhoda – could dislike her; and I – watching her gaze from the windows at Whitstable Bay, or incline her head to catch a story of my father's, or compliment my mother on some ornament or picture (she admired the shawl, above the fireplace!) – I fell in love with her, all over again. And my love was all the warmer, of course, since I had that special, secret knowledge about Tricky, and the contract, and the extra four months.

She had come for tea, and presently we all sat down to it – Kitty marvelling, as we did so, at the table. It was set for a real oyster-supper, with a linen cloth, and a little spirit-lamp with a plate of butter on it, waiting to be melted. On either side of this there were platters of bread, and quartered lemons, and vinegar and pepper castors – two or three of each. Beside every plate there was a fork, a spoon, a napkin, and the all-important oyster-knife; and in the middle of the table there was the oyster-barrel itself, a white cloth bound about its top-most hoop, and its lid loosened by a finger's width – 'Just enough,' as my father would say, 'to let the oysters stretch a little'; but not enough to let them open their shells and sicken. We were rather cramped around the table, for there were eight of us in all, and we had had to bring up extra chairs from the restaurant below. Kitty and I sat close, our elbows almost touching, our shoes side by side beneath the table. When Mother cried, 'Do move along a bit, Nancy, and give Miss Butler some room!', Kitty said that she was quite all right, Mrs Astley, really; and I shifted a quarter of an inch to my right, but kept my foot pressed against hers, and felt her leg, all hot, against my own.

Father handed out the oysters, and Mother offered beer or lemonade. Kitty picked up a shell with one hand and her oyster-knife with the other, and brought them together rather ineffectually. Father saw, and gave a shout.

'Ho, there, Miss Butler, where are our manners! Davy, you take that knife and show the lady how – else she might just job the blade into her hand, and give herself a nasty cut.'

'I can do it,' I said quickly; and I took the oyster from her, and the knife, before my brother could get his fingers on them.

'You do it like this,' I said to her. 'You must hold the oyster in your palm so that the flat shell is uppermost – like this.' I held the shell to show her, and she gazed at it rather gravely. 'Then you must take your blade and put it – not between the

halves, but in the hinge, here. And then you must grasp it, and
prise.' I gave the knife a gentle twist, and the shell eased open.
'You must hold it steady,' I went on, 'because the shell is full
of liquor, and you mustn't spill a drop of it, for that's the tasti-
est part.' The little fish sat in my palm in its bath of
oyster-juice, naked and slippery. 'This here,' I said, pointing
with my knife, 'is called the beard; you must trim that away.'
I gave the blade a flick, and the beard was severed. 'Then you
must just cut your oyster free . . . And now you may eat it.' I
slipped the shell carefully into her hand, and felt her fingers
warm and soft against my own as she cupped them to receive
it. Our heads were very near. She raised the oyster to her lips
and held it for a second before her mouth, her eyes on mine,
unblinking.

I had not been aware of it, but I had spoken softly, and the
others had quietened to listen. Now the table was hushed and
still. When I took my eyes from Kitty's I saw a ring of faces
turned my way, and blushed.

At last, someone spoke. It was Father, and his voice was
very loud. 'No bolting him down whole now, Miss Butler,' he
said, 'like the *gormays* do. We won't have that at this table. You
go on and give him a real good chew.' He said it kindly, and
Kitty laughed. She peered into the shell in her hand.

'And is it really *alive*?' she said.

'Alive alive-oh,' said Davy. 'If you listen very hard, you will
hear him shrieking as he goes down.'

There were protests at that from Rhoda and Alice. 'You will
make the poor girl sick,' said Mother. 'Don't you mind him,
Miss Butler. You just eat your fish, and enjoy it.'

Kitty did so. With no more glances at me she threw the contents of her shell into her mouth, chewed them hard and fast,
and swallowed them. Then she wiped her lips with her
napkin, and smiled at Father.

'Now,' he said, confidentially, 'tell the truth: have you ever
tasted an oyster such as that before, or have you not?'

Kitty said that she had not, and Davy gave a cheer; and for

a while there was no sound at all but the delicate, diminutive sounds of a good oyster-supper: the creak of hinges, the slap of discarded beards, the trickle of liquor and butter and beer.

I opened no more shells for Kitty, for she managed them herself. 'Look at this one!' she said, when she had handled half-a-dozen or so. 'What a brute he is!' Then she looked more closely at it. '*Is* it a he? I suppose they all must be, since they all have beards?'

Father shook his head, chewing. 'Not at all, Miss Butler, not at all. Don't let the beards mislead you. For the oyster, you see, is what you might call a real queer fish – now a he, now a she, as quite takes its fancy. A regular morphodite, in fact!'

'Is that so?'

Tony tapped his plate. 'You're a bit of an oyster, then, yourself, Kitty,' he said with a smirk.

She looked for a moment rather uncertain, but then she smiled. 'Why, I suppose I am,' she said. 'Just fancy! I've never been likened to a fish before.'

'Well, don't take it the wrong way, Miss Butler,' said Mother, 'for spoken in this house, it is something of a compliment.'

Tony laughed, and Father said, 'Oh, it was, it was!'

Kitty still smiled. Then she half-rose to reach a pepper castor; and when she sat again she drew her feet beneath her chair, and I felt my thigh grow cool.

When the oyster-barrel was quite empty, and the lemonade and the Bass had all been drunk, and Kitty declared that she had never had a finer supper in all her life, we moved our chairs away from the table, and the men lit cigarettes, and Alice and Rhoda set out cups, for tea. There was more talk, and more questions for Kitty to answer. Had she ever met Nelly Power? Did she know Bessie Bellwood, or Jenny Hill, or Jolly John Nash? Then, on another tack: was it true that she had no young chap? She said she had no time for it. And had she family, in Kent, and when did she see them? She had none at all, she said, since her grandmother died. Mother tut-tutted

over that, and said it was a shame; Davy said she could help
herself to some of our relations, if she liked, for we had more
than we knew what to do with.

'Oh yes?' said Kitty.

'Yes,' said Davy. 'You must have heard the song:

*'There's her uncle, and her brother, and her sister, and
her mother,*
*And her auntie, and another, who is cousin to her
mother . . .'*

No sooner had he finished the verse, indeed, than there was
the sound of our street-door opening, and a shout up the stairs;
and three of our cousins themselves appeared, followed by
Uncle Joe and Aunt Rosina – all got up in their Sunday best,
and all just popped in, they said, for a 'peek' at Miss Butler, if
Miss Butler had no objection.

More chairs were brought up, and more cups; a fresh round
of introductions was made, and the little room grew stuffy
with heat and smoke and laughter. Somebody said what a
shame it was we had no piano for Miss Butler to give us a song;
then George – my eldest cousin – said, 'Would a harmonica
serve the purpose?' and produced one from his jacket pocket.
Kitty blushed, and said she couldn't; and everyone cried, 'Oh
please, Miss Butler, do!'

'What do you think, Nan?' she said to me. 'Should I shame
myself?'

'You know you won't,' I said, pleased that she had turned to
me at the last, and used my special name before them all.

'Very well, then,' she said. A little space was cleared for her,
and Rhoda ran down to her house, to fetch her sisters to come
and watch.

She sang 'The Boy I Love is Up in the Gallery', and 'The
Coffee Shop Girl' – then 'The Boy' again for Rhoda's sisters,
who had just arrived. Then she whispered to George and to
me, and I fetched her a hat of Father's and a walking-cane, and

she sang us a couple of masher songs, and ended with the ballad with which she finished her set at the Palace, about the sweetheart and the rose.

We cheered her then, and she had her hand shaken, and her back slapped, ten times over. She looked very flushed and hot at the end of it all, and rather tired. Davy said, 'How about a song from you now, Nance?' I gave him a look.

'No,' I said. I wouldn't sing for them with Kitty there, for anything.

Kitty looked at me curiously. 'Do you sing, then?' she said.

'Nancy's got the prettiest voice, Miss Butler,' said one of the cousins, 'you ever heard.'

'Yes, go on, Nance, be a sport!' said another.

'No, no, no!' I cried again – so firmly that Mother frowned, and the others laughed.

Uncle Joe said, 'Well, that's a shame, that is. You should hear her in the kitchen, Miss Butler. She's a regular song-bird, she is, then: a regular lark. Makes your heart turn over, to hear her.' There were murmurs of agreement throughout the room, and I saw Kitty look blinkingly my way. Then George whispered rather loudly that I must be saving my voice for serenading Freddy, and there was a fresh round of laughter that set me gazing and blushing into my lap. Kitty looked bemused.

She asked then, 'Who is Freddy?'

'Freddy is Nancy's young feller,' said Davy. 'A *very* handsome chap. She must've boasted about him to you?'

'No,' said Kitty, 'she has not.' She said it lightly, but I glanced up and saw that her eyes were strange, and almost sad. It was true that I had never mentioned Fred to her. The fact was, I barely thought of him as my beau these days, for since her arrival in Canterbury I had had no evenings spare to spend with him. He had recently sent me a letter to say, Did I still care? And I had put the letter in a drawer, and forgotten to reply.

There was more chaff about Freddy, then; I was glad when

one of Rhoda's sisters caused a fuss, by snatching the harmonica from George and giving us a tune so horrible it made the boys all shout at her, and pull her hair, to make her stop.

While they quarrelled and swore, Kitty leaned towards me and said softly, 'Will you take me to your room, Nan, or somewhere quiet, for a bit – just you and me?' She looked so grave suddenly I feared that she might faint. I got up, and made a path for her across the crowded room, and told my mother I was taking her upstairs; and Mother – who was gazing troubledly at Rhoda's sister, not knowing whether to laugh at her or to scold – gave us a nod, distractedly, and we escaped.

The bedroom was cooler than the parlour, and dimmer, and – although we could still hear shouts, and stamping, and blasts from the harmonica – wonderfully calm compared to the room we had just left. The window was raised, and Kitty crossed to it at once and placed her arms upon the sill. Closing her eyes against the breeze that blew in from the bay, she took a few deep, grateful breaths.

'Are you poorly?' I said. She turned to me and shook her head, and smiled; but again, her smile seemed sad.

'Just tired.'

My jug and bowl were on the side. I poured a little water out and carried it to her, for her to wash her hands and splash her face. The water spotted her dress, and dampened the fringe of her hair into dark little points.

She had a purse swinging at her waist, and now she dipped her fingers into it and drew out a cigarette and a box of matches. She said, 'I am sure your mother would disapprove, but I'm just about busting for a smoke.' She lit the cigarette, and drew upon it heavily.

We gazed at one another not speaking. Then, because we were weary and there was nowhere else for us to sit, we sat upon the bed, side by side, and quite close. It was terribly strange to be with her in the very room – on the very spot! – where I had spent so many hours dreaming of her, so immodestly. I said, 'It ain't half strange—' But as I said it she also spoke; and we laughed. 'You first,' she said, and drew again upon her fag.

'I was just going to say, how funny it is to have you here, like this.'

'And I,' she said, 'was going to say how funny it is to be here! And this is really your room, yours and Alice's? And your bed?' She looked about her, as if in wonder – as if I might have taken her to a stranger's chamber, and be trying to pass it off as my own – and I nodded.

She was silent again, then, and so was I; and yet I sensed that she had more to say, and was only working up to saying it. I thought, with a little thrill, that I knew what it was; but when she spoke again it wasn't about the contract, but about my family – about how kind they were, and how much they loved me, and how lucky I was to have them. I remembered that she was an orphan, of sorts, and bit back my protests, and let her talk; but my silence seemed only to dampen her spirits the further.

At last, when her cigarette was finished and thrown into the grate, she took a breath and said what I had been waiting for. 'Nan, I have something to tell you – a piece of good news, and you must promise to be happy for me.'

I couldn't help myself. I had been longing to smile about it all afternoon, and now I laughed and said, 'Oh Kitty, I know your news already!' She seemed to frown then, so I went on quickly, 'You mustn't be cross with Tony, but he told me – just today.'

'Told you what?'

'That Tricky wants you to stay on, at the Palace; that you will be here till Christmas at least!'

She looked at me rather strangely, then lowered her gaze and gave an awkward little laugh. 'That's not my news,' she said. 'And nobody knows it but me. Tricky *does* want me to stay on – but I've turned him down.'

'Turned him down?' I stared at her. Still she would not catch my eye, but got to her feet, and crossed her arms over her waist.

'Do you remember the gentleman who called on me last night?' she said. 'Mr Bliss?' I nodded. She hadn't mentioned him today; and in all my fussing over her visit, I had forgotten to ask after him. Now she went on: 'Mr Bliss is a manager – not a theatre manager, like Tricky, but a manager for artistes: an agent. He saw my turn and – oh, Nan!' – she couldn't help but be excited now – 'he saw my turn and liked it so much, he has offered me a contract, at a music hall in London!'

'London!' I could only echo her in disbelief. This was terrible beyond all words. Had she gone to Margate or Broadstairs, I might have visited her sometimes. If she went to London I would never see her again; she might just as well go to Africa, or to the moon.

She went talking on, saying how Mr Bliss had friends at the London halls, and had promised her a season at them all; how he had said she was too good for the provincial stage; that she would find fame in the city, where all the big names worked, and all the money was . . . I hardly listened, but grew more and more miserable. At length I placed a hand before my eyes, and bowed my head, and she grew silent.

'You're not happy for me, after all,' she said quietly.

'I am,' I said – my voice was thick – 'but I am more *un*happy, for myself.'

There was a silence then, broken only by the sound of laughter and scraping chairs from the parlour below, and the shriek of gulls outside the open window. The room seemed to have darkened since we entered it, and I felt colder, suddenly, than I had all summer.

I heard her take a step. In a second she was sitting beside me again, and had taken my hand from my brow. 'Listen,' she said. 'I have something to ask you.' I looked at her; her face was pale, except for its cloud of freckles, and her eyes seemed large. 'Do you think that I look handsome today?' she said. 'Do you think I have been kind, and pleasant, and good? Do you think your parents like me?' Her words seemed wild. I did not speak, but only nodded wonderingly. 'I came,' she said, 'to make them. I wore my smartest frock, so they would think me grander than I am. I thought, they might be the meanest and most miserable family in all of Kent; yet I will work so hard at being nice, they'll trust me like a daughter.

'But oh, Nan, they're not miserable or mean, and I didn't have to play at being nice at all! They are the kindest family I ever met; and you are all the world to them. I cannot ask you to give them up . . .'

My heart seemed to stop – and then to pound, like a piston. 'What do you mean?' I said. She looked away.

'I meant to ask you to come with me. To London.'

I blinked. 'To go with you? But how?'

'As my dresser,' she said, 'if you'd care to. As my – any-thing, I don't know. I have spoken to Mr Bliss: he says there will not be much money for you at first – but enough, if you share my diggings.'

'Why?' I said then. She raised her eyes to mine.

'Because I . . . like you. Because you are good for me, and bring me luck. And because London will be strange; and Mr Bliss may not be all that he seems; and I shall have no one . . .'

'And you truly thought,' I said slowly, 'that I would say no?'

'This afternoon – yes. Last night, and this morning, I believed— Oh, it was so different in the dressing-room, when it was just the two of us! I didn't know then how it was for you here. I didn't know then that you had a – a chap.'

Her words made me bold. I drew my hand away from hers and got to my feet. I walked to the head of the bed, where there was a little cabinet, with a drawer in it. I opened it, and took something from it, and showed it to her. 'Do you know this?' I said, and she smiled.

'It's the flower I gave you.' She took it from me, and held it. It was dry and limp, and its petals were brown at the edges and coming loose; and it was rather flat, because I had slept many nights with it beneath my pillow.

'When you threw this to me,' I said to her, 'my life changed.

I think I must have been – asleep – till that moment: asleep, or dead. Since I met you, I've been awake – alive! Do you think I could give that up, now, so easily?'

My words startled her – as well they might, for I had never spoken like this before, to her or to anyone. She looked away from me, about the room, and ran her tongue over her lips. 'And all of *them*, downstairs?' she said, nodding towards the door. 'Your mother and father, your brother, Alice, Freddy?' As she spoke there came a shout, and the sound of voices raised in friendly argument.

They mean nothing to me, I wanted to say, *compared with you* . . . But I only shrugged, and smiled.

She smiled then, too. 'And so you really will come? We must leave on Sunday, you know – a week from today. It doesn't give you long.'

I said it would be long enough; and she placed the faded rose upon the bed, and seized my hands and squeezed them hard.

'Oh Nan! My dear Nan! We'll have such times together, I promise you!' As she spoke, she flung my hands aside, and gripped me in a fierce embrace, and laughed with pleasure, so that I felt her body shudder in my arms.

Then, all too soon, she stepped away, and I had only empty air to clutch at.

There was more noise from below, then the sound of a door opening, followed by the thud of feet upon the staircase, and a cry: 'Nancy!' It was Alice. She paused outside the bedroom door, but was too polite – or fearful – to turn the handle. 'Everyone is leaving,' she called. 'Mother says will Miss Butler just step down for a moment, please, for them to say good-bye.'

I looked at Kitty. 'You go on,' I said, 'without me, and I shall come down in a minute. And don't,' I added in a lower voice, 'say anything to them about – our plans. I'll talk to them about it, later on.'

She nodded, and gave my hand another squeeze; then she

opened the door and joined Alice on the landing, and I heard them step below, together.

I stood in the gathering shadows and put my trembling fingers before my face. I had taken to scrubbing my hands very carefully, since meeting Kitty Butler; and if they were ever a little stained at the creases now, it was as much with paint and hot-black and *blanc-de-perle*, as with vinegar. Even so, there was the scent of oysters on them still, and a slender thread – it might have been the bristle from the back of a lobster, the whisker from a shrimp – beneath one of my nails. How would it be, I thought, to surrender my family, my home, all my oyster-girl's ways?

And how would it be to live at Kitty's side, brim-full of a love so quick, and yet so secret, it made me shake?

Chapter 3

I wish, for sensation's sake, I could say that my parents heard one word of Kitty's proposal and forbade me, absolutely, to refer to it again; that when I pressed the matter, they cursed and shouted; that my mother wept, my father struck me; that I was obliged, in the end, to climb from a window at dawn, with my clothes in a rag at the end of a stick, and a streaming face, and a note pinned to my pillow saying, *Do not try to follow me* . . . But if I said these things, I would be lying. My parents were reasonable, not passionate, people. They loved me, and they feared for me; the idea of allowing their youngest daughter to travel in the care of an actress and a music-hall manager to the grimmest, wickedest city in England was, they knew, a mad one, that no sane parent should entertain for longer than a second. But because they loved me so, they could not bear to have me grieve. Anyone with half an eye could see that my heart lay all with Kitty Butler now; anyone might guess that, having once been offered the chance of a future at her side, and kept from it, I could never return to my father's kitchen and be happy there, as I had been before.

So when, an hour or so after Kitty's departure, I nervously put her plan before my parents, and argued and pleaded for their blessing, they listened to me wonderingly, but carefully;

and when, the next day, Father stopped me on my way down to the kitchen to draw me into the parlour where it was quiet and still, his face was sad and serious, but kind. He asked me, first, whether I had not changed my mind. I shook my head, and he sighed. He said, if I was quite decided, then Mother and he could not keep me; that I was a grown-up woman, almost, and should be allowed to know my own mind; that they had thought to see me marry a Whitstable boy, and settle close at hand, and so have a share in my little happinesses and troubles – but that now, he supposed, I would go and hitch up with some London fellow, who wouldn't understand their ways at all.

But children, he concluded, weren't made to please their parents; and no father should expect to have his daughter at his side for ever . . . 'In short, Nance, even was you going to the very devil himself, your mother and I would rather see you fly from us in joy, than stay with us in sorrow – and grow, maybe, to hate us, for keeping you from your fate.' I had never known him so grave before, nor so eloquent. I had never seen him weep either; but now as he spoke his eyes glistened, and he blinked, twice or thrice, to hold the tears back, and his voice grew thin. I placed my head against his shoulder and let my own tears rise and spill. He put an arm about me, and patted me. 'It breaks our hearts to lose you, dear,' he went on. 'You know it does. Only promise us that you won't forget us, quite. That you'll write to us, and visit us. And that, if things don't turn out as you might, quite, wish them, you won't be too proud to come home to those that love you—' Here his voice failed utterly, and he shuddered; and I could only nod against his neck and say, 'I will, I will; I promise you, I will.'

But oh! Hard-hearted daughter that I was, when he had left me my tears dried at once, and I felt the return of all my gladness of the night before. I hugged myself in pleasure, and danced a jig around the parlour – but delicately, on tiptoe, so that they wouldn't hear me in the dining-room below. Then quickly, before I should be missed, I ran to the post office and sent Kitty a card at the Palace – a picture of a Whitstable oyster-smack, upon whose sail I inked, 'To London', and on the deck of which I drew two girls with bags and trunks and out-size, smiling faces. 'I can come!!!' I wrote upon the back, and added that she must do without her dresser for a few nights while I made all ready . . . and I finished it 'Fondly', and signed it, 'Your Nan'.

I had to be glad only in snatches that day, for the scene that I had passed with Father, after breakfast, had to be undergone again with Mother – who hugged me to her, and cried that they must be fools to let me go; and Davy – who said, quite absurdly, that I was too little to go to London, and would be run down by a tram in Trafalgar Square the minute I set foot in it; and Alice – who said nothing at all when she heard the news, but ran from the kitchen in tears, and could not be per-suaded to take up her duties in the Parlour until lunch-time. Only my cousins seemed happy for me – and they were more jealous than happy, calling me a lucky cat, and swearing that I would make my fortune in the city, and forget them all; or else that I would be ruined utterly, and come sneaking back to them in disgrace.

That week passed quickly. I spent my evenings in calling on friends and family, and bidding them farewell; and in washing and patching and packing my dresses, and sorting out which little items to take with me, which to leave behind. I visited the Palace only once, and that was in the company of my parents, who came to reassure themselves that Miss Butler was still sensible and good, and to ask for further particulars of the shadowy Walter Bliss.

I had Kitty to myself for no more than a minute, while Father chatted with Tony and Tricky, after the show. I had feared all week that I had imagined the words that she had spoken to me on Sunday evening, or misunderstood them entirely. Every night, almost, I had woken sweating from dreams in which I presented myself at her door, with my bags all packed and my hat upon my head, and she looked at me in wonder, and frowned, or laughed with derision; or else I arrived too late at the station, and had to chase the train along the track while Kitty and Mr Bliss gazed at me from their carriage window, and would not lean outside to pull me in . . . That night at the Palace, however, she led me to one side, and pressed my hand, and was quite as kind and excited as she had been before.

'I've had a letter from Mr Bliss,' she said. 'He has found us rooms in a house in a place called Brixton – a place so full, he says, of music-hall people and actors that they call it "Grease-Paint Avenue".'

Grease-Paint Avenue! I saw it instantly and it was marvellous, a street set out like a make-up box, with narrow, gilded houses, each one with a different coloured roof; and ours would be number 3 – with a chimney the colour of Kitty's carmined lips!

'We are to catch the two o'clock train on Sunday,' she went on, 'and Mr Bliss himself will meet us at the station, in a carriage. And I'm due to start the very next day at the Star Music Hall, in Bermondsey.'

'The Star,' I said. 'That's a lucky name.'

She smiled. 'Let's hope so. Oh, Nan, let's only hope so!'

My last morning at home was – like every last morning in history, I suppose – a sad one. We breakfasted together, the five of us, and were bright enough; but there was a horrible sense of expectation in the house that made anything except sighing, and drifting aimlessly from job to job, seem quite impossible. By eleven o'clock I felt as penned and as stifled as a rat in a box, and made Alice walk with me to the beach, and hold my shoes and stockings while I stood at the water's edge one final time. But even this little ritual was a disappointing one. I put my hand to my brow and gazed at the glittering bay, at the distant fields and hedges of Sheppey, at the low, pitch-painted houses of the town, and the masts and cranes of the harbour and the shipyard. It was all as familiar to me as the lines on my own face, and – like one's face when viewed in a glass – both fascinating and rather dull. No matter how hard I studied it, how fiercely I thought, I shall not gaze at you again for months and months, it looked just as it always did; and at last I turned my eyes away, and walked sadly home.

But it was the same there: nothing that I gazed at or touched was as special as I thought it should be, or changed by my going in any way. Nothing, that is, except the faces of my family; and these were so grave, or so falsely merry and stiff, that I could hardly bear to look at them at all.

So I was almost glad, at last, when it was time to say farewell. Father wouldn't let me take the little train to Canterbury, but said I must be driven, and hired a gig from the ostler at the Duke of Cumberland Hotel, to take me there himself. I kissed Mother, and Alice, and let my brother hand me to my seat at Father's side and place my luggage at my feet. There was little enough of it: an old leather suitcase with a strap about it, that held my clothes; a cap-box for my hats; and a little black tin trunk for everything else. The trunk was a good-bye gift from Davy. He had bought it new, and had my initials painted on the lid in swooning yellow capitals; and inside it he had pasted a map of Kent, with Whitstable marked on it with an arrow – to remind me, he said, where home was, in case I should forget.

We did not talk much, Father and I, on the drive to Canterbury. At the station we found the train already in and steaming, and Kitty, her own bags and baskets at her side, frowning over her watch. It wasn't like my anxious dreams at all: she gave a great wave when she saw us, and a smile.

'I thought you might have changed your mind,' she cried, 'at the very last moment.' And I shook my head – in wonder that she could still think such a thing, after all I'd said!

Father was very kind. He greeted Kitty graciously and, when he kissed me good-bye he kissed her, too, and wished her happiness and luck. At the last moment, as I leaned from the carriage to embrace him, he drew a little chamois bag from his pocket and placed it in my hand, and closed my fingers over it. It held coins – sovereigns – six of them, and more, I knew, than he could afford to part with; but by the time I had drawn open the neck of the bag and seen the gleam of the gold inside it, the train had begun to move, and it was too late to thrust them back. Instead, I could only shout my thanks, and kiss my fingers to him, and watch as he raised his hat and waved it; then place my cheek against the window-glass when he was gone from sight, and wonder when I should see him next.

I did not wonder for long, I am afraid to say, for the thrill of being with Kitty – of hearing her talk again of the rooms we were to share, and the kind of life we were to have together in the city, where she was to make her fortune – soon overcame my grief. My family would have thought me cruel, I know, to see me laugh while they were sad at home without me; but oh! I could no more not have smiled, that afternoon, than not drawn breath, or sweated.

And soon, too, I had London to gaze at and marvel over; for in an hour we had arrived at Charing Cross. Here Kitty found a porter to help us with our bags and boxes, and while he loaded them on to a trolley we looked round anxiously for Mr Bliss. At last, 'There he is!' cried Kitty, and her pointing finger showed him striding up the platform, his whiskers and his coat-tails flying and his face very red.

'Miss Butler!' he cried when he reached us. 'What a pleasure! What a pleasure! I feared I would be late; but here you are exactly as we planned, and even more charming than before.' He turned to me, then removed his hat – the silk, again – and made me a low, theatrical bow. '"Off goes his bonnet to an oyster-wench!"' he said, rather loudly. 'Miss Astley – late of Whitstable, I believe?' He took my hand and gripped it briefly. Then he snapped his fingers at the porter, and offered us each an arm.

He had left a carriage waiting for us on the Strand; the driver touched his whip to his cap when we approached, and jumped from his seat to place our luggage on the roof. I looked about me. It was a Sunday and the Strand was rather quiet – but I didn't know it; it might have been the race-track at the Derby to me, so deafening and dizzying was the clatter of the traffic, so swift the passage of the horses. I felt safer in the carriage, and only rather queer, to be so close to a gentleman I did not know, being transported I knew not where, in a city that was vaster and smokier and more alarming than I could have thought possible.

There was much, of course, to look at. Mr Bliss had suggested we take in the sights a little before we headed for Brixton, so now we rolled into Trafalgar Square – towards Nelson on his pillar, and the fountains, and the lovely, bone-coloured front of the National Gallery, and the view down Whitehall to the Houses of Parliament.

'My brother,' I said, as I pressed my face to the window to gaze at it all, 'said I would be run down by a tram in Trafalgar Square, if ever I came to London.'

Mr Bliss looked grave. 'Your brother was very sensible to warn you, Miss Astley – but sadly misinformed. There are no trams in Trafalgar Square – only buses and hansoms, and broughams like our own. Trams are for common people; you should have to go quite as far as Kilburn, I'm afraid, or Camden Town, in order to be struck by a tram.'

I smiled uncertainly. I did not know, quite, what to make of Mr Bliss, to whom my future and my happiness had been so recently, and so unexpectedly, entrusted. While he addressed himself to Kitty, and directed our attention every so often to some scene or character in the street beyond, I studied him. He was a little younger, I saw, than I had taken him to be at first. That night in Kitty's dressing-room I had thought him almost middle-aged; now I guessed him to be one- or two-and-thirty, at the most. He was an impressive, rather than a handsome, man, but for all his flash and his speeches, rather homely: I thought he must have a little wife who loved him, and a baby; and that if he did not – which, in fact, was the case – that he should have. I knew nothing, then, of his history, but learned

later that he came from an old, respectable, theatrical family
(his real name was no more Bliss, of course, than Kitty's was
Butler); that he had left the legitimate stage when he was still
a young man, in order to work the halls as a comic singer; and
that he managed, now, a dozen artistes, but still, on occasion,
took a turn before the footlights – as 'Walter Waters, Character
Baritone' – for sheer love of the profession. I knew none of this
that day in the brougham – but I began to guess a little of it. For
we had reached Pall Mall and turned into the Haymarket,
where the theatres and the music halls begin; and as we rumbled past them he raised his hand and tilted the brim of his hat
in a kind of salute. I have seen old Irishwomen, passing before
a church, do something similar.

'Her Majesty's,' he said, nodding to a handsome building on
his left: 'my father saw Jenny Lind, the Swedish Nightingale,
make her debut there. The Haymarket: managed by Mr
Beerbohm Tree. The Criterion, or Cri: a marvel of a theatre,
built entirely underground.' Theatre upon theatre, hall upon
hall; and he knew all their histories. 'Ahead of us, the London
Pavilion. Down *there*' – we squinted along Great Windmill
Street – 'the Trocadero Palace. On our right, the Prince's
Theatre.' We passed into Leicester Square; he took a breath.
'And finally,' he said – and here he removed his hat entirely,
and held it in his lap – 'finally, the Empire and the Alhambra,
the handsomest music halls in England, where every artiste is
a star, and the audience is so distinguished that even the gay
girls in the gallery – if you'll pardon my French, Miss Butler,
Miss Astley – wear furs, and pearls, and diamonds.'

He tapped on the ceiling of the brougham, and the driver
drew to a halt at a corner of the little garden in the middle of
the square. Mr Bliss opened the carriage door, and led us to its
centre. Here, with William Shakespeare on his marble pedestal
at our backs, we gazed, all three of us, at the glorious façades
of the Empire and the Alhambra – the former with its columns
and its glinting cressets, its stained glass and its soft electric
glow; the latter with its dome, its minarets and fountain. I had

not known there were theatres like this in the world. I had not known that there was such a place as this, at all – this place that was so squalid and so splendid, so ugly and so grand, where every imaginable manner of person stood, or strolled, or lounged, side by side.

There were ladies and gentlemen, stepping from carriages.

There were girls with trays of flowers and fruit; and coffee-sellers, and sherbet-sellers, and soup-men.

There were soldiers in scarlet jackets; there were off-duty shop-boys in bowlers and boaters and checks. There were women in shawls, and women in neckties; and women in short skirts, showing their ankles.

There were black men and Chinamen and Italians and Greeks. There were newcomers to the city, gazing about them as dazed and confounded as I; and there were people curled on steps and benches, people in clothes that were crumpled or stained, who looked as if they spent all their daylit hours here – and all their dark ones, too.

I gazed at Kitty, and my face, I suppose, showed my amazement, for she laughed, and stroked my cheek, then seized my hand and held it.

'We are at the heart of London,' said Mr Bliss as she did so, 'the very *heart* of it. Over there' – he nodded to the Alhambra – 'and all around us' – and here he swept his hand across the square itself – 'you see what makes that great heart beat: *Variety!* Variety, Miss Astley, which age cannot wither, nor custom stale.' Now he turned to Kitty. 'We stand,' he said, 'before the greatest Temple of Variety in all the land. Tomorrow, Miss Butler – tomorrow, or next week, or next month, perhaps, but soon, soon, I promise you – you will stand *within* it, your feet upon its stage. Then it will be *you* that sets the heart of London racing! You that makes the throats of the city shout, "*Brava!*"'

As he spoke he lifted his hat, and punched the air with it; one or two passers-by turned their faces towards us, then looked away quite unconcerned. His words, I thought, were marvellous ones – and I knew Kitty thought so, too, for she gripped my hand at the sound of them, and gave a little shudder of delight; and her cheeks were flushed, as mine were, and her eyes, like mine, were shining and wide.

We didn't linger very long in Leicester Square after that. Mr Bliss hailed a boy, and gave him a shilling to fetch us three foaming glasses from the sherbet-seller, and we sat for a minute in Shakespeare's shadow, sipping our drinks and gazing at the people who passed us by, and at the notices outside the Empire, where Kitty's name, we knew, would soon be pasted in letters three feet high. But when our glasses were empty, he slapped his hands together and said we must be off, for Brixton and Mrs Dendy – our new landlady – awaited; and he led us back to the brougham and handed us to our seats. I felt my eyes, that had been so wide and dazzled, grow small again in the gloom of the coach, and I began to feel not thrilled but rather nervous. I wondered what kind of lodgings he had found for us, and what kind of lady Mrs Dendy would be. I hoped that neither would be very grand.

I need not have worried. Once we had left the West End and crossed the river, the streets grew greyer and quite dull. The houses and the people here were smart, but rather uniform, as if all crafted by the same unimaginative hand: there was none of that strange glamour, that lovely, queer variety of Leicester Square. Soon, too, the streets ceased even to be smart, and became a little shabby; each corner that we passed, each public house, each row of shops and houses, seemed dingier than the one before. Beside me, Kitty and Mr Bliss had fallen into conversation; their talk was all of theatres and contracts, costumes and songs. I kept my face pressed to the window, wondering when we should ever leave behind these dreary districts and reach Grease-Paint Avenue, our home.

At last, when we had turned into a street of tall, flat-roofed houses, each with a line of blistered railings before it and a set of sooty blinds and curtains at its windows, Mr Bliss broke off his talk to peer outside and say that we were almost there. I

had to look away from his kind and smiling face, then, to hide
my disappointment. I knew that my first, excited vision of
Brixton – that row of golden make-up sticks, our house with
the carmine-coloured roof – was a foolish one; but this street
looked so very grey and mean. It was no different really, I suppose, from the ordinary roads that I had left behind in
Whitstable; it was only strange – but therefore slightly sinister.

As we stepped from the carriage I glanced at Kitty to see if
she, too, felt any stirrings of dismay. But her colour was as
high, and her eyes as damp and shining, as before; she only
gazed at the house to which our chaperon now led us, and
gave a little, tight-lipped smile of satisfaction. I understood,
suddenly – what I had only half perceived before – that she
had spent her life in plain, anonymous houses like this one,
and knew no better. The thought gave me a little courage – and
made me ache, as usual, with sympathy and love.

Inside, too, the house was rather cheerier. We were met at
the door by Mrs Dendy herself – a white-haired, rather portly
lady, who greeted Mr Bliss like a friend, calling him 'Wal',
and offering him her cheek to kiss – and shown into her parlour. Here she had us sit and remove our hats, and bade us
make ourselves quite cosy; and a girl was called, then swiftly
dispatched to bring some cups and brew some tea on our
behalf.

When the door was closed behind her Mrs Dendy gave us a
smile. 'Welcome, my dears,' she said – she had a voice as
damp and fruity as a piece of Christmas cake – 'Welcome to
Ginevra Road. I do hope that your stay with me will be a
happy, and a *lucky* one.' Here she nodded to Kitty. 'Mr Bliss
tells me that I'm to have quite a little star twinkling beneath
my eaves, Miss Butler.'

Kitty said modestly that she didn't know about that, and
Mrs Dendy gave a chuckle that turned into a throaty cough. For
a long moment the cough seemed to quite convulse her, and
Kitty and I sat up, exchanging glances of alarm and dismay.
When the fit was passed, however, the lady seemed just as

calm and jolly as before. She drew a handkerchief from her sleeve, and wiped her lips and eyes with it; then she reached for a packet of Woodbines from the table at her elbow, offered us each a cigarette, and took one for herself. Her fingers, I saw then, were quite yellow with tobacco stains.

After a moment the tea things appeared, and while Kitty and Mrs Dendy busied themselves with the tray I looked about me. There was much to look at, for Mrs Dendy's parlour was rather extraordinary. Its rugs and furniture were plain enough; its walls, however, were wonderful, for every one of them was crowded with pictures and photographs – so crowded, indeed, that there was barely enough space between the frames to make out the colour of the wallpaper beneath.

'I can see you are quite taken with my little collection,' said Mrs Dendy as she handed me my tea-cup, and I blushed to find all eyes suddenly turned my way. She gave me a smile, and lifted her yellowed fingers to fiddle with the crystal drop that hung, on a brass thread, from the hole in her ear. 'All old tenants of mine, my dear,' she said; 'and some of them, as you will see, rather famous.'

I looked at the pictures again. They were all, I now saw, portraits – signed portraits most of them – of artistes from the theatres and the halls. There were, as Mrs Dendy had claimed, several faces that I knew – the Great Vance, for instance, had his photograph upon the chimney-breast, with Jolly John Nash, posed as 'Rackity Jack', at his side; and above the sofa there was a framed song-sheet with a sprawling, uneven dedication: 'To Dear Ma Dendy. Kind thoughts, Good wishes. Bessie Bellwood'. But there were many more that I did not recognise, men and women with laughing faces, in gay, professional poses, and with costumes and names so bland, exotic or obscure – Jennie West, Captain Largo, Shinkaboo Lee – I could guess nothing about the nature of their turns. I marvelled to think that they had all stayed here, in Ginevra Road, with comely Mrs Dendy as their host.

We talked until the tea was drunk, and our landlady had

smoked two or three more cigarettes; then she slapped her
knees and got slowly to her feet.

'I dare say you would like to see your rooms, and give your
faces a bit of a splash,' she said pleasantly. She turned to Mr
Bliss, who had risen politely when she had. 'Now, if you could
just apply your obliging arm to the young ladies' boxes and
things, Wal . . .' Then she led us from the parlour, and up the
stairs. We climbed for three flights, the stairwell growing
dimmer as we ascended, then lightening: the last set of steps
were slim and uncarpeted, and had a little skylight above
them, a quartered pane streaked with soot and pigeon-
droppings, through which the blue of the September sky
showed unexpectedly vivid and clear – as if the sky itself were
a ceiling, and, climbing, we had come nearer to it.

At the top of these steps there was a door, and behind this a
very small room – not a bed-sitting room as I had expected, but
a tiny parlour with a pair of ancient, sagging armchairs set
before a hearth, and a shallow, old-fashioned dresser. Beside
the dresser was another door, leading to a second chamber
which a sloping roof made even smaller than the first. Kitty
and I stepped to its threshold and stood, side by side, gazing at
what lay beyond: a wash-hand stand; a lyre-backed chair; an
alcove with a curtain before it; and a bed – a bed with a high,
thick mattress and an iron bedstead, and beneath it a chamber-
pot – a bed rather narrower than the one I was used to sharing
with my sister at home.

'You won't mind doubling up, of course,' said Mrs Dendy,
who had followed us to the bedroom. 'You'll be quite on top of
each other in here, I'm afraid – though not so tight as my boys
downstairs, who only have the one room. But Mr Bliss did
insist on a decent bit of space for the two of you.' She smiled
at me, and I looked away. Kitty, however, said very brightly:
'It's perfect, Mrs Dendy. Miss Astley and I will be as cosy here
as two peg-dolls in a doll's house – won't we, Nan?'

Her cheeks, I saw, had grown a little pink – but that might
have been from the climb up from the parlour. I said, 'We will',

and lowered my gaze again; then moved to take a box from Mr Bliss.

Mr Bliss himself did not stay long after that – as if he thought it indelicate to linger in a lady's chamber, even one he was paying for himself. He exchanged a few words with Kitty regarding her appointment on the morrow at the Bermondsey Star – for she had to meet the manager, and rehearse with the orchestra, in the morning, in preparation for her first appearance in the evening – then he shook her hand, and mine, and bade us farewell. I felt as anxious, suddenly, at the thought of him leaving us, as I had done a few hours before at the prospect of meeting him at all.

But when he had gone – and when Mrs Dendy, too, had closed the door on us and wheezed and coughed her way downstairs behind him – I lowered myself into one of the armchairs and closed my eyes, and felt myself ache with pleasure and relief simply to be alone at last with someone who was more to me than a stranger. I heard Kitty step across the luggage, and when I opened my eyes she was at my side and had raised a hand to tug at a lock of hair which had come loose from my plait and was falling over my brow. Her touch made me stiffen again: I was still not used to the easy caresses, the hand-holdings and cheek-strokings, of our friendship, and every one of them made me flinch slightly, and colour faintly, with desire and confusion.

She smiled, then bent to tug at the straps of the basket at her feet; and after a moment of idling in the armchair, watching her busy herself with dresses and books and bonnets, I rose to help her.

It took us an hour to unpack. My own few poor frocks and shoes and underclothes took up little enough space, and were stowed away in a moment; but Kitty, of course, had not only her everyday dresses and boots to unpack and brush and straighten, but also her suits and toppers. When she started on these, I moved to take them from her. I said, 'You must let me take charge of your costumes now, you know. Look at these

collars! They all need whitening. Look at these stockings! We
must keep a drawer for the ones that have been cleaned, and
another for the ones that need mending. We must keep these
links in a box or they will be lost . . .'

She stepped aside, and let me fuss over the studs and
gloves and shirt-fronts, and for a minute or two I worked in
silence, quite absorbed. I looked up at last to find her watching me; and when I caught her eye she winked and blushed at
once. 'You cannot know,' she said then, 'how horribly smug I
feel. Every second-rate serio longs to have a dresser, Nan.
Every hopeful, tired little actress who ever set foot upon a
provincial stage aches to play the London halls – to have two
nice rooms, instead of one miserable one – to have a carriage
to take her to the show at night, and drive her home, afterwards, while other, poorer, artistes must take the tram.' She
was standing beneath the slope of the ceiling, her face in
shadow and her eyes dark and large. 'And now, suddenly, I
have all these things, that I have dreamed of having for so
long! Do you know how that must feel, Nan, to be given your
heart's desire, like that?'

I did. It was a wonderful feeling – but a fearful one, too, for
you felt all the time that you didn't deserve your own good fortune; that you had received it quite by error, in someone else's
place – and that it might be taken from you while your gaze
was turned elsewhere. And there was nothing you would not
do, I thought, nothing you would not sacrifice, to keep your
heart's desire once you had been given it. I knew that Kitty and
I felt just the same – only, of course, about different things.

I should have remembered this, later.

We unpacked, as I have said, for an hour, and while we worked
I caught the sound of various shouts and stirrings in the rest of
the house. Now – it was six o'clock or so – there came the
creak of footsteps on the landing beneath ours, and a cry: 'Miss
Butler, Miss Astley!' It was Mrs Dendy, come to tell us that
there was a bit of dinner for us, if we wanted it, in the

downstairs parlour – and 'quite a crowd, besides, that'd like to meet you'.

I was hungry, but also weary, and sick of shaking hands and smiling into strangers' faces; but Kitty whispered that we had better go down, or the other lodgers would think us proud. So we called to Mrs Dendy to give us a moment, and while Kitty changed her dress I combed and re-plaited my hair, and beat the dust from the hem of my skirt into the fireplace, and washed my hands; and then we made our way downstairs.

The parlour was a very different room, now, to the one that we had sat and taken tea in on our arrival. The table had been opened out and pulled into the centre of the room, and set for dinner; more importantly, it was ringed with faces, every one of which looked up as we appeared and broke into a smile – the same quick, well-practised smile which shone from all the pictures on the walls. It was as if half-a-dozen of the portraits had come to life and stepped from behind their dusty panes to join Mrs Dendy for supper.

There were eight places set – two of them vacant and waiting, clearly, for Kitty and me, but the rest all taken. Mrs Dendy herself was seated at the head of the table; she was in the process of dishing out slices from a plate of cold meats, but half rose when she saw us, to bid us make ourselves at home, and to gesture, with her fork, to the other diners – first to an elderly gentleman in a velvet waistcoat who sat opposite to her.

'Professor Emery,' she said, without a hint of self-consciousness. 'Mentalist Extraordinary.'

The Professor rose then, too, to make us a little bow.

'Mentalist Extraordinary, ah, *as was*,' he said, with a glance at our landlady. 'Mrs Dendy is too kind. It has been many years since *I* last stood before a hushed and gaping crowd, guessing at the contents of a lady's purse.' He smiled, then sat rather heavily. Kitty said that she was very pleased to know him. Mrs Dendy pointed next to a thin, red-headed boy on the Professor's right.

'Sims Willis,' she said. 'Corner Man—'

'Corner Man Extraordinary, of course,' he said quickly, leaning to shake our hands. 'As *is*. And this' – nodding to another
boy across the table from himself – 'this is Percy, my brother,
who plays the Bones. He's also extraordinary.' As he spoke
Percy gave a wink and, as if to prove his brother's words,
caught up a pair of spoons from the side of his plate, and set
them rattling upon the tablecloth in a wonderful tattoo.

Mrs Dendy cleared her throat above the noise, then gestured to the pretty, pink-lipped girl who had the seat next to
Sims. 'And not forgetting Miss Flyte, our ballerina.'

The girl gave a simper. 'You must call me Lydia,' she said,
extending a hand, 'which is what I am known as at – do cheese
it, Percy! – what I am known as at the Pav. Or Monica, if you
prefer, which is my real name.'

'Or Tootsie,' added Sims, 'which is what her pals all call
her – and if you've read *Ally Sloper's* I'll leave you to work out
why. Only let me say, Miss Butler, that she was in half a panic
when Walter told us he was moving you in, lest you turn out to
be some flashy show-girl with a ten-inch waist. When she
learned you were a male impersonator, why, she turned quite
gentle with relief.'

Tootsie gave him a push. 'Pay no mind to him,' she said to
us, 'he is always teasing. I am very pleased to have another girl
about the place – *two* girls, I should say – flashy or otherwise.'
As she spoke she gave me a quick, satisfied glance that showed
plain enough which kind she thought *I* was; then – as Kitty
took the seat beside her, leaving me with Percy for a neighbour – she went on: 'Walter says you will be very big, Miss
Butler. I hear you're to start at the Star tomorrow night. I
remember that as a very fine hall.'

'So I've heard. Do call me Kitty . . .'

'And what about you, Miss Astley?' asked Percy as they
chatted. 'Have you been a dresser for long? You seem awful
young for it.'

'I'm not really a dresser at all, yet. Kitty is still training me
up—'

'Training you up?' This was Tootsie again. 'Take my advice and don't train her too well, Kitty, or some other artiste'll take her from you. I've seen that happen.'

'Take her from me?' said Kitty with a smile. 'Oh, I couldn't have that. It is Nan that brings me my good luck . . .'

I looked at my plate, and felt myself redden, until Mrs Dendy, still busy with her platter, held a piece of quivering meat my way and coughed: 'A bit of tongue, Miss Astley, dear?'

The supper-talk was all, of course, theatrical tittle-tattle, and terribly dense and strange to my ears. There was no one in that house, it seemed, who had not some link with the profession. Even plain little Minnie – the eighth member of our party, the girl who had brought us tea on our arrival and had returned now to help Mrs Dendy dish and serve and clear the plates – even she belonged to a ballet troupe, and had a contract at a concert hall in Lambeth. Why, even the dog, Bransby, which soon nosed its way into the parlour to beg for scraps, and to lean his slavering jaw against Professor Emery's knee – even he was an old artiste, and had once toured the south coast in a dancing dog act, and had a stage name: 'Archie'.

It was a Sunday night, and nobody had a hall to rush to after supper; no one seemed to have anything to do, indeed, except sit and smoke and gossip. At seven o'clock there was a knock upon the door, and a girl came *halloo*-ing her way into the house with a dress of tulle and satin and a gilt tiara: she was a friend of Tootsie's from the ballet at the Pav come to ask Mrs Dendy's opinion of her costume. While the frock was spread out on the parlour rug, the supper-things were carried off; and when the table was cleared the Professor sat at it and spread a deck of cards. Percy joined him, whistling; his tune was taken up by Sims, who raised the lid of Mrs Dendy's piano and began to strike the melody out on that. The piano was a terrible one – 'Damn this cheesy old thing!' cried Sims as he hit at it. 'You could play Wagner on it, and I swear it would come out sounding like a sea-shanty or a jig!' – but the tune was gay and it made Kitty smile.

'I know this,' she said to me; and since she knew it she couldn't help but sing it, and had soon stepped over the sparkling frock upon the floor to lift her voice for the chorus at Sims's side.

I sat on the sofa with Bransby, and wrote a postcard to my family. 'I am in the queerest-looking parlour you ever saw,' I wrote, 'and everybody is extremely kind. There is a dog here with a stage-name! My landlady says to thank you for the oysters . . .'

It was very cosy on the sofa, with everyone about me so gay; but at half-past ten or so Kitty yawned – and at that I gave a jump, and rose, and said it was my bedtime. I paid a hasty visit to the privy out the back, then ran upstairs and changed into my nightgown double-quick – you might have thought I had been kept from sleeping for a week and was about to die of tiredness. But I was not sleepy at all; it was only that I wanted to be safely abed before Kitty appeared – safely still and calm and ready for that moment that must shortly come, when she would be beside me in the dark, and there would be nothing but the two flimsy lengths of our cotton nightgowns to separate her own warm limbs from mine.

She came about a half-hour later. I didn't look at her or say her name, and she didn't greet me, only moved very quietly about the room – assuming, I suppose, I was asleep, for I was lying very straight on my side and had my eyes hard shut. There was a little noise from the rest of the house – a laugh, and the closing of a door, and the rushing of water through distant pipes. But then all was calm again; and soon there were only the gentle sounds of her undressing: the tiny volley of thuds as she pulled at the buttons on her bodice; the rustle of her skirt, and then of her petticoat; the sighing of the laces through the eyes of her stays. At last there came the slap of her feet on the floorboards, and I guessed that she must be quite naked.

I had turned the gas down, but left a candle burning for her.

I knew that if I opened my eyes now, and tilted my face, I should see her clad in nothing but shadows and the candle-flame's amber glow.

But I did not turn; and soon there was another rustling, that meant she had pulled on her nightgown. In a moment the light was extinguished; the bed creaked and heaved; and she was lying beside me, very warm and horribly real.

She sighed. I felt her breath upon my neck and knew that she was gazing at me. Her breath came a second time, and then a third, then: 'Are you asleep?' she whispered.

'No,' I said, for I could pretend no longer. I rolled on to my back. The movement brought us even closer together – it really was an extremely narrow bed – so I shifted, rather hurriedly, to my left, until I could not have shifted any further without falling out. Now her breath was upon my cheek, and warmer than before.

She said, 'Do you miss your home, and Alice?' I shook my head. 'Not just a little?'

'Well . . .'

I felt her smile. Very gently – but quite matter-of-factly – she moved her hand to my wrist, pulled my arm above the bed-clothes, and ducked her head beneath it to place her temple against my collar-bone, my arm about her neck. The hand that dangled before her throat she squeezed, and held. Her cheek, against my shallow breast, felt hotter than a flat-iron.

'How your heart beats!' she said – and at that, of course, it beat faster. She sighed again – this time her mouth was at the opening of my nightgown, and I felt her breath upon the naked skin beneath – she sighed and said, 'So many times I lay in that dull room at Mrs Pugh's and thought of you and Alice in your little bed beside the sea. Was it just like this, being with her?'

I didn't answer her. I, too, was thinking back to that little bed. How hard it had been, having to lie next to slumbering Alice, my heart and my head all filled with Kitty. How much harder would it be to have Kitty herself beside me, so close and so unknowing! It would be a torture. I thought: I shall pack my trunk tomorrow. I shall get up very early and catch the first train back . . .

Kitty spoke on, not minding my silence. 'You and Alice,' she was saying again. 'Do you know, Nan, how *jealous* I was . . . ?'

I swallowed. 'Jealous?' The word sounded terrible in the darkness.

'Yes, I . . .' She seemed to hesitate; then, 'You see,' she went on, 'I never had a sister like other girls did . . .' She let go of my hand, and placed her arm over my middle, curling her fingers around the hollow of my waist. 'But we're like sisters now, aren't we, Nan? You'll be a sister to me – won't you?'

I patted her shoulder stiffly. Then I turned my face away – quite dazed, with mixed relief and disappointment. I said, 'Oh, yes, Kitty,' and she squeezed me tighter.

Then she slept, and her head and arm grew slack and heavy.

I, however, lay awake – just as I had used to lie at Alice's side. But now I did not dream; I only spoke to myself rather sternly.

I knew that I would not, after all, pack my bags in the morning and bid Kitty farewell; I knew that, having come so far, I could not. But if I were to stay with her, then it must be as she said; I must learn to swallow my queer and inconvenient lusts, and call her 'sister'. For to be Kitty's sister was better than to be Kitty's nothing, Kitty's no one. And if my head and my heart – and the hot, squirming centre of me – cried out at the shame of it, then I must stifle them. I must learn to love Kitty as Kitty loved me; or never be able to love her at all.

And that, I knew, would be terrible.

Chapter 4

The Star, when we reached it at noon the next day, turned out to be not a tenth as smart as those marvellous West End halls before which we had leaned, with Mr Bliss, to dream of Kitty's triumph; even so, however, it was quite alarmingly handsome and grand. Its manager at this time was a Mr Ling; he met us at the stage door and took us to his office, to read aloud the terms of Kitty's contract and secure her signature upon it; but then he rose and shook our hands and shouted for the call-boy, and had us shown, rather briskly, to the stage. Here, self-conscious and awkward, I waited while Kitty spoke with the conductor and ran through her songs with the band. Once a man approached me, with a broom on his shoulder, and asked me rather roughly who I was and what I did there.

'I'm waiting for Miss Butler,' I said, my voice as thin as a whistle.

'Are you, then,' he said. 'Well, sweetheart, you'll have to wait somewhere else, for I've to sweep this spot, and you are in my way. Go on, now.' And I moved away, blushing horribly, and had to stand in a corridor while boys with baskets and ladders and pails of sand lumbered by me, looking me over, or cursing when I blocked their path.

Our return visit, however, in the evening, was an easier one, for then we went straight to the dressing-room, where I knew my part a little better. Even so, when we entered the room I felt my spirits tumble rather, for it was nothing like the cosy little chamber at the Canterbury Palace, which Kitty had had all to herself, and which I was used to keeping so neat and nice. Instead it was dim and dusty, with benches and hooks for a dozen artistes, and one greasy sink that must be shared by all, and a door that must be propped shut or left to sag and let in every glance of every stage-hand and visitor that might be idling in the passageway beyond. We arrived late, and found most of the hooks already taken, and several of the benches occupied by girls and women in varying stages of undress. They looked up when we arrived, and smiled, most of them; and when Kitty took out her packet of Weights and a match, someone cried, 'Thank God, a woman with a cigarette! Give us one, ducks, would you? I'm quite broke till pay-day.'

Kitty was booked to appear, that night, a little way into the first half of the show. While I helped her with her collar and her necktie and her rose, I felt quite steady; but when we walked to the wing to wait for her number to go up, to gaze from the shadows at the unfamiliar theatre and its vast and careless crowd, I felt myself begin to tremble. I looked at Kitty. Her face was white beneath its layer of paint – though whether with fear, or with fierce ambition, I could not tell. With no other motive, I swear, than to comfort her – so mindful was I of that new resolve, to play her sister and nothing more – I took her hand, and pressed it.

When the stage-manager finally gave her his nod, however, I had to turn my eyes away. There was no chairman at this hall to bring the crowd to order, and the act Kitty had to follow was a popular one – a comedian, who had been called back upon the stage four times, and who had had to plead with the audience, in the end, to let him make his exit. They had done so grudgingly; they were disappointed and distracted now when

the orchestra struck up with the first bars of Kitty's opening
song. When Kitty herself stepped out into the glare of the footlights to wave her hat and call 'Hallo!', there was no answering
roar from the gallery, only a half-hearted ripple of applause
from the boxes and stalls – for the sake, I suppose, of her costume. When I forced my gaze at last into the hall I saw that the
audience was restless – that people were on their feet, heading
for the bar or the lavatory; that boys were perched upon the
gallery rail with their backs to us; that girls were calling to
friends three rows away, or gossiping with their neighbours,
looking everywhere but at the stage, where Kitty – lovely,
clever Kitty – sang and strode and sweated.

But slowly, slowly, the mood of the theatre changed – not
tremendously, but enough. When she finished her first song a
man leaned from a balcony to shout, 'Now bring Nibs back
on!' – meaning Nibs Fuller, the comedian whom Kitty had
replaced. Kitty didn't blink; while the band played the warm-
up to her next number she raised her hat to the man and
called, 'Why, does he owe you money?' The crowd laughed –
and listened more carefully to her next song, and clapped
more briskly when she finished it. When, a little later, another
man tried to call for Nibs, he was shushed by his neighbours;
and by the time Kitty got round to her ballad and her bit of
business with the rose, the hall was on her side, attentive and
appreciative.

From my station at the side of the stage I watched her in
wonder. When she stepped into the wing, weary and flushed,
and her place was taken by a comic singer, I put my hand
upon her arm and pressed it hard. Then Mr Bliss appeared
with Mr Ling the manager. They had been watching from the
front, and looked very satisfied; the former took Kitty's hand in
both of his and shook it, crying, 'A triumph, Miss Butler! A triumph, if ever I saw one.'

Mr Ling was more restrained. He gave Kitty a nod, then
said, 'Well done, my dear. A difficult crowd, and you handled it admirably. Once the band has grasped the pacing of

your business and your strolls – well, you will be splendid.'

Kitty only frowned. I had brought a towel with me from the change-room, and this she now caught up, and pressed to her face. Then she took her jacket off, and handed it to me, and unfastened the bow-tie at her throat. 'It wasn't so good,' she said at last, 'as I might have wished it. There was no – *fizz*, no sparkle.'

Mr Bliss gave a snort, then spread his hands. 'My dear, your first night in the capital! A theatre larger than you have ever worked before! The crowd will come to know you, word will spread. You must be patient. Soon they will be buying tickets just for you!' At that I saw the manager glance his way through narrowed eyes; but Kitty, at least, allowed herself to smile. 'That's better,' said Mr Bliss then. 'And now, if you'll permit me, ladies, I believe a light little supper would be welcome. A light little supper – and, perhaps, a heavy large glass with some of that *fizz* in it, Miss Butler, that you seem so keen on.'

The restaurant to which he took us was a theatre people's one, not very far away, and filled with gentlemen in fancy waistcoats just like himself, and with girls and boys like Kitty, with streaks of grease-paint on their cuffs and crumbs of spit-black in the corners of their eyes. He seemed to have a friend at every table, every one of whom saluted him as he passed by; but he did not pause to chat with them, only waved his hat in general greeting, then led us to an empty booth and called to a waiter for a recitation of the bill of fare. When this was done, and we had made our choices, he beckoned the man a little closer and murmured something to him; the waiter withdrew, and returned a minute later with a champagne bottle, which Mr Bliss proceeded ostentatiously to uncork. At that, there was a cheering at the other tables; and a woman began to sing, amidst much laughter and applause, that she *wouldn't call for sherry*, and she *wouldn't call for beer*, and she *wouldn't call for cham because she knew 'twould make her queer* . . .

I thought of the postcard I would write when I got home: 'I have had supper in a theatrical restaurant. Kitty made her debut at the Star and they are calling it a triumph . . .'

Meanwhile, Mr Bliss and Kitty chatted; and when next I concentrated on their talk I realised that it was rather serious.

'Now,' Mr Bliss was saying, 'I am going to ask you to do something which, if I were any other kind of gentleman than a theatrical agent, I should be quite ashamed to. I am going to ask you to go about the city – and you must assist her, Miss Astley,' he added when he saw me looking – 'you must both of you go about the city and *study the men*!'

I gazed at Kitty and blinked, and she smiled back uncertainly. 'Study the men?' she said.

'*Scrutinise* 'em!' said Mr Bliss, sawing at a piece of cutlet. 'Catch their characters, their little habits, their mannerisms and gaits. What are their histories? What are their secrets? Have they ambitions? Have they hopes and dreams? Have they sweethearts they have lost? Or have they only aching feet, and empty bellies?' He waved his fork. 'You must know it; and you must copy them, and make your audience know it in their turn.'

'Do you mean, then,' I asked, not understanding, 'to change Kitty's act?'

'I mean, Miss Astley, to broaden Kitty's repertoire. Her masher is a very fine fellow; but she cannot walk the Burlington Arcade, in lavender gloves, for ever.' He gazed at Kitty again, then wiped his mouth with a napkin and spoke in a more confiding tone. 'What think you of a policeman's jacket? Or a sailor's blouse? What think you of peg-top trousers or a pearly coat?' He turned to me. 'Only imagine, Miss Astley, all the handsome gentlemen's toggery that languishes, at this very minute, at the bottom of some costumier's hamper, waiting, simply waiting, for Kitty Butler to step inside it and lend it life! Only think of all those more than handsome fabrics – those ivory worsteds, those rippling silks, those crimson velvets and scarlet shalloons; only hear the snip of the tailor's scissors, the prick of the sempstress's needle; only imagine her success, decked as a soldier, or a coster, or a prince . . .'

He paused at last, and Kitty smiled. 'Mr Bliss,' she said, 'I do believe you could persuade a one-armed man into a juggling turn, the way you talk.'

He laughed, and struck the table with his hand so that the cutlery rattled: it turned out that he *had* a one-armed juggler for a client, and was billing him – with great success – as 'The Second Cinquevalli: Half the Capacity, Double the Skill!'

And it was all quite as he promised and directed. He sent us to costumiers and tailors, and had Kitty decked out in a dozen different gentlemanly guises; and when the suits were made he sent us to photographers, to have her likeness taken as she held a policeman's whistle to her lip, or shouldered a rifle or a sailor's rope. He found songs to fit the costumes, and brought them round to Ginevra Road himself, to strike them out on Mrs Dendy's terrible old piano for Kitty to try, and for the rest of us to listen to and consider. Most importantly of all he secured contracts, at halls in Hoxton, and Poplar, and Kilburn, and Bow. Within a fortnight, Kitty's London career was fairly launched. Now she did not change into her ordinary girl's clothes when she finished her act at the Star; instead, I stood with her coat and her basket ready, and when she stepped from before the footlights we ran together to the stage door, to where our brougham waited to lumber fitfully with us through the city traffic to the next theatre. Now, instead of wearing one suit for the whole of her turn she wore three or four; and I was her dresser in real earnest, helping her tear at buttons and links while the orchestra played between the songs, and the audience waited, halfway between expectation and impatience, for her to reappear.

The hours we kept now, of course, were rather strange ones, for as long as Kitty continued to work two, three or four halls a night we would arrive back at Ginevra Road at half-past twelve or one, weary and aching but still giddy and hot from our moonlit criss-crossings of the city, our anxious waits in dressing-rooms and wings. Here we would find Sims and Percy, and Tootsie and her girl- and boy-friends, all fresh and flushed and gay as we, making tea and cocoa, Welsh rabbit and pancakes, in Mrs Dendy's kitchen. Then Mrs Dendy herself would appear – for she had kept theatrical lodgers for so long she had begun to keep theatrical hours, too – and suggest a game of cards, or a song or a dance. It could not long be kept secret, in that house, that I liked to sing and had a pretty voice, and so sometimes I might raise a chorus or two, along with Kitty. Now I never went to bed before three, and never woke in the morning before nine or ten o'clock – so swiftly and completely had I forgotten my old oyster-maidish habits.

I did not, of course, forget my family or my home. I sent them cards, as I have said; I sent them notices of Kitty's shows, and gossip from the theatre. They sent me letters in return, and little parcels – and, of course, barrels of oysters, which I passed on to my landlady to let her dish to us all at supper. And yet, somehow, my letters home grew more and more infrequent, my replies to their cards and presents increasingly tardy and brief. 'When are you coming to see us?' they would write at the end of their letters. 'When are you coming home to Whitstable?' And I would answer, 'Soon, soon . . .' or, 'When Kitty can spare me . . .'

But Kitty never could spare me. The weeks passed, the season changed; the nights grew longer and darker and cold. Whitstable became – not dimmer, in my mind, but overshadowed. It was not that I didn't think of Father and Mother, of Alice and Davy and my cousins – just that I thought of Kitty, and my new life, more . . .

For there was so very much to think about. I was Kitty's dresser, but I was also her friend, her adviser, her companion in all things. When she learned a song I held the sheet, to prompt her if she faltered. When tailors fitted her I watched and nodded, or shook my head if the cut was wrong. When she let herself be guided by the clever Mr Bliss – or 'Walter' I

should call him, for so, by now, he had become to us, just as
we were 'Kitty' and 'Nan' to him – when she let herself be
guided by Walter, and spent hours as he had advised in shops
and market squares and stations *studying the men*, I went with
her; and we learned together the constable's amble, the coster's
weary swagger, the smart clip of the off-duty soldier.

And as we did so we seemed to learn the ways and manners of the whole unruly city; and I grew as easy, at last, with
London as with Kitty herself – as easy, and as endlessly fascinated and charmed. We visited the parks – those great,
handsome parks and gardens, that are so queer and verdant in
the midst of so much dust, yet have a little of the pavements'
quickness in them, too. We strolled the West End; we sat and
gazed at all the marvellous sights – not just the grand, celebrated sights of London, the palaces and monuments and
picture galleries, but also the smaller, swifter dramas: the
overturning of a carriage; the escape of an eel from an eel-
man's barrow; the picking of a pocket; the snatching of a
purse.

We visited the river – stood on London Bridge, and
Battersea Bridge, and all the bridges in between, just so that we
might look, and marvel, at the great, stinking breadth of it. It
was the Thames, I knew, which widened at its estuary to form
the kind, clear, oyster-bearing sea I had grown up on. It gave
me an odd little thrill, as I stood gazing at the pleasure-boats
beneath Lambeth Bridge, to know that I had journeyed against
the current – had made the trip from palpitating metropolis to
mild, uncomplicated Whitstable in reverse. When I saw barges
bringing fish from Kent I only smiled – it never made me
homesick. And when the barge-men turned, to make the journey back along the river, I did not envy them at all.

And while we strolled and gazed and grew ever more sisterly
and content, the year drew to a close; we continued to labour
over the act, and Kitty herself became something of a success.
Now, every contract that Walter found her was longer and

more generous than the last; soon she was over-booked, and turning offers down. Now she had admirers – gentlemen, who sent her flowers and dinner invitations (which – to my secret relief – she only laughed over and put aside); boys, who asked for her picture; girls, who gathered at the stage door to tell her how handsome she was – girls I hardly knew whether to pity, patronise or fear, so closely did they resemble me, so easily might they have had my role, I theirs.

And yet, with all this, she did not become what she longed to be, what Walter had promised her she would be: a star. The halls she worked remained the suburban ones, and the better class of East End ones (and once or twice the not-so-nice ones – Foresters, and the Sebright, where the crowd threw boots and trotter-bones at the acts they didn't like). Her name never rose much or grew larger on the music-hall notices; her songs were never hummed or whistled about the streets. The problem, Walter said, lay not with Kitty herself but with the nature of her act. She had too many rivals; male imperson-ation – once as specialised as plate-spinning – had suddenly, inexplicably, become a cruelly overworked routine.

'Why does every young lady who wants to do her bit of business on the stage these days want to do it in trousers?' he asked us, exasperated, when yet another male impersonator made her debut on the London circuit. 'Why does every per-fectly respectable comedienne and serio suddenly want to change her act – to pull a pair of bell-bottoms on, and dance the hornpipe? Kitty, you were born to play the boy, any fool can see it; were you an actress on the legitimate stage you would be Rosalind, or Viola, or Portia. But these tuppeny-ha'penny impersonators – Fannie Leslie, Fanny Robina, Bessie Bonehill, Millie Hylton – they look about as natural in their dinner-jackets as I would, clad in a crinoline or a bustle. It makes me *rage*' – he was seated in our little parlour as he spoke, and here he slapped the arm of his chair, so that the ancient seams gave a fart of dust and hair – 'it makes me *rage* to see girls with a tenth of your talent getting all the bookings that should be yours – and, worse, all the fame!' He stood, and placed his hands upon Kitty's shoulders. 'You are on the very *edge* of stardom,' he said, giving her a little push so that she had to grasp his arms to stop herself from falling. 'There must be something, *something* that we can do to just propel you over – something we can add to your act to set it apart from that of all those other prancing schoolgirls!'

But, however hard we worked, we could not find it; and meanwhile Kitty continued at the lesser theatres, in the humbler districts – Islington, Marylebone, Battersea, Peckham, Hackney – circling Leicester Square, crossing the West End on her nightly trips from hall to hall, but never entering those palaces of her and Walter's dreams: the Alhambra, and the Empire.

To be honest, I didn't much mind. I was sorry, for Kitty's sake, that her great new London career was not quite so great as she had hoped for; but I was also, privately, relieved. I knew how clever and charming and lovely she was, and while a part of me wanted, like Walter, to share the knowledge with the world, a greater part longed only to hug it to myself, to keep it secret and secure. For I was sure that, were she truly famous, I would lose her. I didn't like it when her fans sent flowers, or clamoured at the stage door for photographs and kisses; more fame would bring *more* flowers, *more* kisses – and I could not believe that she would go on laughing at the gentlemen's invitations, could not believe that one day, amongst all those admiring girls, there wouldn't be one she would like better then me . . .

If she were famous, too, then she would also be richer. She might buy a house – we should have to leave Ginevra Road and all our new friends in it; we should have to leave our little sitting-room; we should have to leave our bed, and take separate chambers. I could not bear the thought of it. I had grown used, at last, to sleeping with Kitty at my side. I no longer trembled, or grew stiff and awkward, when she touched me, but had learned to lean into her embraces, to accept her kisses,

chastely, nonchalantly – and even, sometimes, to return them.
I had grown used to the sight of her slumbering or undressed.
I did not hold my breath in wonder when I opened my eyes
upon her face, still and shadowed in the thin grey light of
dawn. I had seen her strip to wash or to change her gown. I
was as familiar with her body, now, as with my own – more so,
indeed, because her head, her neck, her wrists, her back, her
limbs (which were as smooth and as rounded and as freckled
as her cheek), her skin (which she wore with a marvellous,
easy grace, as if it were another kind of handsome suit, perfectly tailored and pleasant to wear), were, I thought, so much
lovelier and more fascinating than my own.

No, I didn't want a single thing to change – not even
when I learned something about Walter that was rather
disconcerting.

Inevitably, we had spent so many hours with Walter – working upon songs at Mrs Dendy's piano, or supping with him
after shows – that we had begun to look upon him less as
Kitty's agent and more as a friend, to both of us. In time it
wasn't only working-days that we were spending with him,
but Sundays, too; eventually, indeed, Sundays with Walter
became the rule rather than the exception, and we began to
listen out for the rumble of his carriage in Ginevra Road, the
pounding of his boots upon our attic stairs, his rap upon our
parlour door, his foolish, extravagant greetings. He would
bring bits of news and gossip; we would drive into town, or
out of it; we would stroll together – Kitty with her hand in the
crook of one of his great arms, me with mine in the crook of the
other, Walter himself like a blustering uncle, loud and lively
and kind.

I thought nothing of it, except that it was pleasant, until
one morning as I sat eating my breakfast beside Kitty and Sims
and Percy and Tootsie. It was a Sunday, and Kitty and I were
rather tardy; when Sims heard who it was that we were rushing for, he gave a cry: 'My word, Kitty, but Walter must be
expecting marvellous things of you! I've never known him

spend so much time with an artiste before. Anyone would think he was your beau!' He seemed to say it guilelessly enough; but as he did so I saw Tootsie smile and give a sideways glance at Percy – and, worse! saw Kitty blush and turn her face away – and all at once I understood what they all knew, and cursed to think I had not guessed it sooner. A half-hour later, when Walter presented himself at the parlour door, offering a gleaming cheek to Kitty and crying 'Kiss me, Kate!', I didn't smile, but only bit my lip, and wondered.

He was a little in love with her; perhaps, indeed, rather more than a little. I saw it now – saw the dampness of the looks he sometimes turned upon her, and the awkwardness of the glances which, more hastily, he turned away. I saw how he seized every foolish opportunity to kiss her hand, or pluck her sleeve, or place his arm, heavy and clumsy with desire, about her slender shoulders; I heard his voice catch, sometimes, or grow thick, when he addressed her. I saw and heard it all, now, because – it was the very reason that had kept me blind and deaf to it before! – because his passion was my own, which I had long grown used to thinking unremarkable, and right.

I almost pitied him; I almost loved him. I did not hate him – or if I did, it was only as one loathes the looking-glass, that shows one one's imperfect form in strict and fearful clarity. Nor did I now begin to resent his presence on those strolls and visits that I should otherwise have made with Kitty on my own. He was my rival, of sorts; but in some queer way it was almost easier to love her in his company, than out of it. His presence gave me a licence to be bold and gay and sentimental, as he was; to be able to *pretend* to worship her – which was almost as good as being able to worship her in earnest.

And if I still longed yet feared to hold her – well, as I have said, the fact that Walter felt the same showed that both my reticence and my love were only natural and proper. She *was* a star – my private star – and I would be content, I thought, like

Walter, to fly about her on my stiff and distant orbit, unswervingly, for ever.

I could not know how soon we would collide, nor how dramatically.

By now it was December – a cold December to match the sweltering August, so cold that the little skylight above our staircase at Ma Dendy's was thick with ice for days at a time; so cold that when we woke in the mornings our breath showed grey as smoke, and we had to pull our petticoats into bed with us and dress beneath the sheets.

At home in Whitstable we hated the cold, because it made the trawler-men's job so much the harder. I remember my brother Davy sitting at our parlour fire on January evenings, and weeping, simply weeping with pain, as the life returned to his split and frozen hands, his chilblained feet. I remember the ache in my own fingers as I handled pail after frigid pail of winter oysters, and transferred fish, endlessly, from icy seawater to steaming soup.

At Mrs Dendy's, however, everybody loved the winter months; and the colder they were, they said, the better. Because frosts, and chill winds, fill theatres. For many Londoners a ticket to the music hall is cheaper than a scuttle of coal – or, if not cheaper, then more fun: why stay in your own miserable parlour stamping and clapping to keep the cold out when you can visit the Star or the Paragon, and stamp and clap along with your neighbours – and with Marie Lloyd as an accompaniment? On the very coldest nights the music halls are full of wailing infants: their mothers bring them to the shows rather than leave them to slumber – perhaps to death – in their damp and draughty cradles.

But we didn't worry much over the frozen babies at Mrs Dendy's house that winter; we were merely glad and careless, because ticket sales were high and we were all in work and a little richer than before. At the beginning of December Kitty got a spot on the bill at a hall in Marylebone, and played there twice a night, all month. It was pleasant to sit gossiping in the green room between shows, knowing that we had no frantic trips to make across London in the snow; and the other artistes – a juggling troupe, a conjuror, two or three comic singers and a dwarf husband-and-wife team, 'The Teeny Weenies' – were all as complacent as we, and very jolly company.

The show ended at Christmas. I should, perhaps, have passed the holiday in Whitstable, for I knew my parents would be disappointed not to have me there. But I knew, too, what Christmas dinner would be like at home. There would be twenty cousins gathered around the table, all talking at once, all stealing the turkey from one another's plates. There would be such a fuss and stir they could not possibly, I thought, miss me – but I knew that Kitty would if I left her for them; and I knew, besides, that I should miss her horribly and only make the occasion miserable for everybody else. So she and I spent it together – with Walter, as ever, in attendance – at Mrs Dendy's table, eating goose, and drinking toast after toast to the coming year with champagne and pale ale.

Of course, there were gifts: presents from home, which Mother forwarded with a stiff little note that I refused to let shame me; presents from Walter (a brooch for Kitty, a hat-pin for me). I sent parcels to Whitstable, and gave gifts at Ma Dendy's; and for Kitty I bought the loveliest thing that I could find: a pearl – a single flawless pearl that was mounted on silver and hung from a chain. It cost ten times as much as I had ever spent on any gift before, and I trembled when I handled it. Mrs Dendy, when I showed it to her, gave a frown. 'Pearls for tears,' she said, and shook her head: she was very superstitious. Kitty, however, thought it beautiful, and had me fasten it about her neck at once, and seized a mirror to watch it swinging there, an inch beneath the hollow of her lovely throat. 'I'll never take it off,' she said; and she never did, but wore it ever after – even on the stage, beneath her neck-ties and cravats.

She, of course, bought me a gift. It came in a box with a bow, and wrapped in tissue, and turned out to be a dress: the most handsome dress I had ever possessed, a long, slim evening dress of deepest blue, with a cream satin sash about the waist, and heavy lace at the bosom and hem; a dress, I knew, that was far too fine for me. When I drew it from its wrappings and held it up against me before the glass, I shook my head, quite stricken. 'It's beautiful,' I said to Kitty, 'but how can I keep it? It's far too smart. You must take it back, Kitty. It's too expensive.'

But Kitty, who had watched me handle it with dark and shining eyes, only laughed to see me so uneasy. 'Rubbish!' she said. 'It's about time you started wearing some decent frocks, instead of those awful old schoolgirlish things you brought with you from home. I have a decent wardrobe – and so should you. Goodness knows we can afford it. And anyway, it can't go back: it was made just for you, like Cinderella's slipper, and is too peculiar a size to fit anybody else.'

Made just for me? That was even worse! 'Kitty,' I said, 'I really cannot. I should never feel comfortable in it . . .'

'You must,' she said. 'And, besides' – she fingered the pearl that I had so recently placed about her neck, and looked away – 'I am doing so well, now. I can't have my dresser running round in her sister's hand-me-downs for ever. It ain't quite the thing, now, is it?' She said it lightly – but all at once I saw the truth of her words. I had my own income now – I had spent two weeks' wages on her pearl and chain; but I had a Whitstable squeamishness, still, about spending money on myself. Now I blushed to think that she had ever thought me dowdy.

And so I kept the dress for Kitty's sake; and wore it, for the first time, a few nights later. The occasion was a party – an end-of-season party at the Marylebone theatre at which we had spent such a happy month. It was to be a very grand affair. Kitty had a new frock of her own made for it, a lovely, low-necked, short-sleeved gown of China satin, pink as the warm

pink heart of a rose-bud. I held it for her to step into, and
helped her fasten it; then watched her as she pulled her gloves
on – aching all the time with the prettiness of her, for the
blush of the silk made her red lips all the redder, her throat
more creamy, her eyes and hair all the browner and more rich.
She wore no jewellery but the pearl that I had given her, and
the brooch that had been Walter's gift. They didn't really
match – the brooch was of amber. But Kitty could have worn
anything – a string of bottle-tops about her neck – and still, I
thought, look like a queen.

Helping Kitty with her buttons made me slow with my own
dressing; I said that she should go on down without me. When
she had done so I pulled on the lovely gown that she had
given me, then stepped to the glass to study myself – and to
frown at what I saw. The dress was so transforming it was
practically a disguise. In the half-light it was dark as midnight;
my eyes appeared bluer above it than they really were, and my
hair paler, and the long skirt, and the sash, made me seem
taller and thinner than ever. I did not look at all like Kitty
had, in her pink frock; I looked more like a boy who had
donned his sister's ball-gown for a lark. I loosened my plait of
hair, then brushed it – then, because I had no time to tie and
loop it, twisted it into a knot at the back of my head, and stuck
a comb in it. The chignon, I thought, brought out the hard
lines of my jaw and cheek-bones, made my wide shoulders
wider still. I frowned again, and looked away. It would have to
do – and would have the merit, I supposed, of making Kitty
look all the daintier at my side.

I went downstairs to join her. When I pushed at the parlour
door I found her chatting with the others; they were all still at
supper. Tootsie saw me first – and must have nudged Percy,
beside her, for he glanced up from his plate and, catching sight
of me, gave a whistle. Sims turned my way, then, and looked at
me as if he had never seen me before, a forkful of food suspended on its journey to his open mouth. Mrs Dendy followed
his gaze, then gave a tremendous cough. 'Well, Nancy,' she

said, 'and look at you! You have become quite the handsome
young lady – and right beneath our noses!'

And at that, Kitty herself turned to me – and showed me
such a look of wonder and confusion that it was as if, just for
a second, *she* had never seen me before; and I do not know
whose cheeks at that moment were the pinker – mine, or hers.

Then she gave a tight little smile. 'Very nice,' she said, and
looked away; so that I thought, miserably, that the dress must
suit me even less than I had hoped, and readied myself for a
wretched party.

But the party was not wretched; it was gay and genial and
loud, and very crowded. The manager had had to build a platform from the end of the stage to the back of the pit, to carry us
all, and he had hired the orchestra to play reels and waltzes,
and set tables in the wings bearing pastries and jellies, and barrels of beer and bowls of punch, and row upon row of bottles
of wine.

We were much complimented, Kitty and I, on our new
dresses; and over me, in particular, people smiled and
exclaimed – mouthing at me across the noisy hall, 'How fine
you look!' One woman – the conjuror's assistant – took my
hand and said, 'My dear, you're so grown-up tonight, I didn't
recognise you!': just what Mrs Dendy had said an hour before.
Her words impressed me. Kitty and I stood side by side all
evening but when, some time after midnight, she moved away
to join a group that had gathered about the champagne tables,
I hung back, rather pensive. I wasn't used to thinking of myself
as a grown-up woman, but now, clad in that handsome frock of
blue and cream, satin and lace, I began at last to feel like one –
and to realise, indeed, that I *was* one: that I was eighteen, and
had left my father's house perhaps for ever, and earned my
own living, and paid rent for my own rooms in London. I
watched myself as if from a distance – watched as I supped at
my wine as if it were ginger beer, and chatted and larked with
the stage-hands, who had once so frightened me; watched as I
took a cigarette from a fellow from the orchestra, and lit it, and

drew upon it with a sigh of satisfaction. When had I started smoking? I couldn't remember. I had grown so used to holding Kitty's fag for her while she changed suits, that gradually I had taken up the habit myself. I smoked so often, now, that half my fingers – which, four months before, had been permanently pink and puckered, from so many dippings in the oyster-tub – were now stained yellow as mustard at the tips.

The musician – I believe he played the cornet – took a small, insinuating step my way. 'Are you a friend of the manager's, or what?' he said. 'I haven't seen you in the hall before.'

I laughed. 'Yes you have. I'm Nancy, Kitty Butler's dresser.'

He raised his eyebrows, and leaned away to look me up and down. 'Well! And so you are. I thought you was just a kid. But here, just now, I took you for an actress, or a dancer.'

I smiled, and shook my head. There was a pause while he sipped at his glass and wiped at his moustache. 'I bet you dance a treat, though, don't you?' he said then. 'How about it?' He nodded to the crush of waltzing couples at the back of the stage.

'Oh, no,' I said. 'I couldn't. I've had too much cham.'

He laughed: 'All the better!' He put his drink aside, gripped his cigarette between his lips, then put his hands on my waist and lifted me up. I gave a shriek; he began to turn and dip, in a clownish approximation of a waltz-step. The louder I laughed and shrieked, the faster he turned me. A dozen people looked our way, and smiled and clapped.

At last he stumbled and almost fell, then put me down with a thump. 'Now,' he said breathlessly, 'tell me I ain't a marvellous dancer.'

'You ain't,' I said. 'You've made me giddy as a fish, and' – I felt at the front of my dress – 'you have spoiled my sash!'

'I'll fix that for you,' he said, reaching for my waist again. I gave a yelp, and stepped out of his grasp.

'No you won't! You can push off and leave me in peace.' Now he seized me, and tickled me so that I giggled. Being tickled always makes me laugh, however little I care for the tickler;

but after several more minutes of this kind of thing he at last gave up on me, and went back to his pals in the band.

I ran my hands over my sash again. I feared he really had spoiled it, but couldn't see well enough to be sure. I finished my drink with a gulp – it was, I suppose, my sixth or seventh glass – and slipped from the stage. I made my way first to the lavatory, then headed downstairs to the change-room. This had been opened tonight only so that the ladies should have a place to hang their coats, and it was cold and empty and rather dim; but it had a looking-glass: and it was to this that I now stepped, squinting and tugging at my dress to pull it straight.

I had been there for no longer than a minute when there came the sound of footsteps in the passageway beyond, and then a silence. I turned my head to see who was there, and found that it was Kitty. She had her shoulder against the door-frame and her arms folded. She wasn't standing as one normally stands – as she usually stood – in an evening gown. She was standing as she did when she was on stage, with her trousers on – rather cockily. Her face was turned towards me and I couldn't see her rope of hair, or the swell of her breasts. Her cheeks were very pale; there was a stain upon her skirt where some champagne had dripped upon it from an over-spilling glass.

'Wot cheer, Kitty,' I said. But she did not return my smile, only watched me, levelly. I looked uncertainly back to the glass, and continued working at my sash. When she spoke at last, I knew at once that she was rather drunk.

'Seen something you fancy?' she said. I turned to her again in surprise, and she took a step into the room.

'What?'

'I said, "Seen something you fancy, Nancy?" Everybody else here tonight seems to have. Seems to have seen something that has rather caught their eye.'

I swallowed, unsure of what reply to make to her. She walked closer, then stopped a few paces from me, and continued to fix me with the same even, arrogant gaze.

'You were very fresh with that horn-player, weren't you?' she said then.

I blinked. 'We were just having a bit of a lark.'

'A bit of a lark? His hands were all over you.'

'Oh Kitty, they weren't!' My voice almost trembled. It was horrible to see her so savage; I don't believe that, in all the weeks that we had spent together, she had ever so much as raised her voice to me in impatience.

'Yes they were,' she said. 'I was watching – me and half the party. You know what they'll be calling you soon, don't you? "Miss Flirt".'

Miss Flirt! Now I didn't know whether to cry or to laugh.

'How can you say such a thing?' I asked her.

'Because it's true.' She sounded all at once rather sullen. 'I wouldn't have bought you such a fine dress, if I'd known you were only going to wear it to go flirting in.'

'Oh!' I stamped my foot, unsteadily – I was as drunk, I suppose, as she was. 'Oh!' I put my fingers to the neck of my gown, and began to fumble with its fastenings. 'I shall take the dam' dress off right here and you shall have it back,' I said, 'if that's how you feel about it!'

At that she took another step towards me and seized my arm. 'Don't be a fool,' she said in a slightly chastened tone. I shook her off and continued to work – quite fruitlessly, since the wine, together with my anger and surprise, had made me terribly clumsy – at the buttons of my frock. Kitty took hold of me again; soon we were almost tussling.

'I won't have you call me a flirt!' I said as she tugged at me. 'How could you call me one? How could you? Oh! If you just knew –' I put my hand to the back of my collar; her fingers followed my own, her face came close. Seeing it, I felt all at once quite dazed. I thought I had become her sister, as she wanted. I thought I had my queer desires cribbed and chilled and chastened. Now I knew only that her arm was about me, her hand on mine, her breath hot upon my cheek. I grasped her – not the better to push her away, but in order to hold her nearer.

Gradually we ceased our wrestling and grew still, our breaths ragged, our hearts thudding. Her eyes were round and dark as jet; I felt her fingers leave my hand and move against my neck.

Then all at once there came a blast of noise from the passageway beyond, and the sound of footsteps. Kitty started in my arms as if a pistol had been fired, and took a half-dozen steps, very rapidly, away. A woman – Esther, the conjuror's assistant – appeared on the other side of the open doorway. She was pale, and looked terribly grave. She said: 'Kitty, Nan, you won't believe it.' She reached for her handkerchief, and put it to her mouth. 'There's some boys just come, from the Charing Cross Hospital. They are saying Gully Sutherland is there' – this was the comic singer who had appeared with Kitty at the Canterbury Palace – 'they are saying Gully is there – that he has got drunk, and shot himself dead!'

It was true – we all heard, next day, how horribly true it was. I should never have suspected it, but had learned since coming to London that Gully was known in the business as something of a lush. He never finished a show without calling into a public-house on his way home; and on the night of our party he had been drinking at Fulham. Here, all hidden in a corner stall, he had overheard a fellow at the bar say that Gully Sutherland was past his best, and should make way for funnier artistes; that he had sat through Gully's latest routine, and all the gags were flat ones. The bar-man said that when Gully heard this he went to the man and shook him by the hand, and bought him a beer, then he bought beer for everyone. Then he went home and took a gun, and fired it at his own heart . . .

We didn't know all of this that night at Marylebone, we knew only that Gully had had a kind of fit, and taken his life; but the news put an end to our party and left us all, like Esther, nervous and grave. Kitty and I, on hearing the news, went up to the stage – she seizing my hand as we stumbled up the steps, but in grief now, I thought, rather than anything warmer. The manager had had all the house-lights lit, and the band had lain their instruments aside; some people were weeping, the cornet-player who had tickled me had his arm about a trembling girl. Esther cried, 'Oh isn't it awful, isn't it *horrible*?' I suppose the wine made everybody feel the shock of it the more.

I, however, did not know what to make of it. I couldn't think of Gully at all: my thoughts were still with Kitty, and with that moment in the change-room, when I had felt her hand on me and seemed to feel a kind of understanding leap between us. She hadn't looked at me since then, and now she had gone to talk to one of the boys who had brought the news of Gully's suicide. After a moment, however, I saw her shake her head and step away, and seem to search for me; and when she saw me – waiting for her, in the shadows of the wing – she came and sighed. 'Poor Gully. They say his heart was shot right through . . .'

'And to think,' I said, 'it was for Gully's sake that I first went to Canterbury and saw you . . .'

She looked at me, then, and trembled; and put a hand to her cheek, as if made weak with sorrow. But I dared not move to comfort her – only stood, miserable and unsure.

When I said that we should go – since other people were now leaving – she nodded. We returned to the change-room for our coats: its jets were all flaring now, and there were white-faced women in it with handkerchiefs before their eyes. Then we stepped to the stage door, and waited while the doorman found a cab for us. This seemed to take an age. It was two o'clock or later before we started on our journey home; and then we sat, on different seats, in silence – Kitty repeating only, now and then: 'Poor Gully! What a thing to do!', and I still drunk, still dazed, still desperately stirred, but still uncertain.

It was a bitterly cold and beautiful night – perfectly quiet, once we had left the clamour of the party behind us, and still. The roads were foggy, and thick with ice: every so often I felt the wheels of our carriage slide a little, and caught the sound of the horse's slithering, uncertain step, and the driver's gentle curses. Beside us the pavements glittered with frost, and each street-lamp glowed, in the fog, from the centre of its own yellow nimbus. For long stretches, ours was the only vehicle on the streets at all; the horse, the driver, Kitty and I might have been the only wakeful creatures in a city of stone and ice and slumber.

At length we reached Lambeth Bridge, where Kitty and I had stood only a few weeks before and gazed at the pleasure-boats below. Now, with our faces pressed to the carriage window, we saw it all transformed – saw the lights of the Embankment, a belt of amber beads dissolving into the night; and the great dark jagged bulk of the Houses of Parliament looming over the river; and the Thames itself, its boats all moored and silent, its water grey and sluggish and thick, and rather strange.

It was this last which made Kitty pull the window down, and call to the driver, in a high, excited voice, to stop. Then she pushed the carriage door open, pulled me to the iron parapet of the bridge, and seized my hand.

'Look,' she said. Her grief seemed all forgotten. Below us, in the water, there were great slivers of ice six feet across, drifting and gently turning in the winding currents, like basking seals.

The Thames was freezing over.

I looked from the river to Kitty, and from Kitty to the bridge on which we stood. There was no one near us save our driver – and he had the collar of his cape about his ears, and was busy with his pipe and his tobacco-pouch. I looked at the river again – at that extraordinary, ordinary transformation, that easy submission to the urgings of a natural law, that was yet so rare and so unsettling.

It seemed a little miracle, done just for Kitty and me.

'How cold it must be!' I said softly. 'Imagine if the whole river froze over, if it was frozen right down from here to Richmond. Would you walk across it?'

Kitty shivered, and shook her head. 'The ice would break,'

she said. 'We would sink and drown; or else be stranded and die of the cold!'

I had expected her to smile, not make me a serious answer. I saw us floating down the Thames, out to sea – past Whitstable, perhaps – on a piece of ice no bigger than a pancake.

The horse took a step, and its bridle jangled; the driver gave a cough. Still we gazed at the river, silent and unmoving – and both of us, finally, rather grave.

At last Kitty gave a whisper. 'Ain't it queer?' she said.

I made no answer, only stared at where the curdled water swirled, thick and unwilling, about the columns of the bridge beneath our feet. But when she shivered again I moved a step closer to her, and felt her lean against me in response. It was icy cold upon the bridge; we should have moved back from the parapet into the shelter of the carriage. But we were loath to leave the sight of the frozen river – loath too, perhaps, to leave the warmth of one another's bodies, now that we had found it.

I took her hand. Her fingers, I could feel, were stiff and cold inside her glove. I placed the hand against my cheek; it did not warm it. With my eyes all the time on the water below I pulled at the button at her wrist, then drew the mitten from her, and held her fingers against my lips to warm them with my breath.

I sighed, gently, against her knuckles; then turned the hand, and breathed upon her palm. There was no sound at all save the unfamiliar lapping and creaking of the frozen river. Then, 'Nan,' she said, very low.

I looked at her, her hand still held to my mouth and my breath still damp upon her fingers. Her face was raised to mine, and her gaze was dark and strange and thick, like the water below.

I let my hand drop; she kept her fingers upon my lips, then moved them, very slowly, to my cheek, my ear, my throat, my neck. Then her features gave a shiver and she said in a whisper: 'You won't tell a soul, Nan – will you?'

I think I sighed then: sighed to know – to know for sure, at last! – that there was *something to be told*. And then I dipped my face to hers, and shut my eyes.

Her mouth was chill, at first, then very warm – the only warm thing, it seemed to me, in the whole of the frozen city; and when she took her lips away – as she did, after a moment, to give a quick, anxious glance towards our hunched and nodding driver – my own felt wet and sore and naked in the bitter December breezes, as if her kiss had flayed them.

She drew me into the shadow of the carriage, where we were hidden from sight. Here we stepped together, and kissed again: I placed my arms about her shoulders, and felt her own hands shake upon my back. From lip to ankle, and through all the fussy layers of our coats and gowns, I felt her body stiff against my own – felt the pounding, very rapid, where we joined at the breast; and the pulse and the heat and the cleaving, where we pressed together at the hips.

We stood like this for a minute, maybe longer; then the carriage gave a creak as the driver shifted in his seat, and Kitty stepped quickly away. I could not take my hands from her, but she seized my wrists and kissed my fingers and gave a kind of nervous laugh, and a whisper: 'You will kiss the life out of me!'

She moved into the carriage, and I clambered in behind her, trembling and giddy and half-blind, I think, with agitation and desire. Then the door was closed; the driver called to his pony, and the cab gave a jerk and a slither. The frozen river was left behind us – dull, in comparison with this new miracle!

We sat side by side. She put her hands to my face again, and I shivered, so that my jaws jumped beneath her fingers. But she didn't kiss me again: rather, she leaned against me with her face upon my neck, so that her mouth was out of reach of mine, but hot against the skin below my ear. Her hand, that was still bare of its glove and white with cold, she slid into the gap at the front of my jacket; her knee she laid heavily against my own. When the brougham swayed I felt her lips, her fingers, her thigh come ever more heavy, ever more hot, ever more close upon me, until I longed to squirm beneath the

pressing of her, and cry out. But she gave me no word, no kiss
or caress; and in my awe and my innocence I only sat steady,
as she seemed to wish. That cab-ride from the Thames to
Brixton was, in consequence, the most wonderful and most
terrible journey I have ever made.

At last, however, we felt the carriage turn, then slow, and
finally stop, and heard the driver thump upon the roof with
the butt of his whip to tell us we were home: we were so quiet,
perhaps he thought we slumbered.

I remember a little of our entry into Mrs Dendy's – the fumbling at the door with the latch-key, the mounting of the
darkened stairs, our passage through that still and sleeping
house. I remember pausing on the landing beneath the skylight, where the stars showed very small and bright, and
silently pressing my lips to Kitty's ear as she bent to unlock our
chamber door; I remember how she leaned against it when
she had it shut fast behind us, and gave a sigh, and reached for
me again, and pulled me to her. I remember that she wouldn't
let me raise a taper to the gas-jet – but made us stumble to the
bedroom through the darkness.

And I remember, very clearly, all that happened there.

The room was bitter cold – so cold it seemed an outrage to
take our dresses off and bare our flesh; but an outrage, too, to
some more urgent instinct to keep them on. I had been clumsy
in the change-room of the theatre, but I was not clumsy now. I
stripped quickly to my drawers and chemise, then heard Kitty
cursing over the buttons of her gown, and stepped to help her.
For a moment – my fingers tugging at hooks and ribbons, her
own tearing at the pins which kept her plait of hair in place –
we might have been at the side of a stage, making a lightning
change between numbers.

At last she was naked, all except for the pearl and chain
about her neck; she turned in my hands, stiff and pimpled
with cold, and I felt the brush of her nipples, and of the hair
between her thighs. Then she moved away, and the bed-
springs creaked; and at that, I didn't wait to pull the rest of my

own clothes off but followed her to the bed and found her shivering there, beneath the sheets. Here we kissed more leisurely, but also more fiercely, than we had before; at last the chill – though not the trembling – subsided.

Once her naked limbs began to strain against my own, however, I felt suddenly shy, suddenly awed. I leaned away from her. 'May I really – touch you?' I whispered. She gave again a nervous laugh, and tilted her face against her pillow.

'Oh, Nan,' she said, 'I think I shall die if you don't!'

Tentatively, then, I raised my hand, and dipped my fingers into her hair. I touched her face – her brow, that curved; her cheek, that was freckled; her lip, her chin, her throat, her collar-bone, her shoulder . . . Here, shy again, I let my hand linger – until, with her face still tilted from my own and her eyes hard shut, she took my wrist and gently led my fingers to her breasts. When I touched her here she sighed, and turned; and after a minute or two she seized my wrist again, and moved it lower.

Here she was wet, and smooth as velvet. I had never, of course, touched anyone like this before – except, sometimes, myself; but it was as if I touched myself now, for the slippery hand which stroked her seemed to stroke me: I felt my drawers grow damp and warm, my own hips jerk as hers did. Soon I ceased my gentle strokings and began to rub her, rather hard. 'Oh!' she said very softly; then, as I rubbed faster, she said 'Oh!' again. Then, 'Oh, oh, oh!': a volley of 'Oh!'s, low and fast and breathy. She bucked, and the bed gave an answering creak; her own hands began to chafe distractedly at the flesh of my shoulders. There seemed no motion, no rhythm, in all the world, but that which I had set up, between her legs, with one wet fingertip.

At last she gasped, and stiffened, then plucked my hand away and fell back, heavy and slack. I pressed her to me, and for a moment we lay together quite still. I felt her heart beating wildly in her breast; and when it had calmed a little she stirred, and sighed, and put a hand to her cheek.

'You've made me weep,' she murmured.

I sat up. 'Not really, Kitty?'

'Yes, really.' She gave a twitch that was half laughter, half a sob, then rubbed at her eyes again, and when I took her fingers from her face I could feel the tears upon them. I pressed her hand, suddenly uncertain: 'Did I hurt you? What did I do that was bad? Did I hurt you, Kitty?'

She shook her head, and sniffed, and laughed more freely. 'Hurt me? Oh, no. It was only – so very sweet.' She smiled. 'And you are – so very good. And I—' She sniffed again, then placed her face against my breast and hid her eyes from me. 'And I – oh, Nan, I do so love you, so very, very much!'

I lay beside her, and put my arms about her. My own desire I quite forgot, and she made no move to remind me of it. I forgot, too, Gully Sutherland – who three hours before had put a gun to his own heart, because a man had sat through his routine unsmiling. I only lay; and soon Kitty slept. And I studied her face, where it showed creamy pale in the darkness, and thought, *She loves me, She loves me* – like a fool with a daisy-stalk, endlessly exclaiming over the same last browning petal.

The next morning we were shy together, at first – and Kitty, I think, was the shyest of all.

'How much we drank last night!' she said, not gazing at me; and for a terrible second I thought it might really have been only the champagne that made her cling to me, and say that she loved me, so very very much . . . But as she spoke she blushed. I said, before I could stop myself: 'If you unsay all those things you said last night, oh, Kitty, I'll die!' and that made her raise her eyes to mine, and I saw that she had simply been anxious, that *I* might only have been drunk . . . And then we gazed and gazed at one another; and for all that I had gazed at her a thousand times before, I felt now that I was looking at her as if for the first time. We had lived and slept and laboured, side by side, for half a year; but there had been a kind of veil between us, that our cries and whispers of the night before had quite torn down. She looked flushed, washed – new-born; so that I could hardly press her skin, for fear of marking it – so that I feared, almost, to kiss her lips again in case they bruised.

But I did kiss them; and then I lay, quite at my leisure, and watched as she splashed water on her face and arms, and fastened on her underclothes and frock, and buttoned her shoes. As she worked at her hair I lit a cigarette: I struck the match and let it burn almost to my fingers, gazing at the flame as it ate its way along the wood. I said, 'When I first knew you, I used to think that, whenever I thought of you, I was all lit up, like a lamp. I was afraid that people would see . . .' She smiled. I gave the match a shake. 'Didn't you know,' I said then, 'didn't you know, that I loved you?'

'I'm not sure,' she answered; then she sighed. 'I didn't like to think of it.'

'Why not?'

She shrugged. 'It seemed easier to be your friend . . .'

'But Kitty, that's just what I thought! And, oh! wasn't it terribly hard! But I thought, that if you knew I liked you as a, as a sweetheart – well, I never heard of such a thing before, did you?'

She moved to the glass to work again at the pins in her plait, and now, without turning, she said, 'It's true I never cared for any other girl, like I care for you . . .' As she said it I saw her neck and ears grow pink, and felt myself grow weak and warm and silly in response; but I caught a glimpse of something, too, behind her words.

'It has happened before, then,' I said flatly, 'with you . . .' She grew redder than ever, but would make me no reply; and I fell silent. But the fact was, I loved her too much to want to fret for very long about the other girls she might have kissed before me. 'When was it,' I asked next, 'that you began to think of me like . . . ? When did you begin to think that you might learn to – to love me?'

Now she did turn, and smiled. 'I remember a hundred little times,' she said. 'I remember how you made my dressing-room so nice and neat; I remember your blushes as I kissed you good-night. I remember how you opened an oyster for me at your father's table – but then, I think I loved you then, already. Indeed, I'm ashamed to say, that it must have been that moment, at the Canterbury Palace, when I first smelled the oyster-liquor on your fingers, that I began to think of you as – as I shouldn't have.'

'Oh!'

'And I'm even more ashamed to say,' she went on in a slightly different tone, 'that it wasn't until last night – when I saw you larking with that boy, and was so jealous – that I learned how much, how much . . .'

'Oh, Kitty . . .' I swallowed. 'I'm glad you learned it, at last.' She looked away, then came to me and took my fag, and gave me one brisk kiss.

'So am I.'

After that she bent to rub with a cloth at the leather of her boots, and I found myself yawning: I was weary, and rather sick from the champagne and the excitements of the night. I said, 'Must we really get up?' and Kitty nodded.

'We must – for it's almost eleven, and Walter will be here soon. Had you forgotten?'

It was a Sunday, and Walter was coming, as usual, to take us driving. I had not forgotten – but had had no time and no desire, yet, to think of ordinary things. Now, at the mention of Walter's name, I grew thoughtful. It would be rather hard on *him*, now that this had happened.

As if Kitty knew what I was thinking, she said, 'You will be sensible with Walter, won't you, Nan?' Then she repeated what she had said the night before upon the bridge: 'You won't let on, will you, to anyone? You will be *careful* – won't you?'

I silently cursed her for being so prudent; but took her hand and kissed it. 'I have been being careful since the first minute I saw you. I am the Queen of Carefulness. I shall go on being careful for ever, if you like – so long as I might be a bit reckless, sometimes, when we are quite alone.'

Her smile, when she gave it, was a little distracted. 'After all,' she said, 'things have not changed so very much.'

But I knew that everything had changed – everything.

At length I rose too, and washed and dressed and used the chamber-pot, while Kitty went downstairs. She came back with a tray of tea and toast – 'I could hardly look Ma Dendy in the eye!' she said, all shy and red again – and we had our breakfast in our own parlour, before the fire, kissing the crumbs and butter from one another's lips.

There was a hamper of suits beneath the window, that we had had sent over from a costumier's and not yet properly examined; and now, as we waited for Walter, Kitty began rather idly to sort through it. She pulled out a black tail-coat, very fine. 'Look at this!' she said. She slipped it on over her dress, and did a stiff little dance; then she began, very lightly, to sing.

'*In a house, in a square, in a quadrant,*' she sang, '*In a street, in a lane, in a road; Turn to the left, on the right hand, You see there my true love's abode.*'

I smiled. This was an old song of George Leybourne's: everyone had used to whistle it in the 'seventies, and I had even once seen it sung by Leybourne himself, at the Canterbury Palace. It was a silly, nonsensical, but rather infectious kind of song, and Kitty sang it all the sweeter for singing it so softly and carelessly.

> '*I go there a courting and cooing,*
> *To my love, like a dove.*
> *And swearing on my bended knee,*
> *If ever I cease to love,*
> *May sheep's heads grow on apple trees,*
> *If ever I cease to love.*'

I listened for a while, then raised my voice with hers for the chorus:

> *'If ever I cease to love,*
> *If ever I cease to love,*
> *May the moon be turned into green cheese,*
> *If ever I cease to love.'*

We laughed, then sang louder. I found a hat in the hamper, and tossed it to Kitty, then pulled out a jacket and a boater for myself, and a walking-cane. I linked my arm with hers, and imitated her dance. The song grew sillier.

> *'For all the money that's in the bank,*
> *For the title of lord or duke,*
> *I wouldn't exchange the girl I love,*
> *There's bliss in every look.*
> *To see her dance the polka,*
> *I could faint with radiant love,*
> *May the Monument a hornpipe dance,*
> *If ever I cease to love!*
> *May we never have to pay the Income Tax,*
> *If ever I cease to love!'*

We finished with a flourish, and I attempted a twirl – then froze. Kitty had left the door ajar, and Walter stood at it watching us, his eyes as wide as if he had had some sort of fright. I felt Kitty's gaze follow mine; she gripped my arm, then dropped it sharply. I thought wildly of what he might have seen. The words of the song were foolish but, unmistakably, we had sung them to one another, and meant them. Had we also kissed? Had I touched Kitty where I shouldn't have?

While I still wondered, Walter spoke. 'My God,' he said. I bit my lip – but he didn't frown, or curse, as I expected. Instead he broke into a great beaming smile, and slapped his hands together, and stepped into the room to seize us both excitedly by the shoulders.

'My God – that's it! That's it! Why, oh why, didn't I see it before? That is what we have been looking for. *This*, Kitty' – he gestured to our jackets, our hats, our gentlemanly poses – '*this* will make us famous!'

And so the day that I became Kitty's sweetheart was also the day that I joined her act, and began my career – my brief, unlooked-for, rather wonderful career – on the music-hall stage.

Chapter 5

At first, the prospect of joining Kitty upon the stage, in a profession for which I had never been trained, never yearned, and had – as I thought – no special talent, filled me with dismay.

'No,' I said to Walter that afternoon, when at last I understood him. 'Absolutely not. I cannot. You, of all people, should know what a fool I would make of myself – and of Kitty!'

But Walter wouldn't listen.

'Don't you see?' he said. 'How long have we been looking for something that will lift the act above the ordinary, and make it really memorable? This is it! A *double* act! A soldier – and his comrade! A swell – together with his chum! Above all: *two* lovely girls in trousers, instead of one! When did you ever see the like of it before? It will be a sensation!'

'It might be a sensation,' I said, 'with two Kitty Butlers in it. But Kitty Butler and Nancy Astley, her dresser, who never sang a song in her life—'

'We have all heard you sing,' said Walter, 'a thousand times – and very prettily, too.'

'Who never danced—' I went on.

'Pooh, dancing! A bit of shuffling about the stage. Any fool with half a leg can do it.'

'Who never raised her voice before a crowd—'

'Patter!' he said carelessly. 'Kitty can take care of the patter!'

I laughed, in sheer exasperation, then turned to Kitty herself. So far she had taken no part in the exchange, only stood at my side, biting at the edge of one of her nails, and frowning. 'Kitty,' I said now, 'for goodness' sake, tell him what madness he is talking!'

She didn't answer at first, but continued to chew distractedly at her fingertip. She looked from me to Walter, then back to me again, and narrowed her eyes.

'It might work,' she said.

I stamped my foot. 'Now you have both lost your minds, entirely! Think what you're saying. You come from families where everybody is an actor. You live all your lives in houses like this, where even the dam' dog is a dancing one. Four months ago I was an oyster-girl in Whitstable!'

'Four months before Bessie Bellwood made *her* debut,' Walter replied, 'she was a rabbit-skinner in the New Cut!' He put his hand upon my arm. 'Nan,' he said kindly, 'I am not pressing you, but let us see if this thing will work, at least. Will you just go and take a suit of Kitty's, and try it on properly? And Kitty, you go and get fitted up, too. And then we'll see what the two of you look like, side by side.'

I turned to Kitty. She gave a shrug. 'Why not?' she said.

It seems strange to think that, in all my weeks of handling so many lovely costumes, I had never thought to try one on myself; but I had not. The piece of sport with the jacket and the boater had been a novel one, born of the gaiety of that marvellous morning; until then Kitty's suits had seemed too handsome, too special – above all, too peculiarly *hers*, too fundamental to her own particular magic and swank – for me to fool with. I had cared for them and kept them neat; but I had never so much as held one up in front of me, before the glass. Now I found myself half-naked in our chilly bedroom, with Kitty beside me with a costume in her hand, and our roles quite reversed.

I had removed my dress and petticoats, and buttoned a shirt over my stays. Kitty had found a morning-suit of black and grey for me to wear, and had a similar costume ready for herself. She looked me over.

'You must take your drawers off,' she said quietly – the door was shut fast, but Walter was audibly pacing the little parlour beyond it – 'or else they'll bunch, beneath the trousers.'

I blushed, then slid the drawers down my thighs and kicked them off, so that I stood clad only in the shirt and a pair of stockings, gartered at the knee. I had once, as a girl, worn a suit of my brother's to a masquerade at a party. That, however, had been many years before; it was quite different, now, to pull Kitty's handsome trousers up my naked hips, and button them over that delicate place that Kitty herself had so recently set smarting. I took a step, and blushed still harder. I felt as though I had never had legs before – or, rather, that I had never known, quite, what it really felt like to have *two* legs, joined at the top.

I reached for Kitty, and pulled her to me. 'I wish Walter were not waiting for us,' I whispered – though, in truth, there was something rather thrilling about embracing her, in such a costume, with Walter so near and so unknowing.

That thought – and the soundless kiss which followed it – made the trousers feel still stranger. When Kitty stepped away to see to her own suit, I looked at her a little wonderingly. I said, 'How can you dress like this, before a hall of strangers, every night, and not feel queer?'

She fastened the clip of her braces, and shrugged. 'I have worn sillier costumes.'

'I didn't mean that it was silly. I meant – well, if I were to be beside you, in these' – I took another couple of steps – 'oh Kitty, I don't think I should be able to keep from kissing you!'

She put a finger to her lips; then pushed at the fringe of her hair. She said, 'You will have to get used to it, for Walter's plan to work. Otherwise – well, what a show *that* would be!'

I laughed; but the words *Walter's plan* had made my stomach lurch in sudden panic, and the laughter sounded rather hollow. I gazed down at my own two legs. The trousers, after all, were far too short for me, and showed my stockings at the ankle. I said, 'It won't do, will it, Kitty? He won't really think that it will do – will he?'

He did. 'Oh, yes!' he cried when we emerged at last together, all dressed up. 'Oh, yes, but what a team you make!' He was more excited than I had ever seen him. He had us stand together, with our arms linked; then he made us turn, and do again the little stiff-legged dance that he had caught us at before. And all the time he walked about us with narrowed eyes, stroking his chin and nodding.

'We shall need a suit for you, of course,' he said to me. 'A number of suits, indeed, to match Kitty's. But that we can easily arrange.' He took my hat from my head, and my plait fell down upon my shoulder. 'Something must be done about your hair; but the colour, at least, is perfect – a wonderful contrast with Kitty's, so the folk in the gallery will have no trouble telling you apart.' He winked, then stood surveying me a little longer with his hands behind his head. He had removed his jacket. He wore a shirt of green with a deep white collar – he was always a fancy dresser – and the armpits of the shirt were dark with sweat. I said, 'You really mean it, Walter?' and he nodded: 'Nancy, I do.'

He kept us busy, that day, all through the afternoon. The outing we had planned, the Sunday stroll, was all forgotten, the driver who was waiting he paid off and sent away. The house being empty, we worked at Mrs Dendy's piano, quite as hard as if it were a weekday morning – except that now I sang too, and not to save Kitty's voice, as I had sometimes done before, but to try out my own alongside it. We sang again the song that Walter had caught us singing, 'If Ever I Cease to Love' – but, of course, we were self-conscious now, and it sounded terribly lame. Then we tried some of Kitty's songs, that I had heard her sing at Canterbury and knew by heart; and they went a little better. And finally we tried a new song, one of the West End songs that were fashionable then – the one about strolling through Piccadilly with a pocket so full of sovereigns all the ladies look, and smile, and wink their eyes. It is sung by mashers even now; but it was Kitty and I who had it first, and when we tried it out together that afternoon – changing the author's 'I' to 'we', linking our arms, and promenading over the parlour-rug with our voices raised in a harmony – well, it sounded sweeter and more comical than I could have thought possible. We sang it once, and then a second time, and then a third and fourth; and each time I grew a little freer, a little gayer, and a little less certain of the foolishness of Walter's plan . . .

At length, when our throats were hoarse and our heads were swimming with sovereigns and winks, he closed the piano lid and let us rest. We made tea, and talked of other things. I looked at Kitty and remembered that I had another, more pressing, reason to be gay and giddy, and I began to wish that Walter would leave us. That, and my tiredness, made me dull with him: I believe he thought he had overworked me. So very soon he did leave; and when the door was closed on him I rose and went to Kitty, and put my arms about her. She wouldn't let me kiss her in the parlour; but after a moment she led me up through the darkening house, back to our bedroom. Here the suit – which I had, indeed, grown rather used to while strolling in it for Walter – began to feel strange again. When Kitty undressed I pulled her to me; and it was lewd to feel her naked hip come pressing in between my trousered legs. She ran her hand once, very lightly, over my buttons, until I began to shake with the wanting of her. Then she drew the suit from me entirely and we lay together, naked as shadows beneath the counterpane; and then she touched me again.

We lay until the front door slammed, and we heard Mrs Dendy's cough, and Tootsie laughing on the stair. Then Kitty said we should rise, and dress, or the others might wonder; and for the second time that day I lay and watched her wash, and pull on stockings and a skirt, through lazy eyes.

As I did so, I put a hand to my breast. There was a dull movement there, a kind of pulling or folding, or melting, exactly as if my chest were the hot, soft wall of a candle, falling in upon a burning wick. I gave a sigh. Kitty heard, and saw my stricken face, and came to me; then she moved my hand away and placed her lips, very softly, over my heart.

I was eighteen, and knew nothing. I thought, at that moment, that I would die of love for her.

We did not see Walter, and there was no more talk about his plan to put me on the stage at Kitty's side, until two evenings later, when he arrived at Mrs Dendy's with a parcel, marked *Nan Astley*. It was the last night of the year: he had come to supper, and to stay to hear the chimes of midnight with us. When at last they came – struck out upon the bells of Brixton church – he raised his glass. 'To Kitty and Nan!' he cried. He gazed at me, and then – more lingeringly – at Kitty. 'To their new partnership, that will bring fame and fortune to us all in 1889, and ever after!' We were at the parlour-table with Ma Dendy and the Professor, and now we joined our voices with his, and took up his toast; but Kitty and I exchanged one swift, secret glance, and I thought – with a little thrill of pleasure and triumph that I couldn't quite suppress – poor man! how could he know what we were really celebrating?

Only now did Walter present me with his package, and smile to see me open it. But I knew already what it would hold: a suit, a stage suit of serge and velvet, cut to my size to the pattern of one of Kitty's – but blue to match my eyes, where hers was brown. I held it up against me, and Walter nodded. 'Now that,' he said, 'will make all the difference. Just you trot upstairs and slip that on, and then we'll see what Mrs Dendy has to say about it.'

I did as he asked; then paused for a moment to study myself in the glass. I had put on a pair of my own plain black boots and piled my hair up inside a hat. I had placed a cigarette behind my ear – I had even taken off my stays, to make my flat chest flatter. I looked a little like my brother Davy – only, per-haps, rather handsomer. I shook my head. Four nights before I had stood in the same spot, marvelling to see myself dressed as a grown-up woman. Now, there had been one quiet visit to a tailor's shop and here I was, a boy – a boy with buttons and a belt. The thought, once again, was a saucy one; I felt I ought not to encourage it. I went down at once to the parlour, put my hands in my pockets and posed before them all, and made ready to receive their praises.

When I stood turning upon the rug, however, Walter was rather subdued, and Mrs Dendy thoughtful. When, at their request, I took Kitty's arm and we sang a quick chorus, Walter stood back, frowned, and shook his head.

'It's not quite right,' he said. 'It grieves me to say it, but – it just won't do.'

I turned, in dismay, to Kitty. She was fiddling with her neck-lace, sucking at the chain and tapping with the pearl upon a tooth. She, too, looked grave. She said, 'There is something queer about it; but I can't say what . . .'

I gazed down at myself. I took my hands from my pockets and folded my arms, and Walter shook his head again. 'It's a perfect fit,' he said. 'The colour is good. And yet there's some-thing – *unpleasing* – about it. What is it?'

Mrs Dendy gave a cough. 'Take a step,' she said to me. I did so. 'Now a turn – that's right. Now be a dear and light me a fag.' I did this for her too, then waited while she drew on her cigar-ette and coughed again.

'She's too real,' she said at last, to Walter.

'Too real?'

'Too real. She looks like a boy. Which I know she is sup-posed to – but, if you follow me, she looks like a *real* boy. Her face and her figure and her bearing on her feet. And that ain't quite the idea now, is it?'

Now I felt more awkward than ever. I looked at Kitty and she gave a nervous kind of laugh. Walter, however, had lost his frown, and his eyes looked blue and wide as a child's. 'Damn it, Ma,' he said, 'but you're right!' He put his hand to his brow, then stepped to the door: we heard his heavy, rapid tread upon the stairs, heard footsteps in the room above our heads – Sims's and Percy's room – and then the slam of a door, higher up. When he returned he held a strange assortment of objects: a pair of gentleman's shoes, a sewing-basket, a couple of ribbons, and Kitty's make-up box. These he dumped about me on the carpet. Then, with a hasty 'Pardon me, Nancy', he pulled the jacket from me, and the boots. The jacket he handed to Kitty, along with the sewing-basket: 'Put a few tucks down the inside of that waist,' he said, pointing to the seam. The boots he cast aside, and replaced with the pair of shoes – Sims's shoes they were, and small, low-heeled and rather dainty; and Walter made them daintier still by tying ribbons in a bow at the laces. To advertise the bows a bit – and because, without my boots, I was now a little shorter – he caught hold of the bottom of my trouser-legs, and gave them cuffs.

Next he seized my head and tilted it back, and worked upon my lips and lashes with carmine and spit-black from Kitty's box: he did this gently as a girl. Then he plucked the cigarette from behind my ear and cast it on to the mantel. Finally he turned to Kitty and snapped his fingers. She, infected by his air of haste and purpose, had begun to sew as he had shown her. Now she raised the jacket to her cheek to bite the final length of cotton from it, and when that was done he took it from her and shrugged me into it and buttoned it over my breast.

Then he stood back, and cocked his head.

I gazed down at myself once again. My new shoes looked quaint and girlish, like a principal boy's in a pantomime. The trousers were shorter, their line rather spoiled. The jacket flared a little, above and below the waist, quite as if I had hips and a bosom – but it felt tighter than before, and not a half as comfortable. My face, of course, I could not see: I had to turn and squint into a picture over the hearth, and saw it reflected there – all eyes and lips – over the red nose and whiskers of 'Rackity Jack'.

I looked at the others. Mrs Dendy and the Professor smiled. Kitty did not look at all nervous, now. Walter was flushed, and seemed awed by his own handiwork. He folded his arms.

'Perfect,' he said.

After that – clad not exactly as a boy but, rather confusingly, as the boy I would have been, had I been more of a girl – my entry into the profession was rather rapid. The very next day Walter sent my costume to a seamstress, and had it properly re-sewn; within a week he had borrowed a hall and a band from a manager who owed him a favour, and had Kitty and me, in our matching suits, practising upon the stage. It was not at all like singing in Mrs Dendy's parlour. The strangers, the dark and empty hall, disconcerted me; I was stiff and awkward, quite unable to master the few simple strolling steps that Kitty and Walter tried patiently to teach me. At last Walter handed me a cane, and said I should just stand and lean upon it, and let Kitty dance; and that was better, and I grew easier, and the song began to sound funny again. When we had finished and were practising our bows, some of the men in the orchestra clapped us.

Kitty sat and took a cup of tea, then; but Walter led me off to a seat in the stalls, away from the others, and looked grave.

'Nan,' he began, 'I told you when all this started that I would not press you, and I meant it; I would give up the business altogether before I forced a girl upon the stage against her will. There are fellows who do that sort of thing, you know, fellows who think of nothing but their own pockets. But I am not one of them; and besides, you are my friend. *But*—' He took a breath. 'We have come this far, the three of us; and you are good – I promise you, you are good.'

'With work, perhaps,' I said doubtfully. He shook his head.

'Not even with that. Haven't you worked, these past six months – harder than Kitty, almost? You know the act as well as she; you know her songs, her bits of business – why, you taught them to her, most of them!'

'I don't know,' I said. 'This is all so new, and strange. All my life I've loved the music hall, but I never thought of getting up upon the stage, myself . . .'

'Didn't you?' he said then. 'Didn't you, really?' Every time you saw some little serio-comic captivate the crowd, at that Palace of yours, in Canterbury, didn't you wish that it was you? Didn't you close your eyes and see your name upon the programmes, your number in the box? Didn't you sing to your – oyster-barrel – as if it were a crowded hall, and you could make those little fishes weep, or shriek with laughter?'

I bit my nail, and frowned. 'Dreams,' I said.

He snapped his fingers. 'The very *stuff* that stages are made of.'

'Where would we start?' I said then. 'Who would offer us a spot?'

'The manager here would. Tonight. I've already spoken with him—'

'Tonight!'

'Just one song. He'll find space for you in his programme; and if they like you, he'll keep you there.'

'Tonight . . .' I looked at Walter in dismay. His face was very kind, and his eyes seemed bluer and more earnest than ever. But what he said made me tremble. I thought of the hall, hot and bright and filled with jeering faces. I thought of that stage, so wide and empty. I thought: I cannot do it, not even for Walter's sake. Not even for Kitty's.

I made to shake my head. He saw, and quickly spoke again – spoke, perhaps for the first time in all the months that I had known him, with something that was almost guile. He said: 'You know, of course, that we cannot throw over the idea of the double act, now that we have hit upon it. If you don't wish to partner Kitty, there'll be some other girl who does. We can spread the word, place notices, audition. You mustn't feel that you are letting Kitty down . . .'

I looked from him to the stage, where Kitty herself sat on the edge of a beam of limelight, sipping at her cup, swinging her

legs, and smiling at some word of the conductor's. The thought
that she might take another partner – might stroll before the
footlights with another girl's arm through hers, another girl's
voice rising and blending with her own – had not occurred to
me. It was more ghastly than the image of the jeering hall;
more ghastly than the prospect of being laughed and hissed off
a thousand, thousand stages . . .

So when Kitty stood in the wing of the theatre that night, waiting for the chairman's cry, I stood beside her, sweating beneath
a layer of grease-paint, biting my lips so hard I thought they
would bleed. My heart had beat fast for Kitty before, in apprehension and passion; but it had never thudded as it thudded
now – I thought it would burst right out of my breast, I thought
I should be killed with fright. When Walter came to whisper to
us, and to fill our pockets with coins, I could not answer him.
There was a juggling turn upon the stage. I heard the creaking
of the boards as the man ran to catch his batons, the clap-gasp-
clap-gasp-*cheer* of the audience as he finished his set; and
then came the clack of a gavel, and the juggler ran by us,
clutching his gear. Kitty said once, very low, 'I love you!' – and
I felt myself half-pulled, half-thrust beneath the rising curtain,
and knew that I must somehow saunter and sing.

At first, so blinded was I by the lights, I couldn't see the
crowd at all; I could only hear it, rustling and murmuring –
loud, and close, it seemed, on every side. When at last I
stepped for a second out of the glare of lime, and saw all the
faces that were turned my way, I almost faltered and lost my
place – and would have done, I think, had not Kitty at that
moment pressed my arm and murmured, 'We have them!
Listen!' under cover of the orchestra. I did listen then – and
realised that, unbelievably, she was right: there were claps,
and friendly shouts; there was a rising hum of expectant pleasure as we worked towards our chorus; there was, finally, a
bubbling cascade of cheers and laughter from gallery to pit.

The sound affected me like nothing I had ever known

before. At once, I remembered the foolish dance that I had failed, all day, to learn, and left off leaning on my stick to join Kitty in her stroll before the footlights. I understood, too, what Walter had wanted of us in the wing: as the new song drew to a close I advanced with Kitty to the front of the stage, drew out the coins that he had tipped into my pocket – they were only chocolate sovereigns, of course, but covered in foil to make them glitter – and cast them into the laughing crowd. A dozen hands reached up to snatch them.

There were calls for an encore, then; but we, of course, had none to make. We could only dance back beneath the dropping curtain while the crowd still cheered and the chairman called for order. The next act – a couple of trick-cyclists – was pushed hurriedly on to take our place; but even at the end of their set there were still one or two voices calling for us.

We were the hit of the evening.

Backstage, with Kitty's lips upon my cheek, Walter's arm about my shoulders, and exclamations of delight and praise greeting me from every corner, I stood quite stunned, unable either to smile at the compliments or to modestly disclaim them. I had passed perhaps seven minutes before that gay and shouting crowd; but in those few, swift minutes I had glimpsed a truth about myself, and it had left me awed and quite transformed.

The truth was this: that whatever successes I might achieve as a girl, they would be nothing compared to the triumphs I should enjoy clad, however girlishly, as a boy.

I had, in short, found my vocation.

Next day, rather appropriately, I got my hair cut off, and changed my name.

The hair I had barbered at a house in Battersea, by the same theatrical hairdresser who cut Kitty's. He worked on me for an hour, while she sat and watched; and at the end of that time I remember he held a glass to his apron and said warningly: 'Now, you will squeal when you see it – I never cropped a girl

before who didn't squeal at the first look,' and I trembled in a
sudden panic.

But when he turned the glass to show me, I only smiled to
see the transformation he had made. He had not clipped the
hair as short as Kitty's, but had left it long and falling,
Bohemian-like, quite to my collar; and here, without the
weight of the plait to pull it flat and lank, it sprang into a
slight, surprising curl. Upon the locks which threatened to
tumble over my brow he had palmed a little macassar-oil,
which turned them sleek as cat's fur, and gold as a ring. When
I fingered them – when I turned and tilted my head – I felt my
cheeks grow crimson. The man said then, 'You see, you *will*
find it queer,' and he showed me how I might wear my severed
plait, as Kitty wore hers, to disguise his barbering.

I said nothing; but it was not with regret that I had blushed.
I had blushed because my new, shorn head, my naked neck,
felt saucy. I had blushed because – just as I had done when I
first pulled on a pair of trousers – I had felt myself stir, and
grow warm, and want Kitty. Indeed, I seemed to want her more
and more, the further into boyishness I ventured.

Kitty herself, however, though she also smiled when the
barber displayed me, smiled more broadly when the plait was
re-affixed. 'That's more like it,' she said, when I stood and
brushed my skirts down. 'What a fright you looked in short
hair and a frock!'

Back at Ginevra Road we found Walter waiting for us, and
Mrs Dendy dishing up lunch; and it was here that I was given
a new name, to match my bold new crop.

For our debut at Camberwell we had thought that our ordinary names would do as well as any, and had been billed by
the chairman as 'Kitty Butler and Nancy Astley'. Now, however, we were a hit: Walter's manager friend had offered us a
four-week contract, and needed to know the names he should
have printed on the posters. We knew we must keep Kitty's, for
the sake of her successes of the past half-year; but Walter said
'Astley' was rather too common, and could we think of a better

one? I didn't mind, only said I should like to keep 'Nan' – since Kitty herself had re-christened me that; and we took our lunch, in consequence, with everybody volunteering names they thought would match it. Tootsie said 'Nan Love', Sims 'Nan Sergeant'. Percy said, 'Nan Scarlet – no, Nan Silver – no, Nan Gold . . .' Every name seemed to offer me some new and marvellous version of myself; it was like standing at the costumier's rail and shrugging on the jackets.

None, however, seemed to fit – till the Professor tapped the table, cleared his throat, and said: 'Nan King'. And although I should like to be able to say – as other artistes do – that there was some terribly clever or romantic story behind the choosing of my stage-name – that we had opened a special book at a certain place, and found it there; that I had heard the word 'King' said in a dream, and quivered at it – I can give no better account of the matter than the truth: which was only that we needed a name, and the Professor said 'Nan King', and I liked it.

It was as 'Kitty Butler and Nan King', therefore, that we returned to Camberwell that evening – to renew, and improve upon our success of the night before. It was 'Kitty Butler and Nan King' that appeared on the posters; and 'Kitty Butler and Nan King' that began to rise, rather steadily, from middle-billing, to second-billing, to top-of-the-list. Not just at the Camberwell hall but, over the next few months, at all the lesser London halls and – slowly, slowly – some of the West End ones, too . . .

I cannot say what it was that made the crowds like Kitty and me together, more than they had liked Kitty Butler on her own. It may just have been, as Walter had foreseen, that we were novel: for though in later years we were rather freely imitated, there was certainly no other act like ours in the London halls in 1889. It may also have been – again, as Walter had predicted – that the sight of a *pair* of girls in gentlemen's suits was somehow more charming, more thrilling, more indefinably *saucy*, than that of a single girl in trousers and topper and spats. We did, I know, go handsomely together – Kitty with her nut-brown crop, me with my head blonde and smooth and gleaming; she raised a little on her one-inch slippers, me in my flat effeminate shoes, my cleverly tailored suits that masked the slender angularity of my frame with girlish curves.

Whatever it was that made the change, however, it worked, and worked extraordinarily. We became not just rather popular, as Kitty had been, but really famous. Our wages rose; we worked three halls a night – four, sometimes – and now, when our brougham was caught in traffic, our driver would yell, 'I've got Kitty Butler and Nan King in here, due at the Royal, Holborn, in fifteen minutes! Clear a way there, can't you?' – and the other drivers would shift a little to let us through, and smile and raise their hats to the windows as we passed! Now there were flowers for me, as well as for Kitty; now *I* received invitations to dinner, and requests for autographs, and letters . . .

It took me weeks to understand that it was really happening, and to me; weeks to let myself believe in it, and to trust the crowd that liked me. But when at last I learned to love my new life, I loved it fiercely. The pleasures of success, I suppose, are rather easy to understand; it was my new *capacity* for pleasure – for pleasure in performance, display and disguise, in the wearing of handsome suits, the singing of ribald songs – that shocked and thrilled me most. I had been content till now to stand in the wings, looking on while Kitty dallied, in the limelight, with the vast, rumbustious crowd. Now, suddenly, it was I who wooed it, me at whom it gazed in envy and delight. I could not help it: I had fallen in love with Kitty; now, *becoming* Kitty, I fell in love a little with myself. I admired my hair, so neat and so sleek. I adored my legs – my legs which, while they had had skirts about them, I had scarcely had a thought for; but which were, I discovered, rather long and lean and shapely.

I sound vain. I was not – then – and could never have been,

while Kitty existed as the wider object of my self-love. The act, I knew, was still all hers. When we sang, it was really she who sang, while I provided a light, easy second. When we danced, it was she who did the tricky steps: I only strolled or shuffled at her side. I was her foil, her echo; I was the shadow which, in all her brilliance, she cast across the stage. But, like a shadow, I lent her the edge, the depth, the crucial definition, that she had lacked before.

It was very far from vanity, then, my satisfaction. It was only love; and the better the act became, I thought, the more perfect that love grew. After all, the two things – the act, our love – were not so very different. They had been born together – or, as I liked to think, the one had been born of the other, and was merely its public shape. When Kitty and I had first become sweethearts, I had made her a promise. 'I will be careful,' I had said – and I had said it very lightly, because I thought it would be easy. I had kept my promise: I never kissed her, touched her, said a loving thing, when there was anyone to glimpse or overhear us. But it was not easy, nor did it become easier as the months passed by; it became only a dreary kind of habit. How *could* it be easy to stand cool and distant from her in the day, when we had spent all night with our naked limbs pressed hot and close together? How could it be easy to veil my glances when others watched, bite my tongue because others listened, when I passed all our private hours gazing at her till my eyes ached of it, calling her every kind of sweet name until my throat was dry? Sitting beside her at supper at Mrs Dendy's, standing near her in the green-room of a theatre, walking with her through the city streets, I felt as though I was bound and fettered with iron bands, chained and muzzled and blinkered. Kitty had given me leave to love her; the world, she said, would never let me be anything to her except her friend.

Her friend – and her partner on the stage. You will not believe me, but making love to Kitty – a thing done in passion, but always, too, in shadow and in silence, and with an ear half-cocked for the sound of footsteps on the stairs – making love to

Kitty, and posing at her side in a shaft of limelight, before a thousand pairs of eyes, to a script I knew by heart, in an attitude I had laboured for hours to perfect – these things were not so very different. A double act is always twice the act the audience thinks it: beyond our songs, our steps, our bits of business with coins and canes and flowers, there was a private language, in which we held an endless, delicate exchange of which the crowd knew nothing. This was a language not of the tongue but of the body, its vocabulary the pressure of a finger or a palm, the nudging of a hip, the holding or breaking of a gaze, that said, *You are too slow – you go too fast – not there, but here – that's good – that's better!* It was as if we walked before the crimson curtain, lay down upon the boards, and kissed and fondled – and were clapped, and cheered, and paid for it! As Kitty had said, when I had whispered that wearing trousers upon the stage would only make me want to kiss her: 'What a show *that* would be!' But, that *was* our show; only the crowd never knew it. They looked on, and saw another turn entirely.

Well, perhaps there were some who caught glimpses . . .

I have spoken of my admirers. They were girls, for the most part – jolly, careless girls, who gathered at the stage door, and begged for photographs, and autographs, and gave us flowers. But for every ten or twenty of such girls, there would be one or two more desperate and more pushing, or more shy and awkward, than the rest; and in them I recognised a certain – something. I could not put a name to it, only knew that it was there, and that it made their interest in me rather special. These girls sent letters – letters, like their stage door manners, full of curious excesses or ellipses; letters that awed, repelled and drew me, all at once. 'I hope you will forgive my writing to say that you are very handsome,' wrote one girl; another wrote: 'Miss King, I am in love with you!' Someone named Ada King wrote to ask if we were cousins. She said: 'I do so admire you and Miss Butler, but especially you. Could you I wonder send a photograph? I *would* like to have a picture of you, beside my bed . . .' The card I sent her was a favourite of mine, a picture of Kitty and me in Oxford bags and boaters, in which Kitty stood with her hands in her pockets and I leaned with my arm through hers, a cigarette between my fingers. I signed it 'To Ada, from one "King" to another'; and it was very odd to think that it would be pinned to a wall, or put in a frame, so that unknown girl might gaze at it while she fastened her frock or lay dreaming.

Then there were other requests, for odder things. Would I send a collar-stud, a button from my suit, a curl of hair? Would I, on Thursday night – or Friday night – wear a scarlet necktie – or a green necktie, or a yellow rose in my lapel; would I make a special sign, or dance a special step? – for then the writer would see, and know that I had received her note.

'Throw them away,' Kitty would say when I showed her these letters. 'They're cracked, those girls, and you mustn't encourage them.' But I knew that the girls were not cracked, as she said; they were only as I had been, a year before – but braver or more reckless. That, in itself, impressed me; what astonished and thrilled me now was the thought that girls might look at me at all – the thought that in every darkened hall there might be one or two female hearts that beat exclusively for me, one or two pairs of eyes that lingered, perhaps immodestly, over my face and figure and suit. Did they know why they looked? Did they know what they looked for? Above all, when they saw me stride across the stage in trousers, singing of girls whose eyes I had sent winking, whose hearts I had broken, *what did they see?* Did they see that – something – that I saw in them?

'They had better not!' said Kitty, when I put my idea to her; and though she laughed as she said it, the laughter was a little strained. She didn't like to talk about such things.

She didn't like it, either, when one night in the change-room of a theatre we met a pair of women – a comic singer and her dresser – who, I thought, were rather like ourselves. The singer was flashy, and had a frock with spangles on it that must be fastened very tightly over her stays. Her maid was an older woman in a plain brown dress; I saw her tugging at the frock, and thought nothing of it. But when she had the hooks fastened tight, she leaned and gently blew upon the singer's throat, where the powder had clogged; and then she whispered something to her, and they laughed together with their heads very close . . . and I knew, as surely as if they had pasted the words upon the dressing-room wall, that they were lovers.

The knowledge made me blush like a beacon. I looked at Kitty, and saw that she had caught the gesture, too; her eyes, however, were lowered, and her mouth was tight. When the comic singer passed us on her way to the stage, she gave me a wink: 'Off to please the public,' she said, and her dresser laughed again. When she came back and took her make-up off, she wandered over with a cigarette and asked for a light; then, as she drew on her fag, she looked me over. 'Are you going,' she said, 'to Barbara's party, after the show?' I said I didn't know who Barbara was. She waved her hand: 'Oh, Barbara won't mind. You come along with Ella and me: you and your friend.' Here she nodded – very pleasantly, I thought – to Kitty. But Kitty, who had had her head bent all this time, working at the fastenings of her skirt, now looked up and gave a prim little smile.

'How nice of you to ask,' she said; 'but we are spoken for tonight. Our agent, Mr Bliss, is due to take us out to supper.'

I stared: we had no arrangement that I knew of. But the singer only gave a shrug. 'Too bad,' she said. Then she looked at me. 'You don't want to leave your pal to her agent, and come on alone, with me and Ella?'

'Miss King will be busy with Mr Bliss,' said Kitty, before I could answer; and she said it so tightly the singer gave a sniff, then turned and went over to where her dresser waited with their baskets. I watched them leave – they didn't look back at me. When we returned to the theatre the next night, Kitty chose a hook that was far from theirs; and on the night after that, they had moved on to another hall . . .

At home, in bed, I said I thought it was a shame.

'Why did you tell them Walter was coming?' I asked Kitty. She said: 'I didn't care for them.'

'Why not? They were nice. They were funny. They were – like us.'

I had my arm about her, and felt her stiffen at my words. She pulled away from me and raised her head. We had left a candle burning and her face, I saw, was white and shocked.

'Nan!' she said. 'They're not like us! They're not like us, at all. They're *toms.*'

'Toms?' I remember this moment very distinctly, for I had never heard the word before. Later I would think it marvellous that there had ever been a time I hadn't known it.

Now, when Kitty said it, she flinched. 'Toms. They make a – a *career* – out of kissing girls. We're not like that!'

'Aren't we?' I said. 'Oh, if someone would only pay me for it, I'd be very glad to make a career out of kissing *you.* Do you think there is someone who would pay me for that? I'd give up the stage in a flash.' I tried to pull her to me again, but she knocked my hand away.

'You would have to give up the stage,' she said seriously, 'and so would I, if there was talk about us, if people thought we were – *like that.*'

But what *were* we like? I still didn't know. When I pressed her, however, she grew fretful.

'We're not like anything! We're just – ourselves.'

'But if we're just ourselves, why do we have to hide it?'

'Because no one would know the difference between us and – women like that!'

I laughed. 'Is there a difference?' I asked again.

She continued grave and cross. 'I have told you,' she said. 'You don't understand. You don't know what's wrong or right, or good . . .'

'I know that this ain't wrong, what we do. Only that the world says it is.'

She shook her head. 'It's the same thing,' she said. Then she

fell back upon her pillow and closed her eyes, and turned her
face away.

I was sorry that I had teased her – but also, I am ashamed to
say, rather warmed by her distress. I touched her cheek, and
moved a little closer to her; then I took my hand from her face
and passed it, hesitantly, down her night-dress, over her
breasts and belly. She moved away, and I slowed – but did not
stop – my searching fingers; and soon, as if despite itself, I felt
her body slacken in assent. I moved lower, and seized the hem
of her shift and drew it high – then did the same with my
own, and gently slid my hips over hers. We fitted together like
the two halves of an oyster-shell – you couldn't have passed so
much as the blade of a knife between us. I said, 'Oh Kitty, how
can this be wrong?' But she did not answer, only moved her
lips to mine at last, and when I felt the tug of her kiss I let my
weight fall heavily upon her, and gave a sigh.

I might have been Narcissus, embracing the pond in which
I was about to drown.

It was true, I suppose, what she said – that I didn't understand her. Always, always, it came down to the same thing:
that however much we had to hide our love, however guard-
edly we had to take our pleasure, I could not long be miserable
about a thing that was – as she herself admitted – so very
sweet. Nor, in my gladness, could I quite believe that anyone
who cared for me would be anything but happy for me, if only
they knew.

I was, as I have said before, very young. The next day, while
Kitty still slept, I rose and made my noiseless way into our parlour. There I did something that I had longed for months to do,
but never had the courage. I took a piece of paper and a pen,
and wrote a letter to my sister, Alice.

I hadn't written home in weeks. I had told them, once, that
I had joined the act; but I had rather played the matter down –
I feared they wouldn't think the life a decent one for their own
daughter. They had sent me back a brief, half-hearted, puzzled

note; they had talked of travelling to London, to reassure themselves that I was quite content – and at that I had written at
once to say, they must not think of coming, I was too busy, my
rooms were too small . . . In short – so 'careful' had Kitty made
me! – I was as unwelcoming as it was possible to be, this side
of friendliness. Since then, our letters had grown rarer than
ever; and the business of my fame upon the stage had been
quite lost – I never mentioned it; they did not ask.

Now, it was not of the act that I wrote to Alice. I wrote to tell
her what had happened between Kitty and me – to tell her that
we loved each other, not as friends, but as sweethearts; that we
had made our lives together; and that she must be glad for me,
for I was happier than I had ever thought it possible to be.

It was a long letter, but I wrote it easily; and when I had finished it I felt light as air. I didn't read it through, but put it in
an envelope at once, and ran with it to the post-box. I was back
before Kitty had even stirred; and when she woke I didn't
mention it.

I didn't tell her about Alice's reply, either. This came a few
days later – came while Kitty and I were at breakfast, and had
to stay unopened in my pocket until I could make time to be
alone and read it. It was, I saw at once, very neat; and knowing
Alice to be no great penwoman, I guessed that this must be the
last of several versions.

It was also, unlike my letter, very short – so short that, to my
great dismay and all unwillingly, I find that I remember it,
even now, in its entirety.

'Dear Nancy,' it began.

'Your letter was both a shock to me and no surprise at all,
for I have been expecting to receive something very like it
from you, since the day you left us. When I first read it I did
not now whether to weep or throw the paper away from me in
temper. In the end I burned the thing, and only hope you will
have sense enough to burn this one, likewise.

'You ask me to be happy on your behalf. Nance, you must
know that I have always only ever had your happiness at my

heart, more nearly even than my own. But you must know too that I can never be happy while your friendship with that woman is so wrong and queer. I can never like what you have told me. You think you are happy, but you are only misled – and that woman, your friend "so-called", is to blame for it.

'I only wish that you had never met her nor ever gone away, but only stayed in Whitstable where you belong, and with those who love you properly.

'Let me just say at the last what you must I hope know. Father, Mother and Davy know nothing of this, and won't from my lips, since I would rather die of shame than tell them. *You must never speak of it to them*, unless you want to finish the job you started when you first left us, and break their hearts completely and for ever.

'Don't burden me, I ask you, with no more shameful secrets. But look to yourself and the path that you are treading, and ask yourself if it is really Right.

'Alice.'

She must have kept her word about not telling our parents, for their letters to me continued as before – still cautious, still rather fretful, but still kind. But now I got even less pleasure from them; only kept thinking, *What would they write, if they knew? How kind would they be then?* My replies, in consequence, grew shorter and rarer than ever.

As for Alice: after that one brief, bitter epistle, she never wrote to me at all.

Chapter 6

The months, that year, seemed to slide by very swiftly; for, of course, we were busier now than ever. We continued to work our hit – the song about the sovereigns and the winks – all through the spring and summer, but there were always new songs, new routines to labour over and perfect, new orchestras to grow familiar with, new theatres, and new costumes. Of the latter, we acquired so many that we found we couldn't manage them without help, and took on a girl to do my old job – to mend the suits and to help us dress in them, at the side of the stage.

We grew rich – or rich, at least, as far as I was concerned. At the Star, in Bermondsey, Kitty had started on a couple of pounds a week, and I had thought my own, small dresser's share of that quite grand enough. Now I earned ten, twenty, thirty times that figure, on my own account, and sometimes more. The sums seemed unimaginable to me: I preferred, perhaps foolishly, not to think of them at all, but let Walter worry over our wages. He, in response to our great successes, had found new agents for his other artistes and was now our manager full-time. He negotiated our contracts, our publicity, and held our money for us; he paid Kitty and she, as before, gave me whatever little cash I needed, when I asked her for it.

It was rather strange with Walter, now that Kitty and I had grown so close. We saw him quite as often as we had before; we still went driving with him; we still spent long hours with him at Mrs Dendy's piano (though the piano itself had been changed, to a more expensive one). He was as kind and as foolish as ever – but a little dimmed, somehow, a little shadowy, now that the blaze of Kitty's charms was more decidedly turned my way. Perhaps it only seemed so to me; but I was sorry for him, and could not help but wonder what he thought. I was sure he hadn't guessed that Kitty and I were sweethearts – for, of course, we were rather cool ourselves, in public, now.

As rich as we became that year, we were never quite rich enough to be so very choosy about the kind of halls we sang in. For the whole of September we played at the Trocadero – a very smart theatre, and one of the ones that Walter had pointed out to us on our first, giddy tour of the West End, more than a year before. When we left the Troc, however, it was to drive to Deacon's Music Hall, in Islington. This was an altogether different place: small and old, with an audience drawn from the streets and courts of Clerkenwell – and inclined, in consequence, to be rather rough.

We didn't mind a rowdy crowd, as a rule, for it could be unnerving to work the prim West End theatres, where the ladies were too gentle or well-dressed to bang their hands together or to stamp, and where only the drunken swells of the promenade really whistled and shouted as a proper musichall audience should. We had never worked Deacon's before, but we had once done a week at Sam Collins', up the road. There the crowd had been humble and gay – working-people, women with babies in their arms – the kind of audience I liked best of all, because it was the kind of which, until very recently, I had myself been a member.

The Deacon's crowd were noticeably shabbier than the folk at Islington Green, but no less kind; if anything, indeed, they were inclined to be kinder, jollier, more willing to be moved

and thrilled and entertained. Our first week there went well –
they packed the hall for us. It was on the Saturday night of the
second week that the trouble came – on a Saturday night at the
end of September, a night of fog – one of those grey-brown
evenings, when all the streets and buildings of the city seem to
waver a little at the edges.

The roads are always choked on such a night, and on this
particular evening the traffic between Windmill Street and
Islington was horribly slow, for there had been an accident
along the way. A van had overturned; a dozen boys had
rushed to sit upon the horse's head, to stop the beast from
rising; and our own carriage could not pass for half an hour or
more. We arrived at Deacon's terribly late, to find the place as
wild as the street we had just left. The crowd had had to wait
for us, and were impatient. Some poor artiste had been sent
on to sing a comic song and keep them occupied, but they had
started to heckle him quite mercilessly; at last – the fellow
had begun a clog dance – two roughs had jumped upon the
stage and pulled the boots from him, and tossed them up to
the gallery. When we arrived, breathless and flustered but
ready to sing, the air was thick with shouts and bellows and
screams of laughter. The two roughs had hold of the comic
singer by the ankles, and were holding him so that his head
dangled over the flames of the footlights, in an attempt to set
fire to his hair. The conductor and a couple of stage-hands had
hold of the roughs, and were trying to pull *them* into the
wings. Another stage-hand stood nearby, dazed, and with a
bleeding nose.

We had Walter with us, for we had arranged to eat with him
later, after the show. Now he looked at the scene before us,
aghast.

'My God,' he said. 'You cannot go on with them in such a
mood as this.'

As he spoke, the manager came running. 'Not go on?' he
said, appalled. 'They must go on, or there will be a riot. It is
entirely because they did not go on when they were meant to

that the damn trouble – excuse me, ladies – started.' He wiped his forehead, which was very damp. From the stage, however, there were signs that the scuffling, at last, was subsiding.

Kitty looked at me, then nodded. 'He's right,' she said to Walter. Then, to the manager: 'Tell them to put our number up.'

The manager pocketed his handkerchief and stepped smartly away before she could change her mind; but Walter still looked grave. 'Are you sure?' he asked us. He glanced back towards the stage. The roughs had been successfully carried off, and the singer had been placed in a chair in the wing across from us and given a glass of water. His clogs must have been thrown back on to the stage, or else some kind soul had delivered or retrieved them; at any rate, they now stood rather neatly beneath his chair and beside his bruised and naked feet. There were still some shrieks and whistles, however, from the hall.

'You don't have to do it,' Walter went on. 'They may hurl something; you might get hurt.'

Kitty straightened her collar. As she did so we heard the great roar, and the thunder of stamping feet, that told us that our number had gone up. In a second, rising doggedly over the din, there came the first few bars of our opening song. 'If they hurl something,' she said quickly, 'we'll duck.' Then she took a step, and nodded for me to follow.

And after all the fuss, indeed, they received us very graciously.

'Wot cheer, Kitty?' someone shouted, as we danced our way into the beam of the limes. 'Did you lose your way in the fog, then, or what?'

'Shocking awful traffic,' she called back – the first verse was about to begin, and she was slipping further into character with every step she took – 'but not so bad as a road my friend and I were a-walking on the other afternoon. Why, it took us quite half a day to get from Pall Mall to Piccadilly . . .' And effortlessly, seamlessly – and with me beside her, closer and more faithful than a shadow – she led us into our song.

When that was over we headed back into the wing, to where Flora, our dresser, waited with our suits. Walter kept his distance, but clasped his hands together before his chest when we emerged, and shook them, in a gesture of triumph. He was pink-faced and smiling with relief.

Our second number – a song called 'Scarlet Fever', for which we dressed in guardsmen's uniforms (red jackets and caps, white belts, black trousers, very smart) – went down a treat; it was during the next routine that all turned sour. There was a man in the stalls: I had noticed him earlier, for he was large, and clearly very drunk; he slept noisily in his seat, with his knees spread wide, his mouth open and his chin glistening slightly in the glow from the stage. For all I know, he might have slept through all the rumpus with the clog-dancer; now, however, by some horrible mischance, he had woken up. It was a very small theatre and I could see him quite distinctly. He had stumbled over his neighbours' legs to get to the end of his row, swearing all the way, and drawing answering curses from everyone he stepped on. He had reached the aisle at last – but there he had grown confused. Instead of heading for the bar, the privy, or wherever it was that he had made up his gin- or whisky-soaked mind to make for, he had wandered down to the side of the stage. Now he stood, peering up at us, with his hands over his eyes.

'What the devil?' he said; he said it during a lull between verses, and it sounded very loud. A few people turned away from us to look at him, and to titter or tut-tut.

I exchanged a glance with Kitty, but kept my voice and steps in time with hers, my eyes still bright, my smile still broad. After a second the man began to curse even louder. The crowd – who were still, I suppose, rather ready for a bit of sport – began to shout at him, to quieten him down.

'Throw the old josser out!' called someone; and, 'Don't you pay no mind to him, Nan, dear!' This was from a woman in the stalls. I caught her eye, and tipped my hat – it was a boater; we were wearing the Oxford bags and boaters, now – and saw her blush.

All the shouting, however, only seemed to enrage and confuse the man still further. A boy stepped up to him, but was knocked away; I saw the fellows in the orchestra begin to gaze a little wildly over the tops of their instruments. At the back of the hall two door-men had been summoned and were squinting into the gloom. Half a dozen hands waved and pointed to where the man leaned over the footlights, his whiskers fluttering in the heat.

He, now, had started banging on the stage with the heel of his hand. I suppressed an urge to dance up to him and stamp upon his wrist (for, apart from anything else, I thought he was quite capable of seizing my ankle and dragging me into the stalls.) Instead, I took my cue from Kitty. She had hold of my arm, and had pressed it, but her brow was smooth and untroubled. At any moment, I thought, she would slow the song, launch into the man, or call for the door-men to come and remove him.

But they, at last, had spotted him, and had begun their advance. He, all unknowing, ranted drunkenly on.

'Call that a song?' he shouted. 'Call that a song? I want my shilling back! You hear me? *I want my bleeding shilling back!*'

'You want your bleeding arse kicked, is what you want!' answered someone from the pit. Then someone else, a woman, yelled, 'Stop your row, can't you? We can't hear the girls for all your racket.'

The man gave a sneer; then he hawked, and spat. 'Girls?' he cried. 'Girls? You call them girls? Why, they're nothing but a couple of – a couple of *toms*!'

He put the whole force of his voice into it – the word that Kitty had once whispered to me, flinching and shuddering as she said it! It sounded louder at that moment than the blast of a cornet – seemed to bounce from one wall of the hall to another, like a bullet from a sharp-shooter's act gone wrong.

Toms!

At the sound of it, the audience gave a great collective flinch. There was a sudden hush; the shouts became mumbles, the shrieks all tailed away. Through the shaft of limelight I saw their faces – a thousand faces, self-conscious and appalled.

Even so, the awkwardness might have lasted no longer than a moment; they might have forgotten it at once, and grown noisy and gay again – but for what happened, simultaneous with their silencing, upon the stage.

For Kitty had stiffened; and then she had stumbled. We had been dancing with our arms linked. Now her mouth flew open. Now it shut. Now it trembled. Her voice – her lovely, shining, soaring voice – faltered and died. I had never known it happen before. I had seen her sail, quite at her ease, through seas of indifference, squalls of heckling. Now, upon that single, dreadful, drunken cry, she had foundered.

I, of course, should have sung all the louder, swept her across the stage, jollied the audience along; but I, of course, was only her shadow. Her sudden silence stopped my throat, and stunned me into immobility, too. I looked from her to the orchestra pit. There, the conductor had seen our confusion. The music had slowed and faded for a second – but now picked up, more briskly than before.

But the melody affected neither Kitty nor the audience. At the side of the stalls, the door-men had reached the drunken man at last, and had hold of his collar. The crowd looked not at him, however, but at us. They looked at us, and saw – what? Two girls in suits, their hair close-clipped, their arms entwined. *Toms!* For all the efforts of the orchestra, the man's cry still seemed to echo about the hall.

Far off in the gallery someone called something that I could not catch, and there was an awkward answering laugh.

If the shout cast a spell over the theatre, the laughter broke it. Kitty shifted, then seemed to see for the first time that our arms were joined. She gave a cry, and drew away from me as if in horror. Then she put her hand to her eyes and stepped, with her head bowed, into the wing.

For a second I stood, dazed and confounded; then I hurried after her. The orchestra rattled on. There were shouts from the hall, at last, and cries of 'Shame!' The curtain, I think, was rung hurriedly down.

Backstage, everything was in a state of the greatest confusion. Kitty had run to Walter: he had his arm about her shoulders and looked grave. Flora stood by with a shoe unlaced and ready, shocked and uncertain but desperately curious. A knot of stage-hands and fly-men looked on, whispering amongst themselves. I stepped up to Kitty and reached for her arm; she flinched as if I had raised my hand to strike her, and instantly I fell back. As I did so the manager appeared, more flustered than ever.

'I should like to know, Miss Butler, Miss King, what the blazes you mean by—'

'*I* should like to know,' interrupted Walter harshly, 'what the blazes *you* mean by sending *my* artistes on before that *rabble* you call your audience. *I* should like to know why a drunken fool is allowed to interfere with Miss Butler's performance for *ten minutes*, while your men gather their scattered wits together, and make up their minds to remove him.'

The manager stamped his foot: 'How *dare* you, sir!'

'How dare *you*, sir!'

The debate went on. I didn't listen to it, only looked at Kitty. Her eyes were dry, but she was white-faced and stiff. She hadn't taken her head from Walter's shoulder, and she had not glanced towards me, at all.

Finally Walter gave a snort, and waved the blustering manager away. He turned to me. He said, 'Nan, I am taking Kitty home, at once. There's no question now of you going on for your final number; I'm afraid, too, that we must forfeit our supper. I shall hail us a hansom; will you follow with Flora and the gear, in the carriage? I should like to get Kitty back to Ginevra Road as swiftly as possible.'

I hesitated, then looked at Kitty again. She raised her eyes to mine at last, very briefly, and nodded.

'All right,' I said. I watched them leave. Walter took up his cloak, and – though it was far too large for her, and trailed upon the dusty floor – he placed it over Kitty's slender shoulders. She clasped it tight at the throat, then let him usher her away, past the angry manager and the knot of whispering boys.

By the time I reached Ginevra Road – after having gathered our boxes and bags together at Deacon's, and delivered Flora to her own house in Lambeth – Walter had gone, our rooms were dark, and Kitty was in bed, apparently asleep. I bent over her, and stroked her head. She did not stir, and I didn't like to wake her to perhaps more upset. Instead, I simply undressed, and lay close beside her, and placed my hand upon her heart – which beat on, very fiercely, through her dreams.

The disastrous night at Deacon's brought changes with it, and made some things a little strange. We did not sing at the hall again, but broke our contract – losing money on the deal. Kitty became choosier about the theatres we worked at; she began to question Walter, too, about the other acts that we must share the bills with. Once he booked us to appear alongside an American artist – a man called 'Paul or Pauline?', whose turn was to dance in and out of an ebony cabinet, dressed now as a woman, now as a man, and singing soprano and baritone by turns. I thought the act was a good one; but when Kitty saw him work, she made us cancel. She said the man was a freak, and would make us seem freakish by association . . .

We lost money on that deal, too. In the end I marvelled at Walter's patience.

For that was another change. I have spoken of the curious dimming of Walter's brightness, of the subtle new distance that had grown between us, since Kitty and I had become sweethearts. Now the dimming and the distance increased. He

remained kind, but his kindness was tempered by a surprising
kind of stiffness; in Kitty's presence, in particular, he grew
easily flustered and self-conscious – and then jolly, with a
horrible, forced kind of jolliness, as if ashamed of himself for
being so awkward. His visits to Ginevra Road grew rarer. At
last we saw him only to rehearse new songs, or in the company of the other artistes we sometimes took supper or drinks
with.

I missed him, and wondered at his change of heart – but
didn't wonder very hard, I must confess, because I thought I
knew what had caused it. That night at Islington he had
learned the truth at last – had heard that drunken man's shout,
seen Kitty's terrible, terrified response, and understood. He
had driven her home – I did not know what had passed
between them then, for neither of them seemed at all inclined
to discuss any part of that dreadful evening – he had driven
her home, but that tender gesture of his, to place his cloak
about her trembling shoulders and see her safely to her door,
had been his last. Now he could not be easy with her – perhaps
because he knew for sure that he had lost her; more probably,
because the idea of our love he found distasteful. And so he
stayed away.

Had we remained very long at Mrs Dendy's house, I think
our friends there would have noticed Walter's absence, and
quizzed us over it; but at the end of September came the
biggest change of all. We said good-bye to our landlady and
Ginevra Road, and moved.

We had talked vaguely of moving since the start of our fame;
but we had always put the crucial moment off – it seemed
foolish to leave a place in which we had been, and were still,
so happy. Mrs Dendy's had become our home. It was the house
in which we had first kissed, first declared our love; it was, I
thought, our honeymoon house – and for all that it was so
cramped and plain, for all that our costumes now took up
more space in the bedroom than our bed, I was terribly loath to
leave it.

But Kitty said it looked queer, us still sharing a room, and a bed, when we had the money to live somewhere ten times the size; and she had a house agent look about for rooms for us, somewhere more seemly.

It was to Stamford Hill that we moved, in the end – Stamford Hill, far across the river, in a bit of London I hardly knew (and thought, privately, a little dull). We had a farewell supper at Ginevra Road, with everyone saying how sorry they were to see us go – Mrs Dendy herself even wept a little, and said her house would never be the same. For Tootsie was also leaving – leaving for France, for a part in a Parisian revue; and her room was being taken by a comedian who whistled. The Professor had developed the beginnings of a palsy – there was talk that he might end up in a home for old artistes. Sims and Percy were doing well, and planned to take our rooms when we had left them; but Percy had found a sweetheart, too, and the girl made quarrels between them – I learned later that they split the act, and found spots as minstrels in rival troupes. It's the way of theatrical houses, I suppose, to break up and re-fashion themselves; but I was almost sadder, on my last day at Ginevra Road, than I had been on leaving Whitstable. I sat in the parlour – my portrait was upon the wall, now, along with all the others – and thought how much had changed since I had sat there first, a little less than thirteen months before; and for a moment I wondered if all the changes had been good ones, and wished that I could be plain Nancy Astley again, whom Kitty Butler loved with an ordinary love she was not afraid to show to all the world.

The street to which we moved was very new, and very quiet. Our neighbours, I think, were city men; their wives stayed at home all day, and their children had nurses, who wheeled them, puffing, up and down the garden steps in great iron per-ambulators. We had the top two floors of a house close to the station; our landlady and her husband lived beneath us, but they were not connected to the business, and we rarely saw

them. Our rooms were smart, we were the first to rent them:
the furniture was all of polished wood, and velvet and bro-
cade, and was far finer than anything either of us was used to –
so that we sat upon the chairs and sofas rather gingerly. There
were three bedrooms, and one of them was mine – which
meant only, of course, that I kept my dresses in its closet, my
brushes and combs upon its wash-hand stand, and my night-
gown beneath the pillow of its bed: this was for the sake of the
girl who came to clean for us, three days a week. My nights
were really spent in Kitty's chamber, the great front bedroom
with its great high bed that the house-builders had meant for a
husband and wife. It made me smile to lie in it. 'We *are* married,' I would say to Kitty. 'Why, we don't have to lie here at
all, if we don't wish to! I could carry you down to the parlour
carpet, and kiss you there!' But I never did. For though we
were at liberty at last to be as saucy and as clamorous as we
chose, we found we couldn't break ourselves of our old habits:
we still whispered our love, and kissed beneath the counterpane, noiselessly, like mice.

That, of course, was when we had time for kisses. We were
working six nights a week now, and there was no Sims and
Percy and Tootsie to keep us lively after shows; often we
would arrive back at Stamford Hill so weary we would simply
fall into the bed and snore. By November we were both so
tired Walter said we must take a holiday. There was talk of a
trip to the Continent – even, to America, where there were
also halls at which we might build up a quiet reputation, and
where Walter had friends who would lodge us. But then,
before the trip could be fixed, there came an invitation to play
in pantomime, at the Britannia Theatre, Hoxton. The pantomime was *Cinderella*, and Kitty and I were wanted for the
First and Second Boy roles; and the offer was too flattering to
resist.

My music-hall career, though brief enough, had been a
happy one; but I do not think that I was ever so content as I
was that winter, playing Dandini to Kitty's Prince, at the

Britannia. Any artiste will tell you that it is their ambition to work in pantomime; it is not until you play in one yourself, however, at a theatre as grand and as famous as the Brit, that you understand why. For the three coldest months of the year you are settled. There is no dashing about from hall to hall, no worrying about contracts. You mix with actors and ballet-girls, and make friends with them. Your dressing-room is large and private and warm – for you are really expected to change and make-up in it, not arrive, breathless, at the stage door, having buttoned on your costume in your brougham. You are handed lines to speak, and you speak them, steps to take, and you take them, costumes to wear – the most wonderful costumes you ever saw in your life, costumes of fur and satin and velvet – and you wear them, then pass them back to the wardrobe-mistress and let her worry about mending them and keeping them neat. The crowds you have to play before are the kindest, gayest crowds there ever were: you will hurl all manner of nonsense at them and they will shriek with laughter, merely because it is Christmas and they are determined to be jolly. It is like a holiday from real life – except that you are paid twenty pounds a week, if you are as lucky as we were then, to enjoy it.

The *Cinderella* in which we played that year was a particularly splendid one. The title role was taken by Dolly Arnold – a lovely girl with a voice like a linnet's, and a waist so slim her trademark was to wear a necklace as a belt. It was rather odd to see Kitty spooning with her upon the stage, kissing her while the clock showed a minute-to-midnight – though it was odder still, perhaps, to think that no one in the audience called out *Toms!* now, or even appeared to think it: they only cheered when the Prince and Cinderella were united at the end, and drawn on stage, by half-a-dozen pygmy horses, in their wedding-car.

Aside from Dolly Arnold, there were other stars – artistes whose turns I had once paid to watch and clap at, at the Canterbury Palace of Varieties. It made me feel very green, to have to work with them and talk to them as equals. I had only ever sung and danced, before, at Kitty's side; now, of course, I had to *act* – to walk on stage with a hunting retinue and say, 'My lords, where is Prince Casimir, our master?'; to slap my thigh and make terrible puns; to kneel before Cinderella with a velvet cushion, and place the slipper of glass upon her tiny foot – then lead the crowd in three rousing cheers when it was found to fit it. If you have ever seen a panto at the Brit, you will know how marvellous they are. For the transformation scene of *Cinderella* they dressed one hundred girls in suits of gauze and bullion fringe, then harnessed them to moving wires and had them swoop above the stalls. On the stage they set up fountains, which they lit, each with a different coloured lime. Dolly, as Cinderella in her wedding-gown, wore a frock of gold, with glitter on the bodice. Kitty had golden pantaloons, a shining waistcoat, and a three-cornered hat, and I wore breeches and a vest of velvet, and square-toed shoes with silver buckles. Standing at Kitty's side while the fountains played, the fairies swooped, and the pygmy horses pranced and trotted, I was never sure I had not died on my way to the theatre and woken up in paradise. There is a particular scent that ponies give off, when they are set too long beneath a too-hot lamp. I smelled it every night at the Brit, mingled with that familiar music-hall reek of dust and grease-paint, tobacco and beer. Even now, if you were to ask me, quickly, 'What is heaven like?' I should have to say that it must smell of over-heated horsehair, and be filled with angels in spangles and gauze, and decorated with fountains of scarlet and blue . . .

But not, perhaps, have Kitty in it.

I did not think this then, of course. I was only extraordinarily glad to have a place in such a business, and with my true love at my side; and everything that Kitty said or did only seemed to show that she felt just the same. I believe we spent more hours at the Brit that winter than at our new home in Stamford Hill – more time in velvet suits and powdered wigs than out of them. We made friends with all the theatre people – with the ballerinas and the wardrobe-girls, the gas-men, the property-men, the carpenters and the call-boys. Flora, our dresser, even found herself a beau amongst them. He was a black fellow, who had run away from a sailing family in Wapping to join a minstrel troupe; not having the voice for it, however, he had become a stage-hand instead. His name, I believe, was Albert – but he paid about as much heed to that as anybody in the business, and was known, universally, as 'Billy-Boy'. He loved the theatre more than any of us, and spent all his hours there, playing cards with the door-men and the carpenters, hanging about in the flies, twitching ropes, turning handles. He was good-looking, and Flora was very keen on him; he spent a deal of time, in consequence, at our dressing-room door, waiting to take her home after the show – and so we came to know him very well. I liked him because he came from the river, and had left his family for the theatre's sake, as I had. Sometimes, in the afternoons or late at night, he and I would leave Kitty and Flora fussing over the costumes and take a stroll through the dim and silent theatre, just for the pleasure of it. He had, somehow, acquired copies of all the keys to all the Britannia's dusty, secret places – the cellars and the attics and the ancient property-rooms – and he would show me hampers full of costumes from the shows of the 'fifties, papier-mâché crowns and sceptres, armour made of foil. Once or twice he led me up the great high ladders at the side of the stage, into the flies: here we would stand with our chins upon the rails, sharing a cigarette, gazing at the ash as it fluttered through the web of ropes and platforms to the boards, sixty feet below us.

It was quite like being at Mrs Dendy's again, with all our friends around us – except, of course, that Walter wasn't one of them. He came only occasionally to the Brit, and hardly at all to Stamford Hill; when he did, I couldn't bear to see him so ill at ease, and so found business of my own to keep me occupied elsewhere, and left Kitty to deal with him. She, I noticed, was as awkward and self-conscious as he when he came calling,

Chapter 7

~

We had opened at the Brit on Boxing Day, and rehearsed all through the weeks before it. Christmas, therefore, had been rather swallowed up; and when Mother had written – as she had the year before – to ask me home for it, I had had to send another apologetic note, to say I was again too busy. It was now almost a year and a half since I had left them; a year and a half since I had seen the sea and had a decent fresh oyster-supper. It was a long time – and no matter how gloomy and spiteful Alice's letter had made me, I could not help but miss them all and wonder how they fared. One day in January I came across my old tin trunk with its yellow enamel inscription. I lifted the lid – and found Davy's map of Kent pasted on the underside, with Whitstable marked with a faded arrow, 'To show me where home was, in case I forgot.' He had meant it as a joke; they had none of them thought I really would forget them. Now, however, it must seem to them that I had.

I closed the trunk with a bang; I had felt my eyes begin to smart. When Kitty came running to see what the noise was, I was weeping.

'Hey,' she said, and put her arm about me. 'What's this? Not tears?'

'I thought of home,' I said, between my sobs, 'and wanted to go there, suddenly.'

She touched my cheek, then put her fingers to her lips and licked them. 'Pure brine,' she said. 'That's why you miss it. I'm amazed you have managed to survive this long away from the sea, without shrivelling up like a bit of old seaweed. I should never have taken you away from Whitstable Bay. Miss Mermaid . . .'

I smiled, at last, to hear her use a name I thought she had forgotten; then I sighed. 'I would like to go back,' I said, 'for a day or two . . .'

'A day or *two*! I shall die without you!' She laughed, and looked away; and I guessed that she was only partly joking, for in all the months that we had spent together, we had not been separated for so much as a night. I felt that old queer tightness in my breast, and quickly kissed her. She raised her hands to hold my face; but again she turned her gaze away.

'You must go,' she said, 'if it makes you sad like this. I shall manage.'

'I shall hate it too,' I said. My tears had dried; it was I, now, who was doing the consoling. 'And anyway, I shan't be able to go until we close at Hoxton – and that is weeks away.' She nodded, and looked thoughtful.

It *was* weeks away, for *Cinderella* was not due to finish until Easter; in the middle of February, however, I found myself suddenly and unexpectedly at liberty. There was a fire at the Britannia. There were always fires in theatres in those days – halls were regularly being burned to the ground, then built up again, better than before, and no one thought anything of it; and the fire at the Brit had been small enough, and no one got injured. But the theatre had had to be evacuated, and there had been problems with the exits; afterwards an inspector came, looked at the building, and said a new escape door must be added. He closed the theatre while the work was done: tickets were returned, apologies pasted up; and for a whole half-week we found ourselves on holiday.

Urged on by Kitty – for she had grown suddenly gallant about letting me go – I took my chance. I wrote to Mother and

told her that, if I was still welcome, I should be home the following day – that was Sunday – and would stay till
Wednesday night. Then I went shopping, to buy presents for
the family: there was something thrilling after all, I found,
about the idea of returning to Whitstable after so long, with a
parcel of gifts from London . . .

Even so, it was hard to part from Kitty.

'You will be all right?' I said to her. 'You won't be lonely
here?'

'I shall be horribly lonely. I expect you will come back and
find me dead from loneliness!'

'Why don't you come with me? We might catch a later
train—'

'No, Nan; you should see your family without me.'

'I shall think about you every minute.'

'And I shall think of you . . .'

'Oh, Kitty . . .'

She had been tapping at her tooth with the pearl of her
necklace; when I put my mouth upon hers I felt it, cold and
smooth and hard, between our lips. She let me kiss her, then
moved her head so that our cheeks touched; then she put her
arms about my waist and held me to her rather fiercely – quite
as if she loved me more than anything.

Whitstable, when I drew into it later that morning, seemed
very changed – very small and grey, and with a sea that was
wider, and a sky that was lower and less blue, than I remembered. I leaned from the carriage window to gaze at it all, and
so saw Father and Davy, at the station, a moment or two before
they saw me. Even they looked different – I felt a rush of
aching love and strange regret, to think it – Father a little older,
a little shrunken, somehow; Davy slightly stouter, and redder
in the face.

When they saw me, stepping from the train on to the platform, they came running.

'Nance! My dearest girl . . . !' This was Father. We

embraced – awkwardly, for I had all my parcels with me, and a hat upon my head with a veil around it. One of the parcels fell to the ground and he bent to retrieve it, then hurried to help me with the others. Davy, meanwhile, took my hand, then kissed my cheek through the mesh of my veil.

'Just look at you,' he said. 'All dressed up to the ninety-nines! Quite the lady, ain't she, Pa?' His cheek grew redder than ever.

Father straightened, and looked me over, then gave a wide smile that seemed to pull, somewhat, at the corners of his eyes.

'Very smart,' he said. 'Your mother won't know you, hardly.'

I did indeed, I suppose, look a little dressy, but I had not thought about it until that moment. All my clothes were good ones, these days, for I had long ago got rid of those girlish hand-me-downs with which I'd first left home. I had only wanted, that morning, to look nice. Now I felt self-conscious.

The self-consciousness did not diminish as I walked, on Father's arm, the little distance to our oyster-shop. The house, I thought, was shabbier than ever. The weather-boards above the shop showed more wood, now, than blue paint; and the sign – *Astley's Oysters, the Best in Kent* – hung on one hinge, and was cracked where the rainwater had soaked it. The stairs we climbed were dark and narrow, the room into which I finally emerged smaller and more cramped than I could have believed possible. Worst of all the street, the stairs, the room, the people in it, all reeked of fish! It was a stink that was as familiar to me as the scent of my own armpit; but I was startled, now, to think that I had ever lived in it and thought it ordinary.

My surprise, I hope, was lost in the general bustle of my arrival. I had expected Mother and Alice to be waiting for me; they were – but so were half-a-dozen other people, each one of whom exclaimed when I appeared, and stepped forward (except for Alice) to embrace me. I had to smile and submit to being squeezed and patted until I grew quite breathless.

Rhoda – still my brother's sweetheart – was there, looking perter than ever; Aunty Ro, too, had come along to welcome me back, together with her son, my cousin George, and her daughter, Liza, and Liza's baby – except that the baby was not a baby at all now, but a little boy in frills. Liza, I saw, was large with child again; I had been told this in a letter, I believe, but had forgotten it.

I took off my hat once all the welcomes had been said, and my heavy coat with it. Mother looked me up and down. She said, 'My goodness, Nance, how tall and fine you look! I do believe you're taller, almost, than your father.' I did feel tall in that tiny, overcrowded room; but I could hardly, I thought, have really grown. It was just that I was standing rather straighter. I gazed around – a little proud, despite my awkwardness – and found a seat, and tea was brought. I still had not exchanged a word with Alice.

Father asked after Kitty, and I said that she was well. Where was she playing now? they asked me. Where were we living? Rosina said there had been talk that I had gone upon the stage myself—? And at that I only answered, that I did 'sometimes join Kitty in the act'.

'Well, fancy that!'

I cannot say what squeamishness still made me keep the fact of my success from them. It was, I think, because the act – as I have said – was so entangled with my love: I could not bear to have them pry at it, or frown at it, or pass the idea of it on to others, carelessly . . .

It was, I suppose now, a kind of priggishness; indeed, I hadn't been amongst them more than half an hour before George, my cousin, gave a cry: 'What's happened to your accent, Nance? You've gone all *lardy-dah*.' I looked at him in real surprise, then listened hard next time I spoke. It was quite true, my voice had changed. I was not posh, as he had claimed, but there is a certain lilt that theatre people have – a rather odd, unpredictable mixture of all the accents of the halls, from coster-man to *lion comique*; and I, all unknowingly, had picked it up. I sounded rather like Kitty – occasionally, even like Walter. I had never realised it till now.

We drank our tea; there was a lot of fussing over the little boy. Someone handed him to me for me to nurse – when I took him, however, he cried.

'Oh *dear*!' said his mother, tickling him. 'Your Aunty Nance will think you a real cry-baby.' She took him from me, then held him near my face: 'Shake hands!' She seized his arm and waved it. 'Shake hands with Aunty Nancy, like a proper little gent!' He jerked at her hip, like some great swollen pistol that at any second might go off; but I dutifully took his fingers in my own, and squeezed them. Of course, he snatched his hand away at once, and only wailed the louder. Everybody laughed. George caught the baby up and swung him high, so that his hair brushed the cracked and yellowed plaster of the ceiling. '*Who's* a little soldier, then?' he cried.

I looked at Alice, and she glanced away.

The baby quietened at last; the room grew warmer. I saw Rhoda lean towards my brother and whisper, and when he nodded, she coughed. She said, 'Nancy, you won't have heard our bit of good news.' I looked at her properly. She had her jacket off and her feet, I noticed, were bare but for a pair of woollen stockings. She seemed very much at home.

Now she held out her hand. On the second finger from the left there was a narrow strip of gold, with a tiny stone – sapphire or diamond, it was too small to tell – mounted upon it. An engagement ring.

I blushed – I don't know why – and forced a smile. 'Oh, Rhoda! I *am* glad. Davy! How nice for you.' I was not glad; it was not nice; the thought of having Rhoda as a sister-in-law – of having any kind of sister-in-law! – was peculiarly horrible. But I must have sounded pleased enough, for they both grew pink and smug.

Then Aunt Rosina nodded towards my own hand. 'No sign of a ring on *your* finger yet, Nance?'

I saw Alice shift in her seat, and shook my head: 'Not yet,

no.' Father opened his mouth to speak; I could not bear, however, for the conversation to run down that particular road. I got up, and retrieved my bags. 'I've bought you all some things,' I said, 'from London.'

There were murmurs and little interested 'Oh's at that. Mother said I shouldn't have, but reached for her spectacles and looked expectant. I went to my aunt, first, and handed her a bag full of packages. 'These are for Uncle Joe, and Mike and the girls. This is for you.' George next: I had bought him a silver hip-flask. Then Liza, and the baby . . . I went all around the crowded room, and finished up at Alice: 'This is for you.' Her parcel – a hat, in a hat box – was the biggest. She took it from me with the smallest, straightest, stiffest smile you ever saw, and began slowly and self-consciously to pull at its ribbons.

Now everybody had a gift but me. I sat and watched as they tore at their packages, chewing at my knuckle and smiling into my hand. One by one the objects appeared, and were turned and examined in the late morning light. The room grew quite hushed.

'My word, Nancy,' said Father at last, 'you have done us proud.' I had bought him a watch-guard, thick and bright as the one that Walter wore; he held it in his hand, and it seemed brighter than ever against the red of his palm, the faded wool of his jacket. He laughed: 'I shall look quite the thing in this, now, shan't I?' The laugh, however, didn't sound quite natural.

I looked at Mother. She had a silver-backed brush and a hand-glass to match: they sat in their wrappers, in her lap, as if she were afraid to pick them up. I thought at once – what had never occurred to me in Oxford Street – how queer they would look beside her cheap coloured perfume bottles, her jar of cold-cream, on her old chest of drawers with its chipped glass handles. She caught my eye, and I saw that she had thought the same. 'Really, Nance . . .' she said; and her words were almost a reproof.

There were murmurs, now, from all around the room, as

people compared presents. Aunt Rosina held up a pair of
garnet earrings, and blinked at them. George fingered his flask,
and asked me, rather nervously, whether I had won the sweep-
stakes. Only Rhoda and my brother seemed really pleased with
their gifts. For Davy I had bought a pair of shoes, hand-sewn
and soft as butter: now he rapped on their soles with his
knuckles, then stepped over the discarded paper and strings to
kiss my cheek. 'What a little star you are,' he said. 'I shall save
these for my wedding-day and be the best-shod bloke in Kent.'

His words seemed to remind everybody of their manners,
and suddenly they all rose to kiss and thank me, and there was
a general, embarrassed shuffling. I looked over their shoulders
to where Alice still sat. She had taken the lid from the hat-box,
but had not removed the hat, only held it, listlessly, in her fingers. Davy saw me looking. 'What've *you* got, Sis?' he called.
When she reluctantly tipped up the box for him to see, he
whistled: 'What a stunner! With an ostrich feather *and* a diamond on the brim. Aren't you going to try it on?'

'I will, later,' she said.

Now everyone turned to look at her.

'Oh, what a beautiful hat!' said Rhoda. 'And what a lovely
shade of red. What shade of red do they call that, Nancy?'

'"Buffalo Red",' I said miserably; I could not have felt more
of a fool if I had given them all a pile of trash – cotton-reels and
candle-stubs, toothpicks and pebbles – wrapped up in tissue
and ribbons and silks.

Rhoda did not notice. '"*Buffalo* Red"!' she cried. 'Oh, Alice,
do be a sport and give us a look at it on you.'

'Yes, go on, Alice.' This was Rosina. 'Nancy'll think you
don't like it, otherwise.'

'It's all right,' I said quickly. 'Let her try it later.' But George
had jumped over to Alice's chair, taken the hat from her, and
now tried to set it on her head.

'Come on,' he said. 'I want to see if you look like a buffalo in
it.'

'Leave off!' said Alice. There was a scuffle. I closed my eyes, heard the rip of stitches, and when next I looked my sister had the bonnet in her lap, and George had half the ostrich feather in his fingers. The chip of diamante had flown off, and been lost.

Poor George began to gulp and cough; Rosina said sternly that she hoped that he was satisfied. Liza took the hat and the feather and tried awkwardly to reunite them: 'Such a pretty bonnet,' she said. Alice started to sniff, then placed her hands before her eyes and hurried from the room. Father said, 'Well, now!'; he still held his gleaming watch-guard. Mother looked at me and shook her head. 'What a shame,' she said. 'Oh, Nancy, what a shame!'

In time Rosina and the cousins left, and Alice, still rather swollen-eyed, went out to call on a friend. I took my bags up to my old room, and washed my face; when I came down a little later, the presents I had brought had all been tidied out of sight, and Rhoda was helping Mother peel and boil potatoes in the kitchen. They shooed me away when I offered to join them, and said I was a guest; and so I sat with Father and Davy – who seemed to think that keeping to their usual habits, and hiding themselves behind the Sunday papers, would put me at my ease.

We had our dinner, then took a walk to Tankerton and sat pitching stones into the water. The sea was grey as lead; far out upon it there were a couple of yawls and barges – bound for London, where Kitty was. What was she doing now, I wondered, apart from missing me?

Later there was tea, after which more cousins appeared, to thank me for their presents and to beg for a look at my handsome new clothes. We sat upstairs and I showed them my frocks, my hat with the veil upon it, and my painted stockings. There was more talk about young men. Alice, I learned – they were surprised she hadn't told me this – had finished with Tony Reeves from the Palace, and had started stepping out with a boy who worked at the shipyard; he was much taller, they said, than Tony, but not as funny. Freddy, my old beau, was also seeing a new girl, and seemed likely to marry her . . . When they asked me, again, if I was courting, I said I wasn't; but I hesitated over it, and they smiled. There *was* someone, they pressed – and just to keep them quiet, I nodded.

'There was a boy. He played the cornet in an orchestra . . .' I looked away, as if it made me sad to think of him, and felt them exchange significant glances.

And what about Miss Butler? Surely she had a young man? 'Yes, a man named Walter . . .' I hated myself for saying it – but thought, too, How Kitty will laugh at this, when I tell her!

I had forgotten what early hours they all kept. The cousins left at ten; at half-past everybody else started yawning. Davy saw Rhoda home, and Alice bade the rest of us good-night. Father rose and stretched, then came to me and put his arm about my neck. 'It's been a treat for us, Nance, to have you home again – and you grown into such a beauty!'

Then Mother smiled at me – the first real smile that I had seen upon her face that day; and I knew then how really glad I was to be at home, amongst them all.

But the gladness didn't last long. In a few minutes more I said my own good-nights, and found myself alone, at last, with Alice, in our – her – room. She was in bed, but the lamp was still high, and her eyes were open. I did not undress, but stood with my back to the door, quite still, until she looked at me.

'I'm sorry about the hat,' she said.

'It doesn't matter.' I stepped to the chair by the fireplace, and began to unbutton my boots.

'You shouldn't have spent so much,' she went on.

I pulled a face: 'I wish I hadn't.' I stepped out of the shoes, kicked them to one side, and started on the hooks of my dress. She had closed her eyes, and seemed disinclined to say anything else. I slowed my hand, and looked at her.

'Your letter,' I said, 'was horrible.'

'I don't want to talk about any of that,' she answered quickly, turning away. 'I told you what I think. I haven't changed.'

'Neither have I.' I tugged harder at the hooks and stepped free of the dress, then slung it over the back of the chair. I felt peevish and not at all tired. I went to one of my bags and got out a cigarette, and when I struck the match to light it Alice raised her head. I shrugged: 'Another nasty little habit Kitty taught me.' I sounded just like some hard-faced bitch of a ballet-girl.

I took off the rest of my clothes, then pulled my night-gown over my head – then remembered my hair. I could not sleep with the plait still fastened to me. I glanced towards Alice again – she had paled at my words, but still watched – then pulled at the hairpins until the chignon came loose. From the corner of my eye I saw her mouth fall open. I ran my fingers through my flat, shorn locks; the action – and the cigarette that I had just smoked – made me feel wonderfully calm.

I said: 'You can't tell, can you, that it's a false one?'

Now Alice sat up with the blankets gripped before her. 'You needn't look so horrified,' I said. 'I told you all, I wrote and told you: I've joined the act; I'm not Kitty's dresser any more. I'm on the stage myself, now, doing what she does. Singing, dancing . . .'

She said, 'You never wrote it like it was really true. If it was true we would have heard! I don't believe you.'

'I don't care whether you believe me or not.'

She shook her head. 'Singing,' she said. 'Dancing. That's a tart's life. You couldn't. You wouldn't . . .'

I said, 'I do'; and just to show her that I meant it, I lifted my nightie and did a little shuffle across the rug.

The dance seemed, like the hair, to frighten her. When she spoke next it was with a show of bitterness – but her voice was thick with rising tears. 'I suppose you lift your skirts like that, do you? And show your legs, on stage, for all the world to look at!'

'My skirts?' I laughed. 'Good heavens, Alice, I don't wear skirts! I didn't get my hair cut off to wear a frock. It's trousers I wear: I wear gentlemen's suits!'

'Oh!' Now she had begun to cry. 'What a thing to do! What a thing to do, in front of strangers!'

I said, 'You thought it good enough when Kitty did it.'

'Nothing she did was ever good! She took you off, and has made you strange. I don't know you at all. I wish you'd never gone with her – or never come back!'

She lay down, pulled the blankets to her chin, and wept; and since I don't know a girl who is not moved to tears by the sight of her own sister weeping, I climbed in beside her, and my own eyes began to sting.

But when she felt me close she gave a jerk. 'Get off me!' she cried, and wriggled away. She said it with such real passion, such horror and grief, I could do nothing but what she asked, and let her lie at the cold edge of the bed. Soon she ceased her shaking, and fell silent; and my own eyes dried, and my face grew hard again. I reached for the lamp, and put it out; then lay on my back and said nothing.

The bed, that had been chill, grew warmer. I began at last to wish that Alice would turn, and talk to me. Then I began to wish that Alice was Kitty. Then I began – I couldn't help it! – to think of all that I would do with her, if she was. The sudden force of my desire unnerved me. I remembered all the times that I had lain here and pictured similar things, before Kitty and I had ever even kissed. I remembered when I had first slept beside her at Ginevra Road, when I was used only to sharing with my sister. Now Alice's body felt strange to me; it seemed queer and wrong, somehow, to lie so close to someone and not kiss and stroke them . . .

I thought suddenly, Suppose I fall asleep, forget that she isn't Kitty, and put a hand upon her, or a leg . . . ?

I got up, put my coat over my shoulders, and smoked another cigarette. Alice did not stir.

I squinted at my watch: half-past eleven. I wondered, again, what Kitty was doing; and sent a mental message through the night, to Stamford Hill, to make her pause – whatever her business was just then – and remember to think of me, in Whitstable.

*

My visit, after that poor start, was not brilliant. I had arrived on a Sunday, and the following days, of course, were working ones. I didn't fall asleep, that first night, until very late, but the next morning I woke when Alice woke, at half-past six, and forced myself to rise and eat my breakfast with the others, at the parlour-table. Then, however, I didn't know whether to offer to take up my old duties in the kitchen, with the oyster-knife – I couldn't tell whether they would like it or expect it, or even whether I could bear to try it. In the end I drifted down with them and found I wasn't needed anyway; for they had a girl, now, to sever and beard the natives, and she was just as quick, it seemed, as I had been. I stood beside her – she was rather pretty – and made some half-hearted passes with my knife at a dozen or so shells . . . But the water chilled and stung me, and soon I preferred to sit and watch – then I closed my eyes and placed my head upon my arms, and listened to the hum of gossip from the restaurant, and the bubble of the pans . . .

In short, I fell asleep; and only woke when Father, hurrying by me, stumbled over my skirts and spilled a pot of liquor. Then it was suggested that I go upstairs – out of their way, they meant. And so I passed the afternoon alone, alternately nodding over the *Illustrated Police News* and pacing the parlour to keep myself awake – and wondering, frankly, why I had come home at all.

The next day, if anything, was worse. Mother said straight out that I must not think of spoiling my dress and hurting my hands by trying to help them in the kitchen; that I was here to have a holiday, not to work. I had read the *Police News* from cover to cover: all there was now was Father's *Fish Trades Gazette*, and I couldn't bear the thought of a day upstairs with that. I put my travelling-dress back on and went out walking; I started out so early that by ten o'clock I had strolled as far as Seasalter and back. At last, desperate for some amusement, I took the train to Canterbury – and while my parents and sister laboured in the oyster-house, I passed the day as a tourist, wandering about the cloisters of a cathedral which, in all the years that I had lived so near to it, I'd never cared to visit.

But on the way back to the station I passed before the Palace. It looked very different to me, now that I had an eye for halls; and when I stepped up to the posters to look at the bill, I saw that all the acts were rather second-rate. The doors, of course, were closed, and the foyer dark; but I couldn't resist it, and wandered round to the stage door and asked for Tony Reeves.

I had my hat and veil on: when he saw me, he didn't recognise me. When he knew me at last, however, he smiled and kissed my hand.

'Nancy! What a treat!' He, at least, had not changed at all. He led me to his office and sat me down. I said I was here on a visit, and had been sent out to keep myself amused. I said, too, that I was sorry to hear about him and Alice.

He shrugged. 'I knew she'd never *marry* me or nothing like that. But I do miss her; and she *was* a lovely looker – though not quite as lovely, if you don't mind my saying so, as her sister has gone and turned out . . .'

I didn't mind, for I knew that he was only flirting – indeed, it was rather pleasant to be flirted with by an old beau of Alice's. Instead I asked him about the hall – about how it did, who he had had there, what they had sung. At the end of it he picked up a pen that lay on his desk, and began to fiddle with it.

'And when are we to have Miss Butler back again?' he asked. 'I gather you and she've teamed up properly now.' I stared, then felt my cheeks grow red; but he only meant, of course, the act: 'I hear you're working the halls together; and are quite a pair, by all accounts.'

Now I smiled. 'How did you find that out? I am very quiet about it with my family.'

'I read the *Era*, don't I? "Kitty Butler and Nan King". I know a stage-name when I see one . . .'

I laughed. 'Oh, isn't it funny, Tony? Isn't it just the most marvellous thing? We are in *Cinderella* at the minute, at the Brit. Kitty's the Prince, and I'm Dandini. I have to speak, sing, dance, slap my thigh, the works, in velvet breeches. And the crowd go mad for it!'

He smiled at my pleasure – it was lovely to be allowed to be pleased with myself, at last! – then shook his head. 'Your folks, from what I've heard them say, don't know the half of it. Why don't you have them up to see you on the stage? Why the big secret?'

I shrugged, then hesitated; then, 'Alice doesn't care for Kitty . . .' I said.

'And you and Kitty: you're still in her pocket? You're still struck with her like you always was?' I nodded. He sniffed. 'Then, she's a lucky girl . . .'

He seemed only to be flirting again; but I had the queerest impression, too, that he knew more than he was letting on – and didn't care a fig about it. I answered, '*I'm* the lucky one,' and held his gaze.

He tapped with his pen again upon his blotter. 'Maybe.' Then he winked.

I stayed at the Palace until it became rather obvious that Tony had other business to get on with, then took my leave of him. Once outside, I stood again before the foyer doors, reluctant to resign the reek of beer and grease-paint and confront the altogether different scents of Whitstable, our Parlour and our home. It had been good to talk of Kitty – so good that, seated at the supper-table later, between silent Alice and nasty Rhoda with her tiny, flashing sapphire, I missed her all the more. I was due to spend another day with them, but now I thought I could not face it. I said, as we started on our puddings, that I had changed my mind and would take the morning, rather than the evening train tomorrow – that I had remembered things that I must do at the theatre, that I shouldn't put off till Thursday.

They didn't seem surprised, though Father said it was a shame. Later, as I kissed them good-night, he cleared his throat. 'There you are,' he said, 'back up to London in the morning, and I've barely had time for a proper look at you.' I smiled. 'Have you had a nice time with us, Nance?'

'Oh, yes.'

'And you will take care of yourself, in London?' asked Mother. 'It seems very far away.'

I laughed. 'It's not so far.'

'Far enough,' she said, 'to keep you from us for a year and a half.'

'I've been busy,' I said. 'We have been terribly busy, both of us.' She nodded, not much impressed: she had heard all this before, in letters.

'Just make sure it's not so long before you come home again. It is very nice to get your parcels; it was very nice to get those gifts; but we would rather have you, than a hairbrush or a pair of boots.' I looked away, abashed; I still felt foolish when I thought about the presents. Even so, I didn't think she needed to be quite so rusty about it, quite so hard.

Having made the decision to leave sooner, I grew impatient. I packed my bags that night, and rose, next morning, even earlier than Alice. At seven, when the breakfast things were cleared away, I was ready to go. I embraced them all, but my parting was not so sad, nor so sweet, as it had been the first time I had left them; and I had no premonition of anything to come, to make it sadder. Davy was kind, and made me promise I would come home for his wedding, and said I might bring Kitty if I liked, which made me love him all the more. Mother smiled, but her smile was tight; Alice was so chill that, in the end, I turned my back on her. Only Father hugged me to him as if really loath to let me go; and when he said that he would miss me, I knew he meant it.

No one could be spared, this time, to walk me to the station, so I made my own way there. I didn't look at Whitstable, or the sea, as my train pulled away from it; I certainly did not think, I shan't see you again, for years and years – and if I had, I am ashamed to say it would not much have troubled me. I thought only of Kitty. It was still only half-past seven; she wouldn't rise, I knew, till ten, and I planned to surprise her – to let myself into our rooms at Stamford Hill, and creep into her bed. The train rolled on, through Faversham and Rochester. I was not impatient now. I did not need to be impatient. I merely sat and thought of her warm, slumbering body that I would soon embrace; I imagined her pleasure, her surprise, her rising love, at seeing me returned so soon.

Our house, when I gazed up at it from the street, was, as I had hoped, quite dark and shuttered. I walked on tip-toe up the steps, and eased my key into the lock. The passageway was quiet: even our landlady and her husband seemed still abed. I laid down my bags, and took off my coat. There was a cloak already hanging from the hat-stand, and I squinted at it: it was Walter's. How queer, I thought, he must have come here yesterday, and forgotten it! – and soon, creeping up the darkened staircase, I forgot it myself.

I reached Kitty's door, and put my ear to it. I had expected silence, but there was a sound from beyond it – a kind of lapping sound, as of a kitten at a saucer of milk. I thought, Damn! She must be awake already and taking her tea; then I caught the creak of the bedstead, and was sure of it. Disappointed, but gay with the expectation of seeing her, I caught hold of the door-handle and entered the room.

She was indeed awake. She sat in bed, propped up against a pillow, with the blankets raised as far as her armpits and her naked arms upon the counterpane. There was a lamp lit, and turned high; the room was not at all dark. At a little wash-hand stand at the foot of the bed there was another figure. Walter. He was jacketless, and collarless; his shirt was tucked roughly into his trousers, but his braces dangled, almost to his knees. He was bending over the bowl of water, bathing his face – that had been the lapping sound that I had heard. His whiskers were dark and gleaming where he had wet them.

It was his eye that I caught first. He gazed at me in sheer surprise, his hands lifted, the water running from them into his sleeves; then his face gave a kind of twitch, horrible to behold – and at the same time, from the corner of my eye, I saw Kitty twitch, too, beneath the bedclothes.

Even then, I think, I didn't quite understand.

'What's this?' I said, and laughed a little, nervously. I looked at Kitty, waiting for her to join in my laughter – to say, 'Oh, Nan! How funny this must look to you! It isn't how it seems, at all.'

But she did not even smile. She gazed at me with fearful eyes, and pulled the blankets higher, as if to hide her nakedness from me. From me!

It was Walter who spoke.

'Nan,' he said hesitantly – I had never heard his voice so dry and bare – 'Nan, you have surprised us. We didn't look for you until tonight.' He took up a towel and rubbed at his face with it. Then he stepped very quickly to the chair, seized his jacket and pulled it on. His hands, I saw, were shaking.

I had never seen him shake before.

I said, 'I caught an earlier train . . .' My mouth, like his, had dried; my voice, in consequence, sounded slow and thick. 'Indeed, I thought it was still very early. How long, Walter, have you been here?'

He shook his head, as if the question pained him, and took a step towards me. Then he said rather urgently: 'Nan, forgive me. This is not for your eyes. Will you come downstairs with me and let us talk . . . ?'

His tone was strange; and hearing it, I knew for certain.

'No!' I folded my hands over my belly: there was a hot, sour churning in there, as if they had fed me poison. At my cry Kitty shivered and grew white. I turned to her. 'It isn't true!' I said. 'Oh tell me, tell me – say it ain't true!' She wouldn't look at me, only placed her hands before her eyes and began to weep.

Walter came closer and put his hand upon my arm.

'Get away!' I cried, and stepped free of him towards the bed. 'Kitty? Kitty?' I knelt beside her, took her hand from her face, and held it to my own lips. I kissed her fingers, her nails, her palm, her wrist; her knuckles, that were damp from her own weeping, were soon drenched with tears and slobber. Walter looked on, appalled, still trembling.

At last, she met my gaze. 'It's true,' she whispered.

I gave a start, and a moan – then heard her shriek, felt Walter's fingers grip my shoulders, and realised that I had bitten her, like a dog. She pulled her hand away and gazed at me in horror. Again I shook Walter off, then turned to scream at him. 'Get away, get out! Get out, and leave us!' He hesitated; I kicked at his ankle with my foot until he stepped away.

'You are not yourself, Nan—'

'Get out!'

'I am afraid to leave you—'

'*Get out!*'

He flinched. 'I shall go beyond the door – no further.' Then he looked at Kitty, and when she nodded he left, closing the door behind him very gently.

There was a silence, broken only by the sound of my ragged breathing, and Kitty's gentle weeping: just so had I seen my sister weep, three days before. *Nothing that Kitty ever did was good!* she had said. I placed my cheek upon the counterpane where it covered Kitty's thighs, and closed my eyes.

'You made me think he was your friend,' I said. 'And then you made me think he didn't care for you, because of us.'

'I didn't know what else to do. He *was* only my friend; and then, and then—'

'To think of you and him – for all that time—'

'It wasn't what you think, before last night.'

'I don't believe you.'

'Oh, Nan, it's true, I swear! Before last night – how could there have been anything? – before last night, there was only talk and – kisses.'

Before last night . . . Before last night I had been glad, beloved, content, secure; before last night I had known myself so full of love and desire I thought I should die of it! At Kitty's words I saw that the pain of my love was not a tenth, not a hundredth, not a thousandth part of the pain I should suffer at her hands now.

I opened my eyes. Kitty herself looked ill and frightened. I said, 'And the – kisses: when did they start?' But even as I asked it, I guessed the answer: 'That night, at Deacon's . . .'

She hesitated – then nodded; and I saw it all again, and understood it all: the awkwardness, the silences, the letters. I had pitied Walter – pitied him! When all the time it had been I who was the fool; when all the time they had been meeting, whispering together, caressing . . .

The thought was a torment to me. Walter was our friend – mine, as well as hers. I knew he loved her, but – he seemed so old, so uncle-ish, still. Could she ever, really, have brought herself to want to lie with him? It was as if I had caught her in bed with my own father!

I began, once more, to weep. 'How could you?' I said through my tears: I sounded like a stage husband in some penny gaff. 'How could you?' Beneath the blankets I felt her squirm.

'I didn't like to do it!' she said miserably. 'At times I could hardly bear it—'

'I thought you loved me! You said that you loved me!'

'I do love you! I do, I do!'

'You said there was nothing you wanted, but me! You said we would be together, for ever!'

'I never said—'

'You let me think it! You made me think it! You said, so many times, how glad you were. Why couldn't we have gone on, as we were . . . ?'

'You *know* why! It is all right, that sort of thing, when you are girls. But as we got older . . . We're not a couple of scullery-maids, to do as we please and have no one notice it. We are known; we are looked at—'

'I don't *want* to be known, then, if it means losing you! I don't want to be looked at, if not by *you*, Kitty . . .'

She pressed my hand. 'But I do,' she said. 'I do. And so long as I am looked at, I cannot bear also to be – *laughed* at; or hated; or scorned, as a . . .'

'As a tom!'

'Yes!'

'But, we could be careful—'

'We should never be careful enough! You are too much – Nan, you are too much like a boy . . .'

'Too much – like a boy? You've never said it before! Too much like a boy – yet, you'd rather go with Walter! Do you – love *him*?'

She looked away. 'He's very – kind,' she said.

'Very kind.' I heard my voice grow hard and bitter at last. I sat up, and leaned away from her. 'And so you had him come, while I was gone; and he was kind to you, in our bed . . .' I got to my feet, suddenly conscious of the soiled sheets and mattress; of her bare flesh, that he had put his hands upon, his mouth . . . 'Oh, God! How long would you have carried on? Would you let me kiss you, *after him*?'

She reached for me, to seize my hand. 'We planned, I swear, to tell you tonight. Tonight was when you were to know it all . . .'

There was something queer about the way she said it. I had been pacing at her side; now I grew still. 'What do you mean?' I said. 'What do you mean, by *all*?'

She took her hand away. 'We are – oh, Nan, don't hate me for it! We are to be – married.'

'*Married?*' If I had had time to think about it I might have expected it; but I had had no time at all, and the word made me giddier and sicker than ever. 'Married? But what – but what about me? Where shall I live? What shall I do? What about, what about . . .' I had thought of something new. 'What about the act? How shall we work . . . ?'

She looked away. 'Walter has a plan. For a new act. He wants to return to the halls . . .'

'To the halls? After *this*? With you and me?'

'No. With me. Just me.'

Just her. I felt myself begin to shake. I said, 'You have killed me, Kitty.' My voice sounded strange even to my own ears; I believe it frightened her, for she glanced a little wildly to the door, and began to speak, very fast, but in a kind of shrill whisper.

'You mustn't say such things,' she said. 'It has been a shock for you. But you will see, in time – we shall be friends again, the three of us!' She reached for me; her voice grew shriller yet quieter still. 'Can you not see how this is for the best? With Walter as my husband, who would think, who would say . . .?' I pulled away; she gripped me tighter – then cried at last, in a kind of panic: 'Oh, you don't think, do you, that I'll let him take me from you?'

At that I pushed her, and she fell back against her pillow. The counterpane was still before her, but it had slipped a little. I caught sight of the swell of her breast, the pink of her nipple. An inch below the downy hollow of her throat – jerking with each breath and pounding heart-beat – hung the pearl that I had bought her, on its silver chain. I remembered kissing it, three days before; perhaps, last night or this morning, Walter had felt it chill and hard against his own tongue.

I stepped towards her, seized the necklace, and – again, just as if I were a character in a novel or a play – I tugged at it. At once the chain gave a satisfying *snap!* and dangled broken from my hand. I gazed at it for a second, then dashed it from me and heard it scutter across the floorboards.

Kitty shouted – I believe she shouted Walter's name. At any rate, the door now opened and he appeared, white-faced above his ginger whiskers, and with his braces still dangling below the hem of his jacket, his collarless shirt still flapping at his throat. He ran to the other side of the bed, and took Kitty in his arms.

'If you have hurt her—' he said. I laughed outright at that.

'Hurt her? Hurt her? I should like to kill her! Had I only a pistol on me now I would shoot her through the heart – and myself as well! And leave you to marry a corpse!'

'You have gone mad,' he said. 'This has driven you quite crazed.'

'And do you wonder at it? Do you know – has she told you – what we are – what we *were* – to one another?'

'Nan!' said Kitty quickly. I kept my eyes fixed upon Walter.

'I know,' he said slowly, 'that you were – sweethearts, of a kind.'

'Of a kind. The kind that – what? Hold hands? Did you think, then, that you were the first to have her, in this bed? Didn't she tell you that I *fuck* her?'

He flinched – and so did I, for the word sounded terrible: I had never said it before, and had not known I was about to use it now. His gaze, however, remained steady: I saw, with increasing misery, that he knew it all, and did not care; that perhaps – who knows? – he even liked it. He was too much the gentleman to make me a foul-mouthed reply, but his expression – a curious mixture of contempt, complacency, and pity – was a speaking one. It said, *That was not fucking, as the world knows it!* It said, *You fucked her so well, that she has left you!* It said, *You may have fucked her first, but I shall fuck her now and ever after!*

He was my rival; and had defeated me, at last.

I took a step away from the bed, and then another. Kitty swallowed, her head still upon Walter's great breast. Her eyes were large and lustrous with unshed tears, her lip red where she had bitten it; her cheeks were pale, and the freckles very dark upon them – there were freckles, too, upon the flesh of her shoulder and chest, where it showed above the blankets. She was about as beautiful as I had ever seen her.

Good-bye, I thought – then I turned and fled.

I ran down the stairs; my skirts snagged about my feet and I almost stumbled. I ran past the open parlour-door; past the hat-stand, where my coat hung next to Walter's; past the suitcase I had brought from Whitstable. I didn't pause to pick anything up, not even so much as a glove or a bonnet. I could touch nothing in that place now – it had become like a plague-house to

me. I ran to the door and pulled it open, then left it wide behind
me as I hurried down the steps and into the street. It was very
cold, but the air was still and dry. I didn't look behind me.

I continued running until my side began to ache; then I half
walked, half trotted, until the pain subsided; then I ran again.
I had reached Stoke Newington and was headed south on the
long straight road that led to Dalston, Shoreditch, and the City.
Beyond that, I could not think: I had wit enough only to keep
Stamford Hill – and *her*, and *him* – continually behind me;
and to run. I was half-blind with weeping; my eyeballs felt
swollen and hot in their sockets, my face was soaked with
slobber, and growing icy. People must have stared as I passed
by them; I believe one or two fellows reached out to pluck me
by the arm; but I saw and heard them not, simply hurried,
stumbling over my skirts, until sheer exhaustion made me
slow my pace and look about me.

I had reached a little bridge over a canal. There were barges on
the water, but they were some way off yet, and the water below
me was perfectly smooth and thick. I thought of that night, when
Kitty and I had stood above the Thames, and she had let me
kiss her . . . I almost cried out at the memory. I placed my hands
upon the iron rail: I believe that, for a second, I really considered
heaving myself over it, and making my escape that way.

But I was as cowardly, in my own fashion, as Kitty herself.
I could not bear the thought of that brown water sucking at my
skirts, washing over my head, filling up my mouth. I turned
away and put my hands before my eyes, and forced my brain
to stop its dreadful whirling. I could not, I knew, keep running
all day. I should have to find a place to hide myself. I had
nothing on me but my dress. I groaned aloud, and gazed about
me again – but this time rather desperately.

Then I held my breath. I recognised this bridge: we had
driven over it every night since Christmas, on our way to
Cinderella. The Britannia Theatre was nearby; and there was
money, I knew, in our dressing-room.

I set off, wiping my face with my sleeve, smoothing my

dress and my hair. The door-man at the theatre eyed me rather curiously when he let me in, but was pleasant enough. I knew him well, and had often stopped to chat with him; today, however, I only nodded to him as I took my key, and hurried by without a smile. I didn't care what he thought; I knew I should not be seeing him again.

The theatre, of course, was still shut up: there were sounds of hammering from the hall as the carpenters finished their work, but apart from that the corridors, the green-room – all were quiet. I was glad: I didn't want to be seen by anyone. I walked very fast but very quietly to the dressing-rooms, until I reached the door that said *Miss Butler and Miss King*. Then very stealthily – for I half-feared, in my fevered state, that Kitty might be on the other side, awaiting me – I unlocked the door and pushed it open.

The room beyond it was dark: I stepped across it in the light from the corridor, struck a match and lit a gas-jet, then closed the door as softly as I could. I knew just what I wanted. In a cupboard beneath Kitty's table there was a little tin box with a pile of coins and notes in it – a portion of our wages went there every week, for us to draw on as we chose. The key to it lay mixed up with her sticks of grease-paint, in the old cigar-box in which she kept her make-up. I took this box, and tipped it up; the sticks fell out, and so did the key – and so, I saw, did something else. There had always been a sheet of coloured paper at the bottom of the box, and I had never thought to lift it. Now it had come loose and behind it was a card. I picked it up with trembling fingers, and studied it. It was creased, and stained with make-up, but I knew it at once. On the front was a picture of an oyster-smack; two girls smiled from its deck through a patina of powder and grease, and on the sail some-one had inked, 'To London'. There was more writing on the back – Kitty's address at the Canterbury Palace, and a message: 'I can come!!! You must do without your dresser for a few nights, though, while I make all ready . . .' It was signed: 'Fondly, Your Nan'.

It was the card that I had sent her, so long ago, before we had even moved to Brixton; and she had kept it, secretly, as if she treasured it.

I held the card between my fingers for a moment; then I returned it to its box and placed the paper sheet above it, as before. Then I laid my head upon the table, and wept, again, until I could weep no more.

I opened the tin box at last, and took, without counting it, all the money that lay inside – about twenty pounds, as it would turn out, and only a fraction, of course, of my total earnings of the past twelve months; but I felt so dazed and ill at that moment I could hardly imagine what I would ever need money for, again. I put the cash into an envelope, tucked the envelope into my belt, and turned to go.

I hadn't glanced about me, yet, at all; now, however, I took a last look round. One thing only caught my eye, and made me hesitate: our rail of costumes. They were all here, the suits that I had worn upon the stage at Kitty's side – the velvet breeches, the shirts, the serge jackets, the fancy waistcoats. I took a step towards them, and ran my hand along the line of sleeves. I would never take them up again . . .

The thought was too much; I couldn't leave them. There were a couple of old sailors' bags nearby – giant great things that we had used once or twice to rehearse with, in the afternoons, when the Britannia stage was quiet and clear. They were filled with rags: very quickly I took one of them and loosened the cord at its neck, and pulled all its stuffing out upon the floor until it was quite empty. Then I stepped to the rail, and began to tear my costumes from it – not all of them, but the ones I could not bear to part with, the blue serge suit, the Oxford bags, the scarlet guardsman's uniform – and stuffed them into the bag. I took shoes, too, and shirts, and neckties – even a couple of hats. I didn't stop to think about it, only worked, sweating, until the bag was full and almost as tall as myself. It was heavy, and I staggered when I lifted it; but it was strangely satisfying to have a real burden upon my shoulders – a kind of counterweight to my terrible heaviness of heart.

Thus laden, I made my way through the corridors of the Britannia. I passed no one; I looked for no one. Only when I reached the stage door did I see a face that I was rather glad to see: Billy-Boy sat in the doorman's office, quite alone, with a cigarette between his fingers. He looked up when I approached, and gazed in wonder at my bag, my swollen eyes, my mottled cheeks.

'Lord, Nan,' he said, getting to his feet. 'Whatever is up with you? Are you sick?'

I shook my head. 'Give me your fag, Bill, will you?' He did so, and I pulled on it and coughed. He watched me warily.

'You don't look right, at all,' he said. 'Where's Kitty?'

I drew on the fag again, and handed it back to him.

'Gone,' I said. Then I pulled at the door and stepped into the street beyond. I heard Billy-Boy's voice, lifted in anxiety and alarm, but the closing door shut off his words. I raised my bag a little higher on my shoulder, and began to walk. I took one turning, and then another. I passed a squalid tenement, entered a busy street, and joined a throng of pedestrians. London absorbed me; and for a little while I ceased, entirely, to think.

PART TWO

Chapter 8

I walked for something like an hour before I rested again; but the course I took was a random one that sometimes doubled back upon itself: my aim was less to run from Kitty than to hide from her, to lose myself in the grey anonymous spaces of the city. I wanted a room – a small room, a mean room, a room that would prove invisible to any pursuing eye. I saw myself entering it and covering my head, like some burrowing or hibernating creature, a wood-louse or a rat. So I kept to the streets where I thought I should find it, the grim and uninviting streets where there were lodging-houses, doss-houses, houses with cards in the window saying *Beds-to-Rent*. Any one of them, I suppose, might have suited me; but I was looking for a sign to welcome me.

And at last it seemed to me I found it. I had strayed through Moorgate, wandered towards St Paul's, then turned and finished up almost at Clerkenwell. Still I had given no thought to the people about me – to the men and the children who stared, or sometimes laughed, to see me trudging, blank-faced, with my sailor's load. My head was bowed, my eyes half-closed; but I became aware now that I had entered some kind of square – grew conscious of a bustle, a hum of business close at hand; grew conscious, too, of a smell: some rank, sweet, sickening odour I vaguely recognised but could not name. I walked more slowly, and felt the road begin to pull, a little stickily, at the soles of my shoes. I opened my eyes: the stones I stood upon were red and running with water and blood. I looked up, and saw a graceful iron building filled with vans and barrows and porters, all bearing carcases.

I was at Smithfield, at the Dead Meat Market.

I gave a kind of sigh to know it. Close at hand there was a tobacconist's booth: I went to it and bought a tin of cigarettes and some matches; and when the boy handed me my change I asked him if there were any lodging-houses nearby, that might have rooms to spare. He gave me the names of two or three – adding, in a warning sort of way: 'They ain't werry smart, miss, the lodgings round these parts.' I only nodded, and turned away; then walked on, to the first address that he had mentioned.

It turned out to be a tall, crumbling house in an unswept row, very close to the Farringdon Street railway. The front yard had a bedstead in it, and a dozen rusty cans and broken-down crates; in the yard next door there was a group of barefoot children, stirring water into pails of earth. But I hardly raised my eyes to any of it. I only stepped to the door, laid my bag upon the step, and knocked. Behind me, in the cut of the railway, a train rumbled and hissed. As it passed, the step on which I rested gave a shake.

My knock was answered by a pale little girl who stared hard at me while I enquired after the vacant rooms, then turned and called into the darkness behind her. After a second, a lady came; and she, too, looked me over. I thought then of how I must appear, in my expensive dress but hatless and gloveless, and with red eyes and a running nose. But I considered this image of myself rather listlessly, as if it did not much concern me; and the lady at last must have thought me harmless enough. She said her name was Mrs Best, that she had one room left for rent; that the charge was five shillings a week – or seven, with attendance; and that she liked her rent in advance.

Would the terms suit me? I gave a quick, half-hearted show of calculation – I felt quite incapable of serious thought – then said that they would.

The room to which she led me was cramped and mean and perfectly colourless; everything in it – the wallpaper, the carpets, even the tiles beside the hearth – having been rubbed or bleached or grimed to some variety of grey. There was no gas, only two oil-lamps with cracked and sooty chimneys. Above the mantel there was one small looking-glass, as cloudy and as speckled as the back of an old man's hand. The window faced the Market. It was all about as different from our house at Stamford Hill as it was possible for any room to be: that, at least, gave me a dreary kind of satisfaction and relief. All I really saw, however, was the bed – a horrible old down mattress, yellow at the edges and blackened in the middle with an ancient bloodstain the size of a saucer – and the door. The bed, for all its rankness, seemed at that moment wonderfully inviting. The door was solid, and had a key in it.

I told Mrs Best therefore that I should like to take the room at once, and drew out the envelope that held my money. When she saw that, she sniffed – I think she took me for a gay girl. 'It is only fair to tell you now,' she said, 'that the house I keep here is a tidy one; and I like my lodgers ditto. I have had trouble with single ladies in the past. I don't care what you do or who you see outside my house; but one thing I won't have, that's men-friends in a single lady's room . . .'

I said that I would give her no trouble on that score.

I must have been a queer sort of tenant for Mrs Best, in those first weeks after my flight from Stamford Hill. I paid my rent very promptly, but never went out. I received no visits, no letters or cards; kept stubbornly to my room, with the shutters closed fast – there to pace the creaking floor, or to mumble or to weep . . .

I think my fellow tenants thought me mad; perhaps I was mad. My life, however, seemed sensible enough to me then.

For where else, in my misery, could I have run to? All my
London friends – Mrs Dendy, Sims and Percy, Billy-Boy and
Flora – were also Kitty's friends. If I went to them, what would
they say? They would only be glad, to know that Kitty and
Walter were lovers at last! And if I went home, to Whitstable,
what would *they* say? I had come away from there so recently,
and been so proud; and it seemed as if they had all been
promising I would be humbled from the very day I left them. It
had been hard to live among them, wanting Kitty. How could
I return to them, and take up my old habits, having *lost* her?

So, though I imagined their letters arriving at Stamford Hill,
and lying there unopened and unanswered; though I guessed
that, recalling my archness, they would think that I had turned
my back on them, and soon stop writing at all, I could not help
it. If I remembered the things I had left behind me – my
women's clothes, and my wages; my letters and cards from
fans and admirers; my old tin trunk with my initials on it – I
remembered them dully, as if they were the pieces of some
other person's history. When I thought of *Cinderella*, and how
I had broken my contract and let them down at the Britannia,
I didn't much care. I was known in my new home as 'Miss
Astley'. If my neighbours had ever seen Nan King upon the
stage, they did not see her now, in me – indeed, I barely recognised her there myself. The costumes I had brought with me I
found myself quite unable, after all, to gaze upon. I placed
them beneath my bed, still in their bag, and left them there to
moulder.

No one came after me, for no one knew where I was. I was
hidden, lost. I had cast off all my friends and joys, and
embraced misery as my career. For a week – and then
another – and another, and another – I did nothing but slumber, and weep, and pace my chamber; or else I would stand
with my brow pressed to the dirty window, gazing at the
Market, watching as the carcases were brought and piled, and
heaved about, and sold, and taken away. The only faces I saw
were those of Mrs Best and Mary – the little skivvy who had

opened the door to me, who changed my pot and brought me coal and water, and who I sometimes sent on errands to buy me cigarettes and food. Her expression as she handed me my packages showed me how strange I had become; but to her fear and her wonder alike, I was indifferent. I was indifferent to everything except my own grief – and this I indulged with a strange and horrible passion.

I believe I barely washed in all those weeks – and certainly I did not change my dress, for I had no other. Very early on I gave off wearing my false chignon, too, and let my hair straggle greasily about my ears. I smoked, endlessly – my fingers grew brown, from the nail to the knuckle; but I ate hardly at all. For all that I liked to watch the carcases being towed about at Smithfield, the thought of meat upon my tongue made me nauseous, and I had stomach for none but the blandest of foods. Like a woman quickening with child I developed a curious appetite: I longed only for sweet, white bread. I gave Mary shilling after shilling, and sent her to Camden Town and Whitechapel, Limehouse and Soho, for bagels, brioches and flat Greek loaves, and buns from the Chinese bakeries. These I would eat dipped in mugs of tea, which I brewed, ferociously strong, in a pot on the hearth, and sweetened with condensed milk. It was the drink I had used to make for Kitty, in our first days together at the Canterbury Palace. The taste of it was like the taste of her; and a comfort, and a frightful torment, all at once.

The weeks, for all my carelessness to their passing, passed by anyway. There is little to say about them, except that they were dreadful. The tenant in the room above my own moved out, and was replaced by a poor couple with a baby: the baby was colicky, and cried in the night. Mrs Best's son found a sweetheart, and brought her to the house: she was given tea and sandwiches in the downstairs parlour; she sang songs, while someone played on the piano. Mary broke a window with a broom, and shrieked – then shrieked again when Mrs

Best rolled up her sleeve and slapped her. Such were the sounds I caught, in my grim chamber. They might have solaced me, except that I was beyond solace. They only kept me mindful of the things – all the ordinary things! The smack of a kiss, the lilt of a voice lifted in pleasure or anger – that I had left behind me. When I gazed at the world from my dusty window, I might as well have been gazing at a colony of ants, or a swarming bee-hive: I could recognise nothing in it that had once been mine. It was only by the lightening and the warming of the days, and the thickening of the reek of blood from Smithfield, that I began to realise that the year was edging slowly into spring.

I might have faded into nothingness, I think, along with the carpet and the wallpaper. I might have died, and my grave gone unvisited and unmarked. I might have remained in my stupor till doomsday – I think I would have – if something hadn't happened, at last, to rouse me from it.

I had been at Mrs Best's for about seven or eight weeks, and had not once stepped beyond her door. I still ate only what Mary brought me; and though I only ever sent her off, as I have said, for bread and tea and milk, she sometimes came with more substantial foods, to try and tempt me into eating them. 'You'll perish, miss,' she would say, 'if you don't get your wittles'; and she'd hand me baked potatoes, and pies, and eels in jelly, which she bought hot from the stalls and pie-shops on the Farringdon Road, and had bound with layers of newsprint into tight little parcels, steaming and damp. I took them – I might have taken arsenic, if she had offered me a packet of that – and it became my habit, as I ate my potato or my pie, to flatten the wrappings across my lap and study the columns of print – the tales of thefts and murders and prize-fights, ten days old. I would do this in the same dull spirit in which I gazed from my window at the streets of East London; but one evening, as I smoothed a piece of newspaper over my knee and brushed the crumbs of pastry from its creases, I saw a name I knew.

The page had been torn from one of the cheap theatrical papers, and bore a feature entitled *Music-Hall Romances*. The words appeared in a kind of banner, held aloft by cherubs; but beneath them there were three or four smaller headlines – they said things like *Ben and Milly Announce Their Engagement*; *Knockabout Acrobats to Wed*; *Hal Harvey and Helen's Heavenly Honeymoon!* I knew none of these artistes, nor did I linger over their stories; for in the very centre of the article there was a column of print and a photograph from which, once I had seen it, I could not tear my eyes.

Butler and Bliss, the column was headed, *Theatreland's Happiest Newly-Weds!* The photograph was of Kitty and Walter in their wedding-suits.

I gazed at it in stupefaction for a moment, then I placed my hand over the page and gave a cry – a quick, sharp, agonised cry, as if the paper was hot and had burned me. The cry became a low, ragged moan that went on, and on, until I wondered that I had breath enough left to make it. Soon I heard footsteps on the stairs: Mrs Best was at the door, calling my name in curiosity and fear.

At that I ceased my racket, and became a little calmer: I did not want her in my room, prying into my grief or offering useless words of comfort. I called to her that I was quite all right – that I had had a dream, merely, which had upset me; and after a moment I heard her take her leave. I looked again at the paper on my knee, and read the story which accompanied the photograph. It said that Walter and Kitty had married at the end of March, and honeymooned on the Continent; that Kitty was currently resting from the stage, but was expected to return to the halls – in an entirely new act, and with Walter as her partner – in the autumn. Her old partner, it said, Miss Nan King, who had been taken ill whilst playing at the Britannia Theatre, Hoxton, was busy with plans for a new career of her own . . .

Reading this I felt a sudden, sickening desire not to moan, or weep – but to laugh. I put my fingers to my lips and held them shut, as if to stem a tide of rising vomit. I had not laughed in what seemed to be a hundred years or more; I feared more than anything to hear the sound of my own mirth now, for I knew it would be terrible.

When this fit had passed, I turned again to the paper. I had wanted at first to destroy it, to tear or crumple it and cast it on the fire. Now, however, I felt I could not let it from my sight. I ran a finger-nail around the edge of the article, then tore, slowly and neatly, where I had scored. The paper that was left over I did cast into the grate; but the slip of newsprint that bore Kitty and Walter's wedding-portrait I held carefully, in the palm of my hand – as carefully as if it were a moth's wing that might tarnish with too much fingering. After a moment's thought I stepped to the looking-glass. There was a gap between the glass itself and the frame which held it, and into this I placed one edge of the piece of paper. Here it was held fast in space, and cut across my own reflection – unmissable, in that tiny room, from any vantage-point.

Perhaps I was a little feverish; yet my head felt clearer than it had in a month and a half. I gazed at the photograph, and then at myself. I saw that I was wasted and grey, that my eyes were swollen and purpled with shadows. My hair, which I had loved before to keep so trim and sleek, was long and filthy; my lips were bitten almost to the blood; my frock was stained, and rancid at the armpits. They, I thought – the smiling couple in the photograph – they had done this to me!

But for the first time in all those long, miserable weeks, I thought, too, what a fool I had been, to let them.

I turned my head away then and stepped to the door, and gave a shout for Mary. When she came running, breathless and a little nervous, I told her I wanted a bath, and soap, and towels. She looked at me rather strangely – I had never called for such a thing before – then she ran to the basement, and soon there came the thump of the tub upon the stairs as she hauled it up behind her, and the clatter of pans and kettles in the kitchen. Soon, too, Mrs Best emerged from her parlour, disturbed once again by the noise. When I explained my sudden longing to bathe she said, 'Oh, Miss Astley, now is that really wise?', and looked pale and shaken. I believe she thought I intended to drown myself, or cut my wrists into the water.

I did, of course, neither. Instead I sat for an hour in the steaming tub, gazing into the fireplace or at Kitty's picture, gently massaging the life back into my aching limbs and joints with a piece of soap and flannel. I washed my hair and cleaned the muck from my eyes; the flesh beneath my ears and behind my knees, in the crooks of my arms and between my legs, I rubbed till it was red and stinging.

At last I think I dozed; and as I did so I had a strange, unsettling vision.

I remembered a woman from Whitstable – an old neighbour of ours – of whom I had not thought in years. She had died while I was still a child, quite unexpectedly, and of a peculiar condition. Her heart, the doctors said, had hardened. The outer skin of it had grown leathery and tough; its valves had turned sluggish, then had begun to falter in their pumping, then ceased entirely. Save a little tiredness and breathlessness there had been no warning; the heart had worked away on its private, fatal, project, at its own secret pace – then stopped.

This story had thrilled and terrified my sister and me, when we first heard it. We were young and well cared for; the idea that one of our organs – our most vital organ, at that – might baulk at its natural role, might conspire with itself to choke, rather than to nurture, us, seemed an appalling one. For a week after the woman's death we talked of nothing else. At night, in bed, we would lie trembling; we would rub and worry at our ribs with sweating fingers, conscious of the unemphatic pulse beneath, terrified that the flimsy rhythm would falter or slow, certain that – like hers, our poor, dead, unsuspecting neighbour's – our hearts were stealthily hardening, hardening, in the tender red cavities of our breasts.

Now, waking to the reality of the cooling tub, the colourless

room, the photograph upon the wall, I found my fingers once
again upon my breast-bone, probing and chafing, searching
for the thickening organ behind it. This time, however, it
seemed to me that I found it. There was a darkness, a heaviness, a stillness at the very centre of me, that I had not known
was growing there, but which gave me, now, a kind of comfort.
My breast felt tight and sore – but I didn't writhe, or sweat,
beneath the pain of it rather, I crossed my arms over my ribs,
and embraced my dark and thickened heart like a lover.

Perhaps, even as I did it, Walter and Kitty were walking
together, on a street in France or Italy; perhaps he leaned to
touch her, as I touched myself; perhaps they kissed; perhaps
they lay in a bed . . . I had thought such things a thousand
times, and wept and bitten my lips to think them; but now I
gazed at the photograph and felt my misery stiffen, as my heart
had stiffened, with rage and frustration. They walked together,
and the world smiled to see it! They embraced on the street,
and strangers were glad! While all the time I lived pale as a
worm, cast out from pleasure, from comfort and ease.

I rose from the bath, all heedless of the spilling water, and
took up the photograph again; but this time I crushed it. I gave
a cry, I paced the floor: but it was not with wretchedness that
I paced, it was as if to try out new limbs, to feel my whole self
shift and snap and tingle with life. I hauled open the window
of my room, and leaned out into the dark – into the never-
quite-dark of the London night, with its sounds and its scents
that, for so long, I had been shut from. I thought, I will go out
into the world again; I will go back into the city – they have
kept me from it long enough!

But oh, how terrible it was, making my way into the streets
next morning – how busy I found them, how dirty and
crowded and dazzling and loud! I had lived for a year and a
half in London, and called it my own. But when I walked in it
before, it was with Kitty or Walter; often, indeed, we had not
walked at all, but taken carriages and cabs. Now, for all that I
had borrowed a hat and a jacket of Mary's to make me seemly,

I felt as though I might as well be stumbling through Clerkenwell in no clothes at all. Part of it was my nervous fear that I would turn a corner and see a face I knew, a face to remind me of my old life, or – worst of all – Kitty's face, tilted and smiling as she walked on Walter's arm. This fear made me falter and flinch, and so I was jostled worse than ever, and had curses thrown at me. The curses seemed as sharp as nettle-stings, and set me trembling.

Then again, I was stared at and called after – and twice or thrice seized and stroked and pinched – by men. This, too, had not happened in my old life; perhaps, indeed, if I had had a baby or a bundle on me now, and was walking purposefully or with my gaze fixed low, they might have let me pass untroubled. But, as I have said, I walked fitfully, blinking at the traffic about me; and such a girl, I suppose, is a kind of invitation to sport and dalliance . . .

The stares and the strokings affected me like the curses: they made me shake. I returned to Mrs Best's and turned the key in my door; then I lay upon my rancid mattress and shivered and wept. I had thought myself brilliant with new life and promise, but the streets that I thought would welcome me had only cast me back into my former misery. Worse, they had frightened me. *How*, I thought, *will I bear it? How will I live?* Kitty had Walter now; Kitty was married! But I was poor and alone and uncared for. I was a solitary girl, in a city that favoured sweethearts and gentlemen; a girl in a city where girls walked only to be gazed at.

I had discovered it, that morning. I might have learned it sooner, from all the songs I'd sung at Kitty's side.

I thought then what a cruel joke it was that I, who had swaggered so many times in a gentleman's suit across the stages of London, should now be afraid to walk upon its streets, because of my own girlishness! If only I were a boy, I thought wretchedly. If only I were really a boy . . .

Then I gave a start, and sat up. I remembered what Kitty had said, that day in Stamford Hill – that I was *too much like a boy*.

I remembered Mrs Dendy's reaction, when I had posed for her in trousers: *She's too real.* The very suit that I had worn then – the blue serge suit that Walter had given me on New Year's Eve – was here, beneath my bed, still crumpled in the sailor's bag with all the other costumes that I'd taken from the Brit. I slid from the mattress and drew the bag free, and in a moment I had all the suits upon the floor. They lay about me, impossible handsome and vivid in that colourless room: all the shades and textures of my former life, with all the scents and songs of the music hall, and my old passion, in their seams and creases.

For a second I sat trembling: I feared the memories would overcome me, and set me weeping again. I almost returned the costumes to the bag – but then I took a breath, and willed my hands to steady and my dampening eyes to dry. I placed my hand upon my breast – upon the heaviness, and the darkness, that had so strengthened me.

I picked up the blue serge suit and shook it. It was horribly creased, but apart from that not damaged at all by its confinement to the bag. I tried it on, with a shirt and a necktie. I had become so thin that the trousers sagged about my waist; my hips were narrower, my breasts even shallower, than before. All that spoilt the illusion of my being a boy was the foolish, tapered jacket – but its seams had not been cut, I saw, only tucked and sewn. There was a knife on the mantel that I used to slice my bread; I seized it, and applied it to the stitches. Soon the jacket was its old, masculine self again. With my hair trimmed, I thought, and a pair of proper boy's shoes upon my feet, anyone – even Kitty herself! – might meet me on the streets of London, and never know me for a girl, at all.

There were one or two obstacles to be overcome, of course, before I could begin to put my daring plan into practice. Firstly, I must properly reacquaint myself with the city: it took another week of wandering every day about the streets of Farringdon and St Paul's, before I could accept the jostling and the roars, and the stares of the men, without smarting.

Then there was the problem of where – if I really was to stroll about in costume – I should change. I did not want to live as a boy full-time; nor did I want, just yet, to give up my room at Mrs Best's. I could imagine that lady's face, however, if I presented myself before her one day in a pair of trousers. She would think that I had lost my mind entirely; she might call for a doctor or a policeman. She would certainly throw me out – and then I would be homeless again. I didn't want that, at all.

I needed somewhere, away from Smithfield; I needed, in fact, a dressing-room. But so far as I knew, there were no such places for hire. The gay girls of the Haymarket, I believe, transformed themselves in the public lavatories of Piccadilly – put their make-up on at the wash-hand basins, and changed into their gaudy frocks while the latch on the door said *Occupied*. This seemed to me a sensible scheme – but hardly one that I could copy, since it would blue my project, rather, to be seen emerging from a ladies' lavatory in a suit of serge and velvet and a boater.

It was indeed amidst the gay life of the West End, however, that I at last found the answer to the problem. I had begun to walk, each day, as far as Soho; and I had noticed there the tremendous number of houses bearing signs that advertised *Beds Let By The Hour*. In my naivety I wondered at first, Who would want to sleep there, for an hour? Then, of course, I realised that no one would: the rooms were for the girls to bring their customers to; to lie abed in, certainly – but not to sleep. I stood one day at a coffee-stall in the mouth of an alley off Berwick Street, and watched the entrance to one of these houses. There was, I saw, a constant flow of men and women over its threshold, and no one paid the slightest heed to any of them save the leering old woman who sat in a chair at the door, taking their coins – and her alertness lasted only until she had palmed her pennies and handed her customers their key. I believe a pantomime horse could have sashayed over that step with a harlot's hand upon its bridle and – so long as the horse had its coin at the ready – no one would have stopped their business to turn and look . . .

A few days later, therefore, I put my costume in a bag, presented myself at the house, and asked for a room. The old woman looked me over and grinned, quite mirthlessly; then, when I gave her my shilling, she thrust a key at me, and nodded me into the darkened passageway behind her. The key was sticky; the handle of my chamber was sticky; indeed, the house was entirely horrible – damp and stinking, and with walls as thin as paper, so that, unpacking my bag and straightening my costume, I heard all the business from the rooms above, below, and on either side of it – all the grunts and slaps and giggles, and pounding mattresses.

I changed very quickly, growing all the time, with every grunt and titter, less certain and less brave. But when I gazed at myself – there was a looking-glass, with a crack across it, and blood in the crack – when I gazed at myself at last, I smiled, and knew my plan was a good one. I had borrowed a flat-iron from my landlady's kitchen, and pressed the suit free of all its creases; I had given my hair a trim with a pair of sewing-shears – now I smoothed it flat with spittle. I left my dress and purse upon a chair, went out upon the landing, and locked the door behind me – my new dark heart, all the time, beating fast as a clock. As I had expected, the old bawd on the step barely raised her eyes as I went past her; and so, a little hesitantly, I began the walk down Berwick Street. With every glance that came my way, I flinched; at any moment I expected the cry to be let up: 'A girl! There is a girl, here, in boy's clothing!' But the glances did not settle on me: they only slithered past me, to the girls behind. There was no cry; and I began to walk a little straighter. At St Luke's Church, on the corner, a man brushed by me with a barrow, calling, 'All right, squire!' Then a woman with a frizzed fringe put her hand upon my arm, and tilted her head and said: 'Well now, pretty boy, you look like a lively one. Fancy payin' a visit, to a nice little place I know . . . ?'

*

The success of that first performance made me bold. I returned to Soho for another turn, and walked further; and then I went again, and then again . . . I became quite a regular at the Berwick Street knocking-shop – the madam kept a room there for me, three days a week. She early on found out the purpose of my visits, of course – though, from a certain narrowing of her gaze when she dealt with me, I think she was never quite sure if I were a girl come to her house to pull on a pair of trousers, or a boy arrived to change out of his frock. Sometimes, I was not sure myself.

For on every visit I found some new trick to better my impersonation. I called at a barber's shop, and had my old effeminate locks quite clipped away. I bought shoes and socks, singlets and drawers and combinations. I experimented with bandages in an effort to get the subtle curves of my bosom more subtle still; and at my groin I wore a handkerchief or a glove, neatly folded, to simulate the bulges of a modest little cock.

I could not say that I was happy – you must not think that I was ever *happy*, now. I had spent too many miserable weeks at Mrs Best's to be anything other than wretched in my room there: I was bleached of hope and colour, like the wallpaper. But London, for all my weeping, could never wash dim; and to walk freely about it at last – to walk as a boy, as a handsome boy in a well-sewn suit, whom the people stared after only to envy, never to mock – well, it had a brittle kind of glamour to it, that was all I knew, just then, of satisfaction.

Let Kitty see me now, I would think. She would not have me when I was a girl – so let her only see me now! And I remembered a book that Mother had had once from the library, in which a woman, cast out, returned to her home to care for her children in the guise of a nurse. If only I could meet Kitty once again, I thought, and woo her as a man – and then reveal myself, to break her heart, as she had broken mine!

But though I thought it, I made no attempt to contact her; and the possibility of accidentally meeting her – of seeing her with Walter – still made me shake. Even when June came, and then July, and she must surely have returned from her gay honeymoon, I never saw her name on any poster outside any hall or theatre; and I never bought a theatrical paper, to look for it there – so never learned how she fared, as Walter's wife. The only glimpses I ever had of her were in my dreams. In those she was still sweet and lovely, still calling my name and offering me her mouth to kiss; but still, at the last, there would come Walter's arm about her freckled shoulders, and she would turn her guilty eyes from me, to him.

I did not wake weeping from such dreams now, however; I would only let them prick me back to Berwick Street. They seemed, I thought, to lend a brilliance to my disguise.

How very fine it was, however, I did not realise until one night, in August, at the hot end of the summer, as I idled in the Burlington Arcade.

It was about nine o'clock. I had been walking, but now stood before the window of a tobacconist's shop, and was gazing at the goods on show – at the cases and cigar-trimmers, the silver toothpicks and the tortoiseshell combs. The month had been a warm one. I was wearing not the blue serge suit, but the costume I had worn to sing the song called 'Scarlet Fever' – a guardsman's uniform, with a neat little cap. I had unfastened the button at my throat, to let the air in.

As I stood there I became aware at last of the presence of a fellow at my side. He had joined me at the window, and seemed slowly to have inched his way towards me; now he was really very close indeed – so close that I could feel the warmth of his arm against my own, and smell the soap on him. I didn't turn to examine his face; I could see that his shoes, however, were highly polished and rather fine.

After a minute or two of silence, he spoke: 'A pleasant evening.'

Still I didn't look round, only agreed – all guilelessly – that it was. There was another silence.

'You are admiring the display, perhaps?' he went on then. I nodded – now I did turn to glance at him – and he looked pleased. 'Then we are kindred spirits, I can tell!' He had the voice of a gentleman, but kept his tone rather low. 'Now, I'm not a smoker; and yet I find myself quite unable to resist the lure of a really good tobacconist's. The cigars, the brushes, the nail-clippers . . .' He gestured with his hand. 'There is something so very *masculine* about a tobacconist's shop – don't you think?' His voice, at the last, had dipped to little more than a murmur. Now he said in the same tone but very fast: 'Are you up for it, Private?'

His words made me blink.

'Pardon?'

He looked about him with an eye that was quick, practised, smooth as a well-oiled castor; then he glanced back to me. 'Are you up for a lark? Have you a room we might go to?'

'I don't know what you mean,' I said – although, to be frank, I felt the stirrings of an idea.

He, at least, must have thought that I was teasing. He smiled, and licked at his moustaches. 'Don't you, now. And I thought all you guardsmen fellows knew the game all right . . .'

'Not me,' I said primly. 'I only joined up last week.'

He smiled again. 'A raw recruit! And you've never done it with another lad, I suppose? A handsome fellow like you?' I shook my head. 'Well' – he swallowed – 'won't you do it now, with me?'

'Do what?' I said. Again there was that swift, well-lubricated glance.

'Put your pretty arse-hole at my service – or your pretty lips, perhaps. Or simply your pretty white hand, through the slit in my breeches. Whatever, soldier, you prefer; only cease your teasing, I beg you. I'm as hard as a broom-handle, and aching for a spend.'

Through all this astonishing exchange our outward show of gazing into the tobacconist's window had barely been disturbed. He had continued to murmur, and made all his lewd proposals in the same swift undertone, his moustaches hardly lifting to let the words out. Any stranger looking on, I thought, would think us two quite unconnected fellows, lost in our own worlds.

The thought made me smile. In the same humouring tone as before, I said: 'How much, then, will you give me for it?'

At that, his face took on a cynical expression, as if he had expected no better of me; but behind the hardness, too, I caught a flash of heat – as if he wouldn't really have wanted me any other way. He said, 'A sovereign, for a suck or for a Robert' – he meant, of course, a Robert Browning. 'Half a guinea for a dubbing.'

I made to shake my head – to tilt my cap to him and move away, with the joke quite finished. But in his impatience he half-turned, and I caught a gleam of something at his middle. It was a fat, gold watch-chain. The waistcoat it swung from was striped and rather flash. And when I looked again at the man's face – there was light upon it, now, from the lamp at the window – I saw that his whiskers and his hair were gingerish and thick. His eyes were brown, his cheeks rather hollow; but for all that, he looked quite unmistakably like Walter. Like Walter, whom Kitty lay with and kissed.

The idea had a peculiar effect on me. I spoke – but it was as if someone else were doing the speaking, not me. I said: 'All right. I'll do it. I'll – touch you; for a sov.'

He grew business-like. When I stepped away I felt him linger a moment at the window, then follow. I went not to my old knocking-shop – I had only the most confused sense of what I was about, but knew I oughtn't to get stuck in a room with him, and risk having him opt for the Robert after all – but to a little court nearby, where there was a nook, above a grating, which the gay girls used as a lavatory. As I approached it, indeed, a woman emerged, pressing her skirts between her legs to dry herself: she gave me a wink. When she had gone, I stood waiting; and a moment later the man appeared. He had a newspaper shielding the fork of his trousers, and when he took the paper away I saw a bulge there the size of a bottle. I had a moment of panic; but then he came and stood before me, and looked expectant. When I began to pull at his buttons, he closed his eyes.

I got his cock out, and studied it: I had never seen one before, so close, and – no disrespect to the gent concerned – it seemed quite monstrous. But there are always jokes about such things in the music hall: I had a pretty good idea of how they worked. Seizing hold of it, I began – very inexpertly, I am sure, though he didn't seem to mind – to pump it.

'How thick and long it is,' I said then – I had heard that it was every man's ambition to be spoken to thus, at such moments. The fellow gave a sigh, and opened his eyes.

'Oh, I do wish you would kiss me there,' he whispered. 'Your mouth is such a perfect one – quite like a girl's.'

I slowed my rhythm, and took another look at his straining cock; and again, when I knelt, it was as if it were someone else who was kneeling, not myself. I thought, This is how *Walter* tastes!

Afterwards I spat his spendings out upon the cobbles, and he thanked me very graciously.

'Perhaps,' he said, buttoning himself up, 'perhaps I shall see you again, in the same spot?'

I could not answer him – the fact was, I felt almost ready to weep. He handed me my sovereign; then, after a moment's hesitation, he stepped to me and kissed my cheek. The gesture made me flinch; and when he felt the shudder, he misunderstood, and looked wistful.

'No,' he said, 'you don't like that, you soldier-boys, do you?' His tone was strange; when I studied him, I saw that *his* eyes were gleaming.

His excitement had stirred me to strangeness, before; his emotion, now, made me terribly thoughtful. When he turned and left the court, I remained there, trembling – not with sadness, but with a creeping kind of relish. The man had looked like Walter; I had pleasured him, in some queer way, for Kitty's sake; and the act had made me sicken. But he was not like Walter, who might take his pleasure where he chose it. His pleasure had turned, at the last, to a kind of grief; and his love was a love so fierce and so secret it must be satisfied, with a stranger, in a reeking court like this. I knew about that kind of love. I knew how it was to bare your palpitating heart, and be fearful as you did so that the beats should come too loudly, and betray you.

I had kept my heart-beats smothered; and had been betrayed, anyway.

And now I had betrayed another, like myself.

I put away the gentleman's sovereign, and walked to Leicester Square.

This was one place which, in all my careless West End wanderings, I had tended to avoid or pass through swiftly: I was always mindful of the first trip I had made there, with Kitty and Walter, and it was not a memory I cared, very often, to revisit. Tonight, however, I walked there rather purposefully. I went to the statue of Shakespeare, where we had stood that time, and I leaned before it, gazing at the view that we had looked on then. I remembered Walter saying that we were at the very heart of London, and did I know what it was that made that great heart beat? *Variety!* I had looked around me that afternoon and seen, astonished, what I thought was all the world's variety, brought together in one extraordinary place. I had seen rich and poor, splendid and squalid, white man and black man, all bustling side by side. I had seen them make a vast harmonious whole, and been thrilled to think that I was about to find my own particular place in it, as Kitty's friend.

How had my sense of the world been changed, since then! I had learned that London life was even stranger and more various than I had ever thought it; but I had learned too that not all its great variety was visible to the casual eye; that not all the pieces of the city sat together smoothly, or graciously, but rather rubbed and chafed and jostled one another, and

overlapped; that some, out of fear, kept themselves hidden,
and only exposed themselves to those upon whose sympathies they could be sure. Now, all unwittingly, I had been
marked out by one such secret element, and claimed by it as a
member.

I looked into the crowds that passed me by on every side.
There were three hundred, four hundred, perhaps five hundred men there. How many of them were like the gentleman
whose parts I had just fingered? Even as I wondered it I saw
one fellow gaze my way, deliberately – and then another.

Perhaps there had been many such looks since I had
returned to the world as a boy; but I had never noticed them or
grasped their import. Now, however, I grasped it very well –
and I trembled again, as I did so, with satisfaction and spite. I
had first donned trousers to avoid men's eyes; to feel myself
the object of *these* men's gazes, however, these men who
thought I was like them, *like that* – well, that was not to be
pestered; it was to be, in some queer way, *revenged*.

For a week or two I continued to wander, and to watch, and
to learn the ways and gestures of the world into which I had
stumbled. Walking and watching, indeed, are that world's
keynotes: you walk, and let yourself be looked at; you watch,
until you find a face or a figure that you fancy; there is a nod,
a wink, a shake of the head, a purposeful stepping to an alley
or a rooming-house . . . At first, as I have said, I took no part
in these exchanges, but only studied others at them, and
received a thousand questing glances on my own account –
some of which I held, rather teasingly, but most of which I
turned aside, after a second, with a show of carelessness. But
then, one afternoon, I was approached once again by a gentleman who, it seemed to me, bore some slight resemblance to
Walter. He wanted my hand upon him, merely, and to have a
string of lewd endearments whispered in his ears as I dubbed
him off – it didn't seem like much. If I hesitated, I don't
believe he saw. I named my terms – a sovereign, again – and
led him to the nook where I had served his predecessor. His

cock seemed rather small; again, however, I said how thick and fine it was.

'You're a beautiful boy,' he whispered to me afterwards. There was no trouble over the coin.

Thus easily – as easily, and fatefully, as I had first begun my music-hall career – thus easily did I refine my new impersonations, and become a renter.

Chapter 9

~

It might seem a curious kind of leap to make, from music-hall masher to renter. In fact, the world of actors and artistes, and the gay world in which I now found myself working, are not so very different. Both have London as their proper country, the West End as their capital. Both are a curious mix of magic and necessity, glamour and sweat. Both have their types – their *ingénues* and *grandes dames*, their rising stars, their falling stars, their bill-toppers, their hacks . . .

All this I learned, slowly but steadily, in the first few weeks of my apprenticeship, just as I had learned my music-hall trade at Kitty's side. Luckily for me, I found a friend and adviser – a boy with whom I fell into conversation late one night, as we sheltered together from a sudden shower in the doorway of a building on the edge of Soho Square. He was a very girlish type – what they call a true mary-anne – and, like many of them, he gave himself a girl's name: Alice.

'That's my sister's name!' I said, when he told me, and he smiled: it was *his* sister's name, too – only his sister, he said, was dead. I said I didn't know if mine was dead or not, and didn't care; and this did not surprise him.

This Alice was, I guessed, about my age. He was as pretty as a girl – prettier, indeed, than most girls (including me), for he had glossy black hair and a heart-shaped face, and eye-lashes impossibly long and dark and thick. He had rented, he said, since he was twelve; renting, now, was the only life he knew, but he liked it well enough. 'It's better, anyway,' he said, 'than working in an office or a shop. I believe that, if I had to work in the same little room all day, perched on the same little stool and staring at the same dull faces, I would go mad, just mad!'

When he asked for my history, I told him that I had come up to London from Kent, that I had been treated rather badly by someone, and was now forced to find my living on the streets; all of which was true enough, in its way. I believe he felt sorry for me – or maybe it was just the coincidence of our sisters' names that warmed him to me – anyway, he began to look out a little for me, and to give me tips and cautions. We would sometimes meet up at the coffee-stalls of Leicester Square, and have a little boast, or grumble, about our fortunes. And while we talked his eyes would be darting, darting, darting all about, looking for new customers, or old ones, or for sweethearts and friends.

'Polly Shaw,' he would say, inclining his head as some slight young man tripped by us, smiling. 'A daisy, an absolute daisy, but *never* let her talk you into lending her a quid.' Or, less kindly: 'My eyes! but doesn't *that* puss always land with her nose in the cream!' as another boy drew up in a hansom, and disappeared into the Alhambra on the arm of a gentleman with a red silk lining to his cape.

Finally, of course, his drifting gaze would settle and harden, and he would give a little nod, or wink, and hastily put down his cup. 'Whoops!' he would say. 'I see a porter who wants to punch Sweet Alice's ticket. *Adieu, cherie.* A thousand kisses on your marvellous eyes!' He would touch his fingertip to his lips, then lightly press it to the sleeve of my jacket; then I would see him picking his careful way across the crowded square to the fellow who had gestured to him.

When he asked me, early on, what my name was, I answered: Kitty.

*

It was Sweet Alice who introduced me to the various renter types, and explained to me their costumes, and their habits, and their skills. Foremost amongst them, of course, were the mary-annes, the other boys like himself, who could be seen strolling up and down the Haymarket at any time of the day or night, with their lips rouged and their throats powdered, and clad in trousers as tight and revealing, almost, as a ballerina's fleshings. These boys took their customers to lodging-houses and hotels; their aim was to be spotted by some manly young gentleman or lord and set up as his mistress in apartments of their own. More succeeded in this ambition than you might think.

Then again, there were the more ordinary-looking fellows, the clerks and shop-boys: they rather despised the mary-annes, and went with gentlemen – or so they claimed – for the money rather than for the thrill of it; some of them, I believe, even kept wives and sweethearts. The aristocracy or leading men of this particular branch of the profession were the guardsmen: it had been as one of these that I had costumed myself, when I had donned that scarlet uniform – all innocently, of course, for I had known nothing of their reputation in this direction, then. These men, I was assured, were cock-handlers and -suckers, almost exclusively. They occasionally obliged a gentleman with a poke or two, when they were feeling friendly; but they never let their own parts be fondled or kissed. They were proud to the point of mania, Sweet Alice said, on that score.

My own renter persona was, of necessity, a rather curious mixture of types. Never a very virile boy, I held no appeal for the kind of gentleman who liked a rough hand through the slit of his drawers, or a bit of a slap in the shadows; equally, how-ever, I could never afford to let myself be seen as one of those lily-white lads whom the working-men go for, and make rather free with. Then again, I was choosy. There were many fellows with curious appetites in the streets round Leicester Square; but not all of them were the sort I was after. Most men, to be frank, will step aside with a renter as you or I might call into a public-house, on our way home from the market: they take their pleasure, give a belch, and think no more of it than that. But still there are always some – they are gentlemen, for the most part; I learned to spot them from afar – who are fretful, or wistful, or romantic – who could, like the fellow from the Burlington Arcade, be brought to kiss me, or thank me, or even weep over me, as I was handling them.

And, as they did so – as they strained and gasped, and whispered their desires to me in some alley or court or dripping lavatory stall – I would have to turn my face away to hide my smiles. If they favoured Walter, then so much the better. If they did not – well, they were all gents and (whatever their own opinion on the matter) with their trousers unbuttoned they all looked the same.

I never felt my own lusts rise, raising theirs. I didn't even need the coins they gave me. I was like a person who, having once been robbed of all he owns and loves, turns thief himself – not to enjoy his neighbours' chattels, but to spoil them. My one regret was that, though I was daily giving such marvellous performances, they had no audience. I would gaze about me at the dim and dreary place in which my gentleman and I leaned panting, and wish the cobbles were a stage, the bricks a curtain, the scuttling rats a set of blazing footlights. I would long for just one eye – just one! – to be fixed upon our couplings: a bold and knowing eye that saw how well I played my part, how gulled and humbled was my foolish, trustful partner.

But that – considering the circumstances – seemed quite impossible.

All continued smoothly for, perhaps, six months or so: my colourless life at Mrs Best's went on, and so did my trips to the West End, and my renting. My little stash of money dwindled, and finally disappeared; and now, since renting was all I knew and cared for, I began to live entirely from what I earned upon the streets.

I still had had no word of Kitty – not a word! I concluded at
last that she must have gone abroad, to try her luck with
Walter – to America, perhaps, where we had planned to go. My
months upon the music-hall stage seemed very distant to me
now, and quite unreal. Once or twice on my trips around the
city I saw someone I knew, from the old days – a fellow with
whom we'd shared a bill at the Paragon, a wardrobe-mistress
from the Bedford, Camden Town. One night I leaned against a
pillar in Great Windmill Street and watched as Dolly Arnold –
who had played Cinderella to Kitty's Prince, at the Britannia –
made her exit from the door of the Pavilion and was helped
into a carriage. She looked at me, and blinked – then looked
away again. Perhaps she thought she knew my face; perhaps
she thought I was a boy that she had worked with; perhaps she
only thought I was a miserable ningle, haunting the shadows
in search of a gent. Anyway, she did not see Nan King in me, I
know it; and if I had an urge to cross to her and reveal myself
and ask for news of Kitty, it lasted for only a moment; and in
that moment the driver shook his horses into life, and the carriage rumbled off.

No, my only contact with the theatre now was as a renter. I
discovered that the music halls of Leicester Square – the very
same halls which Kitty and I had gazed at, all hopefully, two
years before – were rather famous in the renter world as
posing-grounds and pick-up spots. The Empire, in particular,
was always thick with sods: they strolled side-by-side with the
gay girls of the promenade, or stood, in little knots, exchanging
gossip, comparing fortunes, greeting one another with flapping hands and high, extravagant voices. They never looked at
the stage, never cheered or applauded, only gazed at themselves in the mirror-glass or at each other's powdered faces,
or – more covertly – at the gentlemen who, rapidly or rather
lingeringly, passed them by.

I loved to walk with them, and watch them, and be watched
by them in turn. I loved to stroll about the Empire – the handsomest hall in England, as Walter had described it, the hall to

which Kitty had longed so ardently, so uselessly! for an invitation – I loved to stroll about it with my back to its glorious golden stage, my costume bright beneath the ungentle glare of its electric chandeliers, my hair gleaming, my trousers bulging, my lips pink, my figure and pose reeking, as the gay boys say, of lavender, their import bold and unmistakable – but false. The singers and comedians I never looked at once. I had finished with *that* world, entirely.

All, as I have said, went smoothly; then, in the first few warm weeks of 1891 – that is, a year and more after my flight from Kitty – there came a bothersome interruption to my little routine.

I returned to the knocking-shop after an evening of rather heavy renting to find the old proprietress missing, her chair overturned, and the door to my chamber splintered and flung wide. What had happened I never found out for sure; it seemed that the madam had been taken or chased away – though whether by a policeman or a rival bawd, no one professed to know. Anyway, thieves had taken advantage of her absence to steal into the house, to frighten and threaten the girls and their customers, and help themselves to anything that they could lift: the oozing mattresses and rugs, the broken looking-glasses, the few rickety bits of furniture – also my frocks, shoes, bonnet and purse. The loss was not a great one to me; but it meant that I must go home in my masculine attire – I was wearing the old Oxford bags, and a boater – and attempt to reach my room at Mrs Best's without her catching me.

It was quite late, and I walked very slowly to Smithfield, in the hope that all the Bests might be abed and sleeping by the time I got there – and, indeed, when I reached the house, the windows were dark and all seemed still. I let myself in and stepped silently up the stairs – horribly mindful of the last time I had crept, noiselessly, through a slumbering house, and all that the creeping had led to. Perhaps it was the memory that made me blunder: for halfway up I put my hand to my head – and my hat went soaring over the banister to land with a thud in the passageway below. I came, cursing, to a halt. I knew I must go down to fetch it; just as I was about to turn and begin my descent, however, I heard the creaking of a door and saw the bobbing glow of a candle.

'Miss Astley—' It was my landlady's voice, sounding thin and querulous in the darkness. 'Miss Astley, is that you?'

I didn't stop to answer her, but hurled myself up the remaining stairs and ran into my room. With the door closed behind me I tore the jacket from my shoulders and the trousers from my legs, and stuffed them, with my shirt and drawers, into the little curtained alcove where I hung my clothes. I found myself a night-gown, and pulled it on; as I fastened the buttons at the throat, however, I heard what I had dreaded to hear: the sound of rapid, heavy footsteps on the stairs, followed by a hammering at my door and Mrs Best's voice, loud and shrill.

'Miss Astley! Miss Astley! It would oblige me if you would open this door. I have found a peculiar item in the downstairs passage, and believe that you have someone in there as you should not!'

'Mrs Best,' I answered, 'what do you mean?'

'You know what I mean, Miss Astley. I am warning you. I have my son with me!' She caught hold of the door-knob, and shook it. Above our heads there were more footsteps: the baby had been woken by the noise, and begun to cry.

I turned the key, and opened the door. Mrs Best, clad in a night-dress and a tartan wrap, pushed past me, into the room. Behind her, in a shirt and nightcap, stood her son. He had a terrible complexion.

I turned to the landlady. She was gazing about her in frustration. 'I know there is a gentleman in here somewhere!' she cried. She pulled the covers from the bed, then stopped to look beneath it. At last, of course, she headed for the alcove. I darted to stop her, and she curled her lip in satisfaction. 'Now we'll have him!' she said. She reached past me and tweaked the curtain back, then stepped away with a gasp. There were about four suits there, as well as the one that I had just taken off. 'Why, you little strumpet!' she cried. 'I believe you was planning a regular *horgy*!'

'A horgy? A horgy?' I folded my arms. 'They're bits of mending, Mrs Best. It's not a crime, is it, to take in sewing, for gentlemen?'

She picked up the pair of underthings that I had so recently kicked off, and sniffed at them. 'These drawers are still warm!' she said. 'From the heat of your needle, I suppose you'll be telling me? From the heat of *his* needle, more like!' I opened my mouth – but could find no answer to make her. While I hesitated she stepped to the window and looked out of it. 'This, I suppose, is where they made their escape. The villains! Well, they won't get far, that's for sure, in their birthday suits!'

I looked again at her son. He was gazing at my ankles where they showed beneath my night-gown.

'I'm sorry, Mrs Best,' I said. 'I won't do it again, I promise you!'

'You certainly shan't do it again, in my house! I want you out of here, Miss Astley, in the morning. I've always found you a very peculiar tenant, I don't mind admitting – and now, to go and try and play the hussy on me like this! I won't have it; no, certainly I won't! I warned you when you moved in.'

I bowed my head; she turned on her heel. Behind her, her son at last gave me a sneer. 'Tart,' he said. Then he spat, and followed his mother into the darkness.

Being not exactly overburdened with articles to pack, I was out of the house next morning just as soon as I had washed. Mrs Best curled her lip as I passed by her. Mary, however, gazed at me with a kind of admiration in her eyes, as if awed and impressed that I had proved myself so normal – so spectacularly normal – at the last. I gave her a shilling, and patted her hand. Then I took a final turn around Smithfield Market. It was a warm morning, and the reek of the carcases was terrible, the hum of flies about them as deep and steady as the buzz of a

motor; but for all that, I felt a kind of bleak fondness for the
place, which I had gazed at, so often, in my weeks of madness.

I moved on at last, and left the flies to their breakfast. I had
only the vaguest ideas about where I should make for, but I had
heard that the streets around King's Cross were full of rooming-
houses, and thought perhaps that I might try my luck up there.
In the end, however, I did not get even so far as that. In the
window of a shop on the Gray's Inn Road I saw a little card:
Respectible Lady Seeks Fe-Male Lodger, and an address. I
gazed at it for a minute or so. The *Respectible* was off-putting:
I couldn't face another Mrs Best. But there was something very
appealing about that *Fe-Male*. I saw myself in it – in the
hyphen.

I memorised the address. It was for a road named Green
Street, which turned out to be wonderfully near – a narrow
little street off the Gray's Inn Road itself, with a well-kept terrace on one side, and a rather grim-looking tenement on the
other. The number I sought was one of the houses, and looked
very pleasant, with a pot of geraniums upon the step and,
beside that, a three-legged cat, washing its face. The cat gave a
hop as I approached, and lifted its head for me to tickle.

I pulled on the bell, and was greeted by a kind-faced, white-
haired lady in an apron and slippers; she let me in at once
when I explained my visit, introduced herself as 'Mrs Milne',
then spent a moment fussing over the cat. While she did so I
looked about me, and blinked. The hallway was as crowded
with pictures, almost, as Mrs Dendy's old front parlour. These
pictures were not, however, theatrical in theme; indeed, so
far as I could make out, they had nothing in common at all
save the fact that each of them was very brightly hued. Most
seemed rather cheap – some had evidently been cut from
books and papers, and pinned frameless to the wall – but there
were one or two rather famous images. Above the umbrella-
stand, for example, hung a copy of that gaudy painting *The
Light of the World*; beneath it was an Indian picture, of a slender blue god wearing spit-black on the eyes, and holding a

flute. I wondered whether Mrs Milne was perhaps some form of religious maniac – a theosophist, or a Hindoo convert.

When she saw me looking at the walls, however, she smiled in a most Christian-like way. 'My daughter's pictures,' she said, as if that explained it all. 'She does like the colours.' I nodded, then followed her up the stairs.

She took me directly to the room that was for rent. It was a pleasant, ordinary kind of chamber, and everything in it was clean. Its chief attraction was its window: this was long, and split down the middle to form a pair of glass doors; and these opened on to a little iron balcony, that overlooked Green Street and faced the shabby tenement.

'It'll be eight shillings for the rent,' said Mrs Milne as I gazed about me. I nodded. 'You're not the first girl that I've seen,' she went on, 'but, to be honest, I was hoping for an older lady – I thought perhaps a widow. My niece was here until very recently, but had to leave us to get married. You might be thinking of getting married yourself, rather soon?'

'Oh, no,' I said.

'You've no young man?'

'Not one.'

That seemed to please her. She said, 'I am glad. You see, it is just myself and my daughter here, and she is rather an unusual, trusting sort of girl. I wouldn't like to have young fellers, coming in and out . . .'

'There's no young man,' I said firmly.

She smiled again; then seemed to hesitate. 'Might I ask – might I – why you are leaving your present address?' At that *I* hesitated – and her smile grew smaller.

'To be truthful,' I said, 'there was a little bit of unpleasantness with my landlady . . .'

'Ah.' She stiffened a little, and I realised that in telling the truth I had blundered.

'What I mean,' I began – but I could see her mind working. What did she think? That my landlady had caught me kissing her husband, probably.

'You see,' she began again, regretfully, 'my daughter . . .'

This daughter must be a beauty and a half, I thought – or else a complete erotomaniac – if the mother is so eager to keep her safe and close, away from young men's eyes. And yet, just as I had been drawn to that mispelt card in the shopkeeper's window, so, now, there was something about the house and its owner that tugged at me, unaccountably.

I took a chance.

'Mrs Milne,' I said, 'the fact of it is I have a curious occupation – a theatrical occupation, you could call it – that obliges me sometimes to dress in gentlemen's suits. My landlady caught me at it, and took against me. I know for certain that, if I live here, I shall never bring a chap over your threshold. You may wonder how I know that, but I can only say, I do. I shan't ever get behind with my rent; I shall keep myself to myself and you won't hardly know that I am here at all. If you and Miss Milne will only not object to the sight of a girl in a pair of bags and a necktie now and again – well, then I think I might be the lodger you are seeking.'

I had spoken in earnest – more or less – and now Mrs Milne looked thoughtful. 'Gentlemen's suits, you say,' she said – not unkindly or incredulously, but with a rather interested air. I nodded, then pulled at the cord of my bag and drew out a jacket – it happened to be the top half of the guardsman's uniform. I gave it a shake and held it up against myself, rather hopefully. 'My eyes,' she said, folding her arms, 'he's a beauty, in' he? Now my little girl *would* like *him*.' She gestured to the door. 'If you'll permit me . . . ?' She stepped out on to the landing and gave a shout: 'Gracie!' I heard the sound of footsteps below. Mrs Milne tilted her head. 'Now, she's a mote shy,' she said in a low voice, 'but don't you pay no mind to her if she starts being silly on you. It's just her way.' I smiled, uncertainly. In a second Gracie had begun her ascent; a few seconds more, and she was in the room and at her mother's side.

I had expected some extraordinary beauty. Grace Milne was

not beautiful – but she was, I saw at once, rather extraordinary. Her age was hard to judge. She might, I thought, have been anything between seventeen and thirty; her hair, however, was as yellow and fine as flax, and hung loose about her shoulders like a girl's. She was clad in an odd assemblage of clothes – a short blue dress, and a yellow pinafore, and beneath that gaudy stockings with clocks upon them, and red velvet slippers. Her eyes were grey, her cheeks very pale. Her features had a strange, smooth quality to them, as if her face was a drawing to which someone had half-heartedly taken a piece of India rubber. When she spoke her voice was thick and slightly braying. I realised then, what I might have guessed before: that she was rather simple.

I saw all this, of course, in less than a moment. Grace had put her arm through her mother's and, on being introduced to me, had indeed hung back rather shyly. Now, however, she gazed with obvious delight at the jacket that I held before me, and I could see that she was desperate to seize its coloured sleeve and stroke it.

And after all, it *was* a lovely jacket. I asked her, 'Would you like to try it on?'

She nodded, then glanced at her mother: 'If I might.' Mrs Milne said she might. I raised the jacket for her to step into, then moved around her to fasten the buttons. The scarlet serge and the gold trim went bizarrely well with her hair, her eyes, her dress and stockings.

'You look like a lady in a circus,' I said, as her mother and I stood back to study her. 'A ring-master's daughter.' She smiled – then took a clumsy bow. Mrs Milne laughed and clapped.

'May I keep it?' Gracie asked me then. I shook my head.

'To be honest, Miss Milne, I don't believe that I can spare it. Had I only two the same . . .'

'Now, Gracie,' said her mother, 'of course you can't keep it. Miss Astley needs the costume for her theatricals.' Grace pulled a face, but did not seem very seriously dismayed. Mrs

Milne caught my eye. 'She might borrow it, though, mightn't she,' she whispered, 'from time to time . . . ?'

'She can borrow all my suits, all at once, so far as I care,' I said; and when Grace looked up I gave her a wink, and her pale cheeks pinked a little, and her head went down.

Mrs Milne gave a mild *tut-tut*, and folded her arms complacently. 'I do believe that, after all, Miss Astley, you will suit us very well.'

I moved in at once. That first afternoon I passed in unpacking my few little things, with Gracie beside me exclaiming over them all, and Mrs Milne bringing tea, and then more tea, and cake. By supper-time I had become 'Nancy' to them both; and supper itself – which was a pie and peas and gravy, and afterwards, blancmange in a mould – was the first that I had eaten, at a family table, since my last dinner at Whitstable just over a year before.

The next day, Gracie tried my suits, in every combination, and her mother clapped. There were sausages for supper, and later cake. The cake being eaten, I changed for Soho; and when Mrs Milne saw me in my serge-and-velvet, she clapped again. She had had a key cut for me, so that when I came home late I should not wake them . . .

It was like rooming with angels. I could keep the hours I liked, wear the costumes I chose, and Mrs Milne said nothing. I could come home in a jacket crusted, at the collar, with a man's rash spendings – and she would only pluck it from my nervous hands, and wash it at the tap: 'I never *saw* a girl so careless with her soup!' I could wake wretched, plagued with memories, and she would pile my breakfast plate the higher, asking nothing. She was as simple, in her way, as her own simple daughter; she was good to me for Gracie's sake, because I liked her, and was kind to her.

I was patient, for example, over the issue of Grace's interest in the colourful. You could not have spent three minutes in that house without noticing it; but after three days there I began to sense a kind of system to her mania which, if I had had routines of my own, like an ordinary girl, might have proved rather maddening. When, on my first Wednesday there, I went down to breakfast in a yellow waistcoat, Mrs Milne flinched: 'Gracie don't quite like to see yellow in the house,' she said, 'on a Wednesday.' Three days later, however, we had a custard for tea: food on a Saturday, it seemed, must be yellow, or nothing . . .

Mrs Milne had grown so used to the fads, she had almost ceased to notice them; and in time, as I have said, I grew used to them, too – calling, 'What colour today, Grace?' as I dressed in the mornings. 'May I wear my blue serge suit, or must it be the Oxfords?' 'Shall we have gooseberries for supper, or a Battenberg cake?' I didn't mind, it came to seem a kind of game; and Gracie's way was quite as valid a philosophy, I thought, as many others. And her basic passion, for the vivid and the bright, I understood very well. For there *were* so many lovely colours in the city; and in a sense she tutored me to look at them anew. As I strolled about I would keep a watch for pictures and dresses that I knew that she would like, then bring them home for her. She had a number of huge albums, into which she pasted cuttings and scraps: I would find her magazines and little books, to worry at with her scissors; I would buy her flowers from the flower-girls' stalls: violets, carnations, lavender statice and blue forget-me-nots. When I presented them to her – producing them with a flourish, from under my coat, like a conjuror – she would flush with pleasure, and perhaps dip me a playful little curtsey. Mrs Milne would look on, pleased as anything, but shaking her head and pretending to chide.

'*Tut!*' she would say to me. 'You will turn that girl's head right round, one of these days, I swear it!' And I would think for a second how queer it was that she – who had been so careful to keep her daughter from the covetous glances of fresh young men – should encourage Grace and me to play at sweethearts, so blithely, and with such seeming unconcern.

But it was impossible to think very hard about anything in that household, where life was so even and idle and sweet.

And because, since losing Kitty, thinking was the occupation I cared for least, this suited me best of all.

So the months slid by. My birthday arrived: I had not marked its passing at all the year before; but now there were gifts, and a cake with green candles. Christmas came, bringing more presents, and a dinner. I remembered with some small, insistent portion of my brain the two gay Christmases that I had spent with Kitty; and then I thought of my family. Davy, I supposed, would be married by now, and possibly a father – that made me an aunt. Alice would be twenty-five. They would all be celebrating the turning of the year, today, without me – wondering, perhaps, where I was, and how I did; and Kitty and Walter might be doing the same. I thought: *Let them wonder*. When Mrs Milne raised her glass at the dinner-table, and wished the three of us all the luck of the Season and the New Year, I gave her a smile, and then a kiss upon the cheek.

'What a Christmas!' she said. 'Here I am, with my two best girls beside me. What a lucky day it was for me and Grace, Nance, the day you knocked upon our door!' Her eyes glistened a little; she had said this sort of thing before, but never so feelingly. I knew what she was thinking. I knew she had begun to look upon me as a kind of daughter – as a sister, anyway, to her real daughter: a kindly older sister who might be relied upon, perhaps, to care for Gracie when she herself was dead and gone . . .

The idea, at that moment, made me shiver – and yet I had no other plans; no other family, now; no sister of my own; and certainly no sweetheart. So, 'What a lucky day it was for *me*,' I answered. 'If only everything might stay just as it is, for ever!' Mrs Milne blinked her tears away and took my soft white hand in her old, hardened one. Gracie gazed at us, pleased, but distracted by the splendours of the day, her hair shining in the candle-light like gold.

That night I went as usual to Leicester Square. There are
gents there, looking for renters, even at Christmas.

The trade is poor, though, in the winter months. The fogs and
the early darkness are kind to the furtive; but no one likes
unbuttoning himself when there are icicles upon the wall – nor
did I much care for kneeling on slippery cobbles, or wandering
around the West End in a short jacket merely for the sake of
showing off my lovely bum and the roll of the hankie at the
fork of my trousers. I was glad to have a home that was cosy:
gay people go down like skittles in January, with fevers and
influenza, or worse; Sweet Alice coughed all through that
winter – said he was afraid he should do it while he knelt to a
gent, and bite his cock off.

As spring came again, however, the evenings warmed and
my curious gaslit career grew easier; but I, if anything, grew
lazier. Now, more often than I ventured out into the streets, I
kept at home in my room – not sleeping, only lying, open-
eyed, half-clothed; or smoking, while the night grew thicker
and still, and a candle burned low, and trembled, and died. I
took to throwing wide my windows to let the voices of the city
in: the clatter of cabs and vans from the Gray's Inn Road; the
hoots and the rattles and hisses of steam, from King's Cross;
snatches of quarrels and confidences and greetings, from
passers-by – 'Well now, Jenny!'; 'Till Tuesday, till Tuesday . . .'
When the stifling heat of June arrived I got into the habit of
placing a chair on my little balcony high above Green Street,
and sitting there long into the cooling night.

I passed about fifty nights like this that summer, and dare
say I could not distinguish so many as five of them from all
of their fellows. But one of those nights, I remember very
well.

I had set my chair as usual upon my balcony, but had turned
its back to the street and sat lazily straddling it, with my arms
across each other and my chin upon my arms. I was wearing,
I remember, plain linen trousers and a shirt left open at the

neck, and a little straw sailor-hat I had put on against the strong late-afternoon sun, and forgotten to remove. The room behind me I had let darken; I guessed that, apart from the occasional dancing glow of my cigarette tip, I must be quite invisible against its shadows. My eyes were closed, I was thinking of nothing, when all at once I heard music. Someone had begun to strum some kind of sweet, twangy instrument – not a banjo, not a guitar – and a lilting gypsy melody was playing upon the bare evening breezes. Soon a woman's voice, high and quavering, had risen to accompany it.

I opened my eyes to find the source of the sound; it came not, as I had expected, from the street below, but from the building opposite – the old tenement that had used to be so grim and empty, and such a contrast to the pleasant little terrace in which my landlady had her house. Labourers had been at work upon it for a month and more, and I had been dimly aware of them as they hammered and whistled and leaned from ladders; now the building was spruce and mended. In all my time at Green Street the windows opposite mine had been dark. Tonight, however, they were thrown open, and the curtains behind them were drawn quite wide. It was from here that the gay little melody was issuing: the parted drapes gave me a perfect view of the curious scene that was being enacted within.

The player of the instrument – it was, I now saw, a mandolin – was a handsome young woman in a well-tailored jacket, a white blouse, a necktie and spectacles; I put her down at once for a lady clerk or a college girl. As she sang, she smiled; and when her voice fell short of the higher notes, she laughed. She had tied a bunch of ribbons to the neck of her mandolin, and these shook and shimmered as she strummed it.

The little group of people to whom she sang, however, were not quite so gay. A man, in a suit that was rather rough, sat beside her, nodding with a fixed and hopeful smile; on his knee he held a sweet little girl in a patched frock and apron, whose hands he made to clap in approximate time to the melody. At his shoulder leaned a boy, his hair shaved to a stubble around his narrow neck and his large, flushed ears. Behind him stood a tired-looking hard-faced woman – the man's wife, I guessed – and she held another infant listlessly at her breast. The final member of the party, a stocky girl in a smartish jacket, was only partly visible beyond the edge of the curtain. Her face was hidden, but I could see her hands – which were slender and rather pale – with peculiar clarity: they held a card or a pamphlet, which they flapped in the still, warm air like a fan.

All of these figures were gathered around a table, upon which stood a jar of flaccid little daisies and the remains of an economical supper: tea and cocoa, cold meat and pickle, and a cake. Despite the long faces and forced smiles, there was something celebratory about the scene. It was, I supposed, a sort of house-warming party – though I could not fathom the relationship between the lady mandolinist and the poor, drab little family to whom she played. Nor was I sure about the other girl, with the pale hands; she, I thought, could have belonged in either camp.

The tune changed, and I could sense the family growing restless. I lit a cigarette and studied the scene: it was as good a thing to watch, I thought, as any. At length the girl behind the curtain ceased her intermittent fanning and rose. Stepping carefully around the group, she approached the window: it, like my own, opened on to a little balcony, upon which she now stepped, and from which she surveyed, with a mild glance and a yawn, the quiet street beneath.

There were not more than twelve yards between us, and we were almost level; but, as I had guessed, I was only another shadow against my own shadowy chamber, and she hadn't noticed me. I, for my part, had still not seen her face. The window and curtains framed her beautifully, but the light was all from behind. It streamed through her hair, which seemed curly as a corkscrew, and lent her a kind of flaming nimbus, such as a saint might have in the window of a church; her face, however, was left in darkness. I watched her. When the music stopped, and there was a self-conscious smattering of applause and then a bit of desultory chatter, still she kept her place on the balcony and didn't look round.

At last my cigarette burned down, almost to my fingers, and I cast it into the street below. She caught the gesture: gave a start, then squinted at me, then grew stiff. Her confusion – despite the darkness, I could see from the tips of her ears that she flushed – disconcerted me, till I recollected my gentleman's costume. She took me for some insolent *voyeur*! The thought gave me an odd mixture of shame and embarrassment and also, I must confess, pleasure. I took hold of my boater and raised it, politely.

'G'night, sweetheart,' I said in a low, lazy tone. It was the kind of thing rough fellows of the street – costers and road-menders – said to passing ladies all the time. I don't know why, just then, I thought to copy them.

The girl gave another twitch, then opened her mouth as if to make me some rusty reply; at that moment, however, her friend approached the window. She had a hat fixed to her head, and was pulling on her gloves. She said, 'We must go, Florence' – the name sounded very romantic, in the half-light. 'It is time for the children to be put to bed. Mr Mason says he will walk with us as far as King's Cross.'

The girl gave not a glance more my way then, but turned quickly into the room. Here she kissed the children, shook the mother's hand, and politely took her leave; from my place on the balcony I saw her, and her friend, and their rough chaperon Mr Mason, quit the building and make their way up towards the Gray's Inn Road. I thought she might turn to see if I still watched but she did not; and why should I mind it? With the lamplight at last turned upon her face I had seen that she was not at all handsome.

I might have forgotten all about her, indeed, except that a

fortnight or so after I had watched her in the darkness, I saw her again – but this time in daylight.

It was another warm day, and I had woken rather early. Mrs Milne and Grace were out on a visit, and I had in consequence nothing at all in the world to do, and no one to please but myself. Before my money had all run out I had bought myself a couple of decent frocks; and it was one of those that I had put on, today. I had my old plait of false hair, too: it looked wonderfully natural under the shadow of the stiff brim of a black straw hat. I had a mind to make my way to one of the parks – Hyde Park, I thought, then on perhaps to Kensington Gardens. I knew men would pester me along the way; but parks, I have found, are full of women – full of nursemaids wheeling bassinets, and governesses airing babies, and shop-girls taking their lunches on the grass. Any of these, I knew, might be led into a little conversation by a girl with a smile and a handsome dress; and I had a fancy – a rather curious fancy – for women's company that day.

It was in this mood, and with these plans, and in that costume, that I saw Florence.

I recognised her at once, for all that I had seen so little of her before. I had just let myself out of the house, and lingered for a moment on the lowest step, yawning and rubbing my eyes. She was emerging into the sunlight from a passageway on the other side of Green Street, a little way down on my left, and she was dressed in a jacket and skirt the colour of mustard – it was this, struck by the sun and set glowing, that had caught my eye. Like me, she had paused: she had a sheet of paper in her hand, and seemed to be consulting it. The passageway led to the tenement flats, and I guessed she had been visiting the family that had held the party. I wondered idly which way she would go. If she moved towards King's Cross again, I should miss her.

At last she stowed the paper in a satchel that was slung, crosswise, over her chest, and turned – to her left, towards me. I kept to my step and, as I had before, I watched her; slowly she drew level with me until, once again, there was no more than the width of the road between us. I saw her eyes flick once towards mine, then away, and then, as she felt the persistence of my gaze, to mine again. I smiled; she slowed her step and, with a show of uncertainty, smiled back: but I could see that she had not the least idea who I might be. I couldn't let the moment pass. While my eyes still held her questioning, amiable gaze, I lifted my hand to my head and raised my hat, and said in the same low tone that I had used on her before: 'G'mornin'.'

As before, she started. Then she glanced up at the balcony above my head. And then she pinked. 'Oh! It was you then – was it?'

I smiled again, and gave a little bow. My stays creaked; it felt all wrong, being gallant in a skirt, and I had a sudden fear that she might take me not for an impertinent *voyeur*, but for a fool. But when I raised my eyes to hers again her flush was fading, and her face showed neither contempt nor discomfiture, but a kind of amusement. She tilted her head.

A van passed between us, followed by a cart. In lifting my hat to her this time I had thought only, and vaguely, to correct the earlier misunderstanding; perhaps, to make her smile. But when the street was once again clear and she still stood there it seemed a kind of invitation. I crossed, and stood before her. I said, 'I'm sorry if I frightened you the other night.' She seemed embarassed at the memory, but laughed.

'You didn't *frighten* me,' she said, as if she were never frightened. 'You just gave me a bit of a start. If I'd known you were a woman – well!' She blushed again – or it may have been the same blush as before, I couldn't tell. Then she glanced away; and we fell silent.

'Where's your friend the musician?' I said at last. I held an imaginary mandolin to my waist and gave it a couple of strums.

'Miss Derby,' she said with a smile. 'She is back at our office. I do a bit of work with a charity, finding houses for

poor families that've lost their homes.' She had a plain East
End accent, more or less; but her voice was deep and slightly
breathy. 'We have been trying for ages to get our hands on
some of the flats in this block here, and that night you saw me
we had moved our first family in – a bit of a success for us, we
are only a small affair – and Miss Derby thought we should
make a party of it.'

'Oh, yes? Well, she plays very nicely. You should tell her to
come and busk round here more often.'

'You live there then, do you?' she asked, nodding towards
Mrs Milne's.

'I do. I like to sit out on the balcony . . .'

She raised her hand to tuck away a lock of hair beneath her
bonnet. 'And always in trousers?' she asked me then, so that I
blinked.

'Only sometimes in trousers.'

'But always to gaze at the women and give them a start?'

Now I blinked two or three times. 'I never thought to do it,'
I answered, 'before I saw you.' It was the plain truth; but she
laughed at it, as if to say, *Oh, yes.* The laugh, and the exchange
which had provoked it, was unsettling. I studied her more
closely. As I had seen on that first night, she was not what
you might term a beauty. She was thick at the waist and
almost stout, and her face was broad, her chin a firm one. Her
teeth were even, but not perfectly white; her eyes were hazel,
but the lashes not long; her hands, however, seemed graceful.
Her hair was the kind of hair we had all been thankful, as
girls, that we did not have – for though she had bound it into
a bun at her neck, the curls kept springing from it and twisting about her face. With the lamp behind it, too, it had
seemed auburn; but it would really be more truthful to say
that it was brown.

I believe I liked it better that she was not more handsome.
And though there was something wonderfully intriguing about
her tranquillity at my strange behaviour – as if women donned
gents' trousers all the time; as if they made love to girls on

balconies so often that she was used to it, and thought it merely naughty – I did not think I saw that *trick* in her, that furtive *something*, that I had recognised in other girls. Certainly nobody, gazing at her, would ever think to sneer and call out *Tom*! Again, though, I was glad of it. I had quit the business of hearts and kisses; I was in quite another trade altogether, these days!

And yet would it hurt me after all this time to have a – friend?

I said, 'Look here, will you come to the park with me? I was just on my way there when I saw you.'

She smiled, but shook her head: 'I'm working, I couldn't.'

'It's too hot for working.'

'The work must still be done, you know. I have a visit to make at Old Street – a lady Miss Derby knows might have some rooms for us. I should be there now, really.' And she frowned down at a little watch that hung from a ribbon at her breast like a medal.

'Can't you send to Miss Derby and make her go? It seems awfully hard on you. I bet she's sitting in the office with her feet upon her desk, playing a tune on the mandolin; and here are you out in the sun doing all the tramping about. You need a bit of ice-cream, at the least; there's an Italian lady in Kensington Gardens who sells the best ices in London, and she lets me have them at half-price . . .'

She smiled again. 'I cannot. Else, what would happen to all our poor families?'

I didn't care a button about the families; but I did care, suddenly at the thought that I might lose her. I said, 'Well, then I shall have to see you when you come again to Green Street. When will that be?'

'Ah well, you see,' she said, 'it won't. I shall be leaving this post in a couple of days, and I am to help with the running of a hostel, at Stratford. It is better for me, since it's nearer where I live, and I know the local people; but it means I shall be spending most of my days down East . . .'

'Oh,' I said. 'And shall you never be coming into town, at all, after that?'

She hesitated; then: 'Well, I do sometimes come in, in the evenings. I go to the theatre, or to the lectures at the Athenaeum Hall. You might come with me, to one of those places . . .'

I only went to the theatre, now, as a renter; I wouldn't sit in a velvet seat before a stage again, even for her. I said, 'The Athenaeum Hall? I know that place. But lectures – what do you mean? Church stuff?'

'Political stuff. You know, the Class Question, the Irish Question . . .'

I felt my heart sink. 'The Woman Question.'

'Exactly. They have speakers, and readings, and afterwards debates. Look here.' She reached into her satchel and drew forth a slim blue pamphlet. *The Athenaeum Hall Society Lecture Series*, it said; *Women and Labour: An Address by Mr* – and it gave a name I now forget, followed by a little piece of explanatory text, and a date that was for four or five days ahead.

I said, 'Lord!' in an ambiguous sort of way. She lifted her head, took the pamphlet back from me, and said: 'Well, perhaps, after all, you would prefer the ice-cream cart in Kensington Gardens . . .' There was a hint of rustiness about the words, that I found I could not bear to hear. I said at once, 'Good heavens, no: this looks a treat!' But I added, that if they really didn't sell ices in the hall, then I thought we ought to take some refreshment first. There was, I had heard, a little public-house at the King's Cross corner of Judd Street with a ladies' room at the back of it, where they did a very nice, very inexpensive supper. The lecture began at seven – would she meet me there beforehand? At, say, six o'clock? I said – because I thought it would please her – that I might need some instruction, in the ins and outs of the Woman Question.

At that she snorted, and gave me another knowing look; though what it was she thought she knew, I wasn't sure. She did, however, agree to meet me – with a warning that I must not let her down. I said there was not a chance of it, held out my hand; and for a second felt her fingers, very firm and warm in their grey linen glove, clasp my own.

It was only after we had parted that I realised we had not exchanged names; but by then she had turned the corner of Green Street, and was gone. But I had, as a piece of secret knowledge from our earlier, darker encounter, her own romantic christian name, at least. And besides, I knew I should be seeing her again within the week.

Chapter 10

The days that week grew ever warmer, until at last even I began to tire of the heat. All London longed for a break in the weather; and on Thursday evening, when it finally came, crowds took to the streets of the city in sheer relief.

I was amongst them. For two days almost I had kept indoors in a kind of hot stupor, drinking endless cups of lemonade with Mrs Milne and Gracie in their darkened parlour, or dozing naked on my bed with the windows thrown open and the curtains pulled. Now the promise of a night of chilly liberty on the swarming, gaudy streets of the West End drew me like a magnet. My purse, too, was almost empty – and I was mindful of the supper I would have to take care of, with Florence, the following night. So I needed, I thought, to cut something of a dash. I washed, and combed my hair flat and brilliant with Macassar; and when I dressed I put on my favourite costume – the guardsman's uniform, with its brass buttons and its piping, its scarlet jacket and its neat little cap.

I hardly ever wore this outfit. The military pips and buckles meant nothing to me, but I had a vague terror that some real soldier might one day recognise them, and claim me for his regiment; or else that some emergency might occur – the Queen be assaulted while I was strolling by Buckingham

Palace, for instance – and I would be called upon to play some impossible role in its resolution. But the suit was a lucky one, too. It had brought me the bold gentleman of the Burlington Arcade, whose kiss had proved such a fateful one; and it had tipped the wavering balance at my first interview at Mrs Milne's. Tonight, I thought, I should be content enough if it would only net me a sovereign.

And there was a curious quality to the city that night, that seemed all of a piece with the costume I had chosen. The air was cool and unnaturally clear, so that colours – the red of a painted lip, the blue of a sandwich-man's boards, the violet and the green and the yellow of a flower-girl's tray – seemed to leap out of the gloom. It was just as if the city were a monstrous carpet to which a giant hand had applied the beater, to make all glow again. Infected by the mood I had sensed even in my Green Street chamber, people had, like me, put on their finest. Girls in gay dresses walked the pavements in long, intimidating lines, or spooned with their bowler-hatted beaux on steps and benches. Boys stood drinking at the doors of public-houses, their pomaded heads gleaming, in the gas-light, like silk. The moon hung low above the roofs of Soho, pink and bright and swollen as a Chinese lantern. One or two stars winked viciously alongside it.

And through it all sauntered I, in my suit of scarlet; and yet by eleven o'clock, when the streets were thinning, I had had no luck at all. A couple of gents had seemed to like the look of me, and one rough-looking man had set himself to follow me, right the way from Piccadilly to Seven Dials and back again. But the gents, at the last, had been lured by other renters; and the rough man was not the type I cared for. I had given him the slip in a lavatory with two exits.

And then there had been yet another almost-encounter, later, while I was idling beside a lamp-post in St James's Square. A brougham had driven slowly by, then stopped; and then, like me, it had lingered. No one had got out of it, no one had got in. The driver had had a high collar shadowing his face, and had never moved his gaze from his horse – but there had been a certain twitching of the lace at the dark carriage windows, that let me know that I was being observed, carefully, from within.

I had strolled about a bit, and lit a cigarette. I didn't, for obvious reasons, do carriage jobs. Gents on wheels, I knew from my friends at Leicester Square, were demanding. They paid well, but expected correspondingly large favours: bum-work, bed-work – nights, sometimes, in hotels. Even so, it never hurt to show off a bit: the gent inside might remember me on another, more pedestrian, occasion. I had ambled up and down the edges of the Square for a good ten minutes, occasionally reaching down to give a twitch to my groin – for, in the rather flamboyant spirit in which I had dressed that night, I had padded my drawers with a rolled silk cravat, instead of my usual kerchief or glove, and the material was slippery, and kept edging along my thigh. Still, I thought, such a gesture might not prove unpleasing to the distant eye of an interested gent . . .

The carriage, however, with its taciturn driver and bashful occupant, had at last jerked into life and pulled away.

Since then my admirers had all, apparently, been as cautious as that last one; I had sensed a few interested glances slither my way, but had managed to hook none of them with my own more frankly searching one. By now it had grown very dark, and almost chill. It was time, I thought, to pick my slow way home. I felt disappointed. Not with my own performance, but with the evening itself, which had opened with such promise and had finished such a flop. I had not earned so much as a threepenny-bit: I should now have to borrow a little cash from Mrs Milne, and spend longer, more resolute, less choosy hours on the streets over the following week, until my luck turned. The thought did not cheer me: renting, which had seemed such a holiday at first, had come to seem, of late, a little tiresome.

It was in these spirits that I began to make my way back to

Green Street – avoiding, now, the busier routes that I had trod for fun before, and taking back roads: Old Compton Street; Arthur Street; Great Russell Street, which took me by the pale, silent mass of the British Museum; and finally Guilford Street, which would lead me by the Foundling Hospital and on to the Gray's Inn Road.

Even on these quieter routes, however, the traffic seemed unusually heavy – unusually, and puzzlingly, for though few carts and hansoms seemed actually to pass me, the low clatter of wheels and hooves formed a continuous accompaniment to my own slow footfalls. At last, at the entrance to a dim and silent mews, I understood why; for here I paused to tie my lace and, as I stooped, looked casually behind me. There was a carriage moving slowly towards me out of the gloom, a private carriage with a particular, well-greased rumble I now knew for the one that had pursued me all the way from Soho, and a hunched and muffled driver I thought I recognised. It was the brougham that had waited near me in St James's Square. Its shy master, who had watched while I had posed beneath a lamppost and strolled the pavement with my fingers at my crotch, evidently fancied another look.

My lace tied, I straightened up, but cautiously kept my place. The carriage slowed, then – its dark interior still hidden behind the heavy lace at its windows – it passed me by. Then, a little way on, it drew to a halt. I began, uncertainly, to walk towards it.

The driver, as before, was impassive and still: I could see only the curve of his shoulders and the rise of his hat; indeed, as I approached the rear of the vehicle he disappeared from my view completely. In the darkness the brougham seemed quite black, but where the light from a guttering street-lamp spilled on it, it gleamed a deep crimson, touched here and there with gold. The gent inside, I thought, must be a very rich one.

Well, he would be disappointed; he had followed me for nothing. I quickened my step, and made to move past, head down.

But as I drew level with the rear wheel I heard the soft click of a latch undone: the door swung silently open, blocking my path. From the shadows beyond the doorframe drifted a thread of blue tobacco smoke; I heard a breath, a rustle. Now I must either retrace my steps and cross behind the vehicle or squeeze between the swinging door and the wall on my left – and catch a glimpse, perhaps, of its enigmatic occupant. I confess, I was intrigued. Any gent who could bring such a sense of drama to the staging of an encounter which, in the ordinary course of things, might be settled so unspectacularly – by a word, or a nod, or the fluttering of one spit-blacked lash – was clearly someone special. I was also, frankly, flattered; and having been flattered, generous. Since he had had to make do so far with admiring my bottom from a distance, I felt it only fair to give him the chance of a closer look – though he must, of course, be content *only* to look.

I advanced a little towards the open door. Within, all was dark; I saw only the vague outline of a shoulder, an arm, a knee, against the lighter square of the far window. Then briefly the end of a cigarette glowed bright in the blackness, and glimmered redly on a pale gloved hand, and a face. The hand was slender, and had rings upon it. The face was powdered: a woman's face.

I was too surprised even to laugh – too startled, for a moment, to do anything but stand at the rim of gloom that seemed to spill out from the carriage, and gape at her; and in that moment, she spoke.

'Can I offer you a ride?'

Her voice was rich and rather haughty, and somehow arresting. It made me stammer. I said: 'That, that's very kind of you, madam' – I sounded like a mincing shop-boy refusing a tip – 'but I'm not five minutes from home, and I shall get there all the quicker if you'll let me say good-night, and pass on my way.' I tilted my cap towards the dark place where the voice had come from, and, with a tight little smile, I made to move on.

But the lady spoke again.

'It's rather late,' she said, 'to be out on one's own, in streets like these.' She drew on her cigarette, and the tip glowed bright again in the shadows. 'Won't you let me drop you somewhere? I have a very capable driver.'

I thought, I am sure you do: her man was still hunched forward in his seat, his back to me, his thoughts his own. I felt suddenly weary. I had heard stories in Soho about ladies like this – ladies who rode the darkened streets with well-paid servants, on the lookout for idle men or boys like me who'd give them a thrill for the price of a supper. Rich ladies with no husbands, or absent husbands, or even (so Sweet Alice claimed) husbands at home, warming the bed, with whom they shared their startled catches. I had never known quite whether to believe in such ladies; here, however, was one before me, haughty and scented and hot for a lark.

What a mistake she had made this time!

I put my hand on the carriage-door and made to swing it to. But again she spoke. 'If you won't,' she said, 'let me drive you home, then, won't you, as a favour, ride with me a while? As you see, I am quite alone; and I've rather a yearning for company, tonight.' Her voice seemed to tremble – though whether with melancholy, or anticipation, or even laughter, I could not tell.

'Look, missus,' I said then, into the gloom, 'you're on the wrong track. Let me pass, and get your driver to take you another turn around Piccadilly.' Now I laughed: 'Believe me, I haven't got what you're after.'

The carriage creaked; the red end of the cigarette bobbed and brightened and illuminated, once again, a cheek, a brow, a lip. The lip curled.

'On the contrary, my dear. You have exactly what I'm after.'

Still I did not guess, but only thought, Blimey, she's keen! I glanced about me. A few carriages bowled along the Gray's Inn Road, and two or three late pedestrians passed quickly from sight, behind them. A hansom had pulled up at the end of the mews, quite near us, and was letting its passengers dismount; they disappeared into a doorway, and the hansom rolled by and away, and all was still again. I took a breath, and leaned into the dark interior of the coach.

'Madam,' I hissed, 'I ain't a boy at all. I'm—' I hesitated. The end of the cigarette disappeared: she had thrown it out of the window. I heard her give one impatient sigh – and all at once I understood.

'You little fool,' she said. 'Get in.'

Well, what should I have done? I had been weary, but I was not weary now. I had been disappointed, my expectations for the evening dashed; but with this one, unlooked-for invitation the glamour of the night seemed all restored. True, it was very late, and I was alone, and this woman was clearly a stranger of some determination, and with odd and secret tastes . . . But her voice and manner were, as I have said, compelling ones. And she was rich. And my purse was empty. I hesitated for a moment; then she held out her hand and, where the lamplight fell upon her rings, I saw how large the stones were. It was that – only that, just then – which decided me. I took her hand, and climbed into the carriage.

We sat together in the gloom. The brougham lurched forward with a muted creak, and started on its smooth, quiet, expensive way. Through the heavy lace of its windows the streets seemed changed, quite insubstantial. This, I realised, was how the rich saw the city all the time.

I glanced at the woman at my side. She wore a dress or cloak of some sombre, heavy material, indistinguishable from the dark upholstery of the carriage's interior; her face and gloved hands, illuminated by the regular gleam of passing street-lamps, their surface fantastically marbled by the shadow of the drapes, seemed to float, pale as water-lilies, in a pool of gloom. She was, as far as I could tell, handsome, and quite young – perhaps ten years older than myself.

For a full half-minute neither of us spoke; then she tilted

back her head, and looked me over. She said, 'You are, perhaps, on your way home from a costume ball?' Her voice had
a new, slightly arrogant drawl to it.

'A ball?' I answered. To my own surprise I sounded reedy,
rather trembly.

'I thought – the uniform . . .' She gestured towards my suit.
It, too, seemed to have lost some of its bravado, seemed to be
bleeding its crimson into the shadows of the coach. I felt I was
letting her down. I said, with an effort at music-hall sauce, 'Oh,
the uniform is my disguise for the streets, not a party. I find
that a girl in skirts, on her own in the city, gets looked at,
rather, in a way not always nice.'

She nodded. 'I see. And you don't care for that? Being
looked at, I mean. I should never have guessed it.'

'Well . . . It depends, of course, on who's doing the looking.'

I was getting back into my stride at last; and she, I could
sense it, was also warming up. I felt for a second – what I had
not felt, it seemed, for a hundred years – the thrill of performing with a partner at my side, someone who knew the songs,
the steps, the patter, the pose . . . The memory brought with it
an old, dull ache of grief; but it was overlaid, in this new setting, with a keen, expectant pleasure. Here we were, this
strange lady and I, on our way to I knew not what, playing
whore and trick so well we might have been reciting a dialogue
from some handbook of tartery! It made me giddy.

Now she raised her hand to finger the braided collar of my
coat. 'What a little impostor you are!' she said mildly. Then:
'But you have a brother in the Guards, I think. A brother – or,
perhaps, a beau . . . ?' Her fingers trembled slightly, and I felt
the chillest of whispers of sapphire and gold upon my throat.

I said, 'I work in a laundry, and a soldier brought this in. I
thought he wouldn't notice if I borrowed it.' I smoothed out
the creases around my crotch, where the slippery cravat still
rudely bulged. 'I liked the cut,' I added, 'of the trousers.'

After the briefest of pauses her hand – as I knew it must –
moved to my knee, then crept to the top of my thigh, where

she let it rest. Her palm felt extraordinarily hot. It was an age since anyone had touched me there; indeed, I had kept such a close guard over my own lap lately, I had to fight back the urge to brush her fingers away.

Perhaps she felt me stiffen, for she removed the hand herself and said, 'I'm rather afraid that you are something of a tease.'

'Oh,' I said, recovering, 'I can tease all right – if that's what you care for . . .'

'Ah.'

'And besides,' I added pertly, 'it's you who's the tease: I saw you in St James's Square, watching me. Why didn't you stop me then, if you wanted – *company* – so badly?'

'And spoil the fun with hastening it? Why, the wait was half the pleasure!' As she said it she raised the fingers of her other hand – her left hand – to my cheek. The gloves, I thought, were rather damp about the tips; and they were scented with a scent that made me draw back in confusion and surprise.

She laughed. 'But how prim you have turned! You are never so dainty, I'm sure, with the gentlemen of Soho.'

There was a knowingness to the remark. I said, 'You have watched me before – before tonight!'

She answered: 'Well, it is rather marvellous what one may catch, from one's carriage, if one is quick and keen and patient. One may follow one's quarry like a hound with a fox – and all the time the fox not know itself pursued – might think itself only about its little private business: lifting its tail, arching its eye, wiping its lips . . . I might have had you, dear, a dozen times: but oh, as I said, why spoil the chase! Tonight – what was it decided me at last? Perhaps it was the uniform; perhaps the moon . . .' And she turned her face to the carriage window, where the moon showed – higher and smaller than before, but still quite pink, as if ashamed to look upon the wicked world to which it was compelled to lend its light.

I, too, flushed at the lady's words. What she had said was strange, was shocking – and yet, I guessed, might easily be true. In the bustle and swarm of the streets on which I plied my shadowy trade, a stationary or a lingering carriage would be unremarkable – especially to me, who attended to the traffic of the pavements rather than the roads. It made me horribly uneasy to think she really had been observing me, all those times . . . And yet, was it not just such an audience that I had longed for? Had I not lamented, again and again, precisely the fact that my new nocturnal performances must be staged in the dark, under cover, unguessed? I thought of all the parts I had handled, the gents I'd knelt to and the cocks I'd sucked. I had done it all, as cool as Christmas; now, the idea that she had watched me went direct to the fork of my drawers and made me wet.

I said – I didn't know what else to say – I said, 'Am I then so – special?'

'We shall see,' she answered.

After that, we spoke no more.

She took me to her home, in St John's Wood; and the house, as I guessed it must be, was grand – a high, pale villa in a well-swept square, with a wide front door and tall casement windows with many panes of glass. In one of these a single lamp sat gleaming; the neighbouring houses, however, presented only black, shuttered windows, and the clatter of our carriage sounded atrocious, to me, in the stillness – I was not then used to that total, unnatural hush which fills the streets and houses of the rich, when they are sleeping.

She led me to her door, saying nothing. Her knock was answered by a grim-faced servant, who received her mistress's cloak, looked once at me from beneath her lashes, but after that kept her eyes quite lowered. The lady paused to read the cards upon her table; and I, self-conscious, looked about me. We were in a spacious hall, at the bottom of a wide staircase winding up to darker, higher floors. There were doors – closed – to the left and the right of us. The floor was paved with marble, in squares of black and pink. The walls, to match it, were painted a deep, deep rose; and this darkened further, where the staircase curved and lifted, like the interior whorls of a shell.

I heard my hostess say, 'That will do, Mrs Hooper', and the servant, with a bow, took her leave. The lady lifted the lamp from the table at my side and, still with no word for me, began to ascend the stairs. I followed. We climbed to one floor, and then another. At each step the house grew darker, until at last there was only the narrow pool of light from my chaperon's hand to guide my uncertain footsteps through the gloom. She led me down a short passage to a closed door, then turned and stood before it, one hand raised upon the panels, the other with the lamp held at her thigh. Her dark eyes gleamed, with invitation or perhaps with challenge. She looked, to tell the truth, like nothing so much as the 'Light of the World' that hung above the umbrella-stand in Mrs Milne's hallway; but her gesture was not lost on me. This was the third and most alarming threshold I had crossed for her tonight. I felt a prick, now, not of desire, but of fear: her face, lit from beneath by the smoking lamp, seemed all at once macabre, grotesque. I wondered at this lady's tastes, and how they might have decked the room that lay behind this unspeaking door, in this silent house, with its curious, incurious servants. There might be ropes, there might be knives. There might be a heap of girls in suits – their pomaded heads neat, their necks all bloody.

The lady smiled, and turned. The door swung open. She led me in.

It was, after all, a kind of parlour; nothing more. A small fire had burned itself ashy in the grate, and a bowl of browning petals upon the mantel above it made the thick air thicker with a heady perfume. The window was tall, and close-drawn with velvet drapes; against the wall which faced it were two armless, ladder-backed chairs. A door beside the fireplace led into a further room; it was ajar, but I could not see beyond it.

Between the chairs there was a bureau, and now the lady crossed to it. She poured a glass of wine, and took up a rose-tipped cigarette and lit it.

I had seen already that she was older, less handsome, but more striking than I'd thought at first. Her forehead was broad and pale – all the paler for being framed by the rippled blackness of her hair and her heavy dark brows. Her nose was very straight; her mouth was a full mouth that had once, I guessed, been fuller. Her eyes were a deep hazel and, in the dim light of the low-turned gas-jets, seemed all pupil. When she narrowed them – which she did now, the better to study me through the blue haze of tobacco smoke – one noticed the network of wrinkles, fine and not so fine, in which they were set.

The room was terribly warm. I unfastened the button at my throat, then lifted my cap and raked my fingers through my hair – afterwards rubbing my palm against the wool of my thigh, to wipe the oil from it. And all the time she watched me. Then she said, 'You must think me rather rude.'

'Rude?'

'To have brought you so far, without enquiring after your name.'

I said, without hesitation, 'It's Miss Nancy King, and you might at least offer me a cigarette, I think.'

She smiled, and came to me, and placed her own fag, half-smoked and damp at the end, between my lips. I caught the reek of it on her breath, together with the faint spice of the wine that she had swallowed.

'*If you were King of Pleasure*,' she said, '*and I were Queen of Pain* . . .' Then, in a different tone: 'You're very handsome, Miss King.'

I took a long pull on the cigarette: it made me giddy as a glass of cham. I said: 'I know.' At that, she raised her hands to the front of my jacket – she was still wearing gloves, with the rings on top – and ran them over me, delicately and lingeringly, and sighing as she did so. Beneath the wool of my uniform my nipples sprang up stiff as little sergeants; my breasts – which had grown used to being as it were put aside with my corset and chemise – seemed at her touch to rise and swell and strain against their wrappings. I felt like a man being transformed into a woman at the hand of a sorceress. My cigarette smouldered at my lip, forgotten.

Her hands moved lower, and stopped at my lap, which now, as before, began to pulse and heat. The silken cravat lay rolled there; and as she fingered it, I blushed. She said, 'Now you are prim again!' and began to unfasten my buttons. In a moment she had her hand through the slit of my drawers, had seized a corner of the cravat, and began to tug at it. The silk uncurled, and squirmed and susurrated its way out of my trousers, like an eel.

She looked absurdly like a stage magician, producing a handkerchief or a string of flags from a fist, or an ear, or a lady's purse – and, of course, she was too clever not to know it: one dark eyebrow lifted, and her lip gave its ironical curl, and she whispered '*Presto!*' when the cravat was free. But then her look changed. She held the silk to her lips, and gazed at me above it. 'All your promise has come to nothing, after all,' she said. Then she laughed, and stepped away, and nodded to my trousers – now gaping whitely, of course, at the buttons. 'Take them off.' I did so at once, fumbling with my shoes and stockings in my haste. My fag showered me with ash, and I cast it into the grate. 'And the underthings,' she went on. 'But leave the jacket. That's good.'

Now I had a heap of discarded clothes at my feet. My jacket ended at my hips; beneath it, in the dim light, my legs looked very white, the triangle of hair between them very dark. The lady watched me all the while, making no move to touch me further. But when I was finished, she went to a drawer in the bureau; and when she turned back to me she held something in her hand. It was a key.

'In my bedroom,' she said, nodding towards the second door, 'you'll find a trunk, which this will open.' She handed it to me. It felt very chill upon my overheated palm, and for a moment I merely gazed stupidly at it. Then she clapped her hands: 'Presto!' she said again; and this time, she did not smile, and her voice was rather thick.

The room next door was smaller than the parlour, but quite as rich, and just as dim and hot. On one side there was a screen, with a commode behind it; on the other stood a japanned press, its surface hard and black and glossy, like a beetle's back. At the bottom of the bed there was, as she had promised, a trunk: a handsome, antique chest made of some desiccated, perfumed wood – rosewood, I think – with four claw feet and corners of brass, and elaborate carvings on its sides and lid which the dull glow of the fire threw into exaggerated relief. I knelt before it, placed the key in the lock; and felt the shifting, as I turned it, of some deep interior spring.

A movement in the corner of the room made me turn my head. There was a cheval-glass there, big as a door, and I saw myself reflected in it: pale and wide-eyed, breathless and curious, but for all that an unlikely Pandora, with my scarlet jacket and my saucy cap, my crop and my bare bare bum. In the room next door all was hushed and still. I turned to the trunk again, and lifted its lid. Inside was a jumble of bottles and scarves, of cords and packets and yellow-bound books. I didn't pause to gaze upon these objects then, however; indeed, I hardly registered them at all. For on the top of the jumble, on a square of velvet, lay the queerest, lewdest thing I ever saw.

It was a kind of harness, made of leather: belt-like, and yet not quite a belt, for though it had one wide strap with buckles on it, two narrower, shorter bands were fastened to this and they, too, were buckled. For one alarming moment I thought it might be a horse's bridle; then I saw what the straps and the buckles supported. It was a cylinder of leather, rather longer than the length of my hand and about as fat, in width, as I could grip. One end was rounded and slightly enlarged, the other fixed firm to a flattened base; to this, by hoops of brass, the belt and the narrower bands were all also fastened.

It was, in short, a dildo. I had never seen one before; I did not, at that time, know that such things existed and had names.

For all I knew of it, this might be an original, that the lady had
had fashioned to a pattern of her own.

Perhaps Eve thought the same, when she saw her first apple.

Even so, it didn't stop her knowing what the apple was
for . . .

But in case I still wondered, the lady now spoke. 'Put it
on,' she called – she must have caught the opening of the trunk
– 'put it on, and come to me.'

I struggled for a moment or two over the placing of the
straps, and the tightening of the buckles. The brass bit into the
white flesh of my hips, but the leather was wonderfully supple
and warm. I glanced again towards the looking-glass. The base
of the phallus was a darker wedge upon my own triangular
shield of hair, and its lowest tip nudged me in a most insinuating way. From this base the dildo itself obscenely sprang –
not straight out, but at a cunning angle, so that when I looked
down at it I saw first its bulbous head, gleaming in the red
glow of the fire and split by a near-invisible seam of tiny, ivory
stitches.

When I took a step, the head gave a nod.

'Come here,' said the lady when she saw me in the doorway; and as I walked to her, the dildo bobbed still harder. I
lifted my hand to still it; and when she saw me do that she
placed her own fingers over mine, and made them grasp the
shaft and stroke it. Now the base's insinuating nudges grew
more insinuating still: it was not long before my legs began to
tremble and she, sensing my rising pleasure, began to breathe
more harshly. She took her hands away, and turned, and lifted
her hair from the nape of her neck, and gestured for me to
undress her.

I found the hooks of her gown, and then the laces of her
corset: beneath this, I saw, she was mottled scarlet from the
hundred tiny creases of her chemise. She stooped to remove
her petticoats, but retained her drawers, her stockings and her
boots and, still, her gloves. Very daring – for I had not touched
her at all, yet – I slid a hand into the slit of her drawers; and

with the other I caught hold of one of her nipples, and pressed it.

At that, she put her mouth to mine. Our kisses were imperfect ones, as all new lovers' kisses are, and tasted of tobacco; but – again, like all new lovers' kisses – their very strangeness made them thrilling. The more I fingered her the harder she kissed me, and the hotter I grew between my legs, behind my sheath of leather. Finally she pulled away, and seized my wrists.

'Not yet,' she said. 'Not yet, not yet!'

With my hands still clasped in hers she led me to one of the straight-backed chairs and sat me on it, the dildo all the while straining from my lap, rude and rigid as a skittle. I guessed her purpose. With her hands close-pressed about my head and her legs straddling mine, she gently lowered herself upon me; then proceeded to rise and sink, rise and sink, with an ever speedier motion. At first I held her hips, to guide them; then I returned a hand to her drawers, and let the fingers of the other creep round her thigh to her buttocks. My mouth I fastened now on one nipple, now on the other, sometimes finding the salt of her flesh, sometimes the dampening cotton of her chemise.

Soon her breaths became moans, then cries; soon my own voice joined hers, for the dildo that serviced her also pleasured me – her motions bringing it with an ever faster, ever harder pressure against just that part of me that cared for pressure best. I had one brief moment of self-consciousness, when I saw myself as from a distance, straddled by a stranger in an unknown house, buckled inside that monstrous instrument, panting with pleasure and sweating with lust. Then in another moment I could think nothing, only shudder; and the pleasure – mine and hers – found its aching, arching crisis, and was spent.

After a second she eased herself from my lap, then straddled my thigh and rocked gently there, occasionally jerking, and at last growing still. Her hair, which had come loose, was hot against my jaw.

At length she laughed, and moved again against my hip.
'Oh, you exquisite little tart!' she said.

And thus we clasped one another, sated and spent, our legs inelegantly straddling that elegant, high-backed chair; and as the minutes passed I thought with something like dismay of how the night would now proceed. I thought, She's had me fuck her; now she'll send me home. If I'm in luck I might get a pound, for my trouble. It was the prospect of the sovereign, after all, which had lured me to her parlour in the first place. And yet, now, there was something inexpressibly dreary to me at the idea of quitting her company – of surrendering the toy to which I was strapped, and quieting the tommish urges it and its mistress had all unexpectedly revived.

She raised her head and saw, I suppose, my downcast look.

'Poor child,' she said. 'And do you always grow sorry, when your business is complete?' She put a hand to my chin and tilted my face to the lamplight, and I caught her wrist and shook my head free. My cap – which had remained on my head through all our violent kisses – now fell off. She at once returned her hands to my face, and fingered my pomade-stiffened hair; then she laughed, and rose, and walked into her bedroom. 'Pour yourself some wine,' she called. 'And light me a cigarette, will you?' I heard the hiss of water against china, and guessed that she was using the commode.

I moved to the glass, and examined myself. My face was as scarlet, almost, as my jacket, my hair was ruffled, my lips looked bruised and swollen. I remembered the dildo at my hip, and stooped to unfasten it. Its lustre was cloudy now, and its nether straps were sodden and limp from my own lavish spendings; yet it was as indecently rigid and ready as before – *that* never happened with the gents in Soho. There was a handkerchief on the little table before the fire, and with this I wiped first it, and then myself. I lit two cigarettes, and left one smouldering. Then I poured myself a glass of wine and, in between gulps, began to retrieve my stockings, my trousers and my boots from the pile of clothes that lay strewn across the carpet.

The lady reappeared, and seized her fag. She had changed into a dressing-gown of heavy green silk, and her feet were bare; she had that long second toe that you sometimes see on the statues done by the Greeks. Her hair had been properly unfastened, combed out, and rebound into a long, loose plait, and she had at last removed her white kid gloves. The flesh of her hands was almost as pale.

'Do leave all that,' she said, nodding towards the trousers over my arm. 'The maid will deal with it in the morning.' Then she saw the dildo, and caught it up by one of its straps. 'I should, however, remove *this*.'

I was not sure that I had heard her properly. 'The morning?' I said. 'Do you mean that I should stay?'

'Why, of course.' She looked genuinely surprised. 'Are you not able? Will you be missed?' I felt light-headed suddenly. I told her that I lodged with a lady who, though she would wonder at my absence, wouldn't worry over it. Then she asked if I had an employer – perhaps at the laundry I had mentioned? – who would expect me on the morrow. I laughed at that, and shook my head: 'There is no one at all to miss me. I've only myself to think of and please.'

As I said it, the toy at her thigh began to swing.

She said, 'You did, before tonight. Now, however, you have me . . .'

Her words, her expression, made a mockery of my efforts with the handkerchief: I was wet for her anew. I reunited my trousers with her discarded petticoats, and added my jacket to the pile. Next door, the silken counterpane had been turned back, and the sheets beneath looked very white and cool. The chest kept its still, enigmatic place at the foot of the bed. The clock on the mantel showed half-past two.

It was four, or thereabouts, before we slumbered; and perhaps eleven when I woke. I remembered stumbling to the commode some time in the early morning, and recalled the brief renewal of passion which had followed my return to her arms; but my sleep since then had been a heavy, dreamless one, and when next I knew the bed I was alone in it: she had donned her dressing-gown and stood at the half-opened window, smoking, and gazing thoughtfully at the view beyond. I stirred, and she turned and smiled.

'You sleep like a child,' she said. 'I have been up this half-hour, making a fearful row, and still you've slumbered on.'

'I was so very weary.' I yawned – then I recalled all that had wearied me. A slight awkwardness seemed to fall between us. The room last night had been as unreal as a stage-set: a place of lamplight and shadows, and colours and scents of impossible brilliance, in which we had been given a licence to be not ourselves, or more than ourselves, as actors are. Now, in the late morning light that flowed between the partly drawn drapes, I saw that there was nothing fantastic about the chamber at all; I saw that it was really elegant, and rather austere. I felt, all at once, quite horribly out of place. How does a tart take leave of her customer? I did not know; I had never had to do it.

The lady was still gazing at me. She said, 'I have waited for you to wake, before ringing for breakfast.' There was a bell-pull set into the wall beside the fireplace: I had not seen that the night before, either. 'I hope you are hungry?'

I was, I realised, very hungry indeed; but also slightly nauseous. My mouth, moreover, tasted abominable: I hoped she wouldn't try to kiss me again. She didn't, but kept her distance. Soon, piqued by her new, queer, self-conscious air, I began to think that she might, at least, come and put her lips to my hand.

There was a low, respectful knock on the outer door of the adjoining room. At her call the door was opened; I heard footsteps, and the rattle of china. To my amazement the rattle grew louder, the footsteps approached: the servant – who I thought would deposit her burden in the room next door, and discreetly take her leave – appeared in the doorway of ours. I pulled the sheet to my throat and lay quite still; neither the mistress nor the maid, however, appeared in any way discomfited by my presence there. The latter – not the pale-faced woman I had seen the night before, but a girl a little younger than myself – gave a bob and, with her eyes lowered, made space for a tray on the dressing-table. When she had finished with the china she paused with her head bent and her hands folded over her apron.

'Very good, Blake, that will be all for now,' said the lady. 'But have a bath ready for Miss King by half-past twelve. And tell Mrs Hooper I shall speak to her about luncheon, later.' Her tone was quite polite, yet colourless; I had heard ladies and gentlemen use that tone on cabmen and shopgirls and porters a thousand times.

The girl gave another little duck to her head – 'Yes, m'm' – and withdrew. She had not looked towards the bed, at all.

With the breakfast things to busy ourselves over, the next few minutes passed easily. I raised myself into a sitting position – wincing all the time, for my body ached as if it had been pummelled, or stretched on a rack – and the lady fed me coffee, and warm rolls spread with butter and honey. She herself only drank and, later, smoked. She seemed to take pleasure from seeing me eat – as last night she had liked to watch me stand, undress, light cigarettes; but, still, there was that disconcerting thoughtfulness about her, that made me long for her honest, cruel kisses of the night before.

When we had drained the coffee-pot between us, and I had finished all the rolls, she spoke; and her voice was graver than I had yet heard it. She said: 'Last night, upon the street, I invited you to drive with me and you hesitated. Why was that?'

'I was afraid,' I answered honestly.

She nodded. 'You are not afraid now?'

'No.'

'You are glad that I brought you here.'

It was not a question, but as she said it she raised a hand to my throat, and stroked me there until I reddened and swallowed; and I could not help but answer: 'Yes.'

Then the hand was removed. She grew thoughtful again, and smiled. She said: 'There is a Persian story I read as a girl, about a princess and a beggar, and a djinn. The beggar sets the djinn free from a bottle, and is rewarded with a wish; but the wish – they always do, alas! – comes with conditions. The man may live in ordinary comfort for seventy years; or he may live in pleasure – with a princess for a wife, and servants to bathe him, and robes of gold – he may live in pleasure, for five hundred days.' She paused; then said: 'Which would you choose, if you were that beggar?'

I hesitated. 'Those stories are silly,' I said at last. 'Nobody is ever asked—'

'Which would you choose? The comfort; or the pleasure?' She put her hand to my cheek.

'I suppose then, the pleasure.'

She nodded: 'Of course; and so did the beggar. I should be very sorry, if you had said the other thing.'

'Why?'

'Can you not guess?' She smiled again. 'You say that there is no one you must answer to. Have you no – sweetheart, even?' I shook my head, and perhaps looked bitter, for she sighed with a kind of satisfaction. 'Tell me, then: will you stay with me, here – and be pleasured, and pleasure me, in your turn?'

For a second I only gazed stupidly at her. 'Stay with you?' I said. 'Stay as what? Your guest, your servant . . . ?'

'My tart.'

'Your tart!' I blinked; then heard my voice grow a little hard. 'And how should I be paid for that? Rather handsomely, I should think . . .'

'My dear, I have said: you should have pleasure for your wages! You should live with me here, and enjoy my privileges. You should eat from my table, and ride in my brougham, and wear the clothes I will pick out for you – and remove

them, too, when I should ask it. You should be what the sen-
sational novels call *kept*.'

I gazed at her, then looked away – at the silken counterpane
upon the bed, the japanned press, the bell-pull, the rosewood
trunk . . . . I pictured my room at Mrs Milne's, where I had
come so close of late to real happiness; but I remembered too
my growing obligations there, that had made me, more than
once, uneasy. How much freer would I paradoxically be,
bound to this lady – bound to lust, bound to pleasure!

And yet, it was a little sickening, too, that she made such
promises, so easily. I said – and again, my voice was hard –
'And have *you* no fear of sensation, then? You seem rather sure
of me – but you know nothing about me! Don't you worry I'll
raise a row; that I'll tell the papers – the police – your secret?'

'And with it, your own? Oh, no, Miss King. I have no fear of
sensation: on the contrary, I court it! I seek out sensation! And
so do you.' She leaned closer, and fingered a lock of my hair.
'You say I know nothing about you; but I have watched you
upon the streets, remember. How coolly you pose and wander
and flirt! Did you think you could play at Ganymede for ever?
Did you think, if you wore a silken cock, it meant you never
had a cunt at the seam of your drawers?' Her face was very
close to my own; she would not let me turn my eyes from
hers. She said: 'You're like me: you have shown it, you are
showing it now! It is your own sex for which you really
hunger! You thought, perhaps, to stifle your own appetites:
but you have only made them swell the more! And *that* is
why you won't raise a row – why you will stay, and be my tart,
as I desire.' She gave my hair a cruel twist. 'Admit that it is as
I say!'

'It is!'

For it was, it was! What she said was the truth: she had
found out all my secrets; she had shown me to myself. Not just
with the fierce words of that moment, but with all – the kisses,
the caresses, the fuck on the chair – that had made her say
them; and I was glad! I had loved Kitty – I would always love

Kitty. But I had lived with her a kind of queer half-life, hiding from my own true self. Since then I had refused to love at all, had become – or so I thought – a creature beyond passion, driving others to their secret, humiliating confessions of lust; but never offering my own. Now, this lady had torn it from me – had laid me bare, as surely as if she had ripped the shrieking flesh from my white bones. She pressed against me still; and even as her breath came warm against my cheek, I felt my lusts rise up to meet her own, and knew myself in thrall.

After all, there are moments in our lives that change us, that discontent us with our pasts and offer us new futures. That night at the Canterbury Palace, when Kitty had cast her rose at me, and sent my admiration for her tumbling over into love – that had been one such moment. This was another; perhaps, indeed, it had already passed – perhaps it was the second when I was guided into the dark heart of that waiting carriage that was the real start of my new life. Either way, I knew I could not go back to the old one, now. The djinn was out of the bottle at last; and I had settled on pleasure.

I never thought to ask what happened to the beggar in the tale, once the five hundred days came to an end.

Chapter 11

The lady's name, I learned in time, was Diana: Diana Lethaby. She was a widow, and childless, and rich, and venturesome, and thus – though on a considerably grander scale – as accomplished in the habits of self-pleasure as myself, and quite as hard of heart. In that summer of 1892 she would have been eight-and-thirty – younger, that is, than I am now, though she seemed terribly old to me then, at twenty-two. Her marriage had been, I think, a loveless one, for she wore neither wedding-ring nor mourning-ring, nor was there any picture of Mr Lethaby in any room in that large, handsome house. I never asked after him, and she never questioned me about my past. She had created me anew: the old dark days before were nothing to her.

And they must become nothing to me, of course, now that we had settled our bargain. On that first, fierce morning of my time in her house, she had me kiss her again, then bathe, then re-don my old guardsman's uniform; and as I dressed, she stood a little to one side and studied me. She said, 'We shall have to buy you some new suits. This one – for all its charms – will hardly do for very long. I shall ask Mrs Hooper to send to an outfitter's.'

I buttoned my trousers and drew the braces over my arms. 'I have other costumes,' I said, 'at home.'

'But you would rather have new ones.'

I frowned. 'Of course, but – I must fetch my things. I cannot leave them all unsorted.'

'I could send a boy for them.'

I pulled on my jacket. 'I owe my landlady a month in rent.'

'I shall send her the money. How much shall I send? A Pound? Two pounds?'

I didn't answer. Her words had made me understand anew the enormity of the change that was come upon me; and I thought, for the first time, of the visit I should have to make, to Mrs Milne and Gracie. I could hardly shirk my duty there by sending a boy, with a letter and a coin – could I? I knew I could not.

'I must go myself,' I said at last. 'I should like, you know, to say good-bye to my friends.'

She raised an eyebrow: 'As you wish. I shall have Shilling bring the carriage round, this afternoon.'

'I could just as easily catch a tram . . .'

'I shall send for Shilling.' She came to me, and set my guardsman's cap upon my head, and brushed my scarlet shoulders. 'I think it very naughty of you, to want to go from me at all. I must be sure, at least, of having you come swiftly back!'

My visit to Green Street was every bit as dreary as I knew it must be. I could not bear, somehow, for the brougham to draw up at Mrs Milne's front door, so I asked Mr Shilling – Diana's taciturn driver – to drop me at Percy Circus and wait for me there. When I let myself in with my house-key, therefore, it was as if I had just returned from a shopping expedition or a stroll, as I did most days; there was nothing but the length of my absence from them to hint to Mrs Milne and Gracie of my awful change of fortune. I closed the door very softly; still, Grace's sharp ears must have caught the sound, for I heard her – she was in the parlour – give a cry of 'Nance!', and the next moment she had come lolloping down the stairs and had me in a fierce, neck-breaking embrace. Her mother soon followed her to the landing.

'My dear!' she called. 'You're home, and thank goodness! We've been wondering ourselves silly – haven't we, love? – about where you might've got to. Gracie was fretted near half to death, poor soul, but I said to her: "Don't you worry about Nancy, girl; Nancy will've found some friend to take her in, or missed the last bus home, and passed the night in some rooming-house. Nancy will be back all right, tomorrow, you wait and see."' As she spoke she came slowly down the stairs, until at last we were quite level. She gazed at me with real affection; but there was a hint of reproach, I thought, in her words. I felt even more guilty about what I must tell her – but also slightly resentful. I was not her daughter, nor was I Gracie's sweetheart. I owed them nothing – I told myself – but my rent.

Now I drew carefully away from Grace, and nodded to her mother. I said, 'You're right, I did meet a friend. A very old friend I hadn't seen in a long time. What a surprise it was, to meet her! She has rooms over in Kilburn. It was too far to come back so late.' The story sounded hollow to me, but Mrs Milne seemed pleased enough with it.

'There now, Gracie,' she said, 'what did I tell you? Now, just you run downstairs and put the kettle on. Nancy'll be wanting a bit of tea, I don't doubt.' She smiled at me again, while Gracie dutifully lumbered off; then she headed back up the stairs, and I followed.

'The thing is, Mrs Milne,' I began, 'this friend of mine, she's in a bit of a state. You see her room-mate up and moved out last week' – Mrs Milne checked slightly, then stepped steadily on – 'and she can't replace her; and she can't afford all the rent herself, she has only a little part-time work in a milliner's, poor thing . . .' We had reached the parlour. Mrs Milne turned to face me, and her eyes were troubled.

'That is a shame,' she said feelingly. 'A good roomer is hard to find, these days, that I do know. That's why – and I've told you so before, you know I have – that's why me and Gracie've been so glad to have you with us. Why, if you was ever to leave us, Nance –' This seemed the worst possible way for me to tell her, yet I had to speak.

'Oh, don't say that, Mrs M!' I said lightly. 'For you see, I'm sorry to say I *shall* be leaving you. This friend of mine has asked me and, well, I said I would take the other girl's place – just to help her out, you know . . .' My voice grew thin. Mrs Milne looked grey. She sank into a chair and put a hand to her throat.

'Oh, Nance . . .'

'Now don't,' I said, with an attempt at jollity, 'don't be like that; now just don't! I'm not so special a boarder, heaven knows; and you'll soon find another nice girl to take my place.'

'But it ain't me I'm thinking of so much,' she said, 'as Gracie. You have been so good with her, Nance; there's not many as would understand her like you do; not many who would take the trouble over her little ways, the way you have.'

'But I shall come back and visit,' I said reasonably. 'And Grace –' I swallowed as I said it, for I knew there would never be a welcome for Gracie in the stillness and richness and elegance of Diana's villa – 'Grace can come and visit me. It won't be so bad.'

'Is it the money, Nance?' she said then. 'I know you ain't got much—'

'No, of course it ain't the money,' I said. 'Indeed –' I had remembered the coin in my pocket: a pound, placed there by Diana's own fingers. It more than covered the rent I owed, and the fortnight's warning I should have given. I held it out to her; but when she only gazed bleakly at it and made no move to take it, I stepped awkwardly to the mantelpiece and laid it softly there.

There was a silence, broken only by Mrs Milne's sighs. I coughed. 'Well,' I said, 'I had better go and get my things together . . .'

'What! You ain't leaving us *today*? Not so soon?'

'I did promise my friend I would,' I said, trying to suggest by my tone that my friend might have all the blame for it.

'But you'll stay for a bit of tea, at least?'

The thought of the dreary tea-party we would make, with Mrs Milne so ashen and disappointed, and Gracie in all probability in tears, or worse, filled me with dismay. I bit my lip.

'I'd better not,' I said.

Mrs Milne straightened, and her mouth grew small. She shook her head slowly. 'This will break my poor girl's heart.'

There was a flintiness to her tone that was more frightening, more shaming, than her sadness had been; but I found myself, again, vaguely piqued. I had opened my mouth to utter some dreadful pleasantry when there came a scuffling at the door, and Grace herself appeared. 'Tea's hot!' she sang out, all unsuspecting. I could not bear it. I gave her a smile, nodded blindly towards her mother, then made my escape. Her voice – 'Oh, Ma, what's up?' – pursued me up the stairwell, followed by Mrs Milne's murmurs. In a moment I was in my own room again, with the door closed hard behind me.

The little bits and pieces I owned, of course, could be bundled together in a second, in my sailor's bag, and a carpet-bag that Mrs Milne had once given me. My bedclothes I folded and placed neatly at the end of the mattress, and the rug I shook out at the open window; the few little pictures I had pinned to the wall I took down, and burned in the grate. My toilet articles – a cake of cracked yellow soap, a half-used jar of tooth-powder, a tub of face-cream scented with violet – I scooped into the bin. I kept only my toothbrush, and my hair-oil; these, together with an unopened tin of cigarettes and a slab of chocolate, I added to the carpet-bag – though, after a second's hesitation, I took the chocolate out again, and left it on the mantel, where I hoped Grace would find it. In half an hour the room looked quite as it had when I had first moved in. There was nothing at all to mark my stay there save the cluster of pin-holes in the wallpaper where my pictures had been tacked, and a scorch-mark on the bedside cabinet where once, slumbering over a magazine, I had let a candle fall. The thought seemed a miserable one; but I would not grow sad. I didn't go to the window, for a last sentimental look at the view from it. I didn't check the drawers, or go poking under the bed, or pull the cushions from the chair. If I had left anything behind I knew that Diana would replace it with something better.

Downstairs all seemed ominously still, and when I arrived at the parlour it was to find its door shut fast against me. I gave a knock, and turned the handle, my heart beating. Mrs Milne was seated before the table, where I had left her. She was less ashen than before, but still looked grim. The teapot stood cooling on its tray, its contents unpoured; the cups lay huddled on their nest of saucers beside it. Gracie sat stiff and straight on the sofa, her face turned effortfully away, her gaze fixed unswervingly – but also, I thought, unseeingly – on the view beyond the window. I had expected her to weep at my news; instead, it seemed to have enraged her. Her lips were clenched and quite drained of colour.

Mrs Milne, at least, appeared to have reconciled herself a little to my departure, for she addressed me now with something like a smile. 'I'm afraid Gracie is not quite herself,' she said. 'Your tidings've quite upset her. I told her you'll be coming to see us, but – well – she's that stubborn.'

'Stubborn?' I said, as if amazed. 'Not our Gracie?' I took a step towards her and reached out a hand. With something like a yelp she thrust me away, and shuffled to the furthest end of the sofa, her head all the time kept at its stiff, unnatural angle. She had never shown me such displeasure before; when I spoke to her next it was with real feeling.

'Ah, now don't be like that, Gracie, please. Won't you give me a word, or a kiss, before I go? Won't you shake hands with me, even? I shall miss you, so; and I should hate us to part on bad terms, after all our fun together.' And I went on in this fashion, half entreating, half reproachful, until Mrs Milne rose and touched my shoulder, and said quietly, 'Best leave her,

Nance, and be on your way. You come back and see her another day; she'll've come round by then, I don't doubt it.'

So I had to leave, in the end, without Grace's good-bye kiss. Her mother accompanied me to the front door, where we stood awkwardly before the *Light of the World* and the blue effeminate idol, she with her arms folded over her bosom, me hung with bags, and still clad in my scarlet duds.

'I'm sorry, Mrs M, that this has been so sudden,' I tried; but she hushed me.

'Never mind, dear. You must go your own way.' She was too kind to be stern for long. I said that I had left my room in order; that I would send her my address (I never did, I never did!); and lastly that she was the best landlady in the city, and that if her next girl did not appreciate her I would make it my business to find out why.

She smiled in earnest then, and we hugged. Yet, as we drew apart, I could sense that something was troubling her; and as I stood on the step for my final farewell, she spoke.

'Nance,' she said, 'don't mind me asking, but – this friend: it is a girl, ain't it?'

I snorted. 'Oh, Mrs Milne! Did you really think . . . ? Did you really think that I would . . . ?' That I would set up house with a man, was what she meant: me, with my trousers and my barbered hair! She blushed.

'I just thought,' she said. 'A girl can get herself hooked up by a feller, these days, quicker'n that. And what with you moving out so sudden, I was half convinced you'd let some gentleman or other make you a pile of promises. I should've known better.'

My laughter rang a little hollowly then, as I thought of how near her thoughts ran to the truth, while yet remaining so far from it.

I took a firmer grip of my bags. I had told her I was heading for the cab rank on the King's Cross Road, since that was the direction in which I must walk in order to rejoin Diana's driver. Her eyes, which had stayed dry through all her first

shock at my news, now began to glisten. She kept her place on
the doorstep as I made my slow, awkward way down Green
Street. 'Don't forget us, love!' she called out, and I turned to
wave. At the parlour window a figure had appeared. Grace!
She had unbent enough, then, to watch me leave. I widened
the arc of my wave, then caught up my cap and flapped that at
her. Two boys turning somersaults on a broken railing stopped
their game to give me a playful salute: they took me for a soldier, I suppose, whose leave had all run out, and Mrs Milne for
my tearful, white-haired old mother, and Gracie no doubt for
my sister or my wife. But for all that I waved and blew kisses,
she made me no sign, simply stood with her head and her
hands upon the window-pane, which pressed a whiter circle
to the centre of her pale brow, and to the end of each blunt
finger. At last I let my arm slow, and fall.

'*She* don't love yer much,' said one of the boys; and when I
had looked from him back to the house, Mrs Milne had gone.
Gracie, however, still stood and watched. Her gaze – cold and
hard as alabaster, piercing as a pin – pursued me to the corner
of the King's Cross Road. Even up the steep climb to Percy
Circus, where the windows of Green Street are quite hidden
from view, it seemed to prick and worry at the flesh upon my
back. Only when I had seated myself in the shadowy interior
of Diana's carriage, and made fast the latch of the door, did I
feel quite free of it, and secure once again on the path of my
new life.

But even then there was another reminder of my unpaid
debts to the old one. For on our drive along the Euston Road
we neared the corner of Judd Street, and all at once I remembered the appointment I had made, to meet my new friend
Florence. It was for Friday: that, I realised, was today. I had
said that I would see her at the entrance to the public house at
six o'clock, and it must, I thought, be past six now . . . Even as
I thought it, the carriage slowed in the traffic and I saw her
standing there, a little way along the street, waiting for me. The
brougham crawled still slower; from behind the lace of its

windows I could see her perfectly, frowning to her left and
right, then bending her head to look at the watch at her bosom,
then raising a hand to tuck a curl in place. Her face, I thought,
was so very plain and kind. I had a sudden urge to tug at the
latch of the door, and race down the street to her side; I could
at least, I thought, call to the driver to stop his horse, so that I
might shout some apology to her . . .

But while I sat, anxious and undecided, the traffic grew
swift, the carriage gave a jerk, and in a moment Judd Street and
plain, kind Florence were far behind me. I could not bear the
thought, then, of asking the forbidding Mr Shilling to turn the
horse around, for all that I was his mistress for the afternoon.
And besides, what would I say to her? I would never, I supposed, be free to meet with her again; and I could hardly
expect to have her visit me at Diana's. She would be surprised,
I thought, and cross, when I didn't turn up: the third woman to
be disappointed by me that day. I was sorry, too – but, on
reflection, not terribly sorry. Not terribly sorry at all.

When I returned to Felicity Place – for that, I saw now, was the
name of the square in which my mistress had her home – I was
greeted with gifts. I found Diana in the upstairs parlour, bathed
and dressed at last, and with her hair in plaits and elaborately
pinned. She looked handsome, in a gown of grey and crimson,
with her waist very narrow and her back very straight. I
recalled those laces and ties I had fumbled over the night
before: there was no sign of them now beneath the smooth
sheath of her bodice. The thought of that invisible linen and
corsetry, which a maid's steady fingers had fastened and concealed and my own trembling hands, I guessed, would later
uncover and undo, was rather thrilling. I went to her, and put
my hands on her, and kissed her hard upon the mouth, until
she laughed. I had woken tired and sore; I had had a dismal
time at Green Street; but I did not feel dismal now – I felt
limber and hot. If I had had a cock, it would have been twitching.

We embraced for a minute or two; then she moved away and took my hand. 'Come with me,' she said. 'I've had a room made ready for you.'

I was at first a little dismayed to learn that I would not be sharing Diana's chamber; but I could not stay dismayed for long. The room to which she led me – it was a little way along the corridor – was hardly less imposing than her own, and quite as grand. Its walls were bare and creamy-white, its carpets gold, its screen and bedstead of bamboo; its dressing-table, moreover, was crowded with goods – a cigarette-case of tortoise-shell, a pair of brushes and a comb, a button-hook of ivory, and various jars and bottles of oils and perfumes. A door beside the bed led to a long, low-ceilinged closet: here, draped on a pair of wooden shoulders, was a dressing-gown of crimson silk, to match Diana's green one; and here, too, was the suit I had been promised: a handsome costume of grey worsted, terribly heavy and terribly smart. Besides this there was a set of drawers, marked *links* and *neckties*, *collars* and *studs*. These were all full; and on a further rack of shelves, marked *linen*, there was fold after fold of white lawn shirts.

I gazed at all this, then kissed Diana very hard indeed – partly, I must confess, in the hope that she would close her eyes, and thus not see how much I was in awe of her. But when she had gone, I fairly danced about the golden floor in pleasure. I took the suit, and a shirt, and a collar, and a necktie, and laid them all, in proper order, upon the bed. Then I danced again. The bags I had brought with me from Mrs Milne's I carried to the closet and cast, unopened, into the farthest corner.

I wore my suit to supper; it looked, I knew, very well on me. Diana, however, said the cut was not quite right, and that tomorrow she would have Mrs Hooper measure me properly, and send my details to a tailor. I thought her faith in her housekeeper's discretion quite extraordinary; and when that lady had left us – for, as she had at lunch, she filled our plates and

glasses, then stood in grave and (I thought) unnerving attendance until dismissed – I said so. Diana laughed.

'There's a secret to that,' she said; 'can't you guess it?'

'You pay her a fortune in wages, I suppose.'

'Well, perhaps. But didn't you catch Mrs Hooper, gazing
through her lashes at you as she served you your soup? Why,
she was practically drooling into your plate!'

'You don't mean – you can't mean – that she is just – *like
us*?'

She nodded: 'Of course. And as for little Blake – why, I
plucked her, poor child, from a reformatory cell. They had
sent her there for corrupting a house-maid . . .'

She laughed again, while I marvelled. Then she leaned with
her napkin to wipe a splash of gravy from my cheek.

We had been served cutlets and sweetbreads, all very fine. I
ate steadily, as I had eaten at breakfast. Diana, however, did
more drinking than eating, and more smoking than drinking;
and more watching, even, than smoking. After the exchange
about the servants, we fell silent: I found that many of the
things I said produced a kind of twitching at her lips and brow,
as if my words – sensible enough to my ears – amused her; so
at last I said no more, and neither did she, until the only
sounds were the low hiss of the gas-jets, the steady ticking of
the clock upon the mantel, and the clink of my knife and fork
against my plate. I thought involuntarily of those merry dinners in the Green Street parlour, with Grace and Mrs Milne. I
thought of the supper I might be having with Florence, in the
Judd Street public. But then I finished my meal, and Diana
threw me one of her pink cigarettes; and when I had grown
giddy on that, she came to me and kissed me. And then I
remembered that it was hardly for table-talk that I had been
engaged.

That night our love-making was more leisurely than it had
been before – almost, indeed, tender. Yet she surprised me by
seizing my shoulder as I lay on the edge of sleep – my body
delightfully sated and my arms and legs entwined with hers –

and rousing me to wakefulness. The day had been a day of lessons for me; now came the last of all.

'You may go, Nancy,' she said, in exactly the tone I had heard her use on her maid and Mrs Hooper. 'I wish to sleep alone tonight.'

It was the first time she had spoken to me as a servant, and her words drove the lingering warmth of slumber quite from my limbs. Yet I took my leave, uncomplaining, and made my way to the pale room along the hall, where my own cold bed awaited. I liked her kisses, I liked her gifts still more; and if, to keep them, I must obey her – well, so be it. I was used to servicing gents in Soho at a pound a suck; obedience – to such a lady, and in such a setting – seemed at that moment a very trifling labour.

Chapter 12

⌒

For all the strangeness of those first few days and nights at Felicity Place, it did not take me long to settle into my role there and find myself a new routine. This was quite as indolent as the one I had enjoyed at Mrs Milne's; the difference, of course, was that here my indolence had a patron, a lady who paid to keep me well-fed, well-dressed and rested, and demanded only that my vanity should have herself, in return, as its larger target.

At Green Street I was used to waking rather early. Often Grace would bring me tea at half-past seven or so – often, indeed, she would clamber into the warm bed beside me, and we would lie and talk till Mrs Milne called us to breakfast; later I would wash, at the great sink in the downstairs kitchen, and Grace would sometimes come and comb my hair. At Felicity Place, I had nothing to rise for. Breakfast was brought to me, and I received it at Diana's side – or in my own bed, if she had sent me from her the night before. While she was dressing I would drink my coffee and smoke a cigarette, and yawn and rub my eyes; frequently I would fall into a thin kind of slumber, and only wake again when she returned, in a coat and a hat, to slip a gloved hand beneath the counterpane and rouse me with a pinch, or a lewd caress.

'Wake up, and kiss your mistress good-bye,' she'd say. 'I shan't be home till supper-time. You must amuse yourself until I return.'

Then I would frown, and grumble. 'Where are you going?'

'On a visit, to a friend.'

'Take me with you!'

'Not today.'

'I might sit in the brougham while you make your call . . .'

'I would rather you were here, for me to return to.'

'You are cruel!'

She would smile, then kiss me. And then she would go; and I would only sink, again, into stupidity.

When I rose at last, I would call for a bath. Diana's bathroom was a handsome one: I might spend an hour or more in there, soaking in the perfumed water, parting my hair, applying the Macassar, examining myself before the glass for marks of beauty or for blemishes. In my old life I had made do with soap, with cold-cream and lavender scent and the occasional swipe of spit-black. Now, from the crown of my head to the curve of my toe-nails, there was an unguent for every part of me – oil for my eyebrows and cream for my lashes; a jar of tooth-powder, a box of *blanc-de-perle*; polish for my finger-nails and a scarlet stick to redden my mouth; tweezers for drawing the hairs from my nipples, and a stone to take the hard flesh from my heels.

It was quite like dressing for the halls again – except that then, of course, I had had to change at the side of the stage, while the band switched tempo; now, I had entire days to prink in. For Diana was my only audience; and my hours, when out of her company, were a kind of blank. I could not talk to the servants – to strange Mrs Hooper, with her veiled and slithering glances; or to Blake, who flustered me by curtseying to me and calling me 'miss'; or to Cook, who sent me lunch and supper, but never showed her face out-side her kitchen. I might hear their voices, raised in mirth or dispute, if I paused at the green baize door that led to the basement; but I knew myself apart from them, and had my own tight beat to keep to: the bedrooms, and Diana's parlour, and the drawing-room and library. My mistress had said she wouldn't care to have me leave the house, unchaperoned – indeed, she had Mrs Hooper lock the great front door: I heard her turn the key each time she stepped to close it.

I did not much mind my lack of liberty; as I have said, the warmth, the luxury, the kissing and the sleep made me grow stupid, and lazier than ever. I might drift from room to room, soundless and thoughtless, pausing perhaps to gaze at the paintings on the walls; or at the quiet streets and gardens of St John's Wood; or at myself, in Diana's various looking-glasses. I was like a spectre – the ghost, I sometimes imagined, of a handsome youth, who had died in that house and still walked its corridors and chambers, searching, searching, for reminders of the life that he had lost there.

'What a scare you gave me, miss!' the maid might say, hand at her heart, after she had come upon me, lingering at a bend in the stair or in the shadows of some curtain or alcove; but when I smiled and asked what work had she to do there, or, did she know if the day were a fine or a dull one, she would only blush and look frightened: 'I'm sure, miss, I couldn't say.'

The climax of my day, the event to which my thoughts naturally tended, and which gave direction and meaning to the hours before it, was Diana's return. There was drama to be had in the choosing of the chamber, and the pose, in which I would arrange myself for her. She might find me smoking in the library, or dozing, with unfastened buttons, in her parlour; I would feign surprise at her entry, or let her rouse me if I pretended sleep. My pleasure at her appearance, however, was real enough. I at once lost that sense of ghostliness, that feeling of waiting in the wing, and grew warm and substantial again before the blaze of her attention. I would light her a cigarette, pour her a drink. If she was weary I would lead her to a chair and stroke her temples; if she was footsore – she wore high black boots, very tightly laced – I would bare her legs and rub the blood back into her toes. If she was amorous – as she frequently was – I would kiss her. She might have me caress her in the library or drawing-room, heedless of the servants who passed beyond the closed door, or who knocked and, at our breathy answering silence, retired unbidden. Or she might send orders that she was not to be disturbed, and lead me to her parlour, to the secret drawer that held the key that unlocked the rosewood trunk.

The opening of this still enthralled and excited me, though I had soon grown used to handling its contents. They were, perhaps, mild enough. There was, of course, the dildo that I have described (though *the device*, or *the instrument*, was what I learned, following Diana, to call it: I think the unnecessary euphemism, with its particular odour of the surgery or house of correction, appealed to her; only when really heated would she call the thing by its proper name – and even then she was as likely to ask for *Monsieur Dildo*, or simply *Monsieur*). Besides this there was an album of photographs of big-buttocked girls with hairless parts, bearing feathers; also a collection of erotic pamphlets and novels, all hymning the delights of what I would call tommistry but what they, like Diana, called *Sapphic Passion*. They were gross enough, I suppose, in their way; but I had never seen the like of them before, and would gaze at them, squirming, till Diana laughed. Then there were cords, and straps and switches – the kind of thing that might be found, I suppose, in a strict governess's closet, certainly nothing heavier. Lastly, there were more of Diana's rose-tipped cigarettes. They contained, as I guessed very early on, some fragrant French tobacco that was mixed with hashish; and they were, I thought, the pleasantest things of all, since, when used in combination with the other items, they rendered their interesting effects more interesting still.

I might be weary or stupid; I might be nauseous with drink;

I might be sore, at the hips, with the ache of my monthlies, but the opening of this box, as I have said, never ceased to stir me – I was like a dog twitching and slavering to hear his mistress call out *Bone!*

And every jerk, every slaver, made Diana more complacent.

'How vain I am, of my little hoard!' she would say, as we lay smoking in the soiled sheets of her bed. She might be clad in nothing but a corset and a pair of purple gloves; I would have the dildo about me, perhaps with a rope of pearls wound round it. She would reach to the foot of the bed, and run her hand across the gaping box, and laugh. 'Of all the gifts I've given you,' she said once, 'this is the finest, isn't it? Isn't it? Where in London would you find its like?'

'Nowhere!' I answered. 'You're the boldest bitch in the city!'

'I am!'

'You're the boldest bitch, with the cleverest quim. If fucking were a country – well, fuck me, you'd be its queen . . . !'

These were the words which, pricked on by my mistress, I used now – lewd words which shocked and stirred me even as I said them. I had never thought to use them with Kitty. I had not *fucked* her, we had not *frigged*; we had only ever kissed and trembled. It was not a *quim* or a *cunt* she had between her legs – indeed, in all our nights together, I don't believe we ever gave a name to it all . . .

Only let her see me *now*, I thought, as I lay beside Diana, making the necklace of pearls more secure about the dildo; and Diana herself would reach to stroke her box again, and then lean and stroke me.

'Only see what I'm mistress of!' she would say with a sigh. 'Only see – only see what I own!'

I would draw on the cigarette till the bed seemed to tilt; then I'd lie and laugh, while she clambered upon me. Once I let a fag fall on the silken counterpane, and smiled to see it smoulder as we fucked. Once I smoked so much I was sick. Diana rang for Blake and, when she came, cried: 'Look at my tart, Blake, resplendent even in her squalor! Did you ever see a

brute so handsome? Did you?' Blake said that she had not;
then dipped a cloth in water, and wiped my mouth.

It was Diana's vanity, at last, that broke the spell of my confinement. I had passed a month with her – had left the house only
to stroll about the garden, had set not so much as the toe of my
boot upon a London street in all that time – when she declared
one night at supper that I ought to be barbered. I looked up
from my plate, thinking she meant to take me into Soho for it; in
fact, she only rang for the servants: I had to sit in a chair with a
towel about me, while Blake held the comb and the housekeeper plied the scissors. 'Gently with her, gently!' called Diana,
looking on. Mrs Hooper came close to trim the hair above my
brow, and I felt her breath, quick and hot, upon my cheek.

But the hair-cut turned out to be only the prelude to something better. Next morning I woke in Diana's bed to find her
dressed, and gazing at me with her old enigmatic smile. She
said, 'You must get up. I have a treat for you today. Two treats,
indeed. The first is in your bedroom.'

'A treat?' I yawned; the word had lost its charge for me,
rather. 'What is it, Diana?'

'It's a suit.'

'What kind of suit?'

'A coming-out suit.'

'Coming-out . . . ?'

I went at once.

Now, since my very first trouser-wearing days at Mrs
Dendy's, I had sported a wonderful variety of gentlemen's
suits. From the plain to the pantomimic, from the military to
the effeminate, from the brown broad-cloth to the yellow vel-
veteen – as soldier, sailor, valet, renter, errand-boy, dandy and
comedy duke – I had worn them all, and worn them wisely
and rather well. But the costume that awaited me in my bedroom that day in Diana's villa in Felicity Place was the richest
and the loveliest I ever wore; and I can remember it still, in all
its marvellous parts.

There was a jacket and trousers of bone-coloured linen, and a waistcoat, slightly darker, with a silken back. These came wrapped together in a box lined with velvet; in a separate package I found three piqué shirts, each a shade lighter than the one before it, and each so fine and closely woven it shone like satin, or like the surface of a pearl.

Then there were collars, white as a new tooth; studs, of opal, and cuff-links of gold. There was a necktie and a cravat of an amber-coloured, watered silk: they gleamed and rippled as I drew them from their tissue, and slithered from my fingers to the floor like snakes. A flat wooden case held gloves – one pair of kid, with covered buttons, the other of doe-skin and fragrant as musk. In a velvet bag I found socks and drawers and under-shirts – not of flannel, as my linen had been till now, but of knitted silk. For my head there was a creamy Homburg with a trim that matched the neckties; for my feet there was a pair of shoes – a pair of shoes of a chestnut leather so warm and rich I felt compelled at once to apply my cheek to it, and then my lips; and finally, my tongue.

A last, flimsy package I almost overlooked: this held a set of handkerchiefs, each one as fine and fragile as the piqué shirts and each embroidered with a tiny, flowing N.K. The suit, in all its parts, with all its delicate, harmonising textures and hues, enchanted me; but this last detail, and the unmistakable stamp of permanence it conferred upon my relations with the passionate and generous mistress of my curious new home – well, this last detail satisfied me most of all.

I bathed then, and dressed before the glass; and then I threw back the window-shutters, lit a cigarette, and gazed upon myself as I stood smoking. I looked – I think I can say without vanity – a treat. The suit, like all expensive clothes, had a bearing and a lustre all of its own: it would have made more or less anyone look handsome. But Diana had ordered wisely. The bleached linen complemented the dull gold of my hair and the fading renter's tan at my cheek and wrists. The flash of amber at my throat set off my blue eyes and my darkened lashes. The trousers had a vertical crease, and made my legs seem longer and more slender than ever; and they bulged at the buttons, where I had rolled one of the scented doe-skin gloves. I was, I saw, almost unsettlingly attractive. Framed by the wooden surround of the mirror, my left leg slightly bent, one hand hanging loosely at my thigh and the other with its fag arrested halfway on its journey to my faintly carmined lips, I looked not like myself at all, but like some living picture, a blond lord or angel whom a jealous artist had captured and transfixed behind the glass. I felt quite awed.

There came a movement at the door. I turned, and found Diana there: she had been watching me as I gazed at myself – I had been too taken with my own good looks to notice her. In her hand she held a spray of flowers, and now she came to attach them to my coat. She said, 'It should be narcissi, I did not think of it': the flowers were violets. I bent my head to them as she worked at my lapel, and breathed their perfume; a single bloom, come loose from the stem, fluttered to the carpet and was crushed beneath her heel.

When she had finished at my breast she took my cigarette to smoke, and stepped back to survey her handiwork – just as Walter had done, so long ago, at Mrs Dendy's. It seemed my fate to be dressed and fashioned and admired by others. I didn't mind it. I only thought back to the blue serge suit of those innocent days, and gave a laugh.

The laugh brought a hardness to my eyes, that made them sparkle. Diana saw, and nodded complacently.

'We shall be a sensation,' she said. 'They will adore you, I know it.'

'Who?' I asked then. 'Who have you dressed me for?'

'I'm taking you out, to meet my friends. I'm taking you,' she put a hand to my cheek, 'to my club.'

The Cavendish Ladies' Club it was called; and it was situated in Sackville Street, just up from Piccadilly. I knew the road well, I knew all those roads; yet I had never noticed the

building – the slender, grey-faced building – to which Diana
now had Shilling drive us. Its step, I suppose, *is* rather shadowy, and its name-plate is small, and its door is narrow; having
visited it once, however, I never missed it again.

Go to Sackville Street today, if you like, and try to spot it:
you shall walk the length of the pavement, quite three or four
times. But when you find the grey-faced building, rest a
moment looking up at it; and if you see a lady cross its shadowy threshold, mark her well.

She will walk – as I walked with Diana that day – into a
lobby: the lobby is smart-looking, and in it sits a neat, plain,
ageless woman behind a desk. When I first went there, this
woman was named Miss Hawkins. She was ticking entries in
a ledger as we arrived, but looked up when she saw Diana, and
gave a smile. When she saw me, the smile grew smaller.

She said, 'Mrs Lethaby, ma'am, how pleasant! Mrs Jex is
expecting you in the day-room, I believe.' Diana nodded, and
reached to sign her name upon a sheet. Miss Hawkins glanced
again at me. 'Shall the gentleman be waiting for you here?' she
said.

Diana's pen moved smoothly on, and she did not raise her
eyes. She said: 'Don't be tiresome, Hawkins. This is Miss King,
my companion.' Miss Hawkins looked harder at me, then
blushed.

'Well, I'm sure, Mrs Lethaby, I can't speak for the ladies; but
some might consider this a little – irregular.'

'We are here,' answered Diana, screwing the pen together,
'for the sake of the irregular.' Then she turned and looked me
over, raising a hand to twitch at my necktie, licking the tip of
one glove-clad finger to smooth at my brow, and finally pluck-
ing the hat from my head and arranging my hair.

The hat she left for Miss Hawkins to deal with. Then she put
her arm securely through mine, and led me up a flight of stairs
into the day-room.

This room, like the lobby below it, is grand. I cannot say
what colour they have it now; in those days it was panelled in

golden damask, and its carpets were of cream, and its sofas
blue . . . It was decked, in short, in all the colours of my own
most handsome self – or, rather, I was decked to match it. This
idea, I must confess, was disconcerting; for a second, Diana's
generosity began to seem less of a compliment than I had
thought it, posed that morning before the glass.

But all performers dress to suit their stages, I recalled. And
what a stage was this – and what an audience!

There were about thirty of them, I think – all women; all
seated at tables, bearing drinks and books and papers. You
might have passed any one of them upon the street, and
thought nothing; but the effect of their appearance all combined was rather queer. They were dressed, not strangely, but
somehow distinctly. They wore skirts – but the kind of skirts a
tailor might design if he were set, for a dare, to sew a bustle for
a gent. Many seemed clad in walking-suits or riding-habits.
Many wore pince-nez, or carried monocles on ribbons. There
were one or two rather startling coiffures; and there were more
neckties than I had ever before seen brought together at an
exclusively female ensemble.

I did not notice all these details at once, of course; but the
room was a large one and, since Diana took her time to lead me
across it, I had leisure to gaze about me as she did so. We
walked through a hush that was thick as bristling velvet – for,
at our appearance at the door the lady members had turned
their heads to stare, and then had goggled. Whether, like Miss
Hawkins, they took me for a gentleman; or whether – like
Diana – they had seen through my disguise at once, I cannot
say. Either way, there was a cry – 'Good gracious!' – and then
another exclamation, more lingering: 'My *word* . . .' I felt Diana
stiffen at my side, with pure complacency.

Then came another shout, as a lady at a table in the farthest
corner rose to her feet. 'Diana, you old roué! You have done it
at last!' She gave a clap. Beside her, two more ladies looked on,
pink-faced. One of them had a monocle, and now she fixed it
to her eye.

Diana placed me before them all, and presented me – more graciously than she had introduced me to Miss Hawkins, but again as her 'companion'; and the ladies laughed. The first of them, the one who had risen to greet us, now seized my hand. Her fingers held a stubby cigar.

'This, Nancy dear,' said my mistress, 'is Mrs Jex. She is quite my oldest friend in London – and quite the most disreputable. Everything she tells you will be designed to corrupt.'

I bowed to her. I said, 'I hope so, indeed.' Mrs Jex gave a roar.

'But it speaks!' she cried. 'All this' – she gestured to my face, my costume – 'and the creature even speaks!'

Diana smiled, and raised a brow. 'After a fashion,' she said.

I blinked, but Mrs Jex still held my hand, and now she squeezed it. 'Diana is brutal to you, Miss Nancy, but you must not mind it. Here at the Cavendish we have been positively *panting* to see you and make you our particular friend. You must call me "Maria"' – she pronounced it the old-fashioned way – 'and this is Evelyn, and Dickie. Dickie, you can see, likes to think of herself as the boy of the place.'

I bowed to the ladies in turn. The former showed me a smile; the one named Dickie (this was the one with the monocle: I am sure it was of plain glass) only gave a toss to her head, and looked haughty.

'This is the new Callisto then, is it?' she said.

She wore a boiled shirt and a bow-tie, and her hair, though long and bound, was sleek with oil. She was about two- or three-and-thirty, and her waist was thick; but her upper lip, at least, was dark as a boy's. They would have called her terribly handsome, I guessed, in about 1880.

Maria pressed my fingers again, and rolled her eyes; then she tilted her head, and when I bent to her – for she was rather short – she said, 'Now, my dear, you must satisfy our appetite. We want the whole sordid story of your encounter with Diana. She herself will tell us nothing – only that the night was warm; that the streets were gaudy; that the moon was reeling through

the clouds like a drunken woman looking for lovers. Tell us,
Miss Nancy, tell us, do! *Was* the moon really reeling through
the clouds, like a drunken woman looking for her lovers?' She
took a puff of her cigar, and studied me. Evelyn and Dickie
leaned and waited. I looked from them back to Maria; and
then I swallowed.

'It was,' I said at last, 'if Diana said it was.'

And at that, Maria gave a startling laugh, low and loud and
rapid as the rattle of a road-drill; and Diana took my arm and
made a space for me upon the sofa, and called for a waitress to
bring us drinks.

At the rest of the tables the ladies still looked on – some of
them, I could not help but notice, rather fastidiously. There
had come some murmurs, and some whispers; also a titter or
two and a gasp. No one in our party paid the slightest heed to
any of it. Maria kept her eyes fixed upon myself, and when our
drinks arrived, she leered at me over her glass: 'To both ends of
the busk!' she said, and gave me a wink. Diana had her face
turned, to catch a story from the lady named Evelyn. She was
saying, 'Such a scandal, Diana, you never heard! She has
vowed herself to seven women, and sees them all on different
days; one of them is her sister-in-law! She has put together an
album – my dear, I nearly died at the sight of it! – full of bits
and pieces of stuff that she has *cut off* them or *pulled out of*
them: eyelashes, and toe-nail clippings – old sanitary wrappings, from what I could see of it; and she has hair—'

'*Hair*, Diana,' broke in Dickie meaningfully.

'Hair, which she has had made up into rings and aigrettes.
Lord Myers saw a brooch, and asked her where she bought it,
and Susan told him it was from the tail of a fox, and said she
would have one made for him, for his wife! Can you imagine?
Now Lady Myers is to be found at all the fashionable parties
with a sprig of Susan Dacre's sister-in-law's quim-hair at her
bosom!'

Diana smiled. 'And Susan's husband knows it all, and does
not mind it?'

'Mind it? It is he who pays her jewellers' bills! You may hear him boasting – I have heard him myself – of how he plans to rename the estate *New Lesbos*.'

'*New Lesbos!*' Diana said mildly. Then she yawned. 'With that tired old lesbian Susan Dacre in it, it might just as well be the original . . .' She turned to me, and her voice dropped a tone. 'Light me a cigarette, would you, child?'

I took two fags from the tortoise-shell case in my breast pocket, lit them both at my own lip, then passed one over. The ladies watched me – indeed, even while they laughed and chattered, they studied all my movements, all my parts. When I leaned to knock the ash from my cigarette, they blinked. When I ran a hand over the stubble at my hairline, they coloured. When I parted my trouser-clad legs and showed the bulge there, Maria and Evelyn, as one, gave a shift in their chairs; and Dickie reached for her brandy glass and disposed of its contents with one savage swig.

After a moment, Maria came close again. She said, 'Now, Miss Nancy, we are still waiting for your history. We want to know all about you, and so far you have done nothing but tease.'

I said, 'There's nothing to know. You must ask Diana.'

'Diana speaks for the sake of cleverness, not truth. Tell me now' – she had grown confiding – 'where were you born? Was it some hard place? Was it some *rookery*, where you must sleep ten to a bed with your sisters?'

'A *rookery*?' I thought very suddenly, and more vividly than I had in months, of our old front parlour at home – of the cloth with the fringe that dangled, fluttering, above the hearth. I said, 'I was born in Kent, in Whitstable.' Maria only stared. I said again, 'Whitstable – where the oysters come from.'

At that, she threw back her head. 'Why my dear, you're a mermaid! Diana, did you know it? A Whitstable mermaid! Though thankfully,' and here she placed her free hand upon my knee, and patted it, 'thankfully, without the tail. That would never do, now, would it?'

I could not answer. Hot into my head after the image of our parlour had come the memory of Kitty, at her dressing-room door. *Miss Mermaid*, she had called me; and she had said it again that time in Stamford Hill, when she had heard me weeping, come, and kissed my tears . . .

I gave a gulp, and put my cigarette to my lips. It was smoked right down and almost burned me; and as I fumbled with it, it fell. It struck the sofa, bounced, then rolled between my legs. I reached for it – that made the ladies stare again, and twitch – but it was caught, still smouldering, between my buttock and the chair. I leapt up, found the fag at last, then pulled at the linen that covered my bum. I said, 'Hell, if I haven't scorched a hole through these dam' trousers!'

The words came out louder than I meant them to; and as they did, there was an answering cry from the room at my back: 'Really, Mrs Lethaby, this is intolerable!' A lady had risen, and was approaching our table.

'I must protest, Mrs Lethaby,' she said when she arrived at it. 'I really must protest, on behalf of all the ladies present, and absent, at the very great damage you are inflicting upon our club!'

Diana raised languid eyes to her. 'Damage, Miss Bruce? Are you referring to the presence of my companion, Miss King?'

'I am, ma'am.'

'You don't care for her?'

'I don't care for her language, ma'am, or for her clothes!' She herself wore a silk shirt with a cummerbund and a cravat; in the cravat there was a pin, cast in silver, of the head of a horse. Now she stood expectantly at Diana's side; and after a moment, Diana sighed.

'Well,' she said. 'I see we must bow to the members' pleasure.' She rose, then drew me up beside her and leaned rather ostentatiously upon my arm. 'Nancy, dear, your costume has proved too bold for the Cavendish after all. It seems that I must take you home and rid you of it. Now, who will ride with us to Felicity Place, to catch the sport . . .'

There was a ripple around the room. Maria rose at once, and reached for her walking-cane. 'Tantivy, tantivy!' she cried. Then: 'Ho, Satin!' I heard a yelp, and from beneath her chair there came – what I had not seen before, as it lay dozing behind the curtain of her skirts – a handsome little whippet, on a pig-skin leash.

Dickie and Evelyn rose too, then. Diana inclined her head to Miss Bruce, and I made her a deeper bow. All eyes had been upon us as we made our entrance; all eyes were on us still, as we headed for the exit. I heard Miss Bruce return to her seat, and someone call, 'Quite *right*, Vanessa!' But another lady held my gaze as I passed her, and winked; and from a table near the door a woman rose to say to Diana that she hoped that Miss King's trousers had not been too desperately *singed* . . .

The trousers were rather spoiled; back at Felicity Place, Diana had me walk and bend before Maria and Evelyn and Dickie, in order to decide it. She said she would order me another pair, just the same.

'What a find, Diana!' said Maria, as Evelyn patted the cloth. She said it as she might say it about a statue or a clock that Diana had picked up for a song in some grim market. She didn't care whether I overheard or not. Why should it matter that I did? She meant it, she meant it! There was admiration in her eyes. And being admired, by tasteful ladies – well, I knew it wasn't being loved. But it was something. And I was good at it.

Who would ever have thought I should be so good at it!

'Take off your shirt, Nancy,' said Diana then, 'and let the ladies see your linen.'

I did so, and Maria cried again, 'What a find!'

Chapter 13

Diana's wider circle of friends, I believe, thought our union a fantastic one. I would sometimes see them look between us, then overhear their murmurs – 'Diana's *caprice*,' they called me, as if I were an enthusiasm for a wonderful food, that a sensitive palate would tire of. Diana herself, however, once having found me, seemed only increasingly disinclined to let me go. With that one brief visit to the Cavendish Club she had launched me on my new career as her permanent companion. Now came more excursions, more visits, more trips; and more suits for me to make them in. I grew complacent. I had once sat drooping on her parlour chair, expecting her to send me home with a sovereign. Now, when the ladies whispered of 'this *freak* of Diana Lethaby's', I brushed the lint from the sleeve of my coat, drew my monogrammed hankie from my pocket, and smiled. When the autumn of 1892 became the winter, and then the spring of '93, and still I kept my favoured place at Diana's side, the ladies' whispers faded. I became at last not Diana's caprice; but simply, her *boy*.

'Come to supper, Diana.'

'Come for breakfast, Diana.'

'Come at nine, Diana; and bring the boy.'

For it was always as a boy that I travelled with her now,

even when we ventured into the public world, the ordinary world beyond the circle of Cavendish Sapphists, the world of shops and supper-rooms and drives in the park. To anyone who asked after me, she would boldly introduce me as 'My ward, Neville King'; she had several requests for introductions, I believe, from ladies with eligible daughters. These she turned aside: 'He's an Anglo-Catholic, ma'am,' she'd whisper, 'and destined for the Church. This is his final Season, before taking Holy Orders . . .'

It was with Diana that I returned to the theatre again – flinching to find her lead me to a box beside the foot-lights, flinching again as the chandeliers were dimmed. But they were terribly grand, the theatres she preferred. They were lit with electricity rather than gas; and the crowd sat hushed. I could not see the pleasure in it. The plays I liked well enough; but I would more often turn my gaze to the audience – and there was always plenty of eyes and glasses, of course, that were lifted from the stage and fastened on me. I saw several faces that I knew from my old renter days. One time I stood washing my hands in the lavatory of a theatre and felt a gent look me over – he didn't know that he had had my lips on him already, in an alley off Jermyn Street; later I saw him in the audience, with his wife. One time, too, I saw Sweet Alice, the maryanne who had been so kind to me in Leicester Square. He also sat in a box; and when he recognised me, he blew a kiss. He was with two gents: I raised my brows, he rolled his eyes. Then he saw who it was I sat with – it was Diana and Maria – and he stared. I gave a shrug, he looked thoughtful – then rolled his eyes again, as much as to say, *What a business!*

To all these places, as I have said, I went clad as a boy – indeed, the only time I ever dressed as a girl, now, was for our visits to the Cavendish. This was the single spot in the city at which Diana might have put me in trousers and not cared who knew it; but after Miss Bruce's complaint they introduced a new rule, and ever after I was taken there in skirts – Diana having something made up for me, I forget the cut and colour of it now. At the club I would sit and drink and smoke, and be flirted with by Maria, and eyed by other ladies, while Diana met friends or wrote letters. She did this very often, for she was known – I suppose I might have guessed it, in a way – as a philanthropist, and ladies courted her for schemes. She gave money to certain charities. She sent books to girls in prisons. She was involved in the producing of a magazine for the Suffrage, named *Shafts*. She attended to all this, with me at her side. If I leaned to pick up a paper or a list and idly read it, she would take the sheet away, as if gazing too hard at too many words might tire me. In the end, I would settle on the cartoons in *Punch*.

These, then, were my public appearances. There were not too many of them – I am describing here a period that lasted about a year. Diana kept me close, for the most part, and displayed me at home. She liked to limit the numbers who gazed at me, she said; she said she feared that like a photograph I might fade, from too much handling.

When I say *display*, of course, I mean it: it was part of Diana's mystery, to make real the words that other people said in metaphor or jest. I had posed for Maria and Dickie and Evelyn in my trousers with the scorch-mark and my underthings of silk. When they came a second time, with another lady, Diana had me pose for them again in a different suit. After that, it became a kind of sport with her, to put me in a new costume and have me walk before her guests, or among them, filling glasses, lighting cigarettes. Once she dressed me as a footman, in breeches and a powdered wig. It was the costume I had worn for *Cinderella*, more or less – though my breeches at the Brit had not been so snug, nor so large at the groin.

The freak with the breeches inspired her further. She grew tired of gentlemen's suits; she took to displaying me in masquerade – had me set up, behind a little velvet curtain in the drawing-room. This would happen about once a week. Ladies would come for dinner and I would eat with them, in trousers; but while they lingered over their coffee and the trimming of their fags I would leave them, and slip up to my room to change my gear. By the time they made their way into the drawing-room I would be behind the curtain, striking some pose; and when she was ready, Diana would pull a tasselled cord and uncover me.

I might be Perseus, with a curved sword and a head of the Medusa, and sandals with straps that were buckled at the knee. I might be Cupid, with wings and a bow. I was once St Sebastian, tied to a stump – I remember what a job it was to fasten the arrows so they would not droop.

Then, another night I was an Amazon. I carried the Cupid's bow, but this time had one breast uncovered; Diana rouged the nipple. Next week – she said I had shown one, I might as well show both – I was the French Marianne, with a Phrygian cap and a flag. The week after that I was Salome: I had the Medusa head again, but on a plate, and with a beard stuck on it; and while the ladies clapped I danced down to my drawers.

And the week after that – well, that week I was Hermaphroditus. I wore a crown of laurel, a layer of silver grease-paint – and nothing else save, strapped to my hips, Diana's *Monsieur Dildo*. The ladies gasped to see him.

That made him quiver.

And as the quiver did its usual work on me, I thought of Kitty. I wondered if she was still wearing suits and a topper, still singing songs like 'Sweethearts and Wives'.

Then Diana came, and put a pink cigarette between my lips, and led me amongst the ladies and had them stroke the leather. I cannot say if it was Kitty I thought of then, or even Diana herself. I believe I thought I was a renter again, in Piccadilly – or, not a renter, but a renter's gent. For when I twitched and cried out there were smiles in the shadows; and when I shuddered, and wept, there was laughter.

I could help none of it. It was all Diana's doing. She was so bold, she was so passionate, she was so devilishly clever. She was like a queen, with her own queer court – I saw it, at those parties. Women sought her out, and watched her. They brought presents, 'for your collection' – her collection was talked about, and envied! When she made a gesture, they raised their heads to catch it. When she spoke, they listened. It was her voice, I think, which snared them – those low, musical tones, which had once lured me from my random midnight wanderings into the heart of her own dark world. Again and again I heard arguments crumble at a cry or a murmur from Diana's throat; again and again the scattered conversations of a crowded room would falter and die, as one speaker after another surrendered the slender threads of some anecdote or fancy to catch at the more compelling cadences of hers.

Her boldness was contagious. Women came to her, and grew giddy. She was like a singer, shivering glasses. She was like a cancer, she was like a mould. She was like the hero of one of her own gross romances – you might set her in a chamber with a governess and a nun, and in an hour they would have torn out their own hair, to fashion a whip.

I sound weary of her. I was not weary of her then. How could I have been? We were a perfect kind of double act. She was lewd, she was daring – but who made that daring visible? Who could testify to the passion of her; to the sympathetic power of her; to the rare, enchanted atmosphere of her house in Felicity Place, where ordinary ways and rules seemed all suspended, and wanton riot reigned? Who, but I?

I was proof of all her pleasures. I was the stain left by her lust. She must keep me, or lose everything.

And I must keep her, or have nothing. I could not imagine a life beyond her shaping. She had awakened particular appetites in me; and where else, I thought, but with Diana, in the company of Sapphists – where else would those queer hungers be assuaged?

I have spoken of the peculiarly *timeless* quality of my new life, of my removal from the ordinary workings of the hours, the days and the weeks. Diana and I often made love until dawn, and ate breakfast at nightfall; or else, we woke at the regular time, but stayed abed with the drapes close-drawn, and took our lunch by candle-light. Once we rang for Blake, and she came in her night-gown: it was half-past three, we had woken her from her bed. Another time I was roused by bird-song: I squinted at the lines of light around the shutters, and realised I had not seen the sun for a week. In a house kept uniformly warm by the labour of servants, and with a carriage to collect us and deposit us where we wished, even the seasons lost their meanings or gained new ones. I knew winter had arrived only when Diana's walking-dresses changed from silk to corduroy, her cloaks from grenadine to sable; and when my own closet rail sagged with astrakhan, and camel's-hair, and tweed.

But there was one anniversary from the old order of things that, even in the enchanted atmosphere of Felicity Place, surrounded by so much narcotic luxury, I could not quite forget. One day, when I had been Diana's lover for a little less than a year, I was woken by the rustle of news-sheet. My mistress was beside me with the morning paper, and I opened my eyes upon a headline. *Home Rule Bill*, it said; *Irish to Demonstrate June 3rd*. I gave a cry. It was not the words which arrested me – they meant nothing to me. The date, however, was as familiar as my own name. June the third was my birthday; in a week I should be twenty-three.

'Twenty-three!' said Diana when I told her, in a kind of delight. 'What a really glorious age that is! With your youth still hot upon you, like a lover in a pant; and time with his face around the curtain, peeping on.' She could talk like this, even first thing in the morning; I only yawned. But then she said that we must celebrate – and at that, I looked livelier. 'What shall we do,' she said, 'that we haven't done before? Where shall I take you . . . ?'

Where she hit upon, in the end, was the Opera.

The idea sounded a terrible one to me, though I did not like to show it – I had not yet grown sulky with her, as I was later to do. And I was still too much of a child to be anything other than enchanted with my own birthday, when it finally arrived; and of course, there were presents – and presents never lost their charm.

I was given them at breakfast, in two gold parcels. The first was large, and held a cloak – a proper opera-going cloak, it was, and very grand; but then, I had expected that, and hardly considered it a gift at all. The second parcel, however, proved more marvellous. It was small and light: I knew at once it must be some piece of jewellery – perhaps, a pair of links; or a stud for my cravats; or a ring. Dickie wore a ring on the smallest finger of her left hand, and I had often admired it – yes, I was sure it must be a ring, like Dickie's.

But it was not a ring. It was a watch, of silver, on a slender strap of leather. It had two dark arms to show the minutes and the hours, and a faster, sweeping arm to count the seconds. Upon the face, there was glass: the arms were moved by the winder. I turned it in my hands, Diana smiling as I did so. 'It's for your wrist,' she said at last.

I gazed at her in wonder – people never wore wrist-watches then, it was marvellously exotic and new – then tried to buckle the watch upon my arm. I could not manage it, of course: like so many of the things in Felicity Place, you really needed a maid to do it properly. In the end, Diana fastened it for me; and then we both sat gazing at the little face, the sweeping hand, and listened to the ticking.

I said, 'Diana, it's the most wonderful thing I ever saw!', and she pinked, and looked pleased: she was a bitch, but she was human, too.

Later, when Maria came to call, I showed her the watch and she nodded and smiled at it, stroking my wrist beneath the leather of the strap. Then she laughed. 'My dear, the time is wrong! You have it set at seven, and it's only a quarter-past four!'

I looked at the face again, and gave a frown of surprise. I had been wearing it as a kind of bracelet, only: it had not occurred to me to tell the time with it. Now I moved the arms to *4* and *3*, for Maria's sake – but there was really no need, of course, for me ever to wind it at all.

The watch was my finest gift; but there was a present, too, from Maria herself: a walking-cane, of ebony, with a tassel at the top and a silver tip. It went very well with my new opera gear; indeed, we made a very striking couple that night, Diana and I, for her costume was of black and white and silver, to match my own. It came from Worth's: I thought we must look just as if we had stepped out from the pages of a fashion paper. I made sure, when walking, to hold my left arm very straight, so the watch would show.

We dined in a room at the Solferino. We dined with Dickie and Maria – Maria brought Satin, her whippet, and fed him dainties from a plate. The waiters had been told it was my birthday, and fussed around me, offering wine. 'How old is the young gentleman today?' they asked Diana; and the way they asked it showed they thought me younger than I was. They might, I suppose, have taken Diana for my mother; for various reasons, the idea was not a nice one. Once, though, I had stopped at a shoe-black while Diana and her friends stood near to watch it, and the man – catching sight of Dickie and reading tommishness, as many regular people do, as a kind of family likeness – asked me if she, Dickie, were not my Auntie, taking me out for the day; and it had been worth being mistaken for a schoolboy, for the sake of her expression. She once or twice tried to compete with me, on the question of suits. The night of my birthday, for example, she wore a shirt with cuff-links and, above her skirt, a short gent's cloak. At her throat, however, she had a jabot – I should never have worn anything so effeminate. She did not know it – she would have been horrified to know it! – but she looked like nothing so much as a weary old mary-anne – one of the kind you see sometimes holding court, with younger boys, on Piccadilly: they have rented so long they're known as *queens*.

Our supper was a very fine one, and when it was over Diana sent a waiter for a cab. As I have said, I had thought her plan not much of a treat; but even I could not help being excited as our hansom joined the line of rocking carriages at the door of the Royal Opera, and we – Diana, Maria, Dickie and I – entered the crush of gentlemen and ladies in the lobby. I had never been here before; had never, in a year of fitful chaperoning, been part of such a rich and handsome crowd – the gents, like me, all in cloaks and silk hats and carrying glasses; the ladies in diamonds, and wearing gloves so high and slender they might all have just left off dipping their arms, to the armpit, in tubs of milk.

We stood jostling in the lobby for a moment or two, Diana exchanging nods with certain ladies that she recognised, Maria holding Satin at her bosom, out of the crush of heels and trains and sweeping cloaks. Dickie said she would fetch us a tray of drinks, and went off to do so. Diana said, 'Take our coats, Neville, will you?' nodding to a counter where two men stood, in uniform, receiving cloaks. She turned to let me draw the coat from her, Maria did the same, and I picked my way across the lobby with them, then paused to unfasten my own cloak – thinking all the time, only, what a handsome gathering it was, and how well I looked in it! and making sure that the coats I carried weren't falling over my wrist and obscuring the watch. The counter had a queue at it, and as I waited I looked idly at the men whose job it was to collect the cloaks from the gents, and give them tickets. One of them was slim, with a sallow face – he might have been Italian. The other man was a black man. When I reached the desk at last and he tilted his face to the garments I gave him, I saw that he was Billy-Boy, my old smoking-partner from the Brit.

At first, I only stared; I think, actually, that I was considering how I might best make my escape before he saw me. But then, when he tugged at the coats and I failed to release them, he raised his eyes – and I knew that he didn't recognise me at all, only wondered why I hesitated; and the thought made me terribly sorry. I said, 'Bill', and he looked harder. Then he said: 'Sir?'

I swallowed. I said again, 'Bill. Don't you remember me?' Then I leaned and lowered my voice. 'It's Nan,' I said, 'Nan King.' His face changed. He said, 'My God!'

Behind me, the queue had grown longer; now there came a cry: 'What's the delay there?' Bill took the coats from me at last, walked quickly to a hook with them, and gave me a ticket. Then he stepped a little to one side, leaving his friend to struggle with the cloaks, for a minute, on his own. I moved too, away from the jostling gents, and we stood facing each other across the desk, shaking our heads. His brow was shiny with sweat. His uniform was a white bum-shaver jacket and a cheap bow-tie, of scarlet.

He said, 'Lord, Nan, but you gave me a fright! I thought you must be some gentleman I owed money to.' He looked at my trousers, my jacket, my hair. 'What are you up to, wandering about like that, *here*?' He wiped his brow, then looked about him. 'Are you here with an agent? You're not in the *show*, Nan – are you?'

I shook my head; and then I said, very quietly, 'You mustn't say "Nan" now, Bill. The fact is—' The fact was, I hadn't thought what I would tell him. I hesitated; but it was impossible to lie to him: 'Bill, I'm living as a boy just now.'

'As a *boy*?' He said it loudly; then put a hand before his mouth. Even so, one or two of the grumbling gents in the queue turned their heads. I edged a little further away from them. I said again: 'I'm living as a boy, with a lady who takes care of me . . .' And at that, at last, he looked a little more knowing, and nodded.

Behind him, the Italian dropped a gentleman's hat, and the gentleman tutted. Bill said, 'Can you wait?' and stepped to help his friend by taking another couple of cloaks. Then he moved towards me again. The Italian looked sour.

I glanced over to Diana and Maria. The lobby had emptied a bit; they stood waiting for me. Maria had placed Satin on the floor and he was scratching at her skirt. Diana turned to catch my eye. I looked at Bill.

'How *are* you, then?' I asked him.

He looked rueful, and lifted his hand: there was a wedding-ring on it. He said, 'Well, I am married now, for a start!'

'Married! Oh, Bill, I am happy for you! Who's the girl? It's not Flora? Not Flora, our old dresser?' He nodded, and said it was.

'It is on account of Flora,' he added, 'that I am working here. She has a job on round the corner, a month at the Old Mo. She is still, you know' – he looked suddenly rather awk-ward – 'she is still, you know, dressing Kitty . . .'

I stared at him. There came more mutters from the queue of gents, and more sour looks from the Italian, and he stepped back again to help with the cloaks and hats and tickets. I lifted a hand to my head, and put my fingers through my hair, and tried to understand what he had told me. He was married to Flora, and Flora was still with Kitty; and Kitty had a spot at the Middlesex Music Hall. And that was about three streets away from where I stood now.

And Kitty, of course, was married to Walter.

Are they happy? I wanted to call to Bill then. *Does she talk of me, ever? Does she think of me? Does she miss me?* But when he returned – looking even more flustered and damp about the brow – I said only, 'How's – how's the act, Bill?'

'The act?' He sniffed. 'Not so good, *I* don't think. Not so good as the old days . . .'

We gazed at one another. I looked harder at his face, and saw that he had gained a bit of weight beneath his chin, and that the flesh about his eyes was rather darker than I knew it. Then the Italian called, 'Bill, will you come?' And Bill said that he must go.

I nodded, and held my hand out to him. As he shook it, he seemed to hesitate again. Then he said, very quickly, 'You know, we was all really sorry, when you took off like that, from the Brit.' I shrugged. 'And Kitty,' he went on, 'well, Kitty was sorriest of all of us. She put notices, with Walter, in the *Era* and the *Ref*, week after week. Did you never see 'em, Nan, those notices?'

'No, Bill, I never did.'

He shook his head. 'And now, here you are, dressed up like a lord!' But he gave my suit a dubious glance, and added: 'You're sure, though, are you, that you're doing all right?'

I didn't answer him. I only looked over to Diana again. She was tilting her head to gaze after me; beside her stood Maria, and Satin, and Dickie. Dickie held our tray of drinks, and had placed her monocle at her eye. She said, 'The wine will warm, Diana,' in a pettish sort of voice: the lobby was thinned of people, I could hear her very clearly.

Diana tilted her head again: 'What *is* the boy doing?'

'He is talking to the nigger,' answered Maria, 'at the cloaks!'

I felt my cheeks flame red, and looked quickly back at Bill. His gaze had followed mine, but now had been caught by a gentleman offering a coat, and he was lifting the garment over the counter, and already turning with it to the row of hooks.

'Good-bye, Bill,' I said, and he nodded over his shoulder, and gave me a sad little smile of farewell. I took a step away – but then, very quickly, I returned to the counter and put my hand upon his arm. I said: 'What's Kitty's place, on the bill at the Mo?'

'Her place?' He thought about it, folding another cloak. 'I'm not sure. Second half, near the start, half-past nine or so . . .'

Then Maria's voice came calling: 'Is there trouble, Neville, over the tip?'

I knew then that if I lingered near him any longer some terrible sort of scene would ensue. I didn't look at him again but went back to Diana at once, and said it was nothing, I was sorry. But when she raised a hand to smooth back the hair I had unsettled, I flinched, feeling Bill's eyes upon me; and when she pulled my arm through hers, and Maria stepped around me to take my other arm, the flesh upon my back seemed to give a kind of shudder, as if there was a pistol pointed at it.

The hall itself, which was so grand and glorious, I only gazed at rather dully. We did not have a box – there had not been time to book a box – but our seats were very good ones, in the centre of one of the front rows of the stalls. I had made us late, however, and the stalls were almost full: we had to stumble over twenty pairs of legs to reach our seats. Dickie spilled her wine. Satin snapped at a lady with a fox-fur around her throat. Diana, when she sat at last, was thin-lipped and self-conscious: this was not the kind of entrance she had planned for us, at all.

And I sat, numb to her, numb to all of it. I could think only of Kitty. That she was still in the halls, in her act with Walter. That Bill saw her daily – would see her later, after the show, when he fetched Flora. That even now, while the actors in the opera we had come to see were putting on their grease-paint, she was sitting in a dressing-room three streets away, putting on hers.

As I thought all this, the conductor appeared, and was clapped; the lights went down, and the crowd grew silent. When the music started and the curtain went up at last, I gazed at the stage in a kind of stupor. And when the singing began, I flinched. The opera was *Figaro's Wedding*.

I can remember hardly any of it. I thought only of Kitty. My seat seemed impossibly narrow and hard, and I shifted and turned in it, till Diana leaned to whisper that I must be still. I thought of all the times I had walked through the city, fearful of turning a corner and seeing Kitty there; I thought of the disguise I had adopted, to avoid her. Indeed, avoiding Kitty had become, in my renter days, a kind of second nature to me, so that there were whole areas of London through which I automatically never passed, streets at which I didn't have to pause, for thought, before I turned away to find another. I was like a man with a bruise or a broken limb, who learns to walk in a crowd so that the wound might not be jostled. Now, knowing that Kitty was so near, it was as if I was compelled to press the bruise, to twist the shrieking limb, myself. The music grew louder, and my head began to ache; my seat seemed narrower than ever. I looked at my watch, but the lights were too low for me to read it; I had to tilt it so that its face caught the glow from the stage, and in doing so, my elbow caught Diana and made her sigh with pique, and glare at me. The watch showed five to nine – how glad I was that I had wound it, now! The opera was just at that ridiculous point where the countess and the maid have forced the principal boy into a frock and locked him in a closet, and the singing and the rushing about is at its worst. I turned to Diana. I said, 'Diana, I can't bear it. I shall have to wait for you in the lobby.' She put a hand out to grip my arm, but I shook her away, and rose and – saying 'Pardon me, oh! pardon me!' to every tutting lady and gent whose legs I stumbled over or feet I trampled – I made my halting way along the row, towards the usher and the door.

Outside, the lobby was wonderfully quiet after all the shrieking on the stage. At the coat-desk the Italian man sat with a paper. When I went over to him, he sniffed: 'He ain't here,' he said, when I asked after Bill. 'He don't stay once the show starts. Did you want your cloak?'

I said I didn't. I left the theatre, and headed for Drury Lane – very conscious of my suit, and the shine on my shoes, and the flower at my lapel. When I reached the Middlesex I found a group of boys outside it studying the programme and commenting on the acts. I went and peered over their shoulders, looking for the names I wanted, and a number.

Walter Waters and Kitty, I saw at last: it gave me a shock to know that Kitty had lost her *Butler*, and was working under Walter's old stage-name. They were, as Bill had said, placed near the start of the second half – fourteenth on the list, after a singer and a Chinese conjuror.

In the booth inside sat a girl in a violet dress. I went to her window, then nodded to the hall. 'Who's on stage?' I asked.

'What number are they at?' She looked up; and when she saw my suit, she tittered.

'You've lost your way, dearie,' she said. 'You want the Opera, round the corner.' I bit my lip, and said nothing, and her smile faded. 'All right, Lord Alfred,' she said then. 'It's number twelve, Belle Baxter, Cockney Chanteuse.'

I bought a sixpenny ticket – she pulled a face at that, of course: 'Thought we should have the red carpet brung up, at the least.' The truth was, I dared not venture too close to the stage. I imagined Billy-Boy having come to the theatre and told Kitty that he had met me, and how I was dressed. I remembered how near the crowd could seem, from a stage in a small hall, when you stepped out of the limes; and in my coat and my bow-tie, of course, I would be conspicuous. How terrible it would be, to have Kitty see me as I watched her – to have her fix her eyes on mine, as she sang to Walter!

So I went up to the gallery. The stairs were narrow: when I turned a corner and found a couple there, spooning, I had to step around them, very close. Like the girl in the booth, they gazed at my suit and, as she had done, they tittered. I could hear the thumping of the orchestra through the wall. As I climbed to the door at the top of the staircase and the thumps grew louder, my own heart seemed to beat against my breast, in time to them. When I passed into the hall at last – into the lurid half-light, and the heat and the smoke and the reek of the calling crowd – I almost staggered.

On the stage was a girl in a flame-coloured frock, twitching her skirts so her stockings showed. She finished one song while I stood there, clutching at a pillar to steady myself; and then she started on another. The crowd seemed to know it. There were claps, and whistles; and before these had quite died down, I made my way along the aisle to an empty seat. It turned out to be at the end of a line of boys – a bad choice, for, of course, when they saw me there in my opera suit and my flower, they nudged each other, and sniggered. One coughed into his hand – only the cough came out as *Toff!* I turned my

face from them, and looked hard at the stage. Then, after a
moment, I took out a cigarette and lit it. As I struck the match,
my hand trembled.

The Cockney Chanteuse finished her set at last. There were
cheers, then a brief delay, marked by shouts and shuffling and
rustling, before the orchestra struck up with its introduction
for the next act – a tinkling, Chinese melody, which made a
boy in the line along from me stand up, and call out, 'Ninky-
poo!' Then the curtain rose on a magician and a girl, and a
black japanned cabinet – a cabinet not unlike the one that sat
in Diana's bedroom. When the magician snapped his fingers,
there was a flash, and a crack, and a puff of purple smoke; and
at that the boys put their fingers to their lips, and whistled.

I had seen – or felt as if I had seen – a thousand such acts;
and I watched this one now, with my cigarette gripped hard
between my lips, growing steadily more sick and more uncertain. I remembered sitting in my box at the Canterbury Palace,
with my fluttering heart and my gloves with the bows: it
seemed a time immeasurably distant and quaint. But, as I had
used to do then, I clutched the sticky velvet of my seat, and
gazed at where, with a hint of drooping rope and dusty floor-
board, the stage gave way to the wings, and I thought of Kitty.
She was there, somewhere, just beyond the edge of the curtain,
perhaps straightening her costume – whatever that was; perhaps chatting with Walter or Flora; perhaps staring, as
Billy-Boy told her of me – perhaps smiling, perhaps weeping,
perhaps saying only, mildly, 'Fancy that!' – and then forgetting
me . . .

I thought all this, and the magician performed his final trick.
There was another flash, and more smoke: the smoke drifted as
far as the gallery, and left the entire crowd coughing, but cheering through their coughs. The curtain fell, there was another
delay while the number was changed, and then a quiver of
blue, white and amber, as the limes-man changed the filter
across his beam. I had finished my cigarette, and now reached
for another. This time, the boys in my row all saw me do it, so

I held the case to them, and they each took a fag: 'Very generous.' I thought of Diana. Suppose the opera had ended, and she
was waiting for me, cursing, beating her programme against
her thigh?

Suppose she went back to Felicity Place without me?

But then there came music, and the creak of the curtain. I
looked at the stage – and Walter was on it.

He seemed very large – much larger than I remembered.
Perhaps he had grown fatter; perhaps his costume was a little
padded. His whiskers he had teased with a comb, to make
them stand out rather comically. He wore tartan peg-top
trousers and a green velvet jacket; and on his head was a smok-
ing-cap, in his pocket a pipe. Behind him, there was a cloth
with a scene on it representing a parlour. Beside him was an
armchair that he leaned on as he sang. He was quite alone. I
had never seen him in costume and paint before. He was so
unlike the figure I still saw, sometimes, in my dreams – the
figure with the flapping shirt, the dampened beard, the hand
on Kitty – that I looked at him, and frowned: my heart had
barely twitched, to see him standing there.

His voice was a mild baritone, and not at all unpleasant;
there had been a burst of applause at his first appearance, and
there was another round of satisfied clapping now, and one or
two cheers. His song, however, was a strange one: he sang of a
son that he had lost, named 'Little Jacky'. There were a number
of verses, each of them ending on the same refrain – it might
have been, 'Where, oh where, is Little Jacky now?' I thought it
queer he should be there, singing such a song, alone. Where
was Kitty? I drew hard on my cigarette. I couldn't imagine
how she would fit into this routine, in a silk hat, a bow-tie and
a flower . . .

Suddenly a horrible idea began to form itself in my mind.
Walter had taken a handkerchief from his pocket, and was
dabbing at his eye with it. His voice rose on the predictable
chorus, and was joined by not a few from the hall: 'But
where, oh *where*, is Little Jacky now?' I shifted in my seat. I

thought, Let it not be that! Oh please, oh please, let the act not be that!

But it was. As Walter called his plaintive question, there was a piping from the wing: 'Here's your Little Jacky, Father! Here!' A figure ran on to the stage, and seized his hand and kissed it. It was Kitty. She was dressed in a boy's sailor-suit – a baggy white blouse with a blue sash, white knickerbockers, stockings, and flat brown shoes; and she had a straw hat slung over her back, on a ribbon. Her hair was rather longer, and had been combed into a curl. Now the band struck up another tune, and she joined her voice with Walter's in a duet.

The crowd clapped her, and smiled. She skipped, and Walter bent and wagged a finger at her, and they laughed. They liked this turn. They liked seeing Kitty – my lovely, saucy, swaggering Kitty – play the child, with her husband, in stockings to the knee. They could not see me, as I blushed and squirmed; they would not have known why I did it, if they had. I hardly knew it, myself; I only felt myself smart with a terrible shame. I could not have felt worse if they had booed her, or pelted her with eggs. But they liked her!

I looked at her a little harder. Then I remembered my opera glasses, and pulled them from my pocket and lifted them to my eyes, and saw her close before me, as close as in a dream. Her hair, though longer, was still nut-brown. Her lashes were still long, she was still as slender as a willow. She had painted out her own lovely freckles and replaced them with a few comical smudges; but I – who had traced the pattern of them, so often, with my fingers – I thought I could catch the shape of them beneath the powder. Her lips were still full lips, and they gleamed as she sang. She lifted her mouth and placed a kiss, between the verses, on Walter's whiskers . . .

At that, I let the glasses drop. I saw the boys in the row looking enviously at them, so passed them along the line – I think they got thrown, in the end, to a girl at the balcony. When I looked at the stage again, Kitty and Walter seemed very small. He had lowered himself into the chair, and had drawn Kitty down to sit upon his knee; she had her hands clasped at her breast, and her feet, in their flat boy's shoes, were swinging. But I could bear to see no more of it. I started up. The boys called something – their words were lost. I stumbled up the darkened aisle, and found the exit.

Back at the Royal Opera I found the singers still shrieking upon the stage, the horns still blaring. But I only heard this through the doors: I couldn't face picking my way across the stalls to Diana's side, and facing her displeasure. I gave my ticket to the Italian at the cloaks, then sat in the lobby on a velvet chair, watching as the street filled up with waiting hansoms, with women selling flowers, and with gay girls, and renters.

At last there came the cries of 'Bravo', and the shouts for the soprano. The doors were thrown wide, the lobby filled with chattering people, and in time Diana, Maria, Dickie and the dog emerged, and saw me waiting, and came up to yawn and scold and ask me what the trouble was. I said I had been sick in the gentlemen's lavatory. Diana put a hand to my cheek.

'The excitements of the day have proved too much for you,' she said.

But she said it rather coldly; and all through the long ride back to Felicity Place we sat in silence. When Mrs Hooper had let us in and bolted the great front door behind us, I walked with Diana to her bedroom, but then stepped past her, towards my own. As I did so, she put a hand on my arm: 'Where are you going?'

I pulled my arm free. 'Diana,' I said, 'I feel wretched. Let me alone.'

She seized me again. 'You feel wretched,' she said, with scorn in her voice. 'Do you think it matters to me, how *you* feel about anything? Get in my bedroom at once, you little bitch, and take your clothes off.'

I hesitated. Then: 'No, Diana,' I said.

She came closer. 'What?'

There is a way rich people have of saying *What?*: the word is honed, and has a point put on it; it comes out of their mouths like a dagger coming out of a sheath. That is how Diana said it now, in that dim corridor. I felt it pierce me through, and make me sag. I swallowed.

'I said, "*No*, Diana."' It was no more than a whisper. But when she heard it, she seized me by the shirt, so that I stumbled. I said, 'Get off me, you are hurting me! Get off me, get off me! Diana, you will spoil my shirt!'

'What, this shirt?' she answered. And with that, she put her fingers behind the buttons, and pulled it until it ripped, and my breasts showed bare beneath it. Then she caught hold of the jacket, and tore that from me too – all the time panting as she did so, and with her limbs pressed close against my own. I staggered, and reached for the wall, then placed my arm over my face – I thought she would strike me. But when I looked at her at last I saw that her features were livid, not in fury, but in lust. She reached for my hand, and placed my fingers at the collar of her gown; and, miserable as I was, when I understood what it was that she wanted me to do, I felt my own breath quicken, and my cunt gave a kick. I pulled at the lace, heard a few stitches rip, and the sound worked on me like the tip of a whip, snapping against the haunches of a horse. I tore it from her, her gown of black and white and silver, that came from Worth's to match my costume; and when it was wrecked and trampled on the rug, she had me kneel upon it and fuck her, until she came and came again.

Then she sent me to my own room, anyway.

I lay in the darkness and shook, and put my hands before my mouth to keep from weeping. Upon the cabinet beside the bed, gleaming where the starlight struck it, lay my birthday gift, the wrist-watch. I reached for it, and felt it cold between my fingers; but when I placed it to my ear, I shuddered – for all that it would say was: *Kitty, Kitty, Kitty . . .*

I cast it from me, then, and put my pillow over my ears to blot the sound out. I would not weep. I would not weep! I would not even think. I would only surrender myself, for ever, to the heartless, seasonless routines of Felicity Place.

So I thought then; but my days there were numbered. And the arms of my handsome watch were slowly sweeping them away.

Chapter 14

The morning after my birthday I slept late; and when I woke, and rang for Blake to bring me coffee, it was to find that Diana had gone out while I was slumbering.

'Gone out?' I said. 'Gone where? Who with?' Blake gave a curtsey, and said she didn't know. I sat back against my pillow, and took the cup from her. 'What was she wearing?' I asked then.

'She was wearing her green suit, miss, and had her bag with her.'

'Her bag. Then, she might have been going to the Cavendish Club. Didn't she say, that she was going to her club? Didn't she say when she'd be back?'

'Please, miss, she didn't say a thing. She never does say a thing like that, to me. You might ask Mrs Hooper . . .'

I might; but Mrs Hooper had a way about her, of gazing at me as I lay in bed, that I didn't quite care for. I said, 'No, it doesn't matter.' Then, as Blake bent to sweep my hearth and set a fire there, I sighed. I thought of Diana's rough kisses of the night before – of how they had stirred me, and sickened me, while my heart was still smarting after Kitty. I groaned; and when Blake looked up I said, in a half-hearted sort of way: 'Don't you get *tired*, Blake, of serving Mrs Lethaby?'

The question made her cheeks flush pink. She looked back to the hearth, then said, 'I should get tired, miss, with any mistress.'

I answered that I supposed she would. Then, because it was novel to talk to her – and because Diana had gone out without waking me, and I was peevish and bored – I said: 'So you don't think Mrs Lethaby a hard one, then?'

She coloured again. 'They are all hard, miss. Else, how would they be mistresses?'

'Well – but do you *like* it here? Do you *like* being a maid here?'

'I have a room to myself, which is more than most maids get. Besides,' she stood, and wiped her hands on her apron, 'Mrs Lethaby don't half pay a decent wage.'

I thought of how she came every morning with the coffee, and every night with jugs of water for the bowls. I said, 'Don't think me rude, but – whenever do you spent it?'

'I am saving it, miss!' she said. 'I aim to emigrate. My friend says, in the colonies a girl with twenty pounds can set up as a landlady of a rooming-house, with girls of her own.'

'Is that so?' She nodded. 'And you'd like to run a rooming-house?'

'Oh yes! They will always need rooming-houses in the colonies, you see, for the people coming in.'

'Well, that's true. And, how much have you saved?'

She flushed again. 'Seven pounds, miss.'

I nodded. Then I thought and said: 'But the colonies, Blake! Could you bear the journey? You should have to live in a boat – suppose there were storms?'

She picked up the scuttle of coal. 'Oh, I shouldn't mind that, miss!'

I laughed; and so did she. We had never chatted so freely before. I had grown used to calling her only 'Blake' as Diana did; I had grown used to her curtseys; I had grown used to having her see me as I was now: swollen-eyed and swollen-mouthed, naked in a bed with the sheet at my bosom, and the marks of Diana's kisses at my throat. I had grown used to not *looking* at her, not *seeing* her at all. Now, as she laughed, I found myself gazing at her at last, at her pinking cheeks and at her lashes, which were dark, and thinking, *Oh!* – for she was really rather handsome.

And, as I thought it, there came the old self-consciousness between us. She hoisted her scuttle of coal a little higher, then came to take my tray and ask me, 'Would there be anything else?' I answered that she might run me a bath; and she curtseyed.

And when I lay soaking in the bathroom I heard the slam of the front door. It was Diana. She came to find me. She had been to the Cavendish, but only to take a letter that must be signed by another lady.

'I didn't like to wake you,' she said, dipping her hand into the water.

I forgot about Blake, then, and how handsome she was.

I forgot about Blake, indeed, for a month or more. Diana gave dinners, and I posed and wore costumes; we made visits to the club, and to Maria's house in Hampstead. All went on as usual. I was occasionally sulky, but, as on the night of our trip to the opera, she found ways of turning my sulkiness to her own lewd advantage – in the end, I hardly knew if I were really cross or only feigning crossness for the sake of her letches. Once or twice I hoped she would *make* me cross – fucking her in a rage, I found, could at the right moment be more thrilling than fucking her in kindness.

Anyway, we went on like this. Then one night there was some quarrel over a suit. We were dressing for a supper at Maria's, and I would not wear the clothes she picked for me. 'Very well,' she said, 'you may wear what you please!' And she took the carriage, and went off to Hampstead without me. I threw a cup against the wall – then sent for Blake to come and tidy it. And when she came, I remembered how pleasant it had been to chat with her before; and I made her sit with me, and tell me more about her plans.

And after that, she would come and spend a minute or two with me whenever Diana was out; and she became easier with me, and I grew freer with her. And at last I said to her: 'Lord, Blake, you've been emptying my pot for me for more than a year, and I don't even know what your first name is!'

She smiled, and again looked handsome.

Her name was Zena.

Her name was Zena, and her story was a sad one. I had it from her one morning in the autumn of that year, as I lay in Diana's bed, and she came, as usual, to bring breakfast and to see to the fire. Diana herself had risen early, and gone out. I woke to find Zena kneeling at the hearth, working quietly with the coals so as not to disturb me. I shifted beneath the sheets, feeling lazy as an eel. My quim – in the clever way of quims – was still quite slippery, from the passion of the night before.

I lay watching her. She raised a hand to scratch her brow, and when she took the hand away she left a smudge of soot there. Her face, against the smudge, seemed very pale and rather pinched. I said, 'Zena', and she gave a jump: 'Yes, miss?'

I hesitated; then, 'Zena,' I said again, 'don't mind me asking you something, but I can't help but think of it. Diana once told me – well, that she got you out of a prison. Is it true?'

She turned back to the hearth, and continued to pile coals upon the fire; but I saw her ears turn crimson. She said, 'They *call* it a re*form*at'ry. It wasn't a gaol.'

'A reformat'ry, then. But it's true you were in one.' She didn't answer. 'I don't mind it,' I added quickly.

She gave a jerk to her head, and said: 'No, *I* don't mind it, *now* . . .'

Had she said such a thing, in such a tone, to Diana, I think Diana would have slapped her. Indeed, she looked at me now a little fearfully; but when she did so, I grimaced. 'I'm sorry,' I said. 'Do you think me very rude? It's only – well, it is what Diana said, about why they had you in there at all. Is it true, what she said? Or is it only one of her stories? Is it true that they had you in there, because you . . . kissed another girl?'

She let her hands fall to her lap, then sat back upon her heels and gazed into the unlit grate. Then she turned her face to me and gave a sigh.

'I was a year in the reformat'ry,' she said, 'when I was seventeen. It was a cruel enough place, I suppose, though not so hard as other gaols I heard of; its mistress is a lady Mrs Lethaby knows from her club, and that is how she got me. I was sent to the reformat'ry on the word of a girl I was friends with at a house in Kentish Town. We were maids there, together.'

'You were a maid before you came here?'

'I was sent out as a skivvy when I was ten: Pa was rather poor. That was at a house in Paddington. When I was fourteen I went to the place in Kentish Town. It was altogether a better place. I was a housemaid, then; and I got very thick with another girl there, named Agnes. Agnes had a chap, and she threw the chap over, miss, for my sake. *That's* how thick we were . . .'

She gazed very sadly at her hands in her lap, and the room grew still, and I grew sorry. I said, 'And was it Agnes told the story that got you sent to the reformat'ry?'

She shook her head. 'Oh, no! What happened was, Agnes lost her place, because the lady didn't care for her. She went to a house in Dulwich – which, as you will know, is very far from Kentish Town, but not so far that we couldn't meet of a Sunday, and send each other little notes and parcels through the post. But then – well, then another girl came. She was not so nice as Agnes, but she took to me like anything. I think she was a bit soft, miss, in the head. She would look through all my things – and, of course, she found my letters and all my bits. She would make me kiss her! And when at last I said that I wouldn't, for Agnes' sake – well, she went to the lady and told her that *I* had made *her* kiss *me*; and that I touched her, in a peculiar way. When all the time, it was her, only her –! And when the lady wasn't sure whether or not to believe her, she went and took her to my little box of letters, and showed her those.'

'Oh!' I said. 'What a bitch!'

She nodded. 'A bitch is what she was, all right; only, I didn't like to say it before.'

'And it was the lady, then, who got you sent to the reformat'ry?'

'It was, on a charge of tampering and corrupting. And she made sure Agnes lost her place, too; and they would have sent her to prison along with me – except that she took up with another young man again, very sharp. And now she is married to him, and he I hear treats her shabbily.'

She shook her head, and so did I. I said, 'Well, it seems like you were roundly done over by women, all right!'

'*Wasn't* I, though!'

I gave her a wink. 'Come over here, and let's have a fag.'

She stepped over to the bed, and I found us two cigarettes; and for a little while we sat smoking together in silence, occasionally sighing and tutting and still shaking our heads.

At last I saw her gazing at me rather thoughtfully. When I caught her eye, she blushed and looked away. I said, 'What is it?'

'It's nothing, miss.'

'No, there is something,' I said, smiling. 'What are you thinking?'

She took another puff of her cigarette, smoking it as you see rough men on the street smoking, with her fingers cupped around the fag, the burning end of it nearly scorching her palm. Then she said: 'Well, you will think me forwarder than I ought to be.'

'Will I?'

'Yes. But I have been just about busting to know it, ever since I first got a proper look at you.' She took a breath. 'You used to work the halls, didn't you? You used to work the halls, alonger Kitty Butler, and calling yourself plain Nan King. What a turn it give me, when I saw you here first! I never maided for no one famous before.'

I studied the tip of my cigarette, and did not answer her. Her words had given *me* a kind of jolt: they were not what I had been anticipating at all. Then I said, with a show of laughter: 'Well, you know, I am hardly famous now. They were all rather long ago, those days.'

'Not *so* long,' she said. 'I remember seeing you at Camden Town, and another time at the Peckham Palace. That was with Agnes – how we laughed!' Her voice sank a little. 'It was just after that, that my troubles started . . .'

I remembered the Peckham Palace very well, for Kitty and I had only played there once. It had been in the December before we opened at the Brit, so rather near to the start of my own troubles. I said, 'To think of you sitting there, with Agnes beside you; and me upon the stage, with Kitty Butler . . .'

She must have caught something in my tone, for she raised her eyes to mine and said: 'And you don't see Miss Butler at all, these days . . . ?' And when I shook my head, she looked knowing. 'Well,' she said then, 'it's something, ain't it, to have been a star upon the stage!'

I sighed. 'I suppose it is. But—' I had thought of something else. 'You oughtn't to let Mrs Lethaby hear you say it. She, well, she don't quite care for the music hall.'

She nodded. 'I dare say.' Then the clock upon the mantel struck the hour and, hearing it, she rose, and stubbed her fag out, and flapped her hand before her mouth to wave away the flavour of the smoke. 'Lord, look at me!' she cried. 'I shall have Mrs Hooper after me.' She reached for my empty coffee-cup, then picked up her tray and went to her scuttle of coal.

Then she turned, and grew pink again. She said: 'Will there be anything else, miss?'

We gazed at one another for the space of a couple of heart-beats. She still had the smudge of coal-dust at her brow. I shifted beneath the sheets, and felt again that slippery spot between my thighs – only now, it was slipperier than ever. I had been fucking Diana every night, almost, for a year and a half. Fucking had come to seem to me like shaking hands – you might do it, as a kind of courtesy, with anyone. But would

Zena have come and let me kiss her, if I had called her to the bed?

I cannot say. I did not call her. I only said: 'Thank you, Zena; there's nothing else, just now.' And she picked up the scuttle, and went.

I had some squeamishness upon me about such matters, yet.

And Diana, I knew, would have been furious.

This, as I have said, was sometime in the autumn of that year. I remember that time, and the two or three months that followed it, very well, for they were busy ones: it was as if my stay with Diana were acquiring a kind of hectic intensity, as some sick people are said to do, as it hurtled towards its end. Maria, for example, gave a party at her house. Dickie threw a party on a boat – hired it to sail with us from Charing Cross to Richmond, and we danced, till four in the morning, to an all-girl band. Christmas we spent at Kettner's, eating goose in a private room; New Year was celebrated at the Cavendish Club: our table grew so loud and ribald, Miss Bruce again approached us, to complain about our manners.

And then, in January, came Diana's fortieth birthday; and she was persuaded to celebrate it, at Felicity Place itself, with a fancy-dress ball.

We called it a ball, but it was not really so grand as that. For music there was only a woman with a piano; and what dancing there was – in the dining-room with the carpet rolled back – was rather tame. No one, however, came for the sake of a waltz. They came for Diana's reputation, and for mine. They came for the wine and the food and the rose-tipped cigarettes. They came for the scandal.

They came, and marvelled.

The house, for a start, we made wonderful. We hung velvet from the walls and, from the ceiling, spangles; and we shut off all the lamps, and lit the rooms entirely with candles. The drawing-room we cleared of furniture, leaving only the Turkey

rug, on which we placed cushions. The marble floor of the hall
we scattered with roses – we placed roses, too, to smoke upon
the fires: by the end of the night you felt ill with it. There was
champagne to drink, and brandies, and wine with spice in:
Diana had this heated in a copper bowl above a spirit-lamp.
All the food she had sent over from the Solferino. They did her
a cold roast after the manner of the Romans, goose stuffed
with turkey stuffed with chicken stuffed with quail – the quail,
I think, having a truffle in it. There were also oysters, which sat
upon the table in a barrel marked *Whitstable*; however, one
lady, unused to the trick of the shells, tried to open one with a
cigar-knife. The blade slipped, and cut her finger almost to
the bone; and after she had bled into the ice, no one much
cared for them. Diana had them taken away.

Half of the Cavendish Club attended that party – and,
besides them, more women, women from France and from
Germany, and one, even, from Capri. It was as if Diana had sent
a general invitation to all the wealthy circles of the world – but
marked the card, of course, *Sapphists Only*. That was her
prime requirement; her second demand, as I have said, was
that they come in fancy dress.

The result was rather mixed. Many ladies viewed the
evening only as an opportunity at last to leave their riding-
coats at home, and put on trousers. Dickie was one of these:
she came clad in a morning suit, with a sprig of lilac at her
lapel, and calling herself 'Dorian Gray'. Other costumes, however, were more splendid. Maria Jex stained her face and put
whiskers on it, and came robed as a Turkish pasha. Diana's
friend Evelyn arrived as Marie Antoinette – though, another
Marie Antoinette came later and, after her, yet another. That,
indeed, was one of the predicaments of the evening: I counted
fully five separate Sapphos, all bearing lyres; and there were
six Ladies from Llangollen – I had not even *heard* of the Ladies
from Llangollen before I met Diana. On the other hand, the
women who had been more daring in their choices risked
going unrecognised by anyone at all. 'I am Queen Anne!' I

heard one lady say, very cross, when Maria failed to identify her – yet, when Maria addressed another lady in a crown by the same title, she was even crosser. She turned out to be Queen Christina, of Sweden.

Diana herself, that night, I never saw look more handsome. She came as her Greek namesake, in a robe, and with sandals showing her long second toe, and her hair piled high and with a crescent in it; and over her shoulder she wore a quiver full of arrows and a bow. She claimed the arrows were for shooting gentlemen, although later I heard her say they were for piercing young girls' hearts.

My own costume I kept secret, and would not show to anyone: it was my plan to reveal myself, when the guests were all arrived, and present a tribute to my mistress. It was not a very saucy costume; but I thought it a terribly clever one, because it had a connection with the gift I had bought Diana, for her birthday. For that event the year before I had begged the money from her to buy her a present, and had got her a brooch: I think she liked it well enough. This year, however, I felt I had surpassed myself. I had bought her, all by post and in secret, a marble bust of the Roman page Antinous. I had taken his story out of a paper at the Cavendish, and had smiled to read it, because – apart of course from the detail of Antinous being so miserable, and finally throwing himself in the River Nile – it seemed to resemble my own. I had given the bust to Diana at breakfast, and she had adored it at once, and had it set up on a pedestal in the drawing-room. 'Who would have thought the boy had so much cleverness in him!' she had said a little later. 'Maria, you must have chosen it for him – didn't you?' Now, while the ladies all assembled at the party below, I stood in my bedroom, trembling before the glass, garbing myself as Antinous himself. I had a skimpy little toga that reached to my knee, with a Roman belt around it – what they called a zone. I had put powder on my cheeks to make them languorous, and spit-black on my eyes to make them dark. My hair I had covered entirely in a sable wig that curled to my shoulders. About my neck there was a garland of lotus flowers – and I can tell you, the lotus flowers had been harder to organise, in London, in January, than anything.

I had another garland to hand to Diana: this I also placed about my neck. Then I went to the door and listened and, since the moment seemed right, I ran to Diana's closet and took out a cloak of hers and wrapped it tight about me, and raised the hood. And then I went downstairs.

There, in the hall, I found Maria.

'Nancy, dear boy!' she cried. Her lips looked very red and damp where they showed through the slit of her pasha's whiskers. 'Diana has sent me out to find you. The drawing-room is positively pullulating with women, all of them panting for a peek at your *pose plastique*!'

I smiled – a pullulating audience was precisely what I wanted – then let her lead me into the room, still with the cloak about me, and hand me into the alcove behind the velvet curtain. Then, when I had bared my costume and struck my pose, I murmured to her and she pulled the tasselled cord, and the velvet twitched back and uncovered me. As I walked amongst them the guests all fell silent and looked knowing, and Diana – standing just where I could have wished her, beside the bust of Antinous on its little pedestal – raised a brow. Now, at the sight of me in my toga and belt, the ladies sighed and murmured.

I gave them a moment, then stepped over to Diana, lifted the extra garland from around my neck, and wound it about hers. Then I knelt to her, took up her hand, and kissed it. She smiled; the ladies murmured again – and then began, in a delighted sort of way, to clap. Maria stepped up to me, and put a hand to the hem of my toga.

'What a little jewel you look tonight, Nancy – doesn't she, Diana? How my husband would admire you! You look like a picture from a buggers' compendium!'

Diana laughed and said that I did. Then she reached and put her fingers to my chin and kissed me – so hard, I felt her teeth upon the soft flesh of my lips.

And then the music started up in the room across the hall. Maria brought me a glass of the warm spiced wine and, to go with it, a cigarette from Diana's special case. One of the Marie Antoinettes weaved her way through the crowd to take my hand and kiss it. '*Enchantée*,' she said – this one really was French. 'What a spectacle you have provided for us! One would never see such a thing in the salons of Paris . . .'

The entire evening sounds charming; it might, indeed, have been the very high point of my triumph as Diana's boy. And yet, for all my planning, for all the success of my costume and my tableau, I got no pleasure from it. Diana herself – it was her birthday, after all – seemed distant from me, and preoccupied with other things. Only a minute or two after I had placed the garland of lotus flowers about her neck, she took it off, saying it did not match her costume; she hung it from a corner of the pedestal, where it soon fell off – later I saw a lady with one of the flowers from it, at her own lapel. I cannot say why – heaven knows, I had suffered graver abuses at Diana's hand, and only smiled to suffer them! – but her carelessness over the garland made me peevish. Then again, the room was terribly hot and terribly perfumed; and my wig made me hotter than anyone, and itched – yet, I could not remove it, for fear of spoiling *my* costume. After Marie Antoinette, more ladies sought me out to tell me how much they admired me; but each proved drunker and more ribald than the last, and I began to find then wearisome. I drank glass after glass of spiced wine and champagne, in an effort to make myself as careless as they; but the wine – or, more likely, the hashish I had smoked – seemed to make me cynical rather than gay. When one lady reached to stroke my thigh as she stepped past me, I pushed her roughly away. 'What a little *brute*!' she cried, delighted. In the end I stood half-hidden in the shadows, looking on, rubbing my temples. Mrs Hooper was at the table with the hot wine on it, ladling it out; I saw her glance my way, and give a kind of smile. Zena had been sent to move amongst the ladies, bearing dainties on a tray; but when she seemed to want to catch my eye, I looked away. Even from her I felt distant, that night.

So I was almost glad when, at about eleven o'clock, the mood of the party was changed, by Dickie calling for more light to be brought, for the lady on the piano to cease her playing, and for all the women present to gather round and pay attention.

'What's this?' cried one lady. 'Why has it grown bright?'

Evelyn said: 'We are to hear Dickie Reynolds' history, from a book written by a doctor.'

'A doctor? Is she ill?'

'It is her *vie sexuelle*!'

'Her *vie sexuelle*!'

'My dear, I know it already, it is terribly dreary . . .' This was from a woman who stood beside me in the shadows, garbed as a monk; as I turned to her she gave a yawn, then slipped quietly from the room in search of other sport. The rest of the guests, however, looked just as eager as Dickie could wish. She stood beside Diana; the book that Evelyn had referred to was in Diana's hands – it was small and black and densely printed, with not a single illustration: it was not at all the kind of thing that people usually gave Diana, for her box. And yet, she was turning its pages in fascination. A lady dipped her head to read the title from the spine, then cried: 'But the book's in Latin! Dickie, whatever is the point of a filthy story, if the damn thing's written in Latin?'

Dickie now looked a little prim. 'It is only the title that is Latin,' she answered; 'and, besides, it is not a filthy book, it is a very brave one. It has been written by a man, in an attempt to explain our sort so that the ordinary world will understand us.'

A lady dressed as Sappho took the cigar from her mouth, and studied Dickie in a kind of disbelief. She said: 'This book is to be passed among the public; and your story is in it? The story of your life, as a lover of women? But Dick, have you gone mad! This man sounds like a pornographer of the most mischievous variety!'

'She has taken a *nom-de-guerre*, of course,' said Evelyn.

'Even so. Dickie, the folly of it!'

'You misunderstand,' said Dickie. 'This is a new thing entirely. This book will assist us. It will *advertise* us.'

A kind of collective shudder ran right around the drawing-room. The Sappho with the cigar shook her head. 'I have never heard of such a thing,' she said.

'Well,' answered Dickie impressively, 'you will hear more of it, believe me.'

'Let us hear more of it *now*!' cried Maria; and someone else called: 'Yes, Diana, read it to us, do!'

And so more candles were brought, and placed at Diana's shoulder. The ladies settled themselves into comfortable poses, and the reading began.

I cannot remember the words of it now. I know that, as Dickie had promised, they were not at all filthy; indeed, they were rather dry. And yet, her story was lent a kind of lewdness, too, by the very dullness of the prose in which it was told. All the time Diana read, the ladies called out ribald comments. When Dickie's history was complete, they read another, which was rather lewder. Then they read a very saucy one from the gentlemen's section. At last the air was thicker and warmer than ever; even I, in my sulkiness, began to feel myself stirred by the doctor's prim descriptions. The book was passed from lady to lady, while Diana lit herself another cigarette. Then one lady said, 'You must ask Bo about that: she was seven years amongst the Hindoos'; and Diana called, 'What? What must she ask?'

'We are reading the story,' cried the woman in reply, 'of a lady with a clitoris as big as a little boy's prick! She claims she caught the malady from an Indian maid. I said, if only Bo Holliday were here, she might confirm it for us, for she was thick with the Hindoos in her years in Hindoostan.'

'It is not true of Indian girls,' said another lady then. 'But it is of the Turks. They are bred like it, that they might pleasure themselves in the seraglio.'

'Is that so?' said Maria, stroking her beard.

'Yes, it is certainly so.'

'But it is true also of our own poor girls!' said someone else. 'They are brought up twenty to a bed. The continual frotting makes their clitorises grow. I know that for a fact.'

'What rubbish!' said the Sappho with the cigar.

'I can assure you it is not rubbish,' answered the first lady hotly. 'And if we only had a girl from the slums amongst us now, I would pull her drawers down and show you the proof!'

There was laughter at her words, and then the room grew rather quiet. I looked at Diana; and as I did so, she slowly turned her head to gaze at me. 'I wonder . . .' she said thoughtfully, and one or two other ladies began to study me, as she did. My stomach gave a subtle kind of lurch. I thought, *She wouldn't!* And as I thought it, a quite different lady said: 'But Diana, you have just the creature we need! Your maid was a slum-girl, wasn't she? Didn't you have her from a prison or a home? You know what the women get up to in prison, don't you? I should think they must frot until their parts are the size of mushrooms!'

Diana turned her eyes from me, and drew on her pink-tipped fag; and then she smiled. 'Mrs Hooper!' she called. 'Where is Blake?'

'She is in the kitchen, ma'am,' answered the housekeeper from her station at the bowl of wine. 'She is loading her tray.'

'Go and fetch her.'

'Yes, ma'am.'

Mrs Hooper went. The ladies looked at one another, and then at Diana. She stood very calm and steady beside the bust of cold Antinous; but when she raised her glass to her lip, I saw that her hand was trembling slightly. I shifted from one foot to the other, my briefly flaring lust all faded. In a moment, Mrs Hooper had returned, with Zena. When Diana called to her, Zena walked blinkingly into the centre of the room. The ladies parted to let her pass, then stepped together again at the back of her.

Diana said, 'We have been wondering about you, Blake.'

Zena blinked again. 'Ma'am?'

'We have been wondering about your time at the reformatory.'
Now Zena coloured. 'We have been wondering how you filled
your hours. We thought there must be some little occupation, to
which you turned your idle fingers, in your solitary cell.'

Zena hesitated. Then she said, 'Please, m'm, do you mean,
sewing bags?'

At that, the ladies gave a roar of laughter, which made Zena
flinch, and blush worse than ever, and put a hand to her throat.
Diana said, very slowly, 'No, child, I did not mean sewing
bags. I meant, that we thought you must have turned frigstress,
in your little cell. That you must have frigged yourself until
your cunt was sore. That you must have frigged yourself so
long and so hard, you frigged yourself a cock. We think you
must have a cock, Blake, in your drawers. We want you to lift
your skirt, and let us see it!'

Now the ladies laughed again. Zena looked at them, and
then at Diana. 'Please, m'm,' she said, beginning to shake, 'I
don't know what you mean!'

Diana stepped towards her. 'I think you do,' she said. She
had picked up the book that Dickie had given her, and now she
opened it, and held it oppressively close to Zena's face, so
that Zena flinched again. 'We have been reading a book full of
stories of girls like you,' she said. 'And now, what are you
suggesting? That the doctor who wrote this book – this book
that Miss Reynolds gave me, for my birthday – is a fool?'

'No, m'm!'

'Well then. The doctor says you have a cock. Come along,
lift your skirts! Good gracious, girl, we only want to look at
you!'

She had put her hand upon Zena's skirt, and I could see the
other ladies, all gripped, in their turn, by her wildness, making
ready to assist her. The sight made me sick. I stepped out of the
shadows and said, 'Leave her, Diana! For God's sake, leave her
alone!'

The room fell silent at once. Zena gazed at me in fright, and Diana turned, and blinked. She said: 'You wish to raise the skirt yourself?'

'I want you to leave Blake be! Go on, Blake.' I nodded to Zena. 'Go on back to the kitchen.'

'You stay where you are!' cried Diana to her. 'And as for *you*,' she said, fixing me with one narrow, black, glittering eye, 'do you think you are mistress here, to give orders to my servants? Why, you *are* a servant! What is it to you, if I ask my girl to bare her backside for me? You have bared yours for me, often enough! Get back behind your velvet curtain! Perhaps, when we have finished with little Blake, we shall all take turns upon Antinous.'

Her words seemed to press upon my aching head – and then, as if my head were made of glass, it seemed to shatter. I put my hand to the garland of wilting flowers at my throat, and tore it from me. Then I did the same with the sable wig, and flung it to the floor. My hair was oiled flat to my head, my cheeks were flushed with wine and anger – I must have looked terrible. But I didn't feel terrible: I felt filled with power and with light. I said, 'You shall not talk to me in such a way. How dare you talk to me like that!'

Beside Diana, Dickie rolled her eyes. 'Really, Diana,' she said, 'what a bore this is!'

'What a bore!' I turned to her. 'Look at you, you old cow, dressed up in a satin shirt like a boy of seventeen. Dorian Gray? You look more like the bleedin' portrait, after Dorian has made a few trips down the docks!'

Dickie twitched, then grew pale. Several of the ladies laughed, and one of them was Maria. 'My dear boy—!' she began.

'Don't "dear boy" me, you ugly bitch!' I said to her then. 'You're as bad as her, in your Turkish trousers. What are you, looking for your harem? No wonder they are off fucking each other with their enormous parts, if they have you as their master. You have had your fingers all over me, for a year and a half; but if a real girl was ever to uncover her tit and put it in your hand, you would have to ring for your maid, for her to show you what to do with it!'

'That's enough!' This was Diana. She was gazing at me, white-faced and furious, but still terribly calm. Now she turned and addressed the group of goggling ladies. She said: 'Nancy thinks it amusing, sometimes, to kick her little heels; and sometimes, of course, it is. But not tonight. Tonight, I'm afraid, it is only tiresome.' She looked at me again, but spoke, still, as if to her guests. 'She will go upstairs,' she said levelly, 'until she is sorry. Then she will apologise to the ladies she has upset. And then, I shall think of some little punishment for her.' Her gaze flicked over the remains of my costume. 'Something suitably Roman, perhaps.'

'Roman?' I answered. 'Well, you should know about that. How old are you today? You were there, weren't you, at Hadrian's palace?'

It was a mild enough insult, after all that I had said. But as I said it, there came a titter from the crowd. It was only a small one; but if there was ever anyone who could not bear to be tittered at, that person was Diana. I think she would rather have been shot between the eyes. Now, hearing that stifled laugh, she grew even paler. She took a step towards me, and raised her hand; she did it so quickly, I had time only to catch the flash of something dark at the end of her arm – then there came what seemed to be a small explosion at my cheek.

She had still held Dickie's book, all this time; and now she had struck me with it.

I gave a cry, and staggered. When I put a hand to my face, I found blood upon it – from my nose, but also from a gash beneath my eye, where the edge of the leather-bound spine had caught it. I reached for a shoulder or an arm, against which to steady myself; but now all the ladies shrank away from me, and I almost stumbled. I looked once at Diana. She also had reeled, after dealing me the blow; but Evelyn was beside her with her arm about her waist. She said nothing to me; and I, at last, was quite incapable of speech. I think I coughed, or snorted. There came a splatter of blood upon the Turkey rug, that made the ladies draw even further from me, and give little moues of surprise and disgust. Then I turned, and staggered from the room.

At the door stood Maria's whippet, Satin, and when he saw me he barked. Maria had set him there, with a dog's head of papier mâché fixed to each side of his collar, to represent the hound that stood on guard at the gate of Hades.

The marble floor of the hall, as I have said, we had scattered with roses: it was terribly hard to cross it, in bare feet, with my ringing head and my hand at my cheek. Before I had reached the staircase, I heard a step behind me, and a bang. I turned to see Zena there: Diana had sent her from the room in my wake, then had the door shut on us. She gazed at me, then came to put a hand upon my arm: 'Oh, miss . . .'

And I – who had saved her from Diana's wildness only, as it seemed to me then, to have that wildness turned upon myself – I shook her from me. 'Don't you touch me!' I cried. Then I ran from her, to my own room, and closed the door.

And sat there wretched, in the darkness, nursing my oozing cheek. Below me, after a few more minutes of silence, there came the sound of the piano; and then came laughter, and then shouts. They were carrying on their revelling, without me! I could not credit it. The sport with Zena, the insults, the blow and the bleeding nose – these seemed only to have made the marvellous party more gay and marvellous still.

If only Diana had sent her guests home. If only I had placed my head beneath my pillow, and forgotten them. If only I had not grown miserable, and peevish, and vengeful, at the sound of their fun.

If only Zena had not forgiven me my harshness in the hall – had not come creeping to my door, to ask me, was I very hurt, and was there anything that she could do, to comfort me.

*

When I hard her knock, I flinched: I was sure it must be Diana, seeking me out to torture me or – perhaps, who knew? – to caress me. When I saw that it was Zena, I stared.

'Miss,' she said. She had a candle in her hand, and its flame dipped and fluttered, sending shadows dancing crazily about the walls. 'I couldn't go up, knowing you was here all bruised and bleeding – and all, oh, all on my account!'

I sighed. 'Come in,' I said, 'and close the door.' And when she had done that, and stepped nearer to me, I put my head in my hands and groaned. 'Oh Zena,' I said, 'what a night! What a night!'

She set down her candle. 'I've got a cloth,' she said, 'with a little bit of ice in it. If you'll just – permit me –' I lifted my head, and she placed the cloth against my cheek, so that I winced. 'What a corker of an eye you'll have!' she said. Then, in a different tone: 'What a devil that woman is!' She began to wipe away the blood that was crusted about my nostril – lowering herself upon the bed, at my side, and placing her free hand upon my shoulder to brace herself against me, as she did so.

Gradually, however, I became aware that she was trembling. 'It's the cold, miss,' she said. 'Only the cold and, well, the bit of fright I had downstairs . . .' But as she said it, I felt her shudder harder than ever, and she began to weep. 'The truth is,' she said through her tears, 'I could not bear the thought of lying up there in my own room, with them wicked ladies roaming about the place. I thought that they might come and have another go at me . . .'

'There now,' I said. I took the cloth from her and placed it on the floor. Then I drew the counterpane from the bed, and set it about her shoulders. 'You shall stay here with me, where the ladies cannot get you . . .' I put my arm around her, and her head came against my ear. She still wore her servant's cap; now I took the pins from it and drew it from her, and her hair fell to her shoulders. It was scented with burning roses, and with the spice from the wine. Smelling it, with Zena warm

against my shoulder, I began suddenly to feel drunker than I
had all night. Perhaps it was only that my head was reeling,
from the force of Diana's blow.

I swallowed. Zena put a handkerchief to her nose, and grew
a little stiller. There came, from the floors below, the sound of
running feet, a furious thundering upon the piano, and a
scream of laughter.

'Just listen to them!' I said, growing bitter again. 'Partying
like anything! They have forgotten all about us, sitting miserable up here . . .'

'Oh, I hope they have!'

'Of course they have. We might be doing anything, it wouldn't
matter to them! Why, we might be having a party of our own!'
She blew her nose, then giggled. My head gave a sort of tilt. I
said: 'Zena! Why shouldn't we have a party, just the two of
us? How many bottles of champagne are there left, in the
kitchen?'

'There are loads of 'em.'

'Well, then. Just you run down and fetch us one.'

She bit her lip. 'I don't know . . .'

'Go on, you shan't be seen. They are all in the drawing-
room, and you can go by the back stairs. And if anyone does
see you, and asks, you can say you are fetching it for me.
Which is true.'

'Well . . .'

'Go on! Take your candle!' I rose, then took hold of her
hands and pulled her to her feet; and she – infected at last by
my new recklessness – gave another giggle, put her fingers to
her lips, then tip-toed from the room. While she was gone I lit
a lamp, but kept it turned very low. She had left her cap upon
the bed: I picked it up and set it on my own head, and when
she returned five minutes later and saw me wearing it she
laughed out loud.

She carried a dewy bottle and a glass. 'Did you see any
ladies?' I asked her.

'I saw a couple, but they never saw me. They were at the

scullery door and – oh! they was kissing the guts out of each other!'

I imagined her standing in the shadows, watching them. I went to her and took the bottle, then peeled away the lead wrapper from its neck. 'You've shaken it up,' I said. 'It'll go off with a real bang!' She put her hands over her ears, and shut her eyes. I felt the cork squirm in the glass for a second; then it leapt from my fingers, and I gave a yell: 'Quick! Quick! Bring a glass!' A creamy fountain of foam had risen from the neck of the bottle, and now drenched my fingers and soaked my legs – I was still, of course, clad in the little white toga. Zena seized the glass from the tray and held it, giggling again, beneath the spurting wine.

We went and sat upon the bed, Zena with the glass in her hands, me sipping from the frothing bottle. When she drank, she coughed; but I filled her glass again and said: 'Drink up! Just like those cows downstairs.' And she drank, and drank again, until her cheeks were red. I felt my own head grow giddier with every sip I took, and the pulse at my swollen face grow thicker. At last I said, 'Oh! How it hurts!', and Zena set down her glass to put her fingers, very gently, upon my cheek. When she had held them there for a second or two, I took her hand in my own, and leaned and kissed her.

She didn't draw away until I made to lie upon the bed and pull her with me. Then she said: 'Oh, we cannot! What if Mrs Lethaby should come?'

'She won't. She is leaving me, as a kind of punishment.' I touched her knee, and then her thigh, through the layers of her skirts.

'We cannot . . .' she said again; but this time, her voice was fainter. And when I tugged at her frock and said, 'Come on, take this off – or shall I tear the buttons?' she gave a drunken sort of laugh: 'You shall do no such thing! Help me nicely, now.'

Naked she was very thin, and strangely coloured: flaming crimson at the cheeks, a coarser red from her elbows to her fingertips, and palely white – almost bluish-white – on her torso, upper arms, and thighs. The hair between her legs – you can never guess at that kind of thing in advance – was quite ginger.

When I dipped my lips to it, she gave a squeal: 'Oh! What a thing to do!' But then, after a moment, she held my head and pressed it. She didn't seem to be at all sorry about my swollen nose, then. She only said: 'Oh, turn around, turn around quick, that I might do it to you!'

After that, I pulled the counterpane over us, and we drank more champagne, taking turns to sip from the bottle. I put my hand upon her. I said: '*Did* you used to frig yourself in the reformat'ry?' She gave me a slap, saying, 'Oh, you are as bad as them downstairs! I nearly died!' She pushed the blanket back, and squinted at her quim. 'To think of me with a cock! What an idea!'

'What an idea? Oh, Zena, I should love to see you with one! I should love—' I sat up. 'Zena, I should love to see you in Diana's dildo!'

'That thing? She's made you filthy! I should die with shame, before I ever tried such a thing!' Her lashes fluttered.

I said, 'You are blushing! You've fancied it, haven't you? You've fancied a bit of that kind of sport – don't tell me you haven't!'

'Really, a girl like me!' But she was redder than ever, and would not gaze at me. I caught hold of her hand, and pulled her up.

'Come on,' I said. 'You have got me all hot for it. Diana will never know.'

'Oh!'

I pulled her to the door, then peered into the corridor outside. The music and laughter from downstairs was fainter, but still loud and rather furious. Zena fell against me, and put her arms around my waist; then we staggered together, quite naked, and with our hands before our faces to stop ourselves from laughing, to Diana's little parlour.

Here, it was the work of a moment to open the bureau's secret drawer, then take the key to the rosewood trunk, and open that. Zena looked on, all the time casting fearful glances towards the door. When she saw the dildo, however, she coloured again, but seemed unable to tear her eyes from it. I felt a drunken surge of power and pride. 'Stand up,' I said – I sounded almost like Diana. 'Stand up, and fasten the buckles.'

When she had done that, I led her to the looking-glass. I winced, to see my face all red and swollen, and still with crumbs of blood caught in its creases; but the sight of Zena – gazing at herself with the dildo jutting from her, placing a hand upon the shaft of it, and swallowing, to feel the motion of the leather – proved more distracting than the bruise. At last I turned her and placed my hands upon her shoulders, and nudged the head of the dildo between my thighs. If my quim had had a tongue, it could not have been more eloquent; and if Zena's quim had had one, it would now have licked its lips.

She gave a cry. We stumbled to the bed and fell, crosswise, upon the satin. My head hung from it – the blood rushed to my cheek and made it ache – but now Zena had the shaft inside me and, as she began to wriggle and thrust, I found myself compelled to lift my mouth and kiss her.

As I did so, I heard a noise, quite distinct, above the shuddering of the bed-posts and the pounding of the pulse inside my ears. I let my head fall, and opened my eyes. The door of the room was open, and it was full of ladies' faces. And the face, pale with fury, at the centre of them all, was Diana's.

For a second I lay quite frozen; I saw what she must see – the open trunk, the tangle of limbs upon the bed, the pumping, leather-strapped arse (for Zena, alas, had her eyes tight shut, and still thrust and panted even as her outraged mistress gazed on). Then I placed my hands on Zena's shoulders and gripped them hard. She opened her eyes, saw what I saw, and gave a squeal of fright. Instinctively, she tried to rise, forgetful of the shaft which pinned her sweating hips to mine. For a moment we floundered together inelegantly; she let out a burst of nervous laughter, more jarring than her first thin shriek of fear.

At last she gave a wriggle; there was – monstrously distinct in the sudden silence, and horribly incriminating – a kind of sucking sound; then she was free. She stood at the side of the bed, the dildo bobbing before her. One of the ladies at Diana's side said, 'She has a prick, after all!' And Diana answered: 'That prick is mine. These little sluts have stolen it!'

Her voice was thick – with drunkenness, perhaps; but also, I think, with shock. I looked again at the wide and spilling box, that she was so vain and jealous of, and felt a worm of satisfaction wriggle within me.

And I remembered, too, another room, a room I thought that I had carefully forgotten – a room where it was I who stood speechless at the door, while my sweetheart shivered and blushed beside her lover. And the sight of Diana, in my old place, made me smile.

It was the smile, I think, which deranged her at last. 'Maria,' she said – for Maria was with her, too, along with Dickie and Evelyn: perhaps they had all come to the bedroom to retrieve a dirty book – 'Maria, get Mrs Hooper. I want Nancy's things brought here: she is leaving. And a dress for Blake. They are both going back to the gutter, where I got them from.' Her voice was cold; as she took a step towards me, however, it grew warmer. 'You little slut!' she said. 'You little trollop! You whore, you harlot, you strumpet, you bitch!' But they were words that she had used on me a thousand times before, in lust or passion; and now, said in hate, they were curiously devoid of any sting.

Beside me, however, Zena had begun to shake. As she did so, the dildo bobbed; and when Diana caught the motion she gave a roar: 'Take that thing from your hips!' At once, Zena fumbled with the straps; her fingers jumped so that she could barely grasp the buckles, and I stepped to help her. All the time we worked, Diana hurled abuses at her – she was a half-wit, a street-whore, a common little frigstress. The ladies at the door looked on, and laughed. One of them – it might have been Evelyn – nodded to the trunk, and called: 'Use the strap on her, Diana!' Diana curled her lip.

'They will strap her well enough, at the reformatory,' she said; 'when she returns there.'

At that, Zena fell to her knees and began to cry. Diana gave a sneer, and drew her foot away so that the tears should not fall upon her sandal. Dickie – the necktie at her throat pulled loose, the lilac at her lapel squashed flat, and browning – said: 'Can't we see them fuck again? Diana, make them do it, for our pleasure!'

But Diana shook her head; and the gaze that she turned on me was as cold and as dead as the eye of a lantern, when the flame inside has been quite put out. She said: 'They have fucked their last in my house. They can fuck upon the streets, like dogs.'

Another lady, very drunk, said that, in that case, at least they should have the thrill of watching us, from a window. But I looked only at Diana; and, for the first time in all that terrible evening, I began to feel afraid.

Now Maria returned with Mrs Hooper. Mrs Hooper's eyes were bright. She held my old sailor's bag, that I had brought from Mrs Milne's and cast into the furthest corner of my closet, and a rusty black dress, and a pair of thick-soled boots. While the ladies all looked on, Diana threw the dress and boots at Zena; then she dipped her hand fastidiously into the sailor's bag, and pulled out a crumpled frock, and some shoes, which she cast at me. The frock was one I had used to wear in my old life, and thought fine enough. Now it was cold and slightly clammy to the touch, and its seams were rimmed with moth-dust.

Zena began at once to pull on the dreary black dress, and the boots. I, however, kept my own frock in my hands, and gazed at Diana, and swallowed.

'I'm not wearing this,' I said.

'You shall wear it,' she answered shortly, 'or be thrust naked into Felicity Place.'

'Oh, thrust her naked, Diana!' said a woman at her back. It
was a Lady from Llangollen, minus her topper.

'I'm not putting it on,' I said again. Diana nodded. 'Very
well,' she said, 'then I shall make you.' And while I was still
too amazed to raise a hand in my defence, she had crossed the
room, torn the robe from my fingers, and lowered the hem of
its skirts over my head. I writhed, then, and began to kick; she
pushed me to the bed, held me fast upon it with one hand and,
with the other, continued to tug the folds of cloth about me. I
struggled more fiercely; soon there came the rip of a broken
hem.

Hearing it, Diana gave a shout: 'Help me with her, can't
you? Maria! Mrs Hooper! You, girl.' She meant Zena. 'Do you
want to go back to that damn reformatory?'

Instantly, there came upon me what felt like fifty hands, all
pulling at the dress, all pinching me, all grasping at my kicking
legs. For an age, they seemed to be upon me. I grew hot and
faint beneath the layers of wool. My swollen head was
knocked, and began to pulse and ache. Someone placed her
thumb – I remember this very clearly – at the top of my thigh,
in the slippery hollow of my groin. It might have been Maria.
It might have been Mrs Hooper, the housekeeper.

At last I lay panting upon the bed, the dress about me. The
shoes were placed upon my feet, and laced. 'Stand up!' said
Diana; and when I had done so she caught me by the shoulder
and propelled me from her bedroom, through the parlour, and
out into the darkened hall beyond. Behind me, the ladies followed, Mrs Hooper and Maria with Zena gripped between
them. When I hesitated, Diana prodded me forwards, so that I
almost stumbled and fell.

Now, at last, I began to weep. I said, 'Diana, you cannot
mean this!' But her gaze was cold. She seized me, and
pinched me, and made me walk faster. Down we went – all
flushed and panting and fantastically costumed as we were –
down through the centre of that tall house, in a great jagged
spiral, like a tableau of the damned heading for hell. We

passed the drawing-room: there were some ladies there still, lolling upon the cushions, and when they saw us they called, What were we doing? And a lady in our party answered, that Diana had caught her boy and her maid in her own bed, and was throwing them out – they must be sure to come and watch it.

And so, the lower we went, the greater came the press of ladies at my back, and the louder the laughter and the ribald cries. We reached the basement, and it grew colder; when Diana opened the door that led from the kitchen to the garden at the rear of the house, the wind blew hard upon my weeping eyes, and made them sting. I said, 'You cannot, you cannot!' The cold was sobering me. I had had a vision, of my chamber, my closet, my dressing-table, my linen; my cigarette case, my cuff-links, my walking-cane with the silver tip; my suit of bone-coloured linen; my shoes, with the leather so handsome and fine I had once put out my tongue and licked it. My watch, with the strap that secured it to my wrist.

Diana pushed me forward, and I turned and grabbed her arm. 'Don't cast me from you, Diana!' I said. 'Let me stay! I'll be good! Let me stay, and I'll pleasure you!' But as I begged, she kept me marching, backwards; until at last we reached the high wooden gate, beside the carriage-house, at the far end of the garden. There was a smaller door set into the gate, and now Diana stepped to pull it open; beyond seemed perfect blackness. She took Zena from Mrs Hooper, and held her by the neck. 'Show your face in Felicity Place again,' she said, 'or remind me of your creeping, miserable little existence by any word or deed, and I shall keep my promise, and return you to that gaol, and make sure you stay there, till you rot. Do you understand?' Zena nodded. She was thrust into the square of darkness, and swallowed by it. Then Diana turned for me.

She said: 'The same applies to you, you trollop.' She pushed me to the doorway, but here I held fast to the gate, and begged her. 'Please, Diana! Let me only collect my things!' I looked past her, to Dickie, and Maria: the gazes they turned upon me were livid and blurred, with the wine and with the chase, and held not one soft spark of sympathy. I looked at all the ogling ladies in their fluttering costumes. 'Help me, can't you?' I cried to them. 'Help me, for God's sake! How many times have you not gazed at me and wanted me! How many times have you not come to say how handsome I am, how much you envy Diana the owning of me. Any one of you might have me now! Any one of you! Only, don't let her put me into the street, into the dark, without a coin on me! Oh! Dam' you all for a set of bitches, if you let her do such a thing to me!'

So I cried out, weeping all the time I spoke, then turning to wipe my running nose on the sleeve of my cheap frock. My cheek felt twice its ordinary size, and my hair was matted where I had lain upon it; and at last, the ladies turned their eyes from me in a kind of boredom – and I knew myself done for. My hands slid from the gate, Diana pushed me, and I stumbled into the alleyway beyond. Behind me came my sailor's bag, to land with a smack on the cobbles at my feet.

I raised my eyes from it to look once more upon Diana's house. The windows of the drawing-room were rosy with light, and ladies were already picking their way across the grass towards them. I caught a glimpse of Mrs Hooper; of Dickie, fixing her monocle to her watery eye; of Maria; and of Diana. A few strands of her dark hair had come loose from their pins, and the wind was whipping them about her cheeks. Her housekeeper said something to her, and she laughed. Then she closed the door, and turned the key in it; and the lights and the laughter of Felicity Place were lost to me, for ever.

PART THREE

Chapter 15

You might think that, having sunk so low already, I should not have scrupled to have banged upon the door that had been closed on me, or even tried to scale the gate, to plead with my old mistress from the top of it. Perhaps I considered such things, in the moments that I stood, stunned and snivelling, in that dark and lonely alley. But I had seen the look that Diana had turned on me – a look that was devoid of any fire, kind or lustful. Worse, I had seen the expressions upon the faces of her friends. How could I go to them, and ever hope to walk before them again, handsome and proud?

The thought made me weep still harder; I might have sat and wept before that gate, perhaps, till dawn. But after a moment there came a movement at my side, and I looked up to see Zena standing there, with her hands across her breast, her face very pale. In all my agony, I had forgotten her. Now I said, 'Oh, Zena! What an end to it all! What are we to do?'

'What are *we* to do?' she answered: she sounded not at all like her old self. 'What are *we* to do? I know what *I* should do. I should leave you here, and hope that woman comes back for you, and takes you in and treats you nasty. It's all you deserve!'

'Oh, she won't come back for me – will she?'

'No, of course she won't; nor for me, either. See where all your soft talk has landed us! Out in the dark, on the coldest night in January, with not a hat nor even a pair of drawers; nor even a handkerchief! I wish I *was* in gaol. You have lost me my place, you have lost me my character. You have lost me my seven pounds' wages, what I was keeping for the colonies – oh! What a fool I was, to let you kiss me! What a fool *you* was, to think the mistress wouldn't – oh! I could hit you!'

'Hit me then!' I cried, still snivelling. 'Black my other eye for me, I deserve it!' But she only tossed her head, and wrapped her arms still tighter about her, and turned away.

I wiped my eyes upon my sleeve, then, and tried to grow a little calmer. It had been only just midnight when I had staggered from the drawing-room still dressed as Antinous; I guessed it was about half-past now – a terrible time, because it meant we still had the longest, coldest hours to pass, before the dawn. I said, as humbly as I could, 'What *am* I to do, Zena? What *am* I to do?'

She looked over her shoulder at me. 'I suppose, you shall have to go to your folks. You have folks, don't you? You have some friends?'

'I have nobody, now . . .'

I put a hand to my face again; she turned, and began to chew on her lip. 'If you really have no one,' she said at last, 'then we are both quite alike, for I have no one, neither: my family all threw me over, over the business with Agnes and the police.' She gazed at my sailor's bag, and nudged it with her boot. 'Don't you have a bit of cash about you anywhere? What's in there?'

'All my clothes,' I answered. 'All the boy's clothes I came to Diana's with.'

'Are they good ones?'

'I used to think so.' I raised my head. 'Do you mean for us to put them on, and pass as gents . . . ?'

She had bent to the bag, and was squinting into it. 'I mean for us to sell them.'

'Sell them?' Sell my guardsman's uniform, and my Oxford bags? 'I don't know . . .'

She raised her hands to her mouth, to blow upon her fingers. 'You may sell 'em, miss; or you may walk down to the Edgware Road and stand at a lamp-post till a feller offers you a coin . . .'

We sold them. We sold them to an old clothes seller who had a stall in a market off Kilburn Road. He was packing up his bags when Zena found him – the market had been trading till midnight or so, but when we reached it the barrows were mostly empty and the street was filled with litter, and they were shutting down the naphtha lamps and tipping the water from their buckets into the drains. The man saw us coming and said at once: 'You're too late, I ain't selling.' But when Zena opened the bag and pulled the suits from it, he tilted his head and gave a sniff. 'The soldier's duds is hardly worth my keeping on the stall,' he said, spreading the jacket out across his arm; 'but I will take it, for the sake of the serge, which might do for a fancy waistcoat. The coat and trousers is handsome enough, likewise the shoes. I shall take them from you, for a guinea.'

'A guinea!' I said.

'A guinea is as fair a price as you will get tonight.' He sniffed again. 'I dare say they are hot enough.'

'They ain't hot at all,' said Zena. 'But the guinea will do; and if you'll chuck in a couple of ladies' niceties and a pair of hats with bows on, call it a pound.'

The drawers and stockings he gave us were yellowed with age; the hats were terrible; and we were both, of course, still in need of stays. But Zena, at least, seemed satisfied with the deal. She pocketed the money, then led me to a baked-potato stall, and we had a potato each, and a cup of tea between us. The potatoes tasted of mud. The tea was really tinted water. But at the stall there was a brazier, and this warmed us.

Zena, as I have said, seemed very changed since our

expulsion from the house. She did not tremble – it was I who trembled now – and she had an air of wisdom and authority about her, a way of passing through the streets, as if she were quite at her ease upon them. I had been at ease upon them once; now, I think that, if she had let me hold her hand, I would have done it – as it was, I could only stumble at her heels, saying wretchedly, 'What shall we do next, Zena?' and 'Oh, Zena, how cold it is!' and even 'What do you suppose they are doing now, Zena, at Felicity Place? Oh, can you believe that she has really cast me from her!'

'Miss,' she said to me at last, 'don't take it the wrong way; but if you don't shut up, I really shall be obliged to hit you, after all.'

I said: 'I'm sorry, Zena.'

In the end she fell into conversation with a gay girl who had also come to stand beside the brazier; and from her she got the details of a lodging-house nearby, that was said to take people in, all through the night. It turned out to be a dreadful place, with one chamber for the women and another for the men; and everyone who slept there had a cough. Zena and I lay two in a bed – she keeping her dress on, for the sake of the warmth, but me still fretting over the creases in mine, and so placing it beneath the foot of the mattress in the hope that it would press flat overnight.

We lay together very straight and stiff, our heads upon the same prickling bolster, but hers turned from mine and her eyes shut fast. The coughing of the other lodgers, the soreness at my cheek, my general wretchedness and panic, kept me wakeful. When Zena gave a shiver, I put my hand upon her; and when she didn't take the hand away, I moved a little closer to her. I said, very low: 'Oh Zena, I cannot sleep, for thinking of it all!'

'I dare say.'

I trembled. 'Do you hate me, Zena?' She wouldn't answer. 'I shan't blame you, if you do. But oh, do you know how sorry I am?' A woman in the bed beside us gave a shriek – I think she was a drunkard – and that made both of us jump, and brought our faces even closer. Her eyes were still hard shut, but I could tell that she listened. I thought of how differently we had lain together, only a few hours before. My wretchedness since then had knocked the fire right out of me; but because it hadn't been said by either of us, and I thought it ought to be, I whispered now: 'Oh, if only Diana hadn't come when she did! It was fun – wasn't it? – before Diana came and stopped it . . .'

She opened her eyes. 'It was fun,' she said sadly. 'It is always fun before they catch you.' Then she gazed at me, and swallowed.

I said: 'It won't be so bad, Zena – will it? You're the only tom I know in London, now; and since you're all alone, I thought – we might make a go of it, mightn't we? We might find a room, in a rooming-house. You could get work, as a sempstress or a char. I shall buy another suit; and when my face is all healed up – well, I know a trick or two, for making money. We shall have your seven pounds back in a month. We shall have twenty pounds in no time. And then, you can make your trip out to the colonies; and I' – I gave a gulp – 'I might go with you. You said they always need landladies there; surely, they'll always need gentlemen's tarts, too – even in Australia . . . ?'

She gazed at me as I murmured, saying nothing. Then she bent her head and kissed me once, very lightly, upon the lips. Then she turned away again, and at last I slept.

When I woke, it was daylight. I could hear the sounds of women coughing and spitting, and discussing, in low, peevish voices, the nights that they had passed, and the days they must now move on to. I lay with my eyes shut and my hands before my face: I didn't want to look at them, or at any part of the squalid world I was now obliged to share with them. I thought of Zena, and the plan that I had put to her – I thought: It will be hard, it will be terribly hard; but Zena will keep me from the worst of the hardness. Without Zena, it would be hard indeed . . .

Then I took my hands from my face at last, and turned to

gaze at the bed beside me; and it was empty. Zena was gone.
The money was gone. She had risen at dawn, with her servant's habits; and she had left me, slumbering, with nothing.

Understanding it at last left me curiously blank: I think, I was
too giddy already to be dazed any further, too wretched to
descend to greater depths. I rose, and drew my frock from
beneath the mattress – it was creased worse than ever – and
buttoned it on. The drunkard in the neighbouring bed had
spent a ha'penny on a bowl of tepid water, and she let me use
it, after she had stood in it and washed herself down, to wipe
the last remaining flakes of blood from my cheeks, and to flatten my hair. My face, when I gazed at it in the sliver of mirror
that was glued to the wall, looked like a face of wax, that had
been set too near a spirit-lamp. My feet, when I stepped on
them, seemed to shriek: the shoes were ones I had used to
wear as a renter, but either my feet had grown since then, or I
had become too used to gentle leather; I had gained blisters in
the walk to the Kilburn Road, and now the blisters began to
rub raw and wet, and the stockings to fray.

    We were not allowed to linger past the morning in the bed-
room of the lodging-house: at eleven o'clock a woman came,
and chivvied us out with a broom. I walked a little way with
the drunkard. When we parted, at the top of Maida Vale, she
took out the smallest screw of tobacco, rolled two thread-like
cigarettes, and gave me one. Tobacco, she said, was the best
cure for a bruise. I sat on a bench, and smoked till my fingers
scorched; and then I considered my plight.

    My situation, after all, was a ridiculously familiar one: I
had been as cold and as ill and as wretched as this four years
before, after my flight from Stamford Hill. Then, however, I
had at least had money, and handsome clothes; I had had food,
and cigarettes – had all I required to keep me, not happy, but
certainly quick. Now, I had nothing. I was nauseous with
hunger and with the after-effects of wine; and to get so much as
a penny for a cone of eels, I should have to beg for it – or do

what Zena recommended, and try my luck as a tart, up against
some dripping wall. The idea of begging was hateful to me – I
could not bear the thought of trying to extract pity and coins
from the kind of gentlemen who, a fortnight before, had
admired the cut of my suit or the flash of my cuff-links as I
passed amongst them at Diana's side. The thought of being
fucked by one of them, as a girl, was even worse.

I got up: it was too cold to sit upon the bench all day. I
remembered what Zena had said the night before – that I must
go to my folks, that my folks would take me. I had said that I
had no one; but now I thought that there might, after all, be one
place I could try. I did not think of my real family, in Whitstable:
I had finished with them, it seemed to me then, for ever. I
thought instead of a lady who had been like a mother to me,
once; and of her daughter, who had been a kind of sister. I
thought of Mrs Milne, and Gracie. I had had no contact with
them in a year and a half. I had promised to visit them, but had
never been at liberty to do so. I had promised to send them my
address: I had never sent them so much as a note to say I missed
them, or a card on Gracie's birthday. The truth was that, after my
first few, strange days at Felicity Place, I had not missed them at
all. But now I remembered their kindness, and wanted to weep.
Diana and Zena between them had made an outcast of me; but
Mrs Milne – I was sure of it! – was bound to take me in.

And so I walked, from Maida Vale to Green Street – walked
creepingly, in my misery and my shame and my pinching
boots, as if every step were taken barefoot on open swords. The
house, when I reached it at last, seemed shabby – but then, I
knew what it was, to leave a place for something grand, and
come back to find it humbler than you knew. There was no
flower before the door, and no three-legged cat – but then
again, it was winter, and the street very cold and bleak. I could
think only of my own sorry plight; and when I rang the bell
and no one came, I thought: Well, I will sit upon the step, Mrs
Milne is never out for long; and if I grow numb from the cold,
it will serve me right . . .

But then I pressed my face to the glass beside the door and peered into the hall beyond, and I saw that the walls – that used to have Gracie's pictures on them, the *Light of the World* and the Hindoo idol, and the others – I saw that they were bare; that there were only marks upon them, where the pictures had been fastened. And at that, I trembled. I caught hold of the door-knocker and banged it, in a kind of panic; and I called into the letter-box: 'Mrs Milne! Mrs Milne!' and 'Gracie! Grace Milne!' But my voice sounded hollow, and the hall stayed dark.

Then there came a shout, from the tenement behind.

'Are you looking for the old lady and her daughter? They have gone, dear – gone a month ago!'

I turned, and looked up. From a balcony above the street a man was calling to me, and nodding to the house. I went out, and gazed miserably up at him, and said, Where had they gone to?

He shrugged. 'Gone to her sister's, is what I heard. The lady was took very bad, in the autumn; and the girl being a simpleton – you knew that, did you? – they didn't think it clever to leave the pair of them alone. They have took all the furniture; I dare say that the house will come up for sale . . .' He looked at my cheek. 'That's a lovely black eye you have,' he said, as if I might not have noticed. 'Just like in the song – ain't it? Except you only have one of 'em!'

I stared at him, and shivered while he laughed. A little fair-haired girl had appeared on the balcony beside him, and now gripped the rail and put her feet upon the bars. I said, 'Where does the lady live – the sister they've gone to?' and he pulled at his ear and looked thoughtful.

'Now, I *did* know, but have forgotten it . . . I believe it was Bristol; or it may have been Bath . . .'

'Not London, then?'

'Oh no, certainly not London. Now, was it Brighton . . . ?'

I turned away from him, to gaze back up at Mrs Milne's house – at the window of my old room, and at the balcony where I had liked, in summer-time, to sit. When I looked at the man again, he had his little girl in his arms, and the wind had caught her golden hair and made it flap about his cheeks: and I remembered them both, then, as the father and daughter that I had seen clapping their hands to the sound of a mandolin, on that balmy June evening, in the week I met Diana. They had lost their home and been given a new one. They had been visited by that charity-visitor with the romantic-sounding name.

Florence! I did not know that I had remembered her. I had not thought of her at all, for a year and more.

If only I might meet her, now! She found houses for the poor; she might find a house for me. She had been kind to me once – wouldn't she be kind, if I appealed to her, a second time? I thought of her comely face, and her curling hair. I had lost Diana, I had lost Zena; and now I had lost Mrs Milne and Grace. In all of London she was the closest thing I had, at that moment, to a friend – and it was a friend just then that, above all else, I longed for.

On the balcony above me, the man had turned away. Now I called him back: 'Hey, mister!' I walked closer to the wall of the tenement, and gazed up at him: he and his daughter leaned from the balcony rail – she looked like an angel on the ceiling of a church. I said, 'You won't know me; but I lived here once, with Mrs Milne. I am looking for a girl, who called on you when you moved in. She worked for the people that found you your flat.'

He frowned. 'A girl, you say?'

'A girl with curly hair. A plain-faced girl called Florence. Don't you know who I mean? Don't you have the name of the charity she worked for? It was run by a lady – a very clever-looking lady. The lady played the mandolin.'

He had continued to frown, and to scratch at his head; but at this last detail he brightened. 'That one,' he said; 'yes, I remember her. And that gal what helped her, that was your chum, was it?'

I said it was. Then: 'And the charity? Do you remember them, and where their rooms are?'

'Where their rooms are, let me see . . . I did go there wunst; but I don't know as I can quite recall the partic'lar *number*. I do know as it was a place rather close to the Angel, Islington.'

'Near Sam Collins's?' I asked.

'*Past* Sam Collins's, on Upper Street. Not so far as the post office. A little doorway on the left-hand side, somewhere between a public-house and a tailor's . . .'

This was all he could recall; I thought it might be enough. I thanked him, and he smiled. 'What a lovely black eye,' he said again, but to his daughter this time. 'Just like the song – ain't it, Betty?'

By now I felt as if I had been on my feet for a month. I suspected that my boots had worn their way right through my stockings, and had started on the bare flesh of my toes and heels and ankles. But I did not stop at another bench, and untie my laces, in order to find out. The wind had picked up a little and, though it was only two o'clock or so, the sky was grey as lead. I wasn't sure what time the charity offices might close; I wasn't sure how long it would take me to find them; I didn't know if Florence would even be there, when I did. So I walked rather quickly up Pentonville Hill, and let my feet be rubbed to puddings, and tried to plan what I would say to her when I found her. This, however, proved difficult. After all, she was a girl I hardly knew; worse – I could not help but recall this, now – I had once arranged to meet her, then let her down. Would she, even, remember me at all? In that gloomy Green Street passageway I had been certain that she would. But with every burning step, I grew less sure of it.

It did not, as it turned out, take me very long to find the right office. The man's memory was a good one, and Upper Street itself seemed wonderfully unchanged since his last visit there: the public-house and the tailor's were quite as he had described them, close together on the left-hand side of the street, just past the music hall. In between them were three or four doors, leading to the rooms and offices above; and upon one of these was screwed a little enamel plaque, which said: *Ponsonby's Model Dwelling Houses. Directress Miss J. A. D. Derby* – I remembered this very well now as the name of the lady with the mandolin. Beneath the plaque was a hand-written, rain-spattered note with an arrow pointing to a bell-pull at the side of the door. *Please Ring*, it said, *and Enter*. So, with some trepidation, I did both.

The passageway behind the door was very long and very gloomy. It led to a window, which looked out at a view of bricks and oozing drain-pipes; and from here there was only one way to proceed, and that was upwards, via a set of naked stairs. The banister was sticky, but I grasped it, and began to climb. Before I had reached the third or fourth step, a door at the top of the staircase had opened, a head had emerged in the gap, and a lady's voice called pleasantly: 'Hallo down there! It's rather steep, but worth the effort. Do you need a light?'

I answered that I did not, and climbed faster. At the top, a little out of breath, I was led by the lady into a tiny chamber that held a desk, and a cabinet, and a set of mismatched chairs. When she gestured, I sat; she herself perched upon the edge of the desk, and folded her arms. From a room nearby came the fitful *crack-crack-crack* of a typewriting machine.

'Well,' she said, 'what can we do for you? I say, what an eye you have!' I had removed my hat, as if I were a man, and, as she studied my cheek – and then, more warily, my close-clipped head – I fiddled with the ribbon on the hatband, rather awkwardly. She said, 'Have you an appointment with us?' and I answered that I hadn't come about a house, at all. I had come about a girl.

'A girl?'

'A woman, I should say. Her name is Florence, and she works here, for the charity.'

She gave a frown. 'Florence,' she said; then, 'Are you sure? There's really only Miss Derby, myself and another lady.'

'Miss Derby,' I said quickly, 'knows who I mean. She

definitely *used* to work here; for the last time I saw her she said – she said—'

'She said . . . ?' prompted the lady, more warily than ever – for my mouth had fallen open, and my hand had flown to my swollen cheek; and now I cursed, in a hopeless kind of miserable fury.

'She said that she was leaving this post,' I said, 'and moving to another. What a fool I've been! I had forgotten it till now. That means that Florence hasn't worked here for a year and a half, or more!'

The lady nodded. 'Ah, well, you see, that was before my time. But, as you say, Miss Derby is sure to remember her.'

That, at least, was still true. I lifted my head. 'Then, may I see her?'

'You may – but not today; nor even tomorrow, I'm afraid. She won't be in now until Friday—'

'Friday!' That was terrible. 'But I must see Florence today, I really must! Surely you have a list, or a book, or something, that says where she has gone to. Surely somebody here must know.'

The lady seemed surprised. 'Well,' she said slowly, 'perhaps we do . . . But I cannot really give that sort of detail out, you know, to strangers.' She thought for a moment. 'Could you not write her a letter, and let us forward it . . . ?' I shook my head, and felt my eyes begin to prick. She must have seen, and misunderstood, for she said then, rather gently: 'Ah – perhaps you're not very handy with a pen . . . ?'

I would have admitted to anything, for the sake of a kind word. I shook my head again: 'Not very, no.'

She was silent for a moment. Perhaps she thought, that there could be nothing very sinister about my quest, if I could not even read or write. At any rate, she rose at last and said, 'Wait here.' Then she left the room and entered another, across the hall. The sound of the typewriter grew louder for a second, then ceased altogether; in its place I heard the murmur of voices, the prolonged rustling of paper, and finally the slam of a cabinet drawer.

The lady reappeared, bearing a white page – a letter, by the look of it – in her hand. 'Success! Thanks to Miss Derby's beautiful clerking system we have tracked your Florence – or, at least, *a* Florence – down; she left here just before both Miss Bennet and I began, in 1892. However' – she grew grave – 'we really do not think that we can give you her *own* address; but she left here to work at a home for friendless girls, and we can tell you where that is. It's a place called Freemantle House, on the Stratford Road.'

A home for friendless girls! The very idea of it made me tremble and grow weak. 'That must be her,' I said. 'But – Stratford? So far?' I shifted my feet beneath my chair, and felt the leather slide against my bleeding heels. The boots themselves were thick with mud; my skirt had gained a frill of filth, six inches deep, at the hem. Against the window there came the spatter of rain. 'Stratford,' I said again, so miserably that the woman drew near and put her hand upon my arm.

'Have you not the fare?' she asked gently. I shook my head. 'I have lost all my money. I have lost everything!' I placed a hand over my eyes, and leaned in utter weariness against the desk. As I did so, I saw what lay upon it. It was the letter. The lady had placed it there, face upwards, knowing – thinking – that I could not read it. It was very brief; it was signed by Florence herself – Florence Banner, I now saw her full name to be – and was addressed to Miss Derby. *Please accept notice of my resignation* . . . it ran. I didn't read that part. For at the top right-hand corner of the page there was a date, and an address – not that of Freemantle House but, clearly, the home address that I was not allowed to know. A number, followed by the name of a street: *Quilter Street, Bethnal Green, London E.* I memorised it at once.

Meanwhile, the woman talked kindly on. I had scarcely heard her, but now I raised my head and saw what she was about. She had taken a little key from her pocket and unlocked one of the drawers in the desk. She was saying, '. . . not something we make a habit of doing, at all; but I can see that you are *very* weary. If you take a bus from here to Aldgate, you can pick up another there, I believe, that will take you along the Mile End Road, to Stratford.' She held out her hand. There were three pennies in it. 'And perhaps you might get yourself a cup of tea, along the way?'

I took the coins, and mumbled some word of thanks. As I did so a bell rang, close at hand, and we both gave a start. She glanced at a clock upon the wall. 'My last clients of the day,' she said.

I took the hint, and rose and put on my hat. There were footsteps in the passageway below, now, and the sound of stumbling on the stairs. She ushered me to the door, and called to her visitors: 'Come up, that's right. It's rather steep, I know, but worth the effort . . .' A young man, followed by a woman, emerged from the gloom. They were both rather swarthy – Italians, I guessed, or Greeks – and looked terribly pinched and poor. We all shuffled around in the doorway of the office for a moment, smiling and awkward; then at last the lady and the young couple were inside the room, and I was alone at the head of the staircase.

The lady raised her head, and caught my eye.

'Good luck!' she called, a little distractedly. 'I do so hope you find your friend.'

Having no intention at all, now, of travelling to Stratford, I did not, as the lady recommended, catch a bus. I did, however, buy myself a cup of tea, from a stall with an awning to it, on the High Street. And when I gave back my cup to the girl, I nodded. 'Which way,' I asked, 'to Bethnal Green?'

I had never been much further east before – alone, and on foot – than Clerkenwell. Now, limping down the City Road towards Old Street, I felt the beginnings of a new kind of nervousness. It had grown darker during my time in the office, and wet and foggy. The street-lamps had all been lit, and every carriage had a lantern swinging from it; City Road was not, however, like Soho, where light streamed upon the pavements from a thousand flares and windows. For every ten paces of my journey that were illuminated by a pool of gas-light, there were a further twenty that were cast in gloom.

The gloom lifted a little at Old Street itself, for here there were offices, and crowded bus stops and shops. As I walked towards the Hackney Road, however, it seemed only to deepen, and my surroundings to grow shabbier. The crossings at the Angel had been decent enough; here the roads were so clogged with manure that, every time a vehicle rumbled by, I was showered with filth. My fellow pedestrians, too – who, so far, had all been honest working-people, men and women in coats and hats as faded as my own – grew poorer. Their suits were not just dingy, but ragged. They had boots, but no stockings. The men wore scarves instead of collars, and caps rather than bowlers; the women wore shawls; the girls wore dirty aprons, or no apron at all. Everyone seemed to have some kind of burden – a basket, or a bundle, or a child upon their hip. The rain fell harder.

I had been told by the tea-girl at the Angel to head for Columbia Market; now, a little way along the Hackney Road, I found myself suddenly on the edge of its great, shadowy courtyard. I shivered. The huge granite hall, its towers and tracery as elaborate as those on a gothic cathedral, was quite dark and still. A few rough-looking fellows with cigarettes and bottles slouched in its arches, blowing on their hands to keep the cold off.

A sudden clamour in the clock tower made me start. Some complicated pealing of bells – as fussy and useless as the great abandoned market hall itself – was chiming out the hour: it was a quarter-past four. This was far too early to visit Florence's house, if Florence herself was at work all day: so I stood for another hour in one of the arches of the market where the wind was not so cutting and the rain was not so hard. Only when the bells had rung half-past five did I step again into the courtyard, and look about me: I was now almost numb. There was a little girl nearby, carrying a great tray about her neck, filled with bundles of watercresses. I went up to her, and asked how far it was to Quilter Street; and then, because she looked so sad and cold and damp – and also because I had a confused idea that I must not turn up on Florence's doorstep entirely empty-handed – I bought the biggest of her cress bouquets. It cost a ha'penny.

With this cradled awkwardly in the crook of my stiff arm I began the short walk to the street I wanted; soon I found myself at the end of a wide terrace of low, flat houses – not a squalid terrace, by any means, but not a very smart one either, for the glass in some of the street-lamps was cracked, or missing entirely, and the pavement was blocked, here and there, by piles of broken furniture, and by heaps of what the novels politely term *ashes*. I looked at the number of the nearest door: number 1. I started slowly down the street. Number 5 . . . number 9 . . . number 11 . . . I felt weaker than ever . . . 15 . . . 17 . . . 19 . . .

Here I stopped, for now I could see the house I sought quite clearly. Its drapes were drawn against the dark, and luminous with lamplight; and seeing them, I felt suddenly quite sick with apprehension. I placed a hand against the wall, and tried to steady myself; a boy walked by me, whistling, and gave me a wink – I suppose he thought I had been drinking. When he had passed I looked about me at the unfamiliar houses in a kind of panic: I could remember the sense of purpose that had visited me in Green Street, but it seemed a piece of wildness, now, a piece of comedy – I would tell it to Florence, and she would laugh in my face.

But I had come so far; and there was nowhere to turn back to. So I crept to the rosy window, and then to the door; and then I knocked, and waited. I seemed to have presented myself at a thousand thresholds that day, and been cruelly disappointed or repulsed, at all of them. If there was no word of kindness for me here, I thought, I would die.

At last there came a murmur and a step, and the door was opened; and it was Florence herself who stood there – looking remarkably as she had when I had seen her first, peering into the darkness, framed against the light and with the same glorious halo of burning hair. I gave a sigh that was also a shudder – then I saw a movement at her hip, and saw what she carried there. It was a baby. I looked from the baby to the room behind, and here there was another figure: a man, seated in his shirt-sleeves before a blazing fire, his eyes raised from the paper at his knee to gaze at me in mild enquiry.

I looked from him back to Florence.

'Yes?' she said. I saw that she didn't remember me at all. She didn't remember me and – worse – she had a husband, and a child.

I did not think that I could bear it. My head whirled, I closed my eyes – and sank upon her doorstep in a swoon.

Chapter 16

When next I knew myself I was lying flat upon a rug with my feet apparently raised on a little cushion; there was the warmth and the crackling of a fire at my side, and the low murmur of voices somewhere near. I opened my eyes: the room turned horribly and the rug seemed to dip, so I closed them again at once, and kept them tight shut until the floor, like a spinning coin, seemed slowly to cease its lurching and grow still.

After that it was rather wonderful simply to lie in the glow of the fire, feeling the life creep back into my numbed and aching limbs; I forced myself, however, to consider my peculiar situation, and pay a little thoughtful heed to my surroundings. I was, I realised, in Florence's parlour: she and her husband must have lifted me over their threshold and made me comfortable before their hearth. It was their murmurs that I could hear: they stood a little way behind me – they had evidently not caught the flash of my opening eyes – and discussed me, in rather wondering tones.

'But who might she *be*?' I heard the man say.

'I don't know.' This was Florence. There was a creak, followed by a silence, in which I felt her squinting at my features. 'And yet,' she went on, 'there is something a little bit familiar about her face . . .'

'Look at her cheek,' said the man in a lower voice. 'Look at her poor dress and bonnet. Look at her hair! Do you think she might've been in prison? Could she be one of your gals, just come from a reformat'ry?' There was another pause; perhaps Florence shrugged. 'I do think she must've been in prison, though,' the man went on, 'judging by the state of her poor hair . . .' I felt slightly indignant at that; and indignation made me twitch. 'Look out!' said the man then. 'She is waking up.'

I opened my eyes again to see him stooping over me. He was a very gentle-featured man, with short-cut hair of a reddish-golden hue, and a full set of whiskers that made him look a little like the sailor on the Player's packets. The thought made me long all at once for a cigarette, and I gave a dry little cough. The man squatted, and patted my shoulder. 'Ho there, miss,' he said. 'Are you well, dear? Are you well at last? You are quite, you know, amongst friends.' His voice and manner were so very kind that – still weak and slightly bewildered from my swoon – I felt the tears rising to my eyes, and raised a hand to my brow to press them back. When I took the hand away, there seemed blood upon it; I gave a cry, thinking I had set my nose off bleeding once again. But it was not blood. It was only that the rain had soaked into my cheap hat, and the dye had run all down my brows in great wet streaks of crimson.

What a guy Diana had made of me! The thought made me weep at last in earnest, in terrible, shaming gulps. At that, the man produced a handkerchief, and patted me once again upon the arm. 'I expect,' he said, 'that you would like a cup of something hot?' I nodded, and he rose and moved away. In his place came Florence. She must have put her baby down somewhere, for now she had her arms folded stiffly across her chest.

She asked me: 'Are you feeling better?' Her voice was not quite as kind as the man's had been, and her gaze seemed rather sterner. I nodded to her, then with her help raised myself from the floor into an armchair near the fire. The baby, I saw, was lying on its back on another, clasping and unclasping its little hands. From a room next door – the kitchen, I guessed – came the chink of crockery and a tuneless whistle. I blew my nose, and wiped my head; then wept some more; then grew a little calmer.

I looked again at Florence and said, 'I am sorry, to have turned up here in such a state.' She said nothing. 'You will be wondering, I suppose, who I am . . .' She gave a faint smile.

'We have been a little, yes.'

'I'm,' I began – then stopped, and coughed, to mask my hesitation. What could I say to her? I'm the girl who flirted with you once eighteen months ago? I'm the girl who asked you to supper, then left you standing, without a word, on Judd Street?

'I'm a friend of Miss Derby's,' I said at last.

Florence blinked. 'Miss Derby?' she said. 'Miss Derby, from the Ponsonby Trust?'

I nodded. 'Yes. I – I met you once, a long time ago. I was passing through Bethnal Green, on a visit, and thought I might call. I brought you some watercresses . . .' We turned our heads and gazed at them. They had been placed on a table near the door and looked very sad, for I had fallen upon them when I swooned. The leaves were crushed and blackened, the stems broken, the paper damp and green.

Florence said, 'That was kind of you.' I smiled a little nervously. For a second there was a silence – then the baby gave a kick and a yell, and she bent to pick it up and hold it against her breast, saying as she did so: 'Shall Mama take you? There, now.' Then the man reappeared, bearing a cup of tea and a plate of bread and butter which he set, with a smile, on the arm of my chair. Florence placed her chin upon the baby's head. 'Ralph,' she said, 'this lady is a friend of Miss Derby's – do you remember, Miss Derby that I used to work for?'

'Good heavens,' said the man – Ralph. He was still in his shirt-sleeves; now he picked up his jacket from the back of a chair and put it on. I busied myself with my cup and plate. The tea was very hot and sweet: the best tea, I thought, that I had ever tasted. The baby gave another cry, and Florence began to sway and jiggle, and to smooth the child's head, distractedly, with her cheek. Soon the cry became a gurgle, and then a sigh; and hearing it, I sighed too – but turned it into a breath for cooling my tea with, in case they thought I was about to start up weeping again.

There was another silence; then, 'I'm afraid I've forgotten your name,' said Florence. To Ralph she explained: 'It seems we met once.'

I cleared my throat. 'Miss Astley,' I said. 'Miss Nancy Astley.' Florence nodded; Ralph held out his hand for mine, and shook it warmly.

'I'm very glad to meet you, Miss Astley,' he said. Then he gestured to my cheek. 'That's a smart eye you have.'

I said, 'It is, rather, ain't it?'

He looked kind. 'Perhaps it was the blow, as made you faint. You gave us quite a scare.'

'I'm sorry. I think you're right, it must have been the blow. I – I was struck by a man with a ladder, in the street.'

'A ladder!'

'Yes, he – he turned too sharp, not seeing me and—'

'Well!' said Ralph. 'Now, you'd never believe such a thing could happen, would you, outside of a comedy in the theatre!'

I gave him a wan sort of smile, then lowered my eyes and started on the bread and butter. Florence was studying me, I thought, rather carefully.

Then the baby sneezed and, as Florence took a handkerchief to its nose, I said half-heartedly: 'What a handsome child!' At once, his parents turned their eyes upon him and gave identical, foolish smiles of pleasure and concern. Florence lifted him a little way away from her, the lamplight fell upon him; and I saw with surprise that he really was a pretty boy – not at all like his mother, but with fine features and very dark hair and a tiny, jutting pink lip.

Ralph leaned to stroke his son's jerking head. 'He is a beauty,' he said; 'but he is dozier, tonight, than he should be. We leave him in the daytime with a gal across the street, and we are sure that she puts laud'num in his milk, to stop his cries. Not,' he added quickly, 'as I am blaming her. She must take in that many kids, to bring the money in, the noise when they all start up is deafening. Still, I wish she wouldn't. I hardly think it can be very healthful . . .' We discussed this for a moment, then admired the baby for a little longer; then grew silent again.

'So,' said Ralph doggedly, 'you are a friend of Miss Derby's?'

I looked quickly at Florence. She had recommenced her jiggling, but was still rather thoughtful. I said, 'That's right.'

'And how *is* Miss Derby?' said Ralph then.

'Oh, well, you know Miss Derby!'

'Just the same, then, is she?'

'Exactly the same,' I said. 'Exactly.'

'Still with the Ponsonby, then?'

'Still with the Ponsonby. Still doing her good works. Still, you know, playing her mandolin.' I raised my hands, and gave a few half-hearted imaginary strums; but as I did so Florence ceased her swaying, and I felt her glance grow hard. I looked hurriedly back to Ralph. He had smiled at my words.

'Miss Derby's mandolin,' he said, as if the memory amused him. 'How many homeless families must she not've cheered with it!' He winked. 'I had forgotten all about it . . .'

'So had I.' This was Florence, and she did not sound at all ironical. I chewed very hard and fast on a piece of crust. Ralph smiled again, then said, very kindly: 'And where was it you met Flo?'

I swallowed. 'Well—' I began.

'I believe,' said Florence herself, 'I believe it was in Green Street, wasn't it, Miss Astley? In Green Street, just off the Gray's Inn Road?' I put down my plate, and raised my eyes to hers. I knew one second's pleasure, to find that she had not after all quite forgotten the girl who had studied her, so saucily, on that warm June night so long ago; then I saw how hard her expression was, and I trembled.

'Oh dear,' I said, closing my eyes and putting a hand to my brow. 'I think I am not quite well after all.' I felt Ralph take a

step towards me, then grow still: Florence must have stopped
him with some significant look.

'I think Cyril might go up, now, Ralph,' she said quietly.
There was the sound of the baby being passed over, then of a
door opening and shutting, and finally of boots upon a staircase, and the creaking of floorboards in the room above our
heads. Then there was silence; Florence lowered herself into
the other armchair, and sighed.

'Would it really make you very ill, Miss Astley,' she said in
a tired voice, 'to tell me just why it is you're here?' I looked at
her, but couldn't speak. 'I can't believe Miss Derby really recommended you to come.'

'No,' I said. 'I only saw Miss Derby that once, in Green
Street.'

'Then who was it told you where I live?'

'Another lady at the Ponsonby office,' I said. 'At least, she
didn't *tell* me, but she had your address on her desk and I –
saw it.'

'You saw it.'

'Yes.'

'And thought you would visit . . .'

I bit my lip. 'I'm in a spot of trouble,' I said. 'I remembered
you—' Remembered you, I almost added, as rather kinder than
you are proving yourself to be. 'The lady at the office said you
work at a home for friendless girls . . .'

'And so I do! But this ain't it. This is *my* home.'

'But I am quite, quite friendless.' My voice shook. 'I am
more friendless than you can possibly know.'

'You are certainly very changed,' she said after a moment,
'since I saw you last.' I looked down at my crumpled frock, my
terrible boots. Then I looked at her. She, I now saw, was also
changed. She seemed older and thinner, and the thinness
didn't suit her. Her hair, which I remembered as so curly, she
had pulled back into a tight little knot at the back of her head,
and the dress she was wearing was plain and very dark. All in
all, she looked as sober as Mrs Hooper, back at Felicity Place.

I took a breath to steady my voice. 'What can I do?' I said simply. 'I've nowhere to go. I've no money, no home . . .'

'I am sorry for you, Miss Astley,' she answered awkwardly. 'But Bethnal Green is busting with badly-off girls. If I was to let them all come and stay, I should have to live in a castle! Besides, I – I don't know you, or anything about you.'

'Please,' I said. 'Just for one night. If you only knew how many doors I have been turned away from. I really think that, if you send me out into the street, I shall keep walking until I reach a river or a canal; and then I shall drown myself.'

She frowned, then put a finger to her lips and bit at a nail; all her nails, I now noticed, were very short and chewed.

'What kind of trouble are you in, exactly?' she said at last. 'Mr Banner thought you might have come from – well, from gaol.'

I shook my head, and then said wearily: 'The truth is, I've been living with someone; and they have thrown me out. They have kept my things – oh! I had such handsome things! – and they have left me so miserable and poor and bewildered . . .' My voice grew thick. Florence watched me in silence for a moment. Then she said, rather carefully I thought, 'And this person was . . . ?'

But that made me hesitate. If I told her the truth, what would she make of it? I had thought her almost tommish, once; but now – well, maybe she had only ever been an ordinary girl, asking me to a lecture for friendship's sake. Or perhaps she had liked girls once, then turned her back on them – like Kitty! That thought made me cautious: if a tom with a bruise turned up at Kitty's door, I knew very well what a welcome she would get. I put my head in my hands. 'It was a gent,' I said quietly, 'I've been living in the house of a gent, in St John's Wood, for a year and a half. I let him make me a' – I remembered a phrase of Mrs Milne's – 'a pack of promises. He bought me all manner of stuff. And now . . .' I raised my eyes to hers. 'You must think me very wicked. He said he would marry me!'

She looked terribly surprised; but she had also begun to

look sorry, too. 'It was this bloke blacked your eye for you, I suppose,' she said, 'and not a ladder, at all.'

I nodded, and raised a hand to the bruise at my cheek; then I put my fingers to my hair, remembering that. 'What a devil he was!' I said then. 'He was rich as anything, could do what he pleased. He saw me on my balcony, just as you did, in a pair of trousers. He—' I blushed. 'He used to like to make me dress up, as a boy, in a suit like a sailor . . .'

'Oh!' she cried, as if she had never heard anything more awful. 'But the wealthy ones are the worst, I swear it! Have you no family to go to?'

'They – they've all thrown me over, because of this business.'

She shook her head at that; then grew thoughtful again, and glanced quickly at my waist. 'You ain't – you ain't in trouble, are you?' she asked quietly.

'In trouble? I—' I couldn't help it: it was as if she was handing me the play text, for me to read it back to her. 'I *was* in trouble,' I said, with my eyes on my lap, 'but the gent fixed that when he beat me. It was on account of it, I think, that I was so poorly, earlier on . . .'

At that, there came a very queer and kind expression to her face; and she nodded, and swallowed – and I saw I had convinced her.

'If you truly have nowhere, it will not hurt, I suppose, for you to stay a night – just one night – here with us. And tomorrow I shall give you the names of some places where you might find a bed . . .'

'Oh!' I felt ready to swoon all over again, in sheer relief. 'And Mr Banner,' I said, 'won't mind it?'

Mr Banner, it turned out, had no objection to my staying there at all; indeed, as before, he proved pleasanter than his wife, and willing to go to all sorts of trouble for the sake of my comfort. When they ate – for I had interrupted them as they were about to take their tea – it was he who set a plate before me and filled it with stew. He brought me a shawl when I shivered; and, when he saw me limping into the room after a visit to the privy, he made me pull off my boots, and fetched a bowl of salty water for me to soak my blistered feet in. Finally – and most wonderfully of all – he took down a tin of tobacco from the shelf of a bookcase, rolled two neat cigarettes, and offered me one to smoke.

Florence, meanwhile, sat all night a little apart from us, at the supper-table, working through a pile of papers – lists, I fondly supposed them to be, of friendless girls; account-sheets, perhaps, from Freemantle House. When we lit our cigarettes she looked up and sniffed, but made no complaint; occasionally she would sigh or yawn, or rub her neck as if it ached, and then her husband would address her with some word of encouragement or affection. Once the baby cried: she tilted her head, but didn't stir; it was Ralph who, all ungrudgingly, rose to see to it. She simply worked on: writing, reading, comparing pages, addressing envelopes . . . She worked while Ralph yawned, and finally stood and stretched and touched his lips to her cheek and bade us both a polite good-night; she worked while *I* yawned, and began to doze. At last, at around eleven o'clock, she shuffled her papers together and passed her hand over her face. When she saw me she gave a start: I really believe that, in her industry, she had forgotten me.

Now, remembering, she first blushed, then frowned.

'I had better go up, Miss Astley,' she said. 'You won't mind sleeping in here, I hope? I'm afraid there's nowhere else for you.' I smiled. I did not mind – though I thought there must be an empty room upstairs, and wondered, privately, why she did not put me in it. She helped me push the two armchairs together, then went to fetch a pillow, a blanket and a sheet.

'Do you have everything you need?' she asked then. 'The privy is out the back, as you know. There's a jug of clean water kept in the pantry, if you're thirsty. Ralph will be up at six or so, and I shall follow him at seven – or earlier, if Cyril wakes me. You'll have to leave at eight, of course, when I do.' I nodded quickly. I wouldn't think about the morning, just yet.

There was an awkward silence. She looked so tired and ordinary I had a foolish urge to kiss her cheek good-night, as Ralph had. Of course, I did not; I only took a step towards her as she nodded to me and prepared to make her way upstairs, and said, 'I am more grateful to you, Mrs Banner, than I can say. You have been very kind to me – you, who hardly know me; and more especially your husband, who doesn't know me at all.'

As I spoke she turned to me, and blinked. Then she placed her hand on a chair-back, and smiled a curious smile. 'Did you think he was my husband?' she said. I hesitated, suddenly flustered.

'Well, I—'

'He ain't my husband! He's my brother.' Her brother! She continued to smile at my confusion, and then to laugh: for a moment she was the pert girl I had spoken with in Green Street, all those months before . . .

But then the baby, in the room above us, gave a cry, and we both raised our eyes to the sound, and I felt myself blush. And when she saw that, her smile faded. 'Cyril ain't mine,' she said quickly, 'though I call him mine. His mother used to lodge with us, and we took him on when she – left us. He is very dear to us, now . . .'

The awkward way she said it showed there was some story there – perhaps the mother was in prison; perhaps the baby was really a cousin's, or a sister's, or a sweetheart's of Ralph's. Such things happened often enough in Whitstable families: I didn't think much of it. I only nodded; and then I yawned. And seeing me, she yawned too.

'Good-night, Miss Astley,' she said from behind her hand. She did not look like the Green Street girl now. She looked only weary again, and plainer than ever.

I waited a moment while she stepped upstairs – I heard her shuffling above me, and guessed of course that she must share her chamber with the baby – then I took up a lamp, and made my way out to the privy. The yard was very small, and

overlooked on every side by walls and darkened windows; I
lingered for a second on the chilly flags, gazing at the stars,
sniffing at the unfamiliar, faintly riverish, faintly cabbagy,
scents of East London. A rustling from the neighbouring yard
disturbed me and I started, fearing rats. It was not rats, however, but rabbits: four of them, in a hutch, their eyes flashing
like jewels in the light I turned on them.

I slept in my petticoats, half-lying, half-sitting between the
two armchairs, with the blankets wrapped around me and my
dress laid flat upon them for extra warmth. It does not sound
very comfortable; it was, in fact, extraordinarily cosy, and for
all that I had so much to keep me ill and fretful, I found I
could only yawn and smile to feel the cushions so soft beneath
my back, and the dying fire warm beside me. I was woken, in
the night, twice: the first time by the sound of shouting in the
street, and the slam of doors and the rattle of the poker in
the grate, in the house next door; and the second time by the
crying of the baby, in Florence's room. This sound, in the darkness, made me shiver, for it recalled to me all the awful nights
that I had spent at Mrs Best's, in that grey chamber overlooking
Smithfield Market. It did not, however, last for very long. I
heard Florence rise and step across the floor, and then return –
with Cyril, I supposed – to bed. And after that he didn't stir
again, and neither did I.

When I woke next morning it was at the slam of the back door:
this was Ralph, I guessed, leaving for work, for the clock
showed ten to seven. There was movement overhead soon
after that, as Florence rose and dressed, and much activity in
the street outside – amazingly close, it all sounded to me, who
was used to slumbering undisturbed by early risers in Diana's
quiet villa.

I lay quite still, the contentment of the night all seeping
from me. I didn't want to rise and face the day, to pull my
pinching boots back on, bid Florence good-bye, and be a
friendless girl again. The parlour had grown very cold

overnight, and my little makeshift bed seemed the only warm place in it. I pulled the blankets over my head, and groaned; groaning, I found, was rather satisfying, so I groaned still louder . . . I stopped only when I heard the click of the parlour door – then lifted the blankets from my face to see Florence squinting at me, gravely, through the gloom.

'You're not ill again?' she said. I shook my head.

'No. I was only – groaning.'

'Oh.' She looked away. 'Ralph has left some tea. Shall I fetch you some?'

'Yes, please.'

'And then – then you must get up, I'm afraid.'

'Of course,' I said. 'I shall get up now.' But when she had gone I found I could not get up, at all. I could only lie. I needed to visit the privy again, rather badly; I knew that it was dreadfully rude to lie abed like this, in a stranger's parlour. Yet I felt as if I had been visited in the night by a surgeon, who had taken all my bones away and replaced them with bars of lead. I could no nothing at all – except lie . . .

Florence brought me my tea, and I drank it – then lay back again. I heard her moving about in the kitchen, washing the baby; then she returned and pulled the curtains open, meaningfully.

'It's a quarter to eight, Miss Astley,' she said. 'I have to take Cyril across the street. You will be up and dressed, now, won't you, when I come back? You really will?'

'Oh, certainly,' I said; yet when she reappeared, five minutes later, I had not budged an inch. She gazed at me, and shook her head. I gazed back at her.

'You know, don't you, that you cannot stay here. I *must* go to work, and I must go *now*. If you keep me any longer, I shall be late.' With that, she caught hold of the bottom of the blanket. But I caught hold of the top.

'I can't do it,' I said. 'I must be sick, after all.'

'If you're sick, you must go to a place where they will care for you properly!'

'I'm not that sick!' I cried then. 'But if I might only lie a little and get my strength . . . Go on to work, and I'll let myself out, and be long gone by the time you get home. You may trust me in your house, you know. I shan't take anything.'

'There's little enough *to* take!' she cried. Then she threw her end of the blanket at me, and put a hand to her brow. 'Oh,' she said, 'how my head aches!' I looked at her, saying nothing. At last she seemed to force herself into a kind of calmness, and her voice grew stiff: 'You must do as you said, I suppose, and let yourself out.' She caught up her coat from the back of the door, and pulled it on. Then she took up her satchel, reached into it, and brought out a piece of paper and a coin. 'I've made you a list,' she said, 'of hostels and houses you might try to find a bed in. The money' – it was a half-crown – 'is from my brother. He asked me to tell you good-bye and good luck.'

'He's a very kind man,' I said.

She shrugged, then buttoned up her coat, put her hat upon her head, and thrust a pin through it. The coat and the hat were the colour of mud. She said, 'There's a piece of bacon still warm in the kitchen, which you may as well have for your breakfast. Then – oh! Then you really must go.'

'I promise I will!'

She nodded, and pulled at the door. There came a blast of icy air from the street outside that made me shiver. Florence shivered, too. The wind blew the brim of her hat away from her brow, and she narrowed her hazel eyes against it, and tightened her jaw.

I said, 'Miss Banner! I – might I come back, sometime, on a visit? I should like – I should like to see your brother, and thank him . . .' I should like to see *her*, was what I meant. I had come to make a friend of her. But I didn't know how to say it.

She put a hand to her collar, and blinked into the wind. 'You must do as you like,' she said. Then she pulled the door shut, leaving the parlour chill behind her, and I saw her shadow on the lace at the window as she walked away.

After she had gone my leaden limbs seemed all at once,

and quite miraculously, to lighten. I rose, and braved again the
chilly privy; then I found the slice of bacon that had been put
aside for me, and took a piece of bread and a bunch of cress,
and ate my breakfast standing at the kitchen window, gazing
sightlessly at the unfamiliar view beyond it.

After that I rubbed my hands, and glanced about me, and
began to wonder what to do.

The kitchen, at least, was warm, for someone – Ralph, pre-
sumably – had lit a small fire in the range, early on, and the
coals were only half consumed. It did seem a shame to waste
their lovely heat – and it could not hurt, I told myself, to boil
up some water for a bit of a wash. I opened a cupboard door,
looking for a pan to set upon the hob, and came across a flat-
iron; and seeing this I thought: They wouldn't mind, surely, if
I warmed that, too, and gave my battered frock a little
press . . .

While I waited for these things to heat I wandered back into
the parlour, to separate the armchairs that had made my bed,
and set the blankets in a tidy pile. This done, I did what I had
been at first too bewildered, and then too sleepy, to do the
night before: I stood and had a proper look around.

The room, as I have said, was a very small one – far smaller,
certainly, than my old bedroom at Felicity Place – and there
were no gas-jets in it, only oil-lamps and candlesticks. The
furniture and decorations were, I thought, a rather curious
mixture. The walls were bare of paper, like Diana's, but had
been stained a patchy blue, like a workshop's; for decoration
they had only a couple of almanacks – this year's and last
year's – and two or three dull-looking prints. There were two
rugs upon the floor, one ancient and threadbare, the other new
and vivid and coarse and rather rustic: the kind of rug I
thought a shepherd, suffering some disease of the eyes, might
weave to while away the endless gloomy hours of a Hebridean
winter. The mantelpiece was draped with a fluttering shawl,
just as my mother's had been, and upon it were the kind of
ornaments I had seen, as a child, in all my friends' and

cousins' homes: a dusty china shepherdess, her crook broken
and inexpertly mended; a piece of coral, beneath a dome of
soot-spotted glass; a glittering carriage-clock. Besides these,
however, there were other less predictable items on display: a
creased postcard, with a picture of working-men on it and the
words *Dockers' Tanner or Dockers' Strike!*; an oriental idol,
rather tarnished; a colour print of a man and woman in
working-gear, their right hands clasped, their left hands
supporting a billowing banner: *Strength Through Unity!*

These things did not much interest me. I looked next at the
alcove beside the chimney-breast, where there was a set of
home-made shelves, fairly bursting with books and magazines.
This collection was also very mixed, and very dusty. There
was a good supply of shilling classics – Longfellow, Dickens,
that sort of thing – and one or two cheap novels; but there were
also a number of political texts, and two or three volumes of
what might be called interesting verse. At least one of these –
Walt Whitman's *Leaves of Grass* – I had seen before on Diana's
bookshelves at Felicity Place. I had tried to read it once in an
idle moment: I had thought it terribly dull.

These shelves and their contents claimed my attention for a
minute or so; it was seized after that by two pictures which
hung from the rail above. The first of these was a family portrait, and as stiff, as quaint and as marvellously intriguing as
other families' portraits always are. I looked for Florence first,
and found her – aged, perhaps, fifteen or so, and very fresh and
plump and earnest – seated between a white-haired lady and a
younger, darker girl, who had the beginnings of a barmaid's
flash good looks about her and must, I thought, be a sister.
Behind them stood three boys: Ralph, minus his sailor's
whiskers and wearing a very high collar; a rather older brother
who looked very much like him; and an older brother again.
There was no father.

The second portrait was a picture-postcard photograph: it
had been placed in the edge of the large picture's frame, but its
corner curled a little, showing a loop of faded writing on the

back. The subject of the portrait was a woman – a heavy-browed woman with untidy dark hair: she seemed to be sitting very squarely, and her gaze was rather grave. I thought she might be the sister from the family group, grown up; or she might be a friend of Florence's, or a cousin, or – well, anybody. I leaned over to try to read the handwriting that showed where the card curled over; but it was hidden, and I didn't like to pluck it free – it wasn't *that* intriguing. Then I caught the bubbling of the pan of water I had set upon the stove, and hurried out to see to it.

I found a little tin bowl to wash in, and a block of green kitchen soap; and then – since there was no towel, and I didn't think it really polite to use the dish-cloth – I danced about before the range until I was dry enough to climb back into my dirty petticoats. I thought, with a little sigh, of Diana's handsome bathroom – of that cabinet of unguents that I had liked to sample for hours at a time. Even so, it was marvellous to be clean again, and when I had combed my hair and tended my face (I rubbed a bit of vinegar into the bruise, and then a bit of flour); when I had thumped the filth from my skirts and pressed them flat and put them on again, I felt fit and warm and quite unreasonably gay. I walked back into the parlour – it was a matter of some ten steps or so – stood for a second there, then returned to the kitchen. It was, I thought, a very pleasant house; as I had already begun to notice, however, it was not a very clean one. The rugs, I saw, all badly wanted beating. The skirting-boards were scuffed and streaked with mud. Every shelf and picture was as dusty as the sooty mantelpiece. If this was *my* house, I thought, I would keep it smart as a new pin.

Then I had a rather wonderful idea. I ran back into the parlour and looked at the clock. Less than an hour had passed since Florence's departure, and neither she nor Ralph, I guessed, would be home much before five. That gave me about eight whole hours – slightly less, I supposed, if I wanted to be sure of finding myself a room in some lodging-house or hostel while it was still light. How much cleaning could you do in

eight hours? I had no idea: it was generally Alice who had
helped Mother out at home; I had hardly cleaned a thing before
in my life; lately I had had servants to do my cleaning for me.
But I felt inspired, now, to tidy this house – this house where
I had been, albeit briefly, so content. It would be a kind of
parting gift, I thought, for Ralph and Florence. I would be like
a girl in a fairy story, sweeping out the dwarfs' cottage, or the
robbers' cave, while the dwarfs or the robbers were at work.

I believe I laboured, that day, harder than I had ever
laboured over anything before; and I have wondered since,
thinking back to the industry of those hours, whether the thing
that I was really washing was not my own tarnished soul. I
began by lighting a bigger fire in the range, to heat more water
with. Then I found that I had used up all the water in the
house: I had to limp up and down Quilter Street with two
great buckets, looking for a stand-pipe; and when I found one
I also found a line of women at it, and had to wait amongst
them for half an hour, until the tap – which ran no faster than
a trickle, and sometimes only spluttered and choked – was
free. The women looked me up and down, rather – they looked
at my eye, and more especially at my head, for I had placed a
cap of Ralph's upon it in lieu of my damp hat, and they could
see where the hair was shorn and razored beneath. But they
were not at all unfriendly. One or two, who had seen me leave
the house, asked me, was I lodging with the Banners? And I
answered that I was only passing through. They seemed happy
enough with that, as if people passed through, in this district,
very frequently.

When I had staggered home with the water, set it warming
on the stove, and wrapped myself in a great, crusty apron I
found hanging on the back of the pantry door, I began on the
parlour. First I wiped down all the dim and sooty things with
a wet cloth; then I washed the window, and then the skirting-
boards. The rugs I carried out into the yard: here I hung them
over the wash-line, and beat them until my arm ached. As I did
so, the back door of the neighbouring house was pulled open

and a woman, her sleeves rolled up like mine and her own cheeks flushed, emerged to stand upon the step. When she saw me she nodded, and I nodded back.

'A fine job you've taken on,' she said, 'cleaning the Banners' place.' I smiled, glad of the rest, and wiped the sweat from my brow and lip.

'Are they known for their dirt, then?'

'They are,' she said, 'in this street. They do too much in other folks' houses, and not enough in their own. That's the trouble.' She spoke good-humouredly, however: she didn't seem to mean that Ralph and Florence were busy-bodies. I rubbed my aching shoulder. 'You'll be the new lodger, I suppose?' she asked me then. I shook my head, and repeated what I had told the other neighbours – that I was only passing through. She seemed as unimpressed by that as they had been. She watched me for a minute or two while I resumed my beating; then she went indoors, without another word.

When the rugs were beaten I swept the fireplace in the parlour; then I found some blacklead in the pantry, and began to dab at it with that. I had not leaded a grate since I left home – though I had seen Zena blacking Diana's fireplaces a hundred times, and remembered it as rather easy labour. In fact, of course, it was tricky, filthy work, and kept me busy for an hour, and left me feeling not a half so blithe as I had been at first. Still, however, I didn't stop to rest. I swept the floors, and then I scrubbed them; then I washed the kitchen tiles, and then the range, and then the kitchen window. I did not like to venture upstairs, but the parlour and the kitchen, and even the privy and the yard, I worked upon until they fairly gleamed; until every surface that was meant to shine, shone; until every colour was vivid, rather than dulled and paled by dust.

My final triumph was the front doorstep: this I swept and washed, and finally scrubbed with a piece of hearthstone until it was as white as any doorstep in the street – and my arms, which had been black with lead, were streaked with chalk from my fingernails to my elbows. I knelt for a few moments

when I had finished it, admiring the effect and stretching my
aching back, too warmed with work to be bothered by the
January breezes. Then I saw a figure emerge from the house
next door, and looked up to see a little girl in a tattered frock
and a pair of over-large boots pigeon-stepping her way towards
me with a spilling mug of tea.

'Mother says you must be fairly fagged, and to give you
this,' she said. Then she ducked her head. 'But I'm to stay
with you while you drink it, to make sure we get the cup back.'

The tea had been made murky with a bit of skim-milk, and
was terribly sweet. I drank it quickly, while the girl shivered
and stamped her feet. 'No school for you today?' I asked her.

'Not today. It's wash-day, and Mother needs me at home to
keep the babies out from under her heels.' All the while she
talked to me she kept her eyes fixed on my shorn head. Her
own hair was fair, and – much as mine had used to – dribbled
down between her jutting shoulder-blades in a long, untidy
plait.

It was now about half-past three, and when I returned to
Florence's kitchen to wash my filthy hands and arms I found
the house had grown quite dark. I removed my apron, and lit
a lamp; then I took a few minutes to wander between the
rooms, gazing at the transformation I had effected. I thought,
like a child, How pleased they will be! How pleased . . . I was
not quite so gay, however, as I had been six hours before. Like
the darkening day beyond the parlour window, there was a
gloomy knowledge pressing at the edges of my own pleasure –
the knowledge that I must go, and find some shelter of my
own. I picked up the list that Florence had made for me. Her
handwriting was very neat but the ink had stained her fingers, and there was a smudge where she had lain her tired
hand upon the sheet.

I could not bear the idea of going just yet – of working my
way through the list of hostels, of being shown to a bed in
another chamber like the one I had slept in with Zena. I would
go in an hour; for now, I thought again, determinedly, of how

enchanted Ralph and Florence would be, to come home to a tidy house – and then, with more enthusiasm, I thought: And how much more pleased would they be, to come home to their tidy house, and find their supper bubbling on the stove! There was not much food in the cupboards, so far as I could see; but there was, of course, the half-crown that they had left for me . . . I didn't stop to think that I should keep it for my own needs. I picked the coin up – it was just where Florence had placed it, for I had lifted it only to wipe beneath it with a cloth, then put it back again – and hobbled off down Quilter Street, towards the stalls and barrows of the Hackney Road.

A half-hour later I was back. I had bought bread, meat and vegetables and – purely on the grounds that it had looked so handsome on the fruit-man's barrow – a pineapple. For a year and a half I had eaten nothing but cutlets and salmis, *patés* and crystallised fruits; but there was a dish that Mrs Milne had used to make, consisting of mashed potato, mashed cabbage, corned beef and onions – Gracie and I had used to smack our lips at the sight of it placed before us on the table. I thought it couldn't be very hard to make; and I set about cooking it now, for Ralph and Florence.

I had set the potatoes and the cabbage on to boil, and got as far as browning the onions, when I heard a knock at the door. This made me jump, then grow a little flustered. I had made myself so comfortable that I felt, instinctively, that I should answer it; but should I, really? Was there not a point at which helpfulness, if persevered with, became impertinence? I looked down at the pan of onions, my rolled-up sleeves. Had I perhaps crossed over that point, already?'

While I wondered, the knock came again; and this time I didn't hesitate, but went straight to the door and opened it. Beyond it was a girl – a rather handsome girl, with dark hair showing beneath a velvet tam-o'-shanter. When she saw me she said, 'Oh! Is Florrie not at home, then?' and looked quickly at my arms, my dress, my eye, and then my hair.

I said, 'Miss Banner isn't here, no. I'm on my own.' I sniffed, and thought I caught the smell of burning onions. 'Look here,' I went on, 'I'm doing a bit of frying. Do you mind . . . ?' I ran back to the kitchen to rescue my dish. To my surprise I heard the thud of the front door, and found that the girl had followed me. When I looked round she was unbuttoning her coat, and gazing about her in wonder.

'My God,' she said – her voice had a bit of breeding to it, but she was not at all proud. 'I called because I saw the step, and thought Florrie must have had some sort of fit. Now I see she's either lost her head entirely or had the fairies in.'

I said, 'It was me that did it all . . .'

She laughed, showing her teeth. 'Then you, I suppose, must be the fairy king himself. Or is it the fairy queen? I cannot tell if your hair is at odds with your costume, or the other way around. If that' – she laughed again – 'means anything.'

I didn't know what it might mean. I said only, rather primly, that I was waiting for my hair to grow; and she answered, 'Ah', and her smile grew a little smaller. Then she said, in a puzzled sort of way: 'And you're staying with Florrie and Ralph, are you?'

'They let me sleep last night in the parlour, as a favour; but today I have to move on. In fact – what time have you?' She showed me her watch: a quarter to five, and much later than I had expected. 'I really must go very soon.' I took the pan off the stove – the onions had burned a little browner than I wanted – and began to look about me for a bowl.

'Oh,' she said, waving her hand at my haste, 'have a cup of tea with me, at least.' She put some water on to boil, and I began jabbing at the potatoes with a fork. The dish, as I assembled it, did not look quite like the meal that Mrs Milne had used to make; and when I tasted it, it was not so savoury. I set it on the side, and frowned at it. The girl handed me a cup. Then she leaned against a cupboard, quite at her ease, and sipped at her own tea, and then yawned.

'What a day I have had!' she said. 'Do I stink like a rat? I've been all afternoon down a drain-pipe.'

'Down a *drain*-pipe?'

'Down a drain-pipe. I'm an assistant at a sanitary inspector's. You may not pull such a face; it was quite a triumph, I tell you, my getting the position at all. They think women too delicate for that sort of work.'

'I think I would rather be delicate,' I said, 'than do it.'

'Oh, but it's marvellous work! It's only now and then I have to peer into sewers, as I did today. Mostly I measure, and talk to workers, and see if they are too hot or too cold, have enough air to breathe, enough lavatories. I have a government order, and do you know what that means? It means I can *demand* to see an office or a workshop, and if it's not right, I can demand that it be *put* right. I can have buildings closed, buildings improved . . .' She waved her hands. 'Foremen hate me. Greedy masters from Bow to Richmond absolutely loathe the sight of me. I wouldn't swap my work for anything!' I smiled at the enthusiasm in her voice; she might be a sanitary inspector, but she was also, I could tell, something of an actress. Now she took another mouthful of tea. 'So,' she said, when she had swallowed it, 'how long have you been a friend of Florrie's?'

'Well, *friend* isn't quite the word for it, really . . .'

'You don't know her terribly well?'

'Not at all.'

'That's a shame,' she said, shaking her head. 'She's not been herself, these past few months. Not been herself at all . . .' She would have gone on, I think, if there had not, at that moment, come the sound of the front door opening, and then of feet upon the parlour floor.

'Oh *hell!*' I said. I put my cup down, gazed wildly about me for a second, then ran past the girl to the pantry door. I didn't stop to think; I didn't say a word to her or even look at her. I simply hopped inside the little cupboard, and pulled the door shut behind me. Then I put my ear to it, and listened.

'Is there someone out there?' It was Florence's voice. I heard her stepping, cautiously, into the kitchen. Then she must have seen her friend. 'Annie, oh, it's you! Thank goodness. For a moment I thought – what's the matter?'

'I'm not sure.'

'Why do you look so queer? What's going on? What has happened to the step at the front of the house? And what's this mess on the stove?'

'Florrie—'

'What?'

'I think I might as well tell you; indeed, I really think I'm quite obliged to tell you . . .'

'*What?* You're frightening me.'

'There's a girl in your pantry.'

There was a silence then, during which I swiftly surveyed my options. They were, I found, very few; so I decided on the noblest. I took hold of the handle of the pantry door, and slowly pushed it open. Florence saw me, and twitched.

'I was just about to leave,' I said. 'I swear it.' I looked at the girl called Annie, who nodded.

'She was,' she said. 'She was.'

Florence gazed at me. I stepped out of the pantry and edged past her, into the parlour. She frowned.

'What on earth have you been doing?' she asked, as I searched for my hat. 'Why does everything look so strange?' She picked up a box of matches, and lit the two oil-lamps and then a couple of candles. The light was taken up by a thousand polished surfaces, and she started. 'You have cleaned the house!'

'Only the downstairs rooms. And the yard. And the front step,' I said, in increasing tones of wretchedness. 'And I made you supper.'

She gaped at me. '*Why?*'

'Your house was dirty. The woman next door said you were famous for it . . .'

'You met the woman next door?'

'She gave me some tea.'

'I leave you in my home for one day and you quite transform

it. You get yourself in with my neighbours. You're thick, I suppose, with my best friend. And what has *she* been telling you?'

'I haven't told her anything, I'm sure!' called Annie from the kitchen.

I pulled at a thread that had come loose at my cuff. 'I thought you would be pleased,' I said quietly, 'to have a tidy house. I thought –' I had thought that it would make her like me. In Diana's world, it would have. It, or something similar.

'I liked my house the way it was,' she said.

'I don't believe you,' I replied; and then, when she hesitated, I said – what, I suppose, I had been planning to say to her, all along – 'Let me stay, Miss Banner! Oh, please let me stay!'

She gave me a bewildered look. 'Miss Astley, I cannot!'

'I could sleep in here, like I did last night. I could clean and cook, like I did today. I could do your washing.' I was growing more rash and desperate as I spoke. 'Oh, how I longed to do those things, when I was in the house in St John's Wood! But that devil I lived with said I must let the servants do it – that it would spoil my hands. But if I stayed here – well, I could look after your little boy while you are at work. *I* wouldn't give him laudanum when he cried!'

Now Florence's eyes were wider than ever. 'Clean and do my washing? Look after Cyril? I'm sure I couldn't let you do all those things!'

'Why not? I met fifty women in your street today, all doing exactly those things! It's natural, ain't it? If I was your wife – or Ralph's wife, I mean – I should certainly do them then.'

Now she folded her arms. 'In this house, Miss Astley, that's possibly the very worst argument you could have hit upon.' As she spoke, however, the front door opened and Ralph appeared. He had an evening paper under one arm, and Cyril under the other.

'My word,' he said, 'look at the shine on this step! I am frightened to tread on it.' He saw me and smiled – 'Hallo, still here?' – then he glanced about the room. 'And look at all this! I haven't come into the wrong parlour, have I?'

Florence stepped across to him to take the baby, then propelled him out towards the kitchen. Here I heard him exclaiming very warmly – first over Annie, and then over the beef and potatoes, and finally over the pineapple. Florence struggled with Cyril for a moment: he was squirming and fractious and about to cry. I went to her, and – with terrible boldness, for the last baby I had held had been my cousin's child, four years before: and he had screamed in my face – I said, 'Give him to me, babies love me.' She handed him over and, through some extraordinary miracle – perhaps I was holding him so inexpertly, the grip quite stunned him – he fell against my shoulder, and sighed, and grew calm.

I might have thought, if I had had more experience in the matter, that the sight of her foster-son content and still in another girl's arms would be the last thing to convince a mother to allow that girl to stay in her own house; and yet, when I looked at Florence again I saw that her eyes were upon me, and her expression – as it had been once, last night – was strange and almost sad, but also desperately tender. One curl had worked its way out of her knot of hair, and hung, rather limply, over her brow. When she raised a hand to brush it from her eye, it seemed to me that the finger came away a little damp at the tip.

I thought: Blimey, I was wasted in male impersonation, I should have been in melodrama. I bit my lip, and gave a gulp. 'Good-bye, Cyril,' I said, in a voice that shook a little. 'I must put on my damp bonnet now, and head off into the darkening night, and find some bench to sleep on . . .'

But this, after all, proved too much. Florence sniffed, and her face grew stern again.

'All right,' she said. 'You may stay – for a week. And if the week works out, we shall try it for a month: you may have a share of the family salary, I suppose, for the sake of watching Cyril and keeping house. But if it does not work, then you must *promise* me, Miss Astley, that you will go.'

I promised it. Then I hitched the baby a little higher at my shoulder, and Florence turned away. I didn't look to see what her expression was, now. I only smiled; and then I put my lips to Cyril's head – he smelt rather sour – and kissed him.

How thankful I was then, that I had lied about Diana! What did it matter, that I was not all that I pretended? I had been a regular girl once; I could be regular again – being regular, indeed, might prove a kind of holiday. I thought back over my recent history, and gave a shudder; and then I glanced at Florence, and was glad – as I had been glad once before – that she was rather plain, and rather ordinary. She had taken out a handkerchief, and was wiping at her nose; now she was calling out to Ralph, to put the kettle on the stove. My lusts had been quick, and driven me to desperate pleasures: but she, I knew, would never raise them. My too-tender heart had once grown hard, and had lately grown harder – but there was no chance of it softening, I thought, at Quilter Street.

Chapter 17

One of the ladies who had come dressed as Marie Antoinette to Diana's terrible party had come clad, not as a queen, but as a shepherdess, with a crook: I had heard her tell another guest (who had mistaken her for Bo Peep, from the nursery poem) about how Marie Antoinette had had a little cottage built in the garden of her palace, and had thought it droll to play in it, with all of her friends dressed up as dairy-maids and yokels. I remembered that story, in the first few weeks of my time at Quilter Street, a little bitterly. I think I had felt rather like Marie Antoinette, the day that I put on an apron and cleaned Florence's house for her and cooked her supper; I think I even felt like her, the second day I did it. By the third day, however – the third day of waiting in the street for the stand-pipe to spit out its bit of cloudy water, of black-leading the fireplaces and the stove, of whitening the step, of scouring out the privy – I was ready to hang up my crook and return to my palace. But the palace doors, of course, had been closed on me; I must work, now, in earnest. And I must work, too, with a baby squirming on my arm – or rolling about the floor, crack-ing his head against the furniture – or, more usually, shrieking out, from his crib upstairs, for milk and bread-and-butter. For all my promises to Florence, if there had been gin in the house,

I think I would have given it to him – or else, I might have swallowed some of it myself, to make the chores a little gayer. But there was no gin; and Cyril stayed lively, and the chores remained hard. And I could not complain, not even to myself: for I knew that, dreary as they were, they were not so dreary as the habits I should have to learn if I left Bethnal Green to try my luck, all friendless and in winter, upon the streets.

So, I did not complain; but I did think, often, of Felicity Place. I thought of how quiet and how handsome that square was; of how grand Diana's villa was, how pleasant its chambers, how light, how warm, how perfumed, how polished – how different, in short, to Florence's house, which was set in one of the poorest, noisiest quarters of the city; had one dark room to do duty as bed-chamber, dining-room, library and parlour; had windows that rattled and chimneys that smoked, and a door that was continually opening, shutting, or being banged by a fist. The whole street, it seemed to me, might as well be made of India rubber – there was such a passage of shouts and laughter and people and smells and dogs, from one house to its neighbours. I should not have minded it – after all, I had grown up in a street that was similar, in a house where cousins thundered up and down the stairs, and the parlour might be full, on any night of the week, with people drinking beer and playing cards and sometimes quarrelling. But I had lost the habit of enduring it; and now it only made me weary.

Then again, there were so *many* people who came calling. There was, for example, Florence's family: a brother and his wife and children; a sister, Janet. The brother was the oldest of the sons in the family portrait (the middle one was gone to Canada); he worked as a butcher, and sometimes brought us meat; but he was rather boastful – he had moved to a house in Epping, and thought Ralph a fool for remaining in Quilter Street, where the family had all grown up. I didn't like him much. Janet, however, who called oftener, I took to at once. She was eighteen or nineteen, big-boned and handsome; a

born barmaid I had thought her when studying her photograph – so I was rather tickled to learn that she worked as a
tapstress in a City public-house, lodging with the family who
ran it, in their rooms above the bar. Florence fretted over her
like anything: their mother had died while the sisters were
still quite young (their father had died many years before that),
Florence had had all the raising of the girl to do herself and,
like older sisters everywhere, was sure that Janet would be
led astray by the first young man who got his hands on her.
'She will marry without giving it a second's thought,' she said
wearily to me, when Janet paid her first visit after I moved in.
'She'll be dragged down having babies all her life, and her
good looks will be spoiled, and she'll die worn out at forty-
three, like our own mother did.' When Janet came for supper,
she stayed the night; then she would sleep up in Florence's
bed, and I'd hear their murmurs and their laughter as I lay in
the parlour below – the sound made me terribly restless. But
Janet herself seemed marvellously unsurprised to see me dishing up the herrings at the breakfast-table, or putting her
brother's linen, on a wash-day, through the mangle. 'All right,
Nancy,' she would say – she called me 'Nancy' from the start.
The first time we met I still had the bruise at my eye, and
when she saw it, she whistled. She said, 'I bet it was a girl
done that – wasn't it? A girl always goes for the eyes, every
time. A bloke goes for the teeth.'

When the house wasn't being shivered to its foundations by
the thud of Janet's footsteps on the stairs, it was trembling to
the arguments and the laughter of Florence's girl-friends, who
came by regularly to bring books and pamphlets and bits of
gossip, and to take tea. I thought them a very quaint breed,
these girls. They all worked; but, like Annie Page, the sanitary
inspector, not one of them had a dull, straightforward kind of
job – making felt hats, or dressing feathers, or serving in a
shop. Instead they all worked for charities or in homes: they all
had lists of cripples, or immigrants, or orphaned girls, whom
it was their continual ambition to set up in jobs, houses and

friendly societies. Every story they told began the same: 'I had a girl come into the office today . . .'

'I had a girl come into the office today, fresh from gaol, and her mother has taken her baby and disappeared with it . . .'

'I had a poor woman come into the office today: she was brought over from India as a maid, and now the family won't pay her passage back . . .'

'There was a woman come in today: she has been ruined by a gent, and the gent has given her such a thump she . . .' This particular story, however, never got finished: the girl who was telling it caught sight of me, perched on an armchair at Florence's elbow; then she flushed pink, and put her cup to her lips, and turned the subject. They had all had my history – my pretend history – from Florence herself. When they weren't blushing into their tea-cups over it, they were taking me aside to ask me, privately, Was I quite well now? and to recommend some man who would prove helpful if I thought to take my case to court, or else some vegetable treatment that would ease the bruising at my cheek . . .

All of Ralph and Florence's circle, in fact, were quite sickeningly kind and earnest and conscientious over matters like this. As I could not help but find out very early on, the Banners were big in the local labour movement – they always had some desperate project on hand, some plan to get a parliamentary act passed or opposed; the parlour, as a consequence, was always full of people holding emergency meetings or dreary debates. Ralph was a cutter in a silk factory, and secretary of the silk workers' union. Florence – as well as working at the Stratford girls' home, Freemantle House – volunteered for a thing called the Women's Cooperative Guild: it was Guild work (not lists, as I had imagined, of friendless girls) which had kept her up so late on the night of my arrival at her home – and which, indeed, kept her up late on many subsequent nights, balancing budgets and writing letters. In those early days, I would occasionally glance at the pages she worked on; but whatever I saw made me frown. 'What does it mean, *cooperative*?' I asked her once. It was not a word I had ever heard used at Felicity Place.

And yet, there were moments at Quilter Street, when I found myself handing out cups of tea, rolling cigarettes, nursing babies while other people argued and laughed, when I thought I might as well still be in Diana's drawing-room, dressed in a tunic. There, no one had ever asked me anything, because they never thought I might have had an opinion worth soliciting; but at least they had liked to look at me. At Florence's house, no one looked at me at all – and what was worse, they all supposed I must be quite as good and energetic as themselves. I lived in a continual panic, therefore, that I would accidentally disenchant them – that someone would ask me my opinion on the SDF or the ILP, and my reply would make it clear that, not only had I confused the SDF with the WLF, the ILP with the WTUL, but I had absolutely no idea, and never had had, what the initials stood for anyway. When I shyly confessed one time, about six weeks after I moved in there, that I scarcely knew the difference between a Tory and a Liberal, they took it as a kind of clever joke. 'You are so right, Miss Astley!' a man had answered. 'There is no difference at all, and if only everyone were as clear-sighted as yourself, our task would be an easier one.' I smiled, and said no more. Then I collected the cups, and took Cyril into the kitchen with me; and while I waited for the kettle to boil I sang him an old song from the music hall, which made him kick his legs and gurgle.

Then Florence appeared. 'What a pretty song,' she said absently. She was rubbing her eyes. 'Ralph and I are going out – you won't mind watching Cyril, will you? There is a family up the road – they are having the bailiffs in. I said we would go, in case the men get rough . . .' There was always something like this – always some neighbour in trouble, and needing money, or help, or a letter writing or a visit to the police; and it was always Ralph and Florence that they came to – I had not been with them a week before I saw Ralph leave his supper and run along the street in his shirt-sleeves, to give some word of comfort and a couple of coins to some man who had lost his job. I thought them mad to do it. We had been kind enough to our neighbours, back in Whitstable; but the kindness had had limits to it – Mother had never had time for feckless wives, or idlers, or drunkards. Florence and Ralph, however, helped everybody, even – or, it seemed to me, especially – those layabout fathers, those slatternly mothers, whom all the rest of Bethnal Green had taken against. Now, hearing Florence's plans to visit the family that had the bailiffs coming, I grew sour. 'You're a regular pair of saints, you two,' I said, filling a bowl with soapy water. 'You never have a minute for yourselves. You have a pretty house – now that I am here to make it so – and not one moment to enjoy it. You earn a decent wage, between you, and yet you give it all away!'

'If I wanted to close my doors to my neighbours and gaze all night at my pretty walls,' she replied, still passing a hand across her bleary features, 'I would move to Hampstead! I have lived in this house all my life; there's not a family in this street who didn't help Mother out, at one time or another, when we were kids and things were rather hard. You're right: we do draw a fair wage between us, Ralph and me; but do you think I could enjoy my thirty shillings, knowing that Mrs Monks next door must live, with all her girls, on ten? That Mrs Kenny across the street, whose husband is sick, must make do with the *three* shillings she gets making paper flowers, sitting up all night and squinting at the wretched things until she is gone half-blind . . . ?'

'All right,' I said. She made speeches like this often – sounding always, I thought, like a Daughter of the People in some sentimental novel of East End life: Maria Jex had liked to read such novels, and Diana had liked to laugh at her. I didn't say this to Florence, however. I didn't say anything at all. But when she and Ralph and their union friends had gone, I sat down in an armchair in the parlour, rather heavily. The truth was, I hated their charity; I hated their good works, their missions, their orphan protégés. I hated them, because I knew that

I was one of them. I had thought that Florence had let me into her house through some extraordinary favour to myself; but what kind of a compliment was it, when she and her brother would regularly take in any old josser that happened to be staggering about the street, down on his luck, and give him supper? It was not that they were careless with me. Ralph, for example, I knew to be the gentlest man that I should ever meet: no one, not even the most hardened Sapphist in the city, could have lived with Ralph without loving him a little; and I – who liked to think of myself as no very soft tom – learned early on to love him a great deal. Florence, too, was pleasant enough to me, in her own tired, distracted sort of way. But though she ate the suppers I cooked; though she handed me Cyril to wash and dress and cradle; and though, when a month had passed, she had agreed that I might stay if I still cared to, and sent Ralph into the attic to bring me down a little truckle-bed, which she said would be cosier, in the parlour, than the two armchairs – though she did all these things, she never did them as if she really did them for *me*. She did them because the suppers and the baby-minding gave her more hours to devote to her other causes. She had given me work, as a lady might give work to a shiftless girl, come fresh from prison.

I should not have been myself, if her indifference had not rather piqued me. I had spent eighteen months at Felicity Place, shaping my behaviour to the desires of lustful ladies until I was as skilled and as subtle at it as a glove-maker: I could not throw those skills over now, just because I also learned the blacking of a grate. On Florence, however, the skills proved useless. 'She really can't be a tom,' I would say to myself – for, if she never flirted with me, then there were plenty of other girls who passed through our parlour, and I never saw her flirt with a single one of them, not once. But then, I never saw her flirting with a fellow, either. At last, I supposed she was too good to fall in love with anyone.

And, after all, I had not come to Quilter Street to flirt; I had come to be ordinary. And knowing there was no one's eye to charm or set smarting only made me more ordinary still. My hair – which had lost its military sharpness after a week or two, anyway – I let grow; I even began to curl it at the ends. My pinching boots became less stiff, the more I walked in them; but I traded them in, at a second-hand clothes stall, for a pair of shoes with bows on. I did the same with my bonnet and my rusty frock – exchanged them, for a hat with a wired flower and a dress with ribbon at the neck. 'Now, there's a pretty frock!' said Ralph to me, when I put it on for the first time; but Ralph would have told me I looked handsome wrapped in a piece of brown paper, if he thought it would make me smile. The truth was, I had looked awful ever since leaving St John's Wood; and now, in a flowery frock, I only looked extraordinarily awful. The clothes I had bought, they were the kind I'd used to wear in Whitstable and with Kitty; and I seemed to remember that I had been known then as a handsome enough girl. But it was as if wearing gentlemen's suits had magically unfitted me for girlishness, for ever – as if my jaw had grown firmer, my brows heavier, my hips slimmer and my hands extra large, to match the clothes Diana had put me in. The bruise at my eye faded quickly enough, but the brawl with Dickie's book had left me with a scar at my cheek – I have it there still; and this, combined with the new firmness at my shoulders and thighs, got from carrying buckets and whitening steps, gave me something of the air of a rough. When I washed in the mornings in a bowl in the kitchen, and caught sight of myself, from a certain angle, reflected in the darkened window, I looked like a youth in the back-room of some boys' club, rinsing himself down after a boxing match. How Diana would have admired me! At Quilter Street, however, as I have said, there was no one to gasp. By the time Ralph and Florence came down for their breakfasts, I would have my frock upon me and my hair in a curl; and then, more often than not, Florence would only gulp at her tea and say she had no time to eat, she was calling at the Guild on her way to work. Ralph would help himself to the red herrings left on her plate – 'My word, Cyril, but don't these look good!' – and she would leave, without a glance at me, wrapping a muffler about her throat like a woman of ninety.

However much I thought about her – and I spent many hours at it: for there is not much to occupy the brain in house-work, and I might as well puzzle over her, as over anything – I could not figure her out, at all. The Florence I had met first, the Green Street Florence, had been gay; she had had hair that twisted from her head like bed-springs, she had worn skirts as bright as mustard, she had laughed and shown her teeth. Florence Banner of Bethnal Green, however, was only grave, and weary. Her hair was limp, and her dresses were dark, or the colour of rust or dust or ashes; and when she smiled, you found you were surprised by it, and flinched.

For her temper, I discovered, was fickle. She was kind as an angel to the undeserving poor of Bethnal Green; but at home she was sometimes depressed, and very often cross – I would see her brother and her friends tiptoeing about her chair, so as not to rouse her: I thought their patience quite astonishing. She might be gay as you like, for days at a time; but then she would come home from a walk, or wake one morning, as if from trou-bled dreams, dispirited. Strangest of all, to my mind, was her behaviour towards Cyril: for though I knew she loved him as her own, she would sometimes seem to turn her eyes from him, or push his grasping hands away, as if she hated him; then at other times she would seize him and cover him with kisses until he squealed. I had been at Quilter Street for several months when the talk, one evening, turned to birthdays; and I realised with a little start of surprise that Cyril's must have passed and gone uncelebrated. When I asked Ralph about it he answered that, just as I'd thought, it had passed in July, but they had not thought it worthwhile to mark it. I said, laughing, 'Oh, do socialists not keep birthdays, then?' and he had smiled; Florence, however, had risen without a word, and left the room. I wondered again about what story there might be behind the baby; but Florence offered no clue to it, and I did not pry. I thought, if I did, that it might prompt her to ask me again about the gent who had supposedly kept me in luxury, then blacked my eye: she had never referred to him after that first night. I was glad she hadn't. She was so good and honest, after all – I should have hated to have had to lie to her.

Indeed, I should have hated to have had to abuse her, in any way. When she worked so hard and grew so weary, it made me pace about the room and wring my hands, and want to shake her. It was not her job at the girls' home that so exhausted her, it was the endless guild and union work – the piles of lists and ledgers she would place upon the supper-table, when the supper-things had been cleared off it, and squint at, all night long, until her eyes were red, and creased as currants. Sometimes, since I had nothing better to do, I would take a chair and sit beside her, and make her share the chores with me: she gave me envelopes to address, or other little harmless tasks I could not muddle. When, in spring, the Guild set up a local seamstresses' union, and Florence began visiting the home-workers of Bethnal Green – all the poor women who worked long hours, alone, in squalid rooms, for wretched pay – I went with her. The scenes we saw were very miserable, and the women were pleased to be visited, and the Guild was grateful; but it was for Florence's sake I really went. I couldn't bear for her to do the dreary task, and walk the East End streets, at night, alone.

And then – as I have said, a housekeeper will look for any little thing to liven her day – I began to labour for her, in the kitchen. She was thin, and the thinness looked wrong on her: the sight of the shadows at her cheeks made me feel sad. So, while the Women's Cooperative Guild made it their cause to unionise the home-workers of East London, I made it mine to fatten up Florence, with breakfasts and lunches, with sandwich teas, with dinners and suppers and biscuits and milk. I had not much success with this, to start with – for, though I took to haunting the meat stalls of the Whitechapel Market, buying faggots and sausages, rabbits and tripe, and bagfuls of those scraps of flesh we had used to call, in Whitstable, 'bits and ears', I was really rather an indifferent cook, and was as liable to burn the meat, or leave it bloody, as make it savoury; Florence and Ralph did not notice, I think, because they were used to nothing better. But then, one day at the end of August, I saw that the oyster season had started up, and I bought a barrel of natives and an oyster-knife; and as I put the blade to the hinge, it was as if I turned a key which unlocked all my mother's oyster-parlour recipes, and sent them flooding to my finger-ends. I dished up an oyster-pie – and Florence put aside the paper she was writing on, to eat it, then picked at the crust that was left in the bowl, with her fork. The next night I served oyster-fritters, the next night oyster-soup. I made grilled oysters, and pickled oysters; and oysters rolled in flour and stewed in cream.

When I passed a plate of this last dish to Florence, she smiled; and when she had tasted it, she sighed. She took a piece of bread-and-butter, and folded it to mop the sauce with; and the bread left cream upon her lips, that she licked at with her tongue, then wiped with her fingers. I remembered another time, in another parlour, when I had served another girl an oyster-supper, and accidentally wooed her; and as I was thinking of this, Florence lifted a spoonful of fish, and sighed again.

'Oh,' she said, 'I really think, that if there were one dish, and one dish only, that had to be served in paradise, that dish would be oysters – don't you think so, Nance?'

She had never called me 'Nance' before; and I had never, in all the months that I had lived with her then, known her say anything so fanciful. I laughed to hear it; and then so did her brother, and so did she.

'I think it might be oysters,' I said.

'It would be marzipan, in my paradise,' said Ralph: he had a very sweet tooth.

'And there would have,' I said then, 'to be a cigarette beside the dish, otherwise it would be hardly worth eating.'

'That's true. And my supper-table would be set upon a hill,

but overlooking a town – there would not be a chimney in it; every house would be lit and warmed by electricity.'

'Oh, Ralph!' I said. 'But only think how dull it would be, to be able to see into all the corners! There wouldn't be electric lights, or even houses, in my paradise. There would be—' Pygmy ponies and fairies on a wire, was what I wanted to say, thinking back to my nights at the Brit; but I was not up to explaining it.

And while I hesitated, Florence said: 'So, are we all to have a separate paradise?'

Ralph shook his head. 'Well, you, of course, would be in mine,' he said. 'And Cyril.'

'And Mrs Besant, I suppose.' She took another spoonful of her supper, then turned to me: 'And who would be in yours then, Nancy?'

She smiled, and I had been smiling; but even as she asked her question, I felt my smile begin to waver. I gazed at my hands where they lay upon the table: they had grown white as lilies at Felicity Place, but now they were red at the knuckles and split at the nails, and scented with soda; and the cuffs above them had frills, that had got spotted with grease – I hadn't learned the trick of pushing ladies' sleeves back, there seemed never enough material to roll. Now I twitched at one of these cuffs, and bit my lip. The fact was I didn't know who would be beside me in my paradise. The fact was, there was no one who would want to have me in theirs . . .

I looked again at Florence. 'Well, you and Ralph,' I said at last, 'I imagine will be in everybody's paradise, instructing them in how to run it.'

Ralph laughed. Florence tilted her head, and smiled a sad smile of her own. Then, after a moment, she blinked and caught my gaze. 'And you, of course,' she said, 'will have to be in mine . . .'

'Really, Florence?'

'Of course – else, who will stew my oysters?'

I had had better compliments paid me – but not recently. I found myself pinking at her words, and dipped my head.

When I looked at her again, she was gazing over into the
corner of the room. I turned, to see what it was she was looking at: it was the family portrait, and I guessed she must be
thinking of her mother. But in the corner of the frame, of
course, there was the smaller picture, of the grave-looking
woman with the very heavy brows. I had never learned who
she was, after all. Now I said to Ralph: 'Who is that girl, in the
little photo? She don't half need a hairbrush.'

He looked at me, but did not answer. It was Florence who
spoke. 'That's Eleanor Marx,' she said, with a kind of quiver to
her voice.

'Eleanor Marks? Have I met her? Is she that cousin of yours,
who works at the poulterers?'

She gazed at me then as if I had not asked the question, but
barked it. Ralph put down his fork. 'Eleanor Marx,' he said, 'is
a writer and a speaker and a very great socialist . . .'

I blushed: this was worse than asking what *cooperative*
meant. But when Ralph saw my cheeks, he looked kind: 'You
mustn't mind it. Why should you know? I'm sure, you might
mention a dozen writers you have read, and Flo and I would
not know one of them.'

'That's true,' I said, very grateful to him; but though I *had*
read proper books at Diana's, I could think, at that moment,
only of the *im*proper ones – and they all had the same author:
Anonymous.

So I said nothing, and we finished our supper in silence.
And when I looked at Florence again, her eyes were turned
away from me and seemed rather dark. I thought then that,
after all, she would never really want a girl like me in paradise
with her, not even to stew the oysters for her tea; and the
thought, just then, seemed a dreary one.

But I was quite wrong about her. Whether I were in her paradise or not, she wouldn't have noticed; and it was not her
mother she hoped to see there, nor even Eleanor Marx, nor
even *Karl* Marx. It was another person altogether that she had

in mind – but it was not until a few weeks later, one evening in the autumn of that year, that I found out who.

I had begun, as I have said, to accompany Florence on her visits for the Guild, and on this night I found myself in the home of a seamstress at Mile End. It was a terribly poor home: there was no furniture, hardly, in the woman's rooms, only a couple of mattresses, a threadbare rug, and one rickety table and chair. In the chamber that passed for a parlour, a tea-chest was upturned and had the remains of a sad little supper on it: a crust of bread, a bit of dripping in a jar, and a cup half-full of bluish milk. The dinner-table was all covered with the paraphernalia of the woman's trade – with folded garments and tissue wrappers, with pins and cotton reels and needles. The needles, she said, were always dropping on the floor, and the children were always stepping on them; her baby had recently put a pin in his mouth, and the pin had stuck in his palate and almost choked him.

I listened to her story, and then watched while Florence spoke to her about the Women's Guild, and about the seamstresses' union it had established. Would she come to a meeting? Florence asked. The woman shook her head, and said she didn't have the time; that she had no one to mind the children; that she was frightened that the masters at the outfitters for whom she worked would hear about it, and stop her shillings.

'Besides that, miss,' she said at last, 'my husband wouldn't care for me to go. Not but what he ain't a union man himself; but he don't think much of women having a say in all that stuff. He says there ain't the need for it.'

'But what do *you* think, Mrs Fryer? Don't you think the women's union a good thing? Wouldn't you like to see things changed – see the masters *made* to pay you more, and work you kinder?' Mrs Fryer rubbed her eyes.

'They would drop me, miss, that's all, and find a gal to do it cheaper. There are plenty of 'em – plenty gals what envy me even my poor few shillings . . .'

The discussion went on, until at last the woman grew fid-
gety, and said she thanked us, but couldn't spare the time to
hear us any longer. Florence shrugged. 'Think on it a bit, won't
you? I've told you when the meeting is. Bring your babies if
you like – we'll find someone to take care of 'em for an hour or
two.' We rose; I looked again at the table, at the pile of reels
and garments. There was a waistcoat, a set of handkerchiefs,
some gentlemen's linen – I found myself drifting towards it all,
with fingers that itched to pick the garments up and stroke
them. I caught the woman's eye, and nodded at the table-top.

I said, 'What is it you do exactly, Mrs Fryer? Some of these
look very fine.'

'I'm an embroid'rer, miss,' she answered. 'I does the fancy
letters.' She lifted a shirt, and showed me its pocket: there
was a flowery monogram upon it, sewn very neatly in ivory
silk. 'It looks a bit queer, don't it,' she went on sadly, 'seeing all
these scraps of handsomeness in this poor room . . .'

'It does,' I said – but I could hardly get the words out. The
pretty monogram had reminded me suddenly of Felicity Place,
and all the lovely suits that I had worn there. I saw again those
tailored jackets and waistcoats and shirts, those tiny, extravagant *N.K.*s that I had thought so thrilling. I had not known
then that they were sewn in rooms like this, by women as sad
as Mrs Fryer; but if I had, would I have cared? I knew that I
would not, and felt now horribly uncomfortable and ashamed.
Florence had stepped to the door, and stood there, waiting for
me; Mrs Fryer had bent to pick up her youngest child, who had
begun to cry. I reached into the pocket of my coat. There was
a shilling there, and a penny, left over from a marketing trip: I
took them out and placed them on the table amongst the fancy
shirts and hankies, slyly as a thief.

Mrs Fryer, however, saw, and shook her head.

'Oh, now, miss . . .' she said.

'For the baby.' I felt more self-conscious and ill than ever.
'Just for the little one. Please.' The woman ducked her head,
and murmured her thanks; and I did not look at her, or

Florence, until we were both of us out on the street again, and the dismal room was far behind.

'That was kind of you,' said Florence at last. It wasn't kind at all; I felt as if I had slapped the woman, not given her a gift. But I didn't know how to tell any of this to Florence. 'You shouldn't have done it, of course,' she was saying. 'Now she will think the Guild is made of women who are better than her, not women just like herself, trying to help themselves.'

'You're not much like her,' I said – a little stung, despite myself, by her remark. 'You think you are, but you're not, not really.'

She sniffed. 'You're right, I suppose. I'm more like her, however, than I might be. I'm more like her than some of the ladies you see working for the poor and the homeless and the out-of-work.'

'Ladies like Miss Derby,' I said.

She smiled. 'Yes, ladies like that. Miss Derby, your great friend.' She gave me a wink and took my arm; and because it was pleasant to see her so light-hearted I began to forget the little shock that I had had in the seamstress's parlour, and to grow gay again. Arm in arm, we made our slow way, through the sinking autumn night, to Quilter Street, and Florence yawned. 'Poor Mrs Fryer,' she said. 'She is quite right: the women will never fight for shorter hours and minimum wages, while there are so many girls so poorly off that they'll take any work, however miserable . . .'

I was not listening. I was watching the lamplight where, at the edges of her hat, it struck her hair and made it glow; and wondering if a moth might ever come and settle amongst the curls, mistaking them for candle-flames.

We reached our home at last, and Florence hung her coat up and began to busy herself, as usual, with her pile of papers and books. I went quietly upstairs, to gaze at Cyril as he slumbered in his crib; then I went and sat with Ralph, while Florence worked on. It grew chilly, and I set a little fire in the grate: 'The first of autumn,' as Ralph pointed out; and his words – and the idea that I had been at Quilter Street for the turning of three whole seasons – were strangely moving ones. I lifted my eyes to him, and smiled. His whiskers had grown, and he looked more than ever like the sailor on the Player's packets. He looked more than ever like his sister, too, and the likeness made me like him all the more, and wonder how I had ever mistaken him for her husband.

The fire flamed, then grew hot and ashy, and at half-past ten or so Ralph yawned, and slapped his chair and rose from it and wished us both good-night. It was all just as it had been on my first evening there – except that he had a kiss for me, too, these days, as well as for Florence; and there was my little truckle-bed, propped in the corner, and my shoes beside the fire, and my coat upon the hook behind the door.

I gazed at all this in a complacent sort of way, then yawned, and rose to fetch the kettle. 'Stop all that now,' I said to Florence, nodding at her books. 'Come and sit with me and talk.' It was not a strange request – we had got rather into the habit of sitting up when Ralph had gone to bed, chatting over the day's events – and now she looked at me and smiled, and set down her pen.

I swung the kettle over the fire, and Florence rose and stretched – then cocked her head.

'Cyril,' she said. I listened too, and after a second caught his thin, irregular cry. She moved to the stairs. 'I'll shush him, before he wakes Ralph.'

She was gone for a full five minutes or so, and when she returned it was with Cyril himself, his lashes gleaming in the lamplight and his hair damp and darkened with the sweat of fretful slumber.

'He won't settle,' she said. 'I'll let him stay with us a while.' She sat back in the armchair by the fire and the child lay heavily against her. I passed her her tea, and she took a sideways sip at it, and yawned. Then she gazed at me, and rubbed her eyes.

'What a help you've been to me, Nance, these past few months!' she said.

'I only help,' I answered truthfully, 'to stop you wearing
yourself out. You do too much.'

'There's so much to do!'

'I can't believe that all of it should fall to you, though. Do
you never weary of it?'

'I get tired,' she said, yawning again, 'as you can see! But
never *of* it.'

'But Flo, if it's such an endless task, why labour at all?'

'Why, because I must! Because how could I rest, when the
world is so cruel and hard, and yet might be so sweet . . . ? The
kind of work I do is its own kind of fulfilment, whether it's
successful or not.' She drank her tea. 'It's like love.'

Love! I sniffed. 'You think love is its own reward, then?'

'Don't you?'

I gazed into my cup. 'I did once, I think,' I said, 'but . . .' I
had never told her about those days. Cyril wriggled, and she
kissed his head and murmured in his ear, and for a moment all
was very still – perhaps she thought me wondering about the
gent I said I had lived with in St John's Wood. But then she
spoke again, more briskly.

'Besides, I don't believe it is an endless task. Things *are*
changing. There are unions everywhere – and women's unions,
as well as men's. Women do things today their mothers would
have laughed to think of seeing their daughters doing twenty
years ago; soon they will even have the vote! If people like me
don't work, it's because they look at the world, at all the injus-
tice and the muck, and all they see is a nation falling in upon
itself, and taking them with it. But the muck has new things
growing out of it – wonderful things! – new habits of working,
new kinds of people, new ways of being alive and in love . . .'
Love again. I put a finger to the scar upon my cheek, where
Dickie's doctor's book had caught it. Florence bent her head to
gaze at the baby, as he lay sighing upon her chest.

'In another twenty years,' she went on quietly, 'imagine how
the world will be! It will be a new century. Cyril will be a
young man – nearly, but not quite, as old as I am now. Imagine

the things he'll see, the things he'll do . . .' I looked at her, and
then at him; and for a moment I felt almost able to see with her
across the years to the queer new world that would have Cyril
in it, as a man . . .

As I looked, she shifted in her seat, reached a hand out to
the bookcase at her side, and drew a volume from the bulging
shelves. It was *Leaves of Grass*: she turned its pages, and found
a passage that she seemed to know.

'Listen to this,' she said. She began to read aloud. Her tone
was low, and rather self-conscious; but it quivered with passion – I had never heard such passion in her voice, before.

'*O mater! O fils!*' she read. '*O brood continental! O flowers
of the prairies! O space boundless! O hum of mighty prod-
ucts! O you teeming cities! O so invincible, turbulent, proud! O
race of the future! O women! O fathers! O you men of passion
and storm! O beauty! O yourself! O you bearded roughs! O
bards! O all those slumberers! O arouse! the dawn-bird's throat
sounds shrill! Do you not hear the cock crowing?*'

She sat still for a moment, gazing down at the page; then she
raised her eyes to mine, and I saw with surprise that they were
gleaming with unspilled tears. She said, 'Don't you think that
marvellous, Nancy? Don't you think that a marvellous, marvellous poem?'

'Frankly, no,' I said: the tears had unnerved me. 'Frankly,
I've seen better verses on some lavatory walls' – I really had. 'If
it's a poem, why doesn't it rhyme? What it needs is a few good
rhymes and a nice, jaunty melody.' I reached to take the book
from her, and studied the passage she had read – it had been
underlined, at some earlier date, in pencil – then sang it out, to
the approximate tune and rhythm of some music-hall song of
the moment. Florence laughed, and, with one hand upon Cyril,
tried to snatch the book from me.

'You're a beast!' she cried. 'You're a shocking philistine.'

'I'm a purist,' I said primly. 'I know a nice bit of verse when
I see it, and this ain't it.' I flipped through the book, abandon-
ing my attempt to try to force the staggering lines into some

sort of melody, but reading all the ludicrous passages that I could find – there were many of them – and all in the silly American drawl of a stage Yankee. At last I found another underlined section, and started on that. *'O my comrade!'* I began. *'O you and me at last – and us two only; O power, liberty, eternity at last! O to be relieved of distinctions! to make as much of vices as virtues! O to level occupations and the sexes! O to bring all to common ground! O adhesiveness! O the pensive aching to be together – you know not why, and I know not why . . .'*

My voice trailed away; I had lost my Yankee drawl, and spoken the last few words in a self-conscious murmur. Florence had ceased her laughter, and begun to gaze, apparently quite gravely, into the fire: I saw the orange flames of the coals reflected in each of her hazel eyes. I closed the book, and returned it to the shelf. There was a silence, a rather long one.

At last she took a breath; and when she spoke she sounded quite unlike herself, and rather strange.

'Nance,' she began, 'do you remember that day in Green Street, when we talked? Do you remember how we said that we would meet, and how you didn't come . . . ?'

'Of course,' I said, a little sheepishly. She smiled – a curiously vague and inward-seeming kind of smile.

'I never said, did I,' she went on, 'what I did that night?' I shook my head. I remembered very well what *I* had done that night – I had supped with Diana, and then fucked her in her handsome bedroom, and then been sent from it, chilled and chastened, to my own. But I had never stopped to think what Florence might have done; and she, indeed, had never told me.

'What did you do?' I asked now. 'Did you go to that – that lecture, on your own?'

'I did,' she said. She took a breath. 'I – met a girl there.'

'A girl?'

'Yes. Her name was Lilian. I saw her at once, and couldn't take my eyes from her. She was so very – *interesting* looking. You know how it is, with a girl, sometimes? Well, no, perhaps you don't . . .' But I did, I did! And now I gazed at her, and felt myself grow warm; and then rather chill. She coughed, and put a hand to her mouth. Then she said, still gazing at the coals: 'When the lecture was finished Lilian asked a question – it was a very clever question, and the speaker was quite thrown by it. I looked at her then, and knew I must know her. I went over to her, and we began to talk. We talked – we talked, Nance, for an hour, quite without stopping! She had the most unusual views. She'd read, it seemed to me, everything, and had opinions on it all.'

The story went on. They had become friends; Lilian had come calling . . .

'You loved her!' I said.

Florence blushed, and then nodded. 'You couldn't have known her, and not loved her a little.'

'But Flo, you *loved* her! You loved her – like a tom!'

She blinked, and put a finger to her lip, and blushed harder than ever. 'I thought,' she said, 'you might have guessed it . . .'

'Guessed it! I – I am not sure. I never thought you might have – well, I cannot say what I thought . . .'

She turned her head away. 'She loved me, too,' she said, after a moment. 'She loved me, like anything! But not in the same way. I knew it never would be, I didn't mind. The fact is, she had a man-friend, who wished to marry her. But she wouldn't do it, she believed in the free union. Nance, she was the strongest-minded woman I ever knew!'

She sounded, I thought, insufferable; but I had not missed that *was*. I swallowed, and Florence gazed once at me, then looked again at the fire.

'A few months after I first met her,' she went on, 'I began to see that she was not – quite well. One day she turned up here with a suitcase. She was to have a baby, had lost her rooms because of it, and the man – who turned out hopeless, after all – was too ashamed to take her. She had nowhere . . . Of course, we took her in. Ralph didn't mind, he loved her almost as much as I did. We planned to live together, and raise the baby as our own. I was glad – I was glad! – that the man had thrown her over, that the landlady had cast her out . . .'

She gave a grimace, then scraped with a nail at a piece of ash that had come floating from the fire and had fallen on her skirt. 'Those were, I think, the happiest months of all my life. Having Lilian here, it was like – I cannot say what it was like. It was dazzling; I was dazzled with happiness. She changed the house – really changed it, I mean, not just its spirit. She had us strip the walls, and paint them. She made that rug.' She nodded to the gaudy rug before the fire – the one I had thought woven, in a blither moment, by some sightless Scottish shepherd – and I quickly took my feet from it. 'It didn't matter that we weren't lovers; we were so close – closer than sisters. We slept upstairs, together. We read together. She taught me things. That picture, of Eleanor Marx' – she nodded to the little photograph – 'that was hers. Eleanor Marx was her great heroine, I used to say she favoured her; I don't have a photograph of Lily. That book, of Whitman's, that was hers too. The passage you read out, it always makes me think of me and her. She said that we were comrades – if women may be comrades.' Her lips had grown dry, and she passed her tongue across them. 'If women may be comrades,' she said again, 'I was hers . . .'

She grew silent. I looked at her, and at Cyril – at his flushed and sleeping face, with its delicate lashes and its jutting pink lip. I said, with a kind of creeping dread: 'And then . . . ?'

She blinked. 'And then – well, then she died. She was too slight, the confinement was a hard one; and she died. We couldn't even find a midwife who would see to her, because she was unmarried – in the end we had to bring a woman in from Islington, someone who didn't know us, and say that she was Ralph's wife. The woman called her "Mrs Banner" – imagine that! She was good enough, I suppose, but rather strict. She wouldn't let us in the room with her; we had to sit down here and listen to the cries, Ralph wringing his hands and weeping all the while. I thought, Let the baby die, oh, let the baby die, so long as she is safe . . . !

'But Cyril did not die, as you see, and Lilian herself seemed well enough, only tired, and the midwife said to let her sleep. We did so – and, when I went to her a little later, I found that she'd begun to bleed. By then, of course, the midwife had gone. Ralph ran for a doctor – but she couldn't be saved. Her dear, good, generous heart bled quite away . . .'

Her voice failed. I moved to her and squatted beside her, and touched my knuckles to her sleeve; and she acknowledged me kindly, with a slight, distracted smile.

'I wish I'd known,' I said quietly; inwardly, however, it was as if I had myself by the throat, and was banging my own head against the parlour wall. How could I have been so foolish as not to have guessed it all? There had been the business of the birthday – the anniversary, I realised now, of Lilian's death. There had been Florence's strange depressions; her tiredness, her crossness, her brother's gentle forbearance, her friends' concern. There had been her odd ambivalence towards the baby – Lilian's son, yet also, of course, her murderer, whom Florence had once wished dead, so that the mother might be saved . . .

I gazed at her again, and wished I knew some way to comfort her. She was so bleak, yet also somehow so remote; I had never embraced her, and felt squeamish about putting a hand upon her, even now. So I only stayed beside her, stroking gently at her sleeve . . . and at last she roused herself, and gave a kind of smile; and then I moved away.

'How I have talked,' she said. 'I don't know, I'm sure, what made me speak of all this, tonight.'

'I'm glad you did,' I said. 'You must – you must miss her, terribly.' She gazed blankly at me for a moment – as if *missing* was rather a paltry emotion, *terrible* too mild a term, for her great sadness – and then she nodded and looked away.

'It has been hard; I have been strange; sometimes I've wished that I might die, myself. I have, I know, been very poor company for you and Ralph! And I was not very kind when you first came, I think. She had been gone a little under six months then, and the idea of having another girl about the place – especially you, who I had met the very week I had found her – well! And then, your story was like hers, you had been with a gent who had thrown you out, after he'd got you in trouble – it seemed too queer. But there was a moment, when you picked up Cyril – I daresay you don't even remember doing it – but you held Cyril in your arms, and I thought of her, who had never cradled him at all . . . I didn't know whether I could stand to see you do it; or whether I could bear to see you stop. And then you spoke – and you were not like Lily then, of course. And, oh! I've never been gladder of anything, in all my life!'

She laughed; I made some sort of sound that seemed to pass for laughter, some kind of face that could be mistaken, in that dim light, for a smile. Then she gave a terrific yawn, and rose, and shifted Cyril a little higher against her neck, and brushed her cheek across his head; and then, after a moment, she smiled and stepped wearily to the door.

But before she could reach it, I called her name.

I said, 'Flo, there never was a gent who threw me out. It was a lady I was living with; but I lied, so you'd let me stay. I'm – I'm a tom, like you.'

'You *are*!' She gaped at me. 'Annie said it all along; but I never thought much about it, after that first night.' She began to frown. 'And so, if there never was a man, your story wasn't like Lilian's, at all . . .' I shook my head. 'And you were never in trouble . . .'

'Not *that* kind of trouble.'

'And all this time, you have been here, and I've been thinking you one thing, and . . .' She looked at me, then, with a strange expression – I didn't know if she felt angry, or sad, or bewildered, or betrayed, or what.

I said, 'I'm sorry.' But she only shook her head, and put a hand across her eyes for a second; and when she took the hand away, her gaze seemed perfectly clear, and almost amused.

'Annie always said it,' she said again. 'Won't she be pleased, now! Will you mind it, if I tell her?'

'No, Flo,' I said. 'You may tell who you like.'

Then she went, still shaking her head; and I sat, and listened to her climb the stairs and creak about in the room above
my head. Then I took some tobacco and a paper, and rolled
myself a cigarette from a tin upon the mantel, and lit it; then I
ground it upon the hearth, and threw it into the fire, and put
my head against my arm, and groaned.

What a fool I'd been! I had blundered into Florence's life,
too full of my own petty bitternesses to notice her great grief.
I had thrust myself upon her and her brother, and thought
myself so sly and charming; I had thought that I was putting
my mark upon their house, and making it mine. I had believed
myself playing in one kind of story, when all the time, the
plot had been a different one – when all the time, I was only
clumsily rehearsing what the fascinating Lilian had done so
well and cleverly before me! I gazed about the room – at the
washed blue walls, the hideous rug, the portraits: I saw them
suddenly for what they were – details in a shrine to Lilian's
memory, that I, all unwittingly, had been tending. I caught
hold of the little picture of Eleanor Marx – except it was not
Eleanor Marx I saw, of course; it was *her*, with Eleanor Marx's
features. I turned it in my hands, and read the back of it: *F.B.,
my comrade*, it said, in large, looped letters, *my comrade for
ever. L.V.*

I groaned still louder. I wanted to chuck the damn picture
into the grate along with my half-smoked fag – I had to return
it quickly to its frame in case I did so. I was jealous of Lilian!
I was more jealous than I had ever been of anyone! Not because
of the house; not because of Cyril, or even Ralph – who had
been kind to me, but who had wept for her, and wrung his
hands in grief when she lay dying; but because of Florence.
Because it was Florence, above all, whom Lilian's story
seemed both to have given me and to have robbed me of for
ever. I thought of my labours of the past few months. I had not
made Florence fat and happy, as I had supposed: it had only
been time, making her grief less keen, her memories duller. *Do*

you remember how we said that we would meet, she had asked
me tonight, *and how you didn't come . . . ?* Her eyes had shone
as she had asked it, for I had done her some sort of wonderful
favour by not turning up that night, two years before.

I had done her a wonderful favour – and done myself, it
seemed to me now, the worst kind of disservice. I thought
again of how I had spent that night, and the nights following it;
I thought of all the lickerish pleasures of Felicity Place – all the
suits, the dinners, the wine, the *poses plastiques.* I would have
traded them all in, at that moment, for the chance to have been
in Lilian's place at that dull lecture, and had Florence's hazel
eyes upon me, fascinated!

Chapter 18

In the days and weeks following Florence's sad disclosure I became aware that things at Quilter Street were rather changed. Florence herself seemed gayer, lighter – as if, in telling me her history, she had rid herself of some huge burden, and was now flexing limbs that had been cramped and numbed, straightening a back that had been bowed. She was still gloomy, sometimes, and she still went off for walks, alone, and came back wistful. But she did not try to hide her melancholy now, or to disguise its cause – letting me know, for example, that her trips were (as I might have guessed) to Lilian's grave. In time she even began to speak of her dead friend, quite routinely. 'How Lilian would have laughed to hear of that!' she would say; or, 'Now, if Lily were only here, we might ask her, and she'd be sure to know.'

Her new, sweeter mood had an effect upon us all. The atmosphere of our little house – which I had always thought easy enough, before, but which I now saw to have been quite choked with the memory of Lilian, and with Ralph and Florence's sorrow – seemed to clear and brighten: it was as if we were passing not into the fogs and frosts of winter, but into springtime, with all its mildnesses and balms. I would see Ralph gazing at his sister as she smiled or hummed or caught at Cyril and tickled him, and his gaze would be soft, and he would sometimes lean to kiss her cheek, in pleasure. Even Cyril himself seemed to feel the change, and to grow bonnier and more content.

And I, in contrast, became ever more pinched and secretive and fretful.

I could not help it. It was as if, in casting off her own old load, Florence had burdened me with a new one; my feelings – which had been stirred, on the night of her confession, into such a curious mixture – only seemed to grow queerer and more contradictory as the weeks went by. I had been sorry for her, and was as glad as her brother to see her rather lighter-hearted now; I was also pleased and touched that she had confided in me at last, and told me all. But oh, how I wished her story had been different! I could never learn to like the tragic Lilian, and had to bite back my crossness when she was spoken of so reverently. Perhaps I pictured her as Kitty – it was certainly Walter's face I saw, whenever I thought of her cow-ardly man-friend; but it made me hot and giddy to think of her, commanding Florence's passion, sleeping beside her night after night – and never so much as turning her face to her friend, to kiss her mouth. Why had Florence cared for her so much? I would gaze at the photograph of Eleanor Marx – I could never shake off the confused conviction that it was really Lilian's features printed there – until the face began to swim before my eyes. She was so different from me – hadn't Florence herself told me that? She said she had never been gladder of anything, than that I was so different from Lilian! She meant, I suppose, that Lilian was clever, and good; that she knew the meaning of words like *cooperative*, and so never had to ask. But I – what was I? I was only tidy, and clean.

Well, I think I was never quite so tidy, after that night. I cer-tainly never beat the dirt from Lilian's gaudy rug again – but smiled when people stepped on it, and took a dreadful plea-sure in watching its colours grow dim.

But then I would imagine Lilian in paradise, weaving more

carpets so that Florence might one day come and sit on them and rest her head against her knee. I imagined her stocking up the bookshelves with essays and poems, so that she and Florence might walk, side by side, reading together. I saw her preparing a stove in some small back kitchen in heaven, so that I should have somewhere to stew the oysters while she and Flo held hands.

I began to look at Florence's hands – I had never done such a thing before – and imagine all the occupations *I* would have set them to, had I been in Lilian's place . . .

Again, I couldn't help it. I had persuaded myself that Florence was a kind of saint, with a saint's dimmed, unguessable limbs and warmths and wantings; but now, in telling me the story of her own great love, it was as if she had suddenly shown herself to me, robeless. And I could not tear my eyes from what I saw.

One night, for example – one dark night, quite late, when Ralph was out with his union friends and Cyril was quiet upstairs – she bathed and washed her hair, then sat in the parlour with her dressing-gown about her, and fell asleep. I had helped her tip her tub of soapy water down the privy, then gone to warm some milk for us to drink; and when I returned with the mugs, I found her slumbering there, before the fire. She was sitting, slightly twisted, and her head had fallen back, and her arms were slack and heavy, and her hands were loose and vaguely folded in her lap. Her breaths were deep, and almost snores.

I stood before her, holding the steaming mugs. She had taken the towel from her head, and her hair was spread out over the bit of lace on the back of her chair, like the halo on a Flemish madonna. I did not think that I had ever seen her hair so full and loose before, and I studied it now for a long time. I remembered when I had thought it was a dreary auburn; but it was not auburn, there were a thousand tints of gold and brown and copper in it. It rose and curled, and grew ever more rich and lustrous, as it dried.

I looked from her hair to her face – to her lashes, to her wide pink mouth, to the line of her jaw, and the subtle weight of flesh beneath it. I looked at her hands – I remembered seeing them at Green Street, beating the hot June air; I remembered taking her hand in mine, a little later – I remembered the exact pressure of her fingers, in their warm linen glove, against my own. Her hands were pink, tonight, and still a little puckered from her bath. Her nails – which she had used, I remembered now, to chew – were neat and quite unbitten.

I looked at her throat. It was smooth, and very white; beneath it – just visible in the spreading V at the neck of her dressing-gown – was the hint of the beginnings of the swell of a breast.

I looked – and looked – and felt a curious movement in my own breast, a kind of squirming or turning, or flexing, that I seemed not to have felt there for a thousand years. It was followed almost immediately by a similar sensation, rather lower down . . . The mugs of milk began to quiver, until I feared they would spill. I turned, and placed them carefully upon the supper-table; and then I crept, very quietly, from the room.

With every step I took away from her, the movement at my heart and between my legs grew more defined: I felt like a ventriloquist, locking his protesting dolls into a trunk. When I reached the kitchen I stood and leaned against a wall – I was still trembling, worse than ever. I did not return to the parlour until I heard Florence wake and exclaim, a half-hour later, over the mugs of milk that I had left upon the table to grow cool and scummy; and even then I was so flushed and shaken that she looked at me and said, 'What's wrong with you?', and I had to answer, 'Nothing, nothing . . .' – all the time averting my gaze from that white V of curving flesh beneath her throat, because I knew that, if I looked at it again, I would be compelled to step to her and kiss it.

I had come to Quilter Street to be ordinary; now I was more of a tom than ever. Indeed, once I had made my own confession

on the matter and begun to look about me, I saw that I was
quite surrounded by toms, and couldn't believe I had not
noticed them before. Two of Florence's charity-worker friends,
it seemed, were sweethearts: I suppose she must have tipped
them off about me, for the next time they came calling, I
thought they gazed at me in quite a different sort of way. As for
Annie Page: when next I saw her she put her arm about my
shoulder and said, 'Nancy! Florrie tells me you're a cousin! My
dear, I never was less surprised by anything, nor more
delighted . . .'

And, for all that my bewildering new interest in Flo was
such a troublesome one, it *was* rather marvellous to feel my
lusts all on the rise again – to have my tommish parts all
greased and purring, like an engine with a flame set to the
coals. I dreamed one night that I was walking in Leicester
Square in my old guardsman's uniform, with my hair clipped
military-style and a glove behind the buttons of my trousers
(in fact, one of Florence's gloves: I could never look at it
again, without blushing). I had had such dreams before, at
Quilter Street – minus the detail of the glove, of course; but
this time, when I woke, there was a prickling at my scalp
and a tickling at the inside of my thighs that remained insistent, and I fingered my drab little curls and my flowery frock
in a kind of disgust. I went, that day, to the Whitechapel
Market; and on the way home I found myself lingering at the
window of a gentlemen's outfitters, with my forehead and
my fingertips pressing smears of sweat and longing against
the glass . . .

And then I thought, Why not? I went in – perhaps the tailor
thought me shopping for my brother – and bought a pair of
moleskin trousers, and a set of drawers and a shirt, and a pair
of braces and some lace-up boots; then, back at Quilter Street,
I knocked on the door of a girl who was known for doing haircuts for a penny and said: 'Cut it off, cut it all off, quick, before
I change my mind!' She scissored the curls away, and – toms
grow easily sentimental over their haircuts, but I remember

this sensation very vividly – it was not like she was cutting hair, it was as if I had a pair of wings beneath my shoulder-blades, that the flesh had all grown over, and she was slicing free . . .

Florence came home distracted that night, and hardly seemed to notice whether I had hair upon my head or not – though Ralph said, in a hopeful way, 'Now, there's a handsome hair-cut!' She didn't see me in my moleskins, either: for I had promised myself that, for the sake of the neighbours, I would only wear them to do the housework in; and by the time she came home from Stratford each night, I had changed back into my frock and put an apron on. But then, one day, she came home early. She came home the back way, through the yard behind the kitchen; and I was at the window, cleaning the glass. It was a large window, divided into panes: I had covered the panes with polish, and was wiping them clear, one by one. I was dressed in the moleskin bags and the shirt – I had left the collar off – my sleeves were rolled above my elbows, and my arms were dusty and my fingernails black. My throat was damp at the hollow, and my top lip wet – I paused to wipe it. My hair I had combed flat, but it had shaken itself loose: there was a long front lock which kept tumbling into my eyes, so that I had to push out my lip to blow it back, or swipe at it with my wrist. I had cleaned all the panes except the one before my face; and when I wiped at this I jumped, for Florence was standing on the other side of it, very still. She was clad in her coat and hat, and had her satchel over her arm; but she was gazing at me as if – well, I had had too many admiring glances come my way, in the years since I had first walked before Kitty Butler in a party-gown and not known why it was she flushed to look at me, not to know why it was that Florence, studying me in my moleskins and my crop, flushed now.

But, like Kitty, her desire seemed almost as painful to her as it was pleasant. When she caught my eye, she lowered her head and walked into the house; and all that she would say was: 'Why, what a shine you have put upon the glass!' And while it was glorious to know that – at last, and all unwittingly! – I had made her look at me and want me; while I had felt, for the second that her gaze had met mine, the leaping of my own new passion, and an answering passion in her; and while that passion had left me giddy, and aching, and hot, it was as much with nervousness as with lust that I trembled and grew weak.

Anyway, when I met her later her eyes were dim and she kept them turned from me; and I thought, again, Why would she ever care for me, while she still grieved for somebody like Lilian?

And so we went on, and the year grew colder. When Christmas came I spent it not at Quilter Street, but at Freemantle House, where Florence had organised a dinner for her girls and needed extra hands to baste the goose and wash the dishes. At New Year we drank a toast to 1895, and another to 'absent friends' – she meant Lilian, of course; I'd never told her about all the friends that I had lost. In January there was Ralph's birthday to celebrate. It fell, in the most uncanny fashion, on the same day as Diana's; and as I smiled to see him opening his gifts, I remembered the bust of Antinous, and wondered if it was still casting its frigid glances over the warm transactions at Felicity Place, and whether Diana ever looked at it and remembered me.

But by now I had grown so at home in Bethnal Green that I could barely believe I had ever lived anywhere else, or imagine a time when Quilter Street routines were not my own. I had become used to the neighbours' racket, and to the clamour of the street. I bathed once a week, like Florence and Ralph, and the rest of the time was content to wash in a bowl: Diana's bathroom had become a strange and distant memory to me – as of paradise, after the fall. I kept my hair short. I wore my trousers, as I had planned, to do the housework in – at least, for a month or so I did: after that, the neighbours had all caught glimpses of me in them, and since I had become known in the district as something of a trouser-wearer, it seemed rather a fuss to take the trousers off at night and put a frock on. No one appeared to mind it; in some houses in Bethnal Green, after all, it was a luxury to have any sort of clothes at all, and you regularly saw women in their husbands' jackets, and sometimes a man in a shawl. Mrs Monks' daughters, next door, would run squealing when they saw me. Ralph's union colleagues tended to look me over, as they debated, and then lose the thread of their text. Ralph himself, however, would sometimes wander downstairs with a shirt or a flannel waistcoat in his hand, saying vaguely: 'I found this, Nance, in the bottom of my cupboard, and wondered, would the thing be any use to you . . . ?'

As for Florence – well, increasingly I seemed to catch her gazing at me as she had gazed at me that day through the glass of the window; but always – always – she would look away again, and her eyes would grow dark. I longed to keep them fixed upon me, but didn't know how. I had made myself saucy, for Diana's sake; I had flirted heartlessly with Zena; but with Florence I might as well have been eighteen again, sweating and anxious – afraid, of trespassing upon her fading sorrow. If only, I would think, we were mary-annes. If only I were a renter again, and she some nervous Soho gent, and I could simply lead her to some shabby shady place and there unbutton her . . .

But we were not mary-annes; we were only a couple of blushing toms, hesitating between desire and the deed, while the winter slid by, and the year grew slowly older – and Eleanor Marx stayed fixed to the wall, grave and untidy and ageless.

The change came in February, on quite an ordinary day. I went to Whitechapel, to the market – a very regular thing to do, I did it often. When I came home, I came through the yard; I found the back door slightly open, and so entered the house quite noiselessly. As I put my parcels down upon the kitchen floor I heard voices in the parlour – Florence's, and Annie's. The doors between were all ajar, and I could hear them perfectly: 'She works at a printer's,' Annie was saying. 'The handsomest woman you ever saw in your life.'

'Oh Annie, you always say that.'

'No, *really*. She was sitting at a desk at a page of text, and the sun was on her and making her shine. When she raised her eyes to me I held my hand out to her. I said, "Are you Sue Bridehead? My name's Jude . . ."'

Florence laughed: they had all just been reading the latest chapter of that novel, in a magazine; I dare say Annie would not have made the joke, had she known how the story would turn out. Now Florence said: 'And what did she say to that? That she wasn't sure, but thought Sue Bridehead might work at the other office . . . ?'

'Not at all. What she said was: "*Allelujah!*" Then she took my hand and – oh, then I knew I was in love, for sure!'

Flo laughed again – but in a thoughtful kind of way. After a second she murmured something that I did not catch, but which made her friend laugh. Then Annie said, still with a smile to her voice: 'And how *is* that handsome uncle of yours?'

Uncle? I thought, moving to warm my hands against the stove. What uncle is that? I didn't feel like an eavesdropper. I heard Florence give a tut. 'She's not my uncle,' she said – she said it very clearly. 'She's not my uncle, as you well know.'

'Not your uncle?' cried Annie then. 'A girl like that – with hair like that – growling about in your parlour in a pair of chamois trousers like a regular little bricksetter . . .'

At that, I didn't care if I were eavesdropping or not: I took a swift silent step into the passageway, and listened rather harder. Florence laughed again.

'I promise you,' she said, 'she's not my uncle.'

'Why not? Why ever not? Florrie, I despair of you. It's unnatural, what you're doing. It's like – like having a roast in the pantry, and eating nothing but bits of crusts and cups of water.

What I say is, if you're not going to make an uncle of her, then, really, consider your friends, and pass her on to somebody who will.'

'*You* ain't having her!'

'I don't want anyone, now I've found Sue Bridehead. But there, you see, you do care for her!'

'Of course I care for her,' said Florence quietly. Now I was listening so hard I felt I could hear her blinking, pursing her lips.

'Well then! Bring her to the boy tomorrow night' – I was sure that's what she said. 'Bring her to the boy. You can meet my Miss Raymond . . .'

'I don't know,' answered Florence. The words were followed by a silence. And when Annie spoke next, it was in a slightly different tone.

'You cannot grieve for her for ever,' she said. 'She would never have wanted that . . .'

Florence tutted. 'Being in love, you know,' she said, 'it's not like having a canary, in a cage. When you lose one sweetheart, you can't just go out and get another to replace her.'

'I thought that's exactly what you were supposed to do!'

'That's what *you* do, Annie.'

'But Florence – you might just let the cage door open, just a little . . . There is a new canary in your own front room, banging its handsome head against the bars.'

'Suppose I let the new one in,' said Flo then, 'then find I don't care for it, as much as I did the old one? Suppose— Oh!' I heard a thump. 'I can't believe that you have got me here, comparing *her* to a budgie!' I knew she meant Lilian, not me; and I turned my head away, and wished I hadn't listened after all. The parlour remained quiet for a second or two, and I heard Florence dip her spoon into her cup, and stir it. Then, before I had quite tiptoed back into the kitchen, her voice came again, but rather quietly.

'Do you think it's true, though, what you said, about the new canary and the bars . . . ?'

My foot caught a broom, then, and sent it falling; and I had to give a shout and slap my hands, as if I had just that moment come home. Annie called me in and said that tea was brewed. Florence seemed to raise her eyes to mine, a little thoughtfully.

Annie left soon after, and Florence busied herself, all night, with paperwork: she had lately got herself a pair of spectacles, and with them flashing firelight all night, I could not even see which way her glances tended – to me, or to her books. We said good-night in our usual way, but then we both lay wakeful. I could hear her creaking about in her bed upstairs, and once she went out to the privy. I thought she might have paused on her way, outside my door, to listen for my snores. I didn't call out to her.

Next morning I was too tired to study her terribly hard; but as I set the pan of bacon on the stove, she came to me. She came very close, and then she said, quite low – perhaps so that her brother, who was in the room across the passageway, might not hear: 'Nance, will you come out with me tonight?'

'Tonight?' I said, yawning, and frowning at the bacon, which I had put too wet into a too-hot pan, so that it hissed and steamed. 'Where to? Not collecting subscriptions again, surely?'

'Not subscriptions, no. Not work at all, in fact, but – pleasure.'

'Pleasure!' I had never heard her say the word before, and it seemed, all of a sudden, a terribly lewd one. Perhaps she thought the same, for now she blushed a little, and took up a spoon and began to fiddle with it.

'There's a public-house near Cable Street,' she went on, 'with a ladies' room in it. The girls call it "The Boy in the Boat . . ."'

'Oh, yes?'

She looked once at me, and then away again. 'Yes. Annie will be there, she says, with a new friend of hers; and perhaps Ruth and Nora.'

'Ruth and Nora too!' I said lightly: they were the two girl-friends who had turned out sweethearts. 'Is it to be all toms, then?'

To my surprise she nodded, quite seriously: 'Yes.'

All toms! The thought sent me into a fever. It was twelve months since I had last passed an evening in a room full of woman-lovers: I was not sure I still possessed the knack. What would I wear? What attitude would I strike? *All toms!* What would they make of me? And what would they make of Florence?

'Will you still go,' I asked, 'if I don't?'

'I rather thought I might . . .'

'Then I'll certainly come,' I said – and had to look quickly to the pan of smoking bacon, and so didn't see whether she looked pleased, or satisfied, or indifferent.

I passed a fretful day, picking through my few dull frocks and skirts in the hope of finding some forgotten tommish gem amongst them. Of course, there was nothing except my work-stained moleskins; and these – while they might have caused something of a sensation at the Cavendish Club – I thought must be rather too bold for an East End audience, so I cast them regretfully aside in favour of a skirt, and a gentleman's shirt and collar, and a tie. The shirt and collar I cleaned and starched myself, and rinsed in washing-blue to make them shine; the necktie was of silk – a very fine silk, with only a slight imperfection to the weave, which Ralph had brought me from his workshop, and which I had had made up at a Jewish tailor's. The silk was of blue, and showed off my eyes.

I didn't change, of course, until after we had cleared the supper things; and when I did – banishing poor Ralph and Cyril to the kitchen while I washed and dressed before the parlour fire – it was with a kind of anxious thrill, an almost queasy gaiety. For all that it was skirts and stays and petticoats that I pulled on, I felt as I thought a young man must feel, when dressing for his sweetheart; and all the time I buttoned my costume, and fumbled blindly with my collar-stud and necktie, there came a creaking of the boards above my head, and a swishing of material, until at last I could hardly believe that it was not my sweetheart up there, dressing for me.

When she pushed at the parlour door and stepped into the room at last, I stood blinking at her for a moment, quite at a loss. She had changed out of her work-dress into a shirt-waist, and a waistcoat, and a skirt. The skirt was of some heavy winter stuff, but damson-coloured, and very warm upon the eye. The waistcoat was a lighter shade, the shirt-waist almost red; at her throat was pinned a brooch: a few chips of garnet, in a golden surround. It was the first time in a year that I had seen her out of her sober suits of black and brown, and she seemed quite transformed. The reds and damsons brought out the blush of her lip, the gold shine of her curling hair, the white-ness of her throat and hands, the pinkness and the pale half-moons at her thumb-nails.

'You look,' I said awkwardly, 'very handsome.' She flushed.

'I have grown too stout,' she said, 'for all my newer clothes . . .' Then she gazed at my own gear. 'You look very smart. How well that necktie becomes you – doesn't it? Except, you have tied it crooked. Here.' She came towards me, and took hold of the knot to straighten it; the pulse at my throat began at once to knock against her fingers, and I started a fruit-less fumbling at my hips for a pair of pockets in which to thrust my hands. 'What a fidget you are,' she said mildly, quite as if she were addressing Cyril; but her cheeks, I noticed, had not paled – nor was her voice, I thought, quite steady.

She finished at my throat at last, then stepped away again.

'There is just my hair,' I said. I took two brushes and damp-ened them in my water-jug, and combed the hair away from my face till it was flat and sleek; then I greased my palms with Macassar – I had Macassar, now – and ran them over my head until the hair felt heavy, and the little, overheated room was thick with scent. And all the time, Florence leaned against the frame of the parlour door and watched me; and when I had fin-ished, she laughed.

'My word, what a pair of beauties!' This was Ralph, come that moment along the passageway, with Cyril at his feet. 'We didn't recognise them, did we, son?' Cyril held up his arms to Florence, and she lifted him with a grunt. Ralph put his hand upon her shoulder and said, in an altogether softer tone, 'How fair you look, Flo. I haven't seen you look so fair, for a year and more.' She tilted her head, graciously; they might for a moment have been a knight and his lady, in some medieval portrait. Then Ralph looked my way, and smiled; and I didn't know who it was that I loved more, then – his sister, or him.

'Now, you will manage with Cyril, won't you?' said Florence anxiously, when she had handed the baby back to Ralph and begun to button her coat.

'I should think I will!' said her brother.

'We won't be late.'

'You must be as late as you like; we shall not wonder. Only mind you are careful. They are rather rough streets, that you must cross . . .'

The trip from Bethnal Green to Cable Street did indeed take us through some of the roughest, poorest, squalidest districts in the city, and could never, ordinarily, be very cheerful. I knew the route, for I had walked it often with Florence: I knew which courts were grimmest, which factories sweated their workers hardest, which tenements housed the saddest and most hopeless families. But we were out that night together – as Florence herself had admitted – for pleasure's sake; and though it might seem strange to say it, our journey was indeed a pleasant one, and seemed to take us over a rather different landscape to the one we normally trod. We passed gin-palaces and penny-gaffs, coffee-shops and public-houses: they were not the grim and dreary places that they sometimes were, tonight, but luminous with warmth and light and colour, thick with laughter and shouts, and with the reeking odours of beer and soup and gravy. We saw spooning couples; and girls with cherries on their hats, and lips to match them; and children bent over hot, steaming packets of tripe, and trotters, and baked potatoes. Who knew to what sad homes they might be returning, in an hour or two? For now, however, there was a queer kind of glamour to them, and to the very streets – Diss Street, Sclater Street, Hare Street, Fashion Street, Plumbers Row, Coke Street, Pinckin Street, Little Pearl Street – in which they walked.

'How gay the city seems tonight!' said Florence wonderingly.

It is for you, I wanted to reply: for you and your new costume. But I only smiled at her and took her arm; then, 'Look at that coat!' I said, as we passed a boy in a yellow felt jacket that was bright, in the Brick Lane shadows, as a lantern. 'I knew a girl once – oh, she would have loved that coat . . .'

It did not take us long, after that, to reach Cable Street. Here we turned left, then right; and at the end of this road I saw the public-house that was, I guessed, our destination: a squat, flat-roofed little building with a gas-jet in a plum-coloured shade above the door, and a garish sign – *The Frigate* – that reminded me how near our walk had brought us to the Thames.

'It's this way,' said Florence self-consciously. She led me past the door and around the building to a smaller, darker entrance at the back. Here a set of rather steep and treacherous-looking steps took us downwards, to what must once have been a cellar; at the bottom there was a door of frosted glass, and behind this was the room – the Boy in the Boat, I remembered to call it – that we had come for.

It was not a large room, but it was very shady, and it took me a time to gauge its breadth and height, to see beyond its spots of brightness – its crackling fire, its gas-lamps, the gleam of brass and glass and mirror and pewter at its bar – into the pools of gloom that lay between them. There were, I guessed, about twenty persons in it: they were seated in a row of little stalls, or standing propped against the counter, or gathered in the furthest, brightest corner, about what seemed to be a billiard table. I didn't like to gaze at them for long, for at our appearance they all, of course, looked up, and I felt strangely shy of them and their opinion.

Instead I kept my head down, and followed Florence to the bar. There was a square-chinned woman standing behind it, wiping at a beer-glass with a cloth; when she saw us coming she put both glass and towel down, and smiled.

'Why, Florence! How grand to see you here again! And how bonny you are looking!' She held out her hand and took Florence's fingers in her own, and looked her over with pleasure. Then she turned to me.

'This is my friend, Nancy Astley,' said Flo, rather shyly. 'This is Mrs Swindles, who keeps bar here.' Mrs Swindles and I exchanged nods and smiles. I took off my coat and hat, and ran my fingers through my hair; and when she saw me do that her brow lifted a little and I hoped that she was thinking, as Annie Page had: *Well, Florence has a fancy new uncle, all right!*

'What will you have, Nance?' Florence asked me then. I said I would have whatever she cared for, and she hesitated, then asked for two rum hots. 'Let's take them to a stall.' We stepped across the room – there was sand upon the floor-boards, and our boots crunched upon it as we walked – to a table, set between two benches. We sat, across from one another, and stirred sugar into our glasses.

'You were a regular here once, then?' I asked Flo.

She nodded. 'I haven't been here for an age . . .'

'No?'

'Not since Lily died. It's a bit of a monkey-parade, to tell the truth. I haven't had the heart for it . . .'

I gazed into my rum. All at once there came a burst of laughter from the stall at my back that made me jump.

'I said,' came a girl's voice, '"I only does *that* sort of thing, sir, with my friends." "Emily Pettinger," he said, "said you let her flat fuck you for an hour and a half" – which is a lie, but anyway, "Flat fucking is one thing, sir," I said, "and this quite another. If you want me to — her"' – here she must have made a gesture – '"you shall have to pay me for it, rather dear."'

'And did he, then?' came another voice. The first speaker paused, perhaps to take a sip from her glass; then, 'Swipe me!' she said, 'if the bastard didn't put his hand in his pocket and pull out a sov, and lay it on the table-top, all cool as you like . . .'

I looked at Florence, and she smiled. 'Gay girls,' she said. 'Half the girls who come in here are gay. Do you mind it?' How could I mind it, when I had been a gay girl – well, a gay boy – once, myself? I shook my head.

'Do *you* mind it?' I asked her.

'No. I'm only sorry that they must do it . . .'

I didn't listen: I was too taken with the gay girl's story. She was saying now: 'We flat fucked for a half an hour; then tipped the velvet while the gent looked on. Then Susie took a pair of vampers, and . . .'

I looked again at Florence, and frowned. 'Are they French, or what?' I asked. 'I can't understand a thing they're saying.' And indeed, I could not; for I had never heard such words before, in all my time upon the streets. I said, '*Tipped the velvet*: what does that mean? It sounds like something you might do in a theatre . . .'

Florence blushed. 'You might try it,' she said; 'but I think the chairman would chuck you out . . .' Then, while I still frowned, she parted her lips and showed me the tip of her tongue; and glanced, very quickly, at my lap. I had never known her do such a thing before, and I found myself terribly startled by it, and terribly stirred. It might just as well have been her lips that she had dipped to me: I felt my drawers grow damp, and my cheeks flush scarlet; and had to look away from her own warm gaze, to hide my confusion.

I looked at Mrs Swindles at the bar, and at the pewter mugs that hung, in one long gleaming row, above her; and then I looked at the group of figures at the billiard table. And then, after a moment or two, I studied them a little harder. I said to Florence, 'I thought you said it was to be all toms here? There are blokes over there.'

'Blokes? Are you sure?' She turned to where I pointed, and gazed with me at the billiard players. They were rather rowdy, and half of them were clad in trousers and waistcoats, and sported prison crops. But as Florence studied them, she laughed. 'Blokes?' she said again. 'Those are not blokes! Nancy, how could you think it?'

I blinked, and looked again. I began to see . . . They were not men, but girls; they were girls – and they were rather like myself . . .

I swallowed. I said, 'Do they live as men, those girls?'

Florence shrugged, not noticing the thickness in my voice. 'Some do, I believe. Most dress as they please, and live as others care to find them.' She caught my gaze. 'I had rather thought, you know, that you must've done the same sort of thing, yourself . . .'

'Would you think me very foolish,' I answered, 'if I said that I had thought I was the only one . . . ?'

Her gaze grew gentle, then. 'How queer you are!' she said mildly. 'You have never tipped the velvet—'

'I didn't say that I had never done it, you know; only that I never called it that.'

'Well. You use all sorts of peculiar phrases, then. You seem never to have seen a tom in a pair of trousers. Really, Nance, sometimes – sometimes I think you must've been born quite grown – like Venus in the sea-shell, in the painting . . .'

She put a finger to the side of her glass, to catch a trickle of sugary rum; then put the finger to her lip. I felt my throat grow even thicker, and my heart give a strange kind of lurch. Then I sniffed, and gazed again at the trousered toms beside the billiard table.

'To think,' I said after a second, 'that I might have worn my moleskins, after all . . .' Florence laughed.

We sat sipping at our rums a little longer; more women arrived, and the room became hotter and noisier and thick with smoke. I went to the bar to have our glasses re-filled, and when I walked with them back to our stall I found Annie there, with Ruth and Nora and another girl, a fair-haired, pretty girl, who was introduced to me as Miss Raymond. 'Miss Raymond works in a print-shop,' said Annie, and I had to pretend surprise to hear it. When, after half an hour or so, she went off to find the lavatory, Annie made us rearrange our places so that she might sit next to her.

'Quick, quick!' she cried. 'She'll be back in a moment! Nancy, over there!' I found myself placed between Florence and the wall; and for lovely long moments at a time I let the other women talk, and savoured the press of her damson thigh against my own more sober, more slender one. Every time she turned to me I felt her breath upon my cheek, hot and sugary and scented with rum.

The evening passed: I began to think that I had never spent a pleasanter one. I gazed at Ruth and Nora, and saw them lean together and laugh. I looked at Annie: she had her hand upon Miss Raymond's shoulder, her eyes upon her face. I looked at Florence, and she smiled. 'All right, Venus?' she said. Her hair had sprung right out of its pins, and was curling about her collar.

Then Nora began one of those earnest stories – 'This girl came into the office today, listen to this . . .' – and I yawned, and looked away from her, towards the billiard players; and was very surprised to find the knot of women there all turned away from their table, and gazing at me. They seemed to be debating me – one nodded, another shook her head, yet another squinted at me, and thumped her billiard cue upon the floor emphatically. I began to grow a little uncomfortable: perhaps – who knew? – I had breached some tommish etiquette, coming here in short hair and a skirt. I looked away; and when I looked again, one of the women had disentangled herself from her neighbours, and was stepping purposefully towards our stall. She was a large woman, and she had her sleeves rolled up to her elbows. On her arm there was a rough tattoo, so green and smudged it might have been a bruise. She reached our booth, placed the tattooed arm across the back of it, and leaned to catch my eye.

'Excuse me, sweetheart,' she said, rather loudly. 'But my pal Jenny will have it that you're that Nan King gal, what used to work the halls with Kitty Butler. I've a shilling on it that you ain't her. Now, will you settle it?'

I looked quickly around the table. Florence and Annie had looked up in mild surprise. Nora had broken off her story and now smiled and said, 'I should make the most of this, Nance. There might be a free drink in it.' Miss Raymond laughed. No one believed that I really might be Nan King; and I, of course, had spent five years in hiding from that history, denying I had ever been her, myself.

But the rum, the warmth, my new, unspoken passion seemed to work in me like oil in a rusted lock. I turned back to the woman. 'I'm afraid,' I said, 'that you must lose your bet. I *am* Nan King.' It was the truth, and yet I felt like an impostor – as if I had just said, 'I *am* Lord Rosebery.' I did not look at Florence – though out of the corner of my eye I saw her mouth fly open. I looked at the tattooed woman, and gave her a modest little shrug. She, for her part, had stepped back; now she slapped our stall until it shook, and called, laughing, to her friend.

'Jenny, you have won your coin! The gal says she is Nan King, all right!'

At her words the group at the billiard table let up a cry, and half the room fell silent. The gay girls in the neighbouring stall got up, to peer over at me; I heard 'Nan King, it is Nan King there!' whispered at every table. The tattooed tom's friend – Jenny – came stepping over, and held her hand out to me.

'Miss King,' she said, 'I knew it was you the moment you come in. What happy times I used to have, watching you and Miss Butler at the Paragon!'

'You're very kind,' I said, taking her hand. As I did so, I caught Florence's eye.

'Nance,' she asked, 'what is all this? Did you really work the halls? Why did you never say?'

'It was all rather long ago . . .' She shook her head, and looked me over.

'You don't mean you didn't know your friend was such a star?' asked Jenny now, overhearing.

'We didn't know that she was any kind of star,' said Annie.

'Her and Kitty Butler – what a team! There never was a pair o' mashers like 'em . . .'

'Mashers!' said Florence.

'Why yes,' continued Jenny. Then: 'Why, just a minute – I believe there is the very thing to show it, here . . .' She pushed her way through the crowd of gaping women to the bar, and here I saw her catch the barmaid's eye, then gesture towards the wall behind the rows of upturned bottles. There was a faded piece of baize there, with a hundred old notes and picture-postcards fastened to it; I saw Mrs Swindles reach into the layers of curling paper for a second, then draw out something small and bent. This she handed to Jenny; in a moment it had been placed before me, and I found myself gazing at a photograph: Kitty and me, faint but unmistakable, in Oxford bags and boaters. I had my hand upon her shoulder, and a cigarette, unlit, between the fingers.

I looked and looked at the picture. I remembered very clearly the weight and scent of that suit, the feel of Kitty's shoulder beneath my hand. Even so, it was like gazing into someone else's past, and it made me shiver.

The postcard was seized from me, then, first by Florence – who bent her head to it and studied it almost as intently as I had – then by Ruth and Nora, and Annie and Miss Raymond, and finally by Jenny, who passed it on to her friends.

'Fancy us still having that pinned up,' she said. 'I remember the gal what put it there: she was rather keen on you – indeed, you was always something of a favourite, at the Boy. She got it from a lady in the Burlington Arcade. Did you know there was a lady there, selling pictures such as yours, to interested gals?' I shook my head – in wonder, to think of all the times that I had trolled up and down the Burlington Arcade for interested *gents*, and never noticed that particular lady.

'What a treat, Miss King,' cried someone else then, 'to find you *here . . .*' There was a general murmuring as the implications of this comment were digested; 'I cannot say I never wondered,' I heard someone say. Then Jenny leaned near to me again, and cocked her head.

'What about Miss Butler, if you don't mind my asking? I heard she was a bit of a tom, herself.'

'That's right,' said another girl, 'I heard that too.'

I hesitated. Then: 'You heard wrong,' I said. 'She wasn't.'

'Not just a bit . . . ?'

'Not at all.'

Jenny shrugged. 'Well, that's too bad.'

I looked at my lap, suddenly upset; worse, however, was to follow, for at that moment one of the gay girls thrust her way between Ruth and Nora to call, 'Oh, Miss King, won't you give us a song?' Her cry was taken up by a dozen throats – 'Oh, yes, Miss King, do!' – and, as in a terrible dream, a broken-down old piano was suddenly produced, it seemed, from nowhere, and wheeled over the gritty floorboards. At once, a woman sat down before it, cracked her knuckles, and played a staggering scale.

'Really,' I said, 'I can't!' I looked wildly at Florence – she was studying me as if she had never seen my face before. Jenny cried carelessly: 'Oh, go on, Nan, be a sport, for the gals at the Boy. What was that one you used to sing – about winking at the pretty ladies, with your hand hanging on to your sovereign . . . ?'

One voice, and then another and another, picked it up. Annie had taken a swig of her beer, and now almost choked on it. 'Lord!' she said, wiping her mouth. 'Did you sing that? I saw you once at the Holborn Empire! You threw a chocolate coin at me – it was half-melted from the heat of your pocket – I ate it, and thought I should die! Oh, *Nancy*!'

I gazed at her and bit my lip. The billiard players had all set down their cues and moved to stand about the piano; the pianist was picking out the chords of the song, and about twenty women were singing it. It was a silly song, but I remembered Kitty's voice lilting upwards at the chorus, and giving the tune a kind of sweet liquidity, as if the foolish phrases turned to honey on her tongue. It sounded very different here, in this rough cellar – and yet, it had a certain trueness, too, and a new sweetness all of its own. I listened to the boisterous girls, and found myself beginning to hum . . . In a moment I had knelt upon my seat and joined my voice with theirs; and afterwards they cheered and clapped me, and I found I had to put my head upon my arm, and bite my lip, to stop the tears from coming.

They started on another song, then – not one of mine and Kitty's, but a new one that I didn't know, and so could not join in with. I sat down, and let my head fall back against the panels of the stall. A girl arrived at the end of our table with a pork pie on a plate, sent over from Mrs Swindles and 'on the house'. I picked at the pastry of this for a while, and grew a little calmer. Ruth and Nora now had their elbows on the table, their heads on their chins, and were gazing at me, their story forgotten. Annie, I could hear in the pauses of the new song, was explaining to an incredulous Miss Raymond: 'No, I swear, we had no idea. Arrived on Florrie's doorstep with a black eye and a bunch of cresses, and has never left it. *Quite* a dark horse . . .'

Florence herself had her face turned my way, and her eyes in shadow.

'You were really famous?' she asked me, as I found a cigarette and lit it. 'And you really sang?'

'Sang, and danced. And acted, once, in a pantomime at the Britannia.' I slapped my thigh. '"My lords, where is the Prince, our master?"' She laughed, though I did not.

'How I wish I'd seen you! When was all this?'

I thought for a moment; then, 'Eighteen eighty-nine,' I said.

She stuck her lip out. 'Ah. Strikes all that year: no time for the music hall. I think, one night, I might have stood outside the Britannia, collecting money for the dockers . . .' She smiled. 'I should have liked a chocolate sovereign, though.'

'Well, I should have made sure to throw you one . . .'

She lifted her glass to her lips, then thought of something else. 'What happened,' she asked, 'to make you leave the theatre? If you were doing so well, why did you stop? What did you do?'

I had admitted to some things; but I wasn't ready to admit to them all. I pushed my plate towards her. 'Eat this pie for me,' I said. Then I leaned past her and called down the table. 'I say, Annie, give me a cigarette, will you? This one's a dud.'

'Well, since you're a *celebrity* . . .'

Florence ate the pie, helped out by Ruth. The singers at the piano grew weary and hoarse, and went back to their billiards. The gay girls in the stall next door got up, and pinned on their hats: they were off, I suppose, to start work, in the more ordinary publics of Wapping and Limehouse. Nora yawned and, seeing her, we all yawned, and Florence gave a sigh.

'Shall we go?' she asked. 'I think it must be very late.'

'It is almost midnight,' said Miss Raymond. We stood, to button our coats on.

'I must just have a word with Mrs Swindles,' I said, 'to thank her for my pie'; and when I had done that – and been seized and saluted by half-a-dozen women on the way – I wandered over to the billiard corner, and nodded to Jenny.

'Good-night to you,' I said. 'I'm glad you won your shilling.'

She took my hand and shook it. 'Good-night to you, Miss King! The shilling was nothing compared to the pleasure of having you here among us all.'

'Shall we see you here again, Nan?' her friend with the tattoo called then. I nodded: 'I hope so.'

'But you must sing us a proper song next time, on your own, in all your gentleman's toggery.'

'Oh yes, you must!'

I made no answer, only smiled, and took a step away from them; then I thought of something, and beckoned to Jenny again.

'That picture,' I said quietly when she was close. 'Do you think – would Mrs Swindles mind – do you think that I might

have it, for myself?' She put her hand to her pocket at once, and
drew out the creased and faded photograph, and passed it to me.

'You take it,' she said; then she could not help but ask, a
little wonderingly, 'But have you none of your own? I
should've thought . . .'

'Between you and me,' I said, 'I left the business rather fast.
I lost a lot of stuff, and never cared to think of it till now. This,
however . . .' I gazed down at the photo. 'Well, it won't hurt me,
will it, to have this little reminder?'

'I hope it won't, indeed,' she answered kindly. Then she
looked past me, to Florence and the others. 'Your girl is a-
waiting for you,' she said with a smile. I put the picture in the
pocket of my coat.

'So she is,' I said absently. 'So she is.'

I joined my friends; we picked our way across the crowded
room, and hauled ourselves up the treacherous staircase into
the aching cold of the February night. Outside The Frigate the
road was dark and quiet; from Cable Street, however, came a
distant row. Like us, the customers of all the other publics and
gin palaces of the East End were beginning to make their tipsy
journeys home.

'Is there never trouble,' I said as we started to walk,
'between women at the Boy and local people, or roughs?'

Annie turned her collar up against the cold, then took Miss
Raymond's arm. 'Sometimes,' she said. 'Sometimes. Once
some boys dressed a pig in a bonnet, and tipped it down the
cellar stairs . . .'

'No!'

'Yes,' said Nora. 'And once a woman got her head broken, in
a fight.'

'But this was over a girl,' said Florence, yawning, 'and it
was the girl's husband who hit her . . .'

'The truth is,' Annie went on, 'there is such a mix round
these parts, what with Jews and Lascars, Germans and Poles,
socialists, anarchists, salvationists . . . The people are surprised at nothing.'

Even as she spoke, however, two fellows came out of a house at the end of the street and, seeing us – seeing Annie and Miss Raymond arm in arm, and Ruth with her hand in Nora's pocket, and Florence and I bumping shoulders – gave a mutter, and a sneer. One of them hawked as we passed by him, and spat; the other cupped his hand at the fork of his trousers, and shouted and laughed.

Annie looked round at me and gave a shrug. Miss Raymond, to make us all smile, said, 'I wonder if any woman will ever get her head broken on *my* account . . .'

'Only her heart, Miss Raymond,' I called gallantly; and had the satisfaction of seeing both Annie and Florence look my way and frown.

Our group got smaller as we journeyed, for at Whitechapel Ruth and Nora left us to pick up a cab to take them to their flat in the City, and at Shoreditch, where Miss Raymond lived, Annie looked at the toe of her boot and said, 'Well, I think I shall just walk Miss Raymond to her door, since it's so late; but you be sure to go on without me, and I'll catch you up . . .'

So then it was only Florence and me. We walked quickly, because it was so cold, and Florence linked her hands around my arm and held me very close. When we reached the end of Quilter Street we stopped, as I had done on my first journey there, to gaze for a moment at the dark and eerie towers of Columbia Market, and to peer up at the starless, moonless, fog- and smoke-choked London sky.

'I don't believe Annie will catch us up, after all,' murmured Florence, looking back towards Shoreditch.

'No,' I said. 'I don't believe she will . . .'

The house, when we entered it, seemed hot and stuffy enough; we soon grew chilled, however, once we had taken our coats off and visited the privy. Ralph had left my truckle-bed made up for me, and fixed a note to the mantel to say there was a pot of tea for us inside the oven. There was: it was as thick and brown as gravy, but we drank it anyway – carrying our mugs back into the parlour, where the air was warmest, and holding our hands before the last few glowing coals in the ashy hearth.

The chairs had been pushed back to make room for my bed, so now, rather shyly, we sat upon it, side by side: as we did so, it moved a little on its castors, and Florence laughed. There was a lamp turned low upon the table but, apart from that, the room was very dim. We sat, and sipped our tea, and gazed at the coals: now and then the ash would shift a little in the grate, and the coal give a pop. 'How still it seems,' said Florence quietly, 'after the Boy!'

I had drawn my knees to my chin – the bed was very low upon the rug – and now turned my cheek upon them, and smiled at her.

'I'm glad you took me there,' I said. 'I don't believe I've had such a pleasant night since – well, I cannot say.'

'Can't you?'

'I can't. For half my pleasure, you know, was seeing you so gay . . .'

She smiled, then yawned. 'Didn't you think Miss Raymond very handsome?' she asked me.

'Pretty handsome.' Not as handsome as you, I wanted to say, looking again at all the features I had once thought plain. Oh, Flo, there's no one as handsome as you!

But I didn't say it. And meanwhile, she had smiled. 'I remember another girl Annie courted once. We let them stay with us, because Annie was sharing with her sister then. They slept in here, and Lilian and I were upstairs; and they were so noisy, Mrs Monks came round to ask, "Was someone poorly?" We had to say that Lily had the toothache – when in fact, she had slept through it all, with me beside her . . .'

Her voice grew quiet. I put a hand to my necktie, to loosen it: the idea of Flo lying at Lilian's side, stirred to a useless passion, made me bitter; but, as usual, it also made me rather warm. I said, 'Wasn't it hard, sharing a bed with someone you loved like that?'

'It was terribly hard! But also rather marvellous.'

'Did you never – never kiss her?'

'I sometimes kissed her as she slept; I kissed her hair. Her hair was handsome . . .'

I had a very vivid memory, then, of lying beside Kitty, in the days before we had ever made love. I said, in a slightly different tone: 'Did you watch her face, as she lay dreaming – and hope she dreamed of you?'

'I used to light a candle, just to do it!'

'Didn't you ache to touch her, as she lay at your side?'

'I thought I *would* touch her! I was frightened half to death by it.'

'But didn't you sometimes touch yourself – and wish the fingers were hers . . . ?'

'Oh, and then blush to do it! One time, I moved against her in the bed and she said, still sleeping, "*Jim!*" – Jim was the name of her man-friend. And then she said it again: "*Jim!*" – and in a voice I'd never heard her use before. I didn't know whether to weep about it, or what; but what I really wanted – oh, Nance! what I really wanted was for her to sleep on, like a girl in a trance, so I could touch her and have her think me him, and call out again, in that voice, as I did it . . . !'

She drew in her breath. A coal in the hearth fell with a rattle, but she did not turn to it, and neither did I. We only stared: it was as if her words, that were so warm, had melted our gazes the one into the other, and we could not tear them free. I said, almost laughing: 'Jim! Jim!' She blinked, and seemed to shiver; and then I shivered, too. And then I said, simply, 'Oh, Flo . . .'

And then, as if through some occult power of its own, the space between our lips seemed to grow small, and then to vanish; and we were kissing. She lifted her hand to touch the corner of my mouth; and then her fingers came between our pressing lips – they tasted, still, of sugar. And then I began to shake so hard I had to clench my fists and say to myself, Stop shaking, can't you? She'll think you've never been kissed before, at all!

When I raised my hands to her, however, I found that she was shaking just as badly; and when, after a moment, I moved my fingers from her throat to the swell of her breasts, she twitched like a fish – then smiled, and leaned closer to me. 'Press me harder!' she said.

We fell back together upon the bed, then – it shifted another inch across the carpet, on its wheels – and I undid the buttons of her shirt and pressed my face to her bosom, and sucked at one of her nipples, through the cotton of her chemise, till the nipple grew hard and she began to stiffen and pant. She put her hands to my head again, and lifted me to where she could kiss me; I lay and moved upon her, and felt her move beneath me, felt her breasts against my own, till I knew I should come, or faint – but then she turned me, and raised my skirt, and put her hand between my legs, and stroked so slowly, so lightly, so teasingly, I hoped I might never come at all . . .

At last, I felt her hand settle at the very wettest part of me, and she breathed against my ear. 'Do you care for it,' she murmured then, 'inside?' The question was such a gentle, such a gallant one, I almost wept. 'Oh!' I said, and again she kissed me; and after a moment I felt her move within me, first with one finger, then with two, I guessed, then three . . . At last, after a second's pressure, she had her hand in me up to the wrist. I think I called out – I think I shivered and panted and called out, to feel the subtle twisting of her fist, the curling and uncurling of her sweet fingers, beneath my womb . . .

When I reached my crisis I felt a gush, and found that I had wet her arm, with my spendings, from fingertip to elbow – and that she had come, out of a kind of sympathy, and lay weak and heavy against me, with her own skirts damp. She drew her hand free – making me shiver anew – and I seized it and held it, and pulled her face to me and kissed her; and then we lay very quietly with our limbs pressed hard together until, like cooling engines, we ceased our pulsings and grew still.

When she rose at last, she cracked her head upon the supper-table: we had jerked the truckle-bed from one side of the parlour to the other, and not noticed. She laughed. We shuffled off our clothes, and she turned down the lamp, and we lay beneath the blankets in our damp petticoats. When she fell asleep I put my hands to her cheeks, and kissed her brow where she had bruised it.

I woke to find it still the night, but a little lighter. I didn't know what had disturbed me; when I looked about me, however, I saw that Florence had raised herself a little on the pillow, and was gazing at me, apparently quite wide awake. I reached for her hand again, and kissed it, and felt my insides give a kind of lurch. She smiled; but there was a darkness to the smile, that made me feel chill.

'What's up?' I murmured. She stroked my hair.

'I was only thinking . . .'

'What?' She wouldn't answer. I propped myself up beside her, quite wide awake myself, now. '*What*, Florence?'

'I was looking at you in the darkness: I have never seen you sleep before. You looked like quite a stranger to me. And then I thought, you *are* a stranger to me . . .'

'A stranger? How can you say that? You have lived with me for more than a year!'

'And last night,' she answered, 'for the first time, I discovered you were once a music-hall star! How can you keep a thing like that a secret? Why would you want to? What else have you done that I don't know about? You might have been in prison, for all I know. You might have been mad. You might have been gay!'

I bit my lip; but then, remembering how kind she had been about the gay girls at the Boy, I said quickly, 'Flo, I did go on the streets one time. You won't hate me for it, will you?'

She took her hand away at once. 'On the streets! My God! Of course I won't hate you, but – oh, Nance! To think of you as one of them sad girls . . .'

'I wasn't sad,' I said, and looked away. 'And to tell the truth I – well, I wasn't quite a girl, either.'

'Not a girl?' she said. 'What can you mean?'

I scraped at the silken edge of the blanket with my nail. Should I tell my story – the story I had kept so close, so long? I saw her hand upon the sheet and, as my stomach gave another slide, I remembered again her fingers, easing me open, and her fist inside me, slowly turning . . .

I took a breath. 'Have you ever,' I said, 'been to Whitstable . . . ?'

Once I began it, I found I could not stop. I told her every-thing – about my life as an oyster-girl; about Kitty Butler, whom I had left my family for, and who had left me, in her turn, for Walter Bliss. I told her about my madness; my mas-querade; my life with Mrs Milne and Grace, in Green Street, where she had seen me first. And finally I told her about Diana, and Felicity Place, and Zena.

When I stopped talking it was almost light; the parlour seemed chillier than ever. Through all my long narrative Florence had been silent; she had begun to frown when I had reached the part about the renting, and after that the frown had deepened. Now it was very deep indeed.

'You wanted to know,' I said, 'what secrets I had . . .'

She looked away. 'I didn't think there would be quite so many.'

'You said you wouldn't hate me, over the renting.'

'It's so hard to think you did those things – for fun. And – oh, Nance, for such a cruel kind of fun!'

'It was very long ago.'

'To think of all the people you have known – and yet you have no friends.'

'I left them all behind me.'

'Your family. You said when you came here that your family had thrown you over. But it was *you* threw *them* over! How they must wonder over you! Do you never think of them?'

'Sometimes, sometimes.'

'And the lady who was so fond of you, in Green Street. Do you never think to call on her, and her daughter?'

'They have moved away; and I tried to find them. And anyway, I was ashamed, because I had neglected them . . .'

'Neglected them, for that – what was her name?'

'Diana.'

'Diana. Did you care for her, then, so very much?'

'Care for her?' I propped myself upon my elbow. 'I hated her! She was a kind of devil! I have told you—'

'And yet, you stayed with her, so long . . .'

I felt suffocated, all at once, by my own story, and by the meanings she was teasing from it. 'I can't explain,' I said. 'She had a power over me. She was rich. She had – things.'

'First you told me it was a gent that threw you out. Then you said it was a lady. I thought, that you had lost some girl . . .'

'I had lost a girl; but it was Kitty, and it was years before.'

'And Diana was rich; and blacked your eye and cut you, and you let her. And then she chucked you out because you – kissed her maid.' Her voice had grown steadily harder. 'What happened to *her*?'

'I don't know. I don't know!'

We lay a while in silence, and the bed seemed suddenly terribly slim. Florence gazed at the lightening square of curtain at the window, and I watched her, miserably. When she put a finger to her mouth to chew at a nail I lifted my hand to stop her; but she pushed my arm away, and made to rise.

'Where are you going?' I asked.

'Upstairs. I want to sit a little while and think.'

'No!' I cried; and as I cried it, Cyril, in his crib upstairs, woke up, and began to call out for his mother. I reached for Florence and seized her wrist and, all heedless of the baby's cries, pulled her back and pressed her to the bed. 'I know what you mean to do,' I said. 'You mean to go and think of Lilian!'

'I cannot *help* but think of Lilian!' she answered, stricken. 'I cannot *help* it. And you – you're just the same, only I never knew it. Don't say – don't say you weren't thinking of her, of Kitty, last night, as you kissed me!'

I took a breath – but then I hesitated. For it was true, I

couldn't say it. It was Kitty I had kissed first and hardest; and
it was as if I had had the shape or the colour or the taste of her
kisses upon my lips, ever after. Not the spendings and the
tears of all the weeping sods of Soho, nor the wine and the
damp caresses of Felicity Place, had quite washed those kisses
away. I had always known it – but it had never mattered with
Diana, nor with Zena. Why should it matter with Florence?

What should it matter who she thought of, as she kissed me?

'All I know is,' I said at last, 'if we had not lain together last
night, we would have died of it. And if you tell me now we
shall never lie together again, after that, that was so
marvellous . . . !'

I still held her to the bed, and Cyril still cried; but now, by
some miracle, his cries began to die – and Florence, in her
turn, grew slack in my arms, and turned her head against me.

'I liked to think of you,' she said quietly, 'as Venus in a sea-
shell. I never thought of the sweethearts you had, before you
came here . . .'

'Why must you think of them now?'

'Because *you* do! Suppose Kitty were to show up again, and
ask you back to her?'

'She won't. Kitty's gone, Flo. Like Lilian. Believe me, there's
more chance of *her* coming back!' I began to smile. 'And if she
does, you can go to her, and I won't say a word. And if Kitty
comes for me, you can do similar. And then, I suppose, we
shall have our paradises – and will be able to wave to one
another from our separate clouds. But till then – till then, Flo,
can't we go on kissing, and just be glad?'

As lovers' vows go, this one was, I suppose, rather curious;
but we were girls with curious histories – girls with pasts like
boxes with ill-fitting lids. We must bear them, but bear them
carefully. We should do very well, I thought, as Florence
sighed and raised her hand to me at last; we should do very
well, so long as the boxes stayed unspilled.

Chapter 19

That afternoon, we put the truckle-bed back in the attic – I think its castors had got permanently skewed – and I moved my night-things to Florence's room, and put my gown beneath her pillow. We did it while Ralph was out; and when he came home, and gazed at the place where the bed had used to be propped, and then at us, with our blushes and our shadowy eyes and swollen lips, he blinked about a dozen times, and swallowed, and sat and raised an issue of *Justice* before his face; but when he rose to go to his room that night, he kissed me very warmly. I looked at Florence.

'Why doesn't Ralph have a sweetheart?' I said, when he had left us. She shrugged.

'Girls don't seem to care for him. Every tom friend of mine is half in love with him, but regular girls – well! He goes for dainty ones; the last one gave him up for the sake of a boxer.'

'Poor Ralph,' I said. Then: 'He is remarkably forbearing on the matter of your – leanings. Don't you think?'

She came and sat on the arm of my chair. 'He's had a long time to get used to them,' she said.

'Have you always had them, then?'

'Well, I suppose there was always a girl or two, somewhere about the place. Mother never was able to figure it out. Janet don't care – she says it leaves more chaps for her. But Frank' – this was the older brother, who came visiting from time to time with his family – 'Frank never liked to see girls calling for me, in the old days: he slapped me over it once, I've never forgotten it. He wouldn't be at all tickled to see you here, now.'

'We can pretend it's otherwise, if you like,' I said. 'We can bring the truckle-bed back, and pretend—'

She leaned away from me as if I had sworn at her. 'Pretend? Pretend, and in my own house? If Frank doesn't like my habits, he can stop visiting. Him, and anyone else with a similar idea. Would you have people think we were ashamed?'

'No, no. It was only that Kitty—'

'Oh, Kitty! Kitty! The more you tell me about that woman, the less I care for her. To think she kept you cramped and guilty for so long, when you might have been off, having your bit of fun as a real gay tom . . .'

'I wouldn't have been a tom at all,' I said, more hurt by her words than I was willing to show, 'if it hadn't been for Kitty Butler.'

She looked me over: I had my trousers on. 'Now *that*,' she said, 'I cannot believe. You would have met some woman, sooner or later.'

'When I was married to Freddy, probably, and had a dozen kids. I should certainly never have met *you*.'

'Well, then I suppose I have *some*thing to thank Kitty Butler for.'

The name, when spoken aloud like that, still grated on my nerves a little and set them tingling; I think she knew it. But now I said lightly, 'You do. Be sure you remember it. In fact, I have something that will remind you . . .' I went to the pocket of my coat, and drew out the photograph of Kitty and me, that I had got from Jenny, at the Boy in the Boat; and I carried it to the bookcase and set it there, beneath the other portraits. 'Your Lilian,' I said, 'may have got a thrill from gazing at Eleanor Marx. Sensible girls used to put pictures of me on their bedroom walls, five years ago.'

'Stop boasting,' she answered. 'All this talk about the music hall. I've never heard you sing a song to *me*.'

She had taken my place in the armchair, and now I went and nudged at her knees with my own. '*Tommy*,' I sang – it was an old song of W. B. Fair's – '*Tommy, make room for your uncle.*'

She laughed. 'Is that a song you used to sing with Kitty?'

'I should say not! Kitty would have been too afraid, in case there was a real tom in the crowd who got the joke and thought we meant it.'

'Sing me one of the ones you sang with Kitty, then.'

'Well . . .' I was not sure I liked the idea; but I sang her a few lines of our song about the sovereigns – strolling about the parlour as I did so, and kicking my moleskinned legs. When I finished, she shook her head.

'How proud she should have been of you!' she said softly. 'If I'd been her . . .' She didn't finish. She only rose, and came to me, and drew back the shirt where it flapped beneath my throat, and kissed the flesh that showed there, until I trembled.

She had seemed chaste as a plaster saint to me, once; she had seemed plain. But she was not chaste now – she was marvellously bold and frank and ready; and the boldness made her bonny, made her gleam, like a kind of polish. I could not look at her and not want to touch her. I could not see the shine upon her pink lips, without wanting to step to her and press my mouth to it; I couldn't look at her hand as it lay limp upon some table-top, or held a pen, or carried a cup, or did any kind of ordinary business, without longing to take it in my own and kiss the knuckles or put my tongue to the palm, or press it to the fork at my trousers. I would stand beside her in a crowded room and feel the hairs lift on my arms – and see her own flesh pimple, and her cheeks grow warm, and know she ached for me, to match my aching; but she would take a dreadful satisfaction, too, in lengthening the visits of her friends – in handing out a second cup of tea, and then a third – and all while I looked on, tortured and damp.

'You made me wait, for two years and a half,' she said to me once; I had followed her into the kitchen, and put my shaking arms about her as she lifted a kettle to the stove. 'It won't hurt you, to wait an hour till the parlour clears . . .' But when she said a similar thing another night, I touched her through the folds of her skirt until her voice grew weak – and then she led me into the pantry, and put a broom across the door, and we caressed amongst the packets of flour and tins of treacle while the kettle whistled and the kitchen grew woolly with steam, and Annie called out from the parlour, What *were* we doing?

The fact was, we had both gone kissless for so long that, having once begun to kiss again, we could not stop.

Our boldness made us marvel.

'I had you down for one of those terrible grudging girls,' she said to me one night, a week or two after our visit to the Boy. 'One of those dry-rub-it-on-the-hip-don't-touch-me sorts . . .'

'Are there such girls?' I asked her.

She coloured. 'Well, I have lain with one or two . . .'

The thought that she had lain with different girls – with so many girls that she could put them into categories, like breeds of fish – was wonderfully astonishing and stirring. I put my hand upon her – we were lying together, naked despite the cold, because we had bathed in a steaming tub and were still warm and prickling from it – and stroked her, from the hollow at her throat to the hollow of her groin; then I stroked her again, and felt her shiver.

'Who would ever have thought that I should touch you so, and talk to you so!' I asked her – whispering, because Cyril lay beside us, asleep in his crib. 'I was sure you would prove prim and awkward. I was sure you would be shy. Indeed, I didn't see how you could fail to be, being so political and good as you are!'

She laughed. 'It ain't the Salvation Army, you know,' she answered, 'socialism.'

'Well, maybe . . .'

We said nothing more, then; only kissed and murmured. But the next night she produced a book, and had me read it. It was *Towards Democracy*, the poem by Edward Carpenter; and as I turned the pages, with Florence warm beside me, I found myself growing damp.

'Did you used to look at this with Lilian?' I asked her.

She nodded. 'She used to like to have me read it to her, as we lay in bed. She couldn't have known, I suppose, that it was sometimes hard to do it . . .'

Perhaps she did know, I thought – and the idea made me damper. I handed the book to her. 'Read it to me, now,' I said.

'You have already read it.'

'Read me the bits you used to read to her . . .'

She hesitated, then did so; and as she murmured, I put my hand between her legs and touched her, and her voice grew less steady, the more firmly I stroked.

'There are books written especially for this sort of thing,' I said to her, thinking back to the many times I had lain doing something similar with Diana – on the very same nights, probably, that Florence had lain squirming next to Lilian. 'Wouldn't you rather I bought you a book like that? I can't believe Mr Carpenter really intended his poem to be enjoyed in such a way.'

She put her lips against my throat. 'Oh, I think Mr Carpenter would approve all right.'

She had let the book fall on to her breast. Now I pushed it aside, and rolled upon her.

'And this,' I said, moving my hips, 'is really contributing to the social revolution?'

'Oh, yes!'

I wriggled lower. 'And this, too?'

'Oh, certainly!'

I slid beneath the sheet. 'And how about this?'

'*Oh!*'

'Lord,' I said a little later. 'To think I have been part of the

socialist conspiracy all these years, and never knew it till
now . . .'

We kept *Towards Democracy* beside the bed permanently,
after that; and just as Florence would sometimes say to me,
when the house was quiet, 'Sing me a song, in your moleskins, Uncle . . .', so I would occasionally lean to whisper to
her, over supper or as we walked side by side: 'Shall we be
democratic tonight, Flo . . . ?' Of course, there were certain
songs – 'Sweethearts and Wives' was one of them – I would
never have sung for her. And *Leaves of Grass*, I noticed, stayed
downstairs, on the shelf beneath the photographs of Eleanor
Marx and Kitty. I didn't mind it. How could I mind it? We had
struck a kind of bargain. We had fixed to kiss for ever. We had
never once said, *I love you*.

'Isn't it marvellous to be in love, in spring-time?' Annie asked
us one evening in April: she and Miss Raymond were sweethearts now, and spent long hours in our parlour, sighing over
one another's charms. 'I went visiting a factory today, and it was
the grimmest, most broken-down old place you ever saw. But I
came out into its yard and there was a piece of pussy willow
growing there – just a piece of common old pussy-willow, but
with a bit of yellow sun on it, and it looked so exactly like my
dear Emma I thought for a moment I would fall down and kiss
it, and weep.'

Florence snorted. 'They should never have let women into
the civil service, I said it all along. Weeping over pussy willow?
I never heard such rubbish in my life; I really wonder, sometimes, how Emma can bear you. If I heard Nancy likening me to
a sprig of catkins, I should be sick.'

'Oh, for shame! Nancy, have you never seen Florrie's face in
a chrysanthemum, or a rose?'

'Never,' I said. 'Though there was a flounder for sale on a
fishmonger's barrow, in Whitechapel yesterday, and the likeness was quite uncanny. I very nearly brought it home . . .'

Annie took Miss Raymond's hand in hers, and gazed at us in

wonder. 'I swear,' she said, 'you two are the most unsenti-
mental sweethearts I've ever known.'

'We are too sensible for sentiment, aren't we, Nance?'

'Too busy, more like,' I said, with a yawn.

Florence grew sheepish. 'And, well, we shall be even busier
before long, I'm afraid. For, you know, I promised Mrs Macey
at the Guild that I would help with the organising of the
Workers' Rally—'

'Oh, Florence,' I cried, 'you didn't!'

'What's this?' asked Miss Raymond.

'Some wretched scheme,' I said, 'dreamed up by all the
guilds and unions of East London, to fill Victoria Park with
socialists—'

'A demonstration,' interrupted Florence. 'A wonderful
thing, if it works. It is to be at the end of May. There will be
tents, and speeches and stalls, and a pageant; we hope to get
visitors and speakers from all over Britain – and some, even,
from Germany and France.'

'And now you have said you will help to run it. Which
means,' I said bitterly to Miss Raymond, 'that she will have
taken far more duties upon herself than she should have, and
so, as usual, I shall be obliged to help her – to sit up late at
night writing letters to the president of the Hoxton Fur and
Feather Dressers' Union, or the Wapping Small Metal Workers'
Society. And all at a time—' All at a time, I wanted to say,
when I longed only to tip her satchel of papers into the fire,
and lie kissing her before its blaze.

I thought Florence looked at me a little sadly then. She said,
'You needn't help, if you don't care to.'

'Needn't help?' I cried. 'In this house?'

And it was just as I had supposed. Florence had committed
herself to a thousand duties, and I, to stop her working herself
into a fit, took on half of them – wrote letters and figured sums
at her direction, and delivered bags of posters and pamphlets
to grubby union offices, and visited carpenters' shops, and sat
sewing tablecloths and flags, and costumes for the workers'

pageant. Our house in Quilter Street grew quite dusty again; our suppers became ever more hasty and under-prepared – I had no time for stewing oysters now, but served them raw, and we swallowed them as we worked. Half of the flags I sewed, half of the letters Florence wrote, were stained at the edges with liquor, and spotted with grease.

Even Ralph was involved in it. He had been asked, as secretary of his union, to write a little address for the day itself, and deliver it – in between the grander speeches – before the crowd. The title of the address was to be 'Why Socialism?', and the composing and rehearsing of this threw Ralph – who was no very keen public speaker – into a fever. He would sit at the supper-table for hours at a time, writing until his arm grew sore – or more often gazing bleakly at the empty page before him, then dashing to the bookcase to check a reference in some political tract, and cursing to find it lent out or lost: 'What has happened to *The White Slaves of England*? Who has borrowed my Sidney Webb? And where the blazes is *Towards Democracy*?'

Florence and I would gaze at him and shake our heads. 'Give the thing up,' we would say, 'if you don't want to do it, or feel you can't. No one will mind.' But Ralph would always stiffen and answer, 'No, no. It is for the sake of the union. I almost have it.' Then he would frown at his page again, and chew on his beard; and I would see him imagining himself standing before a crowd of staring faces, and he would sweat and start to tremble.

But here, at least, I felt I could help. 'Let me hear you read a bit of your speech,' I said to him one night when Florence was out. 'Don't forget I was an actress of sorts, once. It's all the same, you know, whether it's a stage or a platform.'

'That's true,' he said, struck by the idea. Then he flapped his sheets. 'But I am rather shy of reading it out before you.'

'Ralph! If you are shy with me, in our parlour, what will you be like before five hundred people, in Victoria Park?' The thought set him biting at his beard again; but he held his speech before him as requested, stood before the curtained window, and cleared his throat.

'"Why Socialism?"' he began. I jumped to my feet.

'Well, that is hopeless, for a start. You can't mumble into your hands like that, and expect the folk in the gallery – I mean, at the back of the tent – to be able to hear you.'

'You are rather harsh, Nancy,' he said.

'You will thank me for it, in the end. Now, straighten your back and lift up your head, and start again. And talk from *here*' – I touched the buckle on his trousers, and he twitched – 'not from your throat. Go on.'

'"Why Socialism?"' he read again, in a deep, unnatural voice. 'That is the question I have been invited to discuss with you this afternoon. "Why Socialism?" I shall keep my answer rather brief.'

I sucked at my lip. 'Some joker is sure to shout "Hurrah" at that point, you know.'

'Not really, Nance?'

'You may count on it. But you mustn't let it unsettle you, or you'll be done for. Go on, now, let's hear the rest.'

He read the speech – it was a matter of two or three pages, no more – and I listened, and frowned.

'You *will* talk into the paper,' I said at the end. 'No one will be able to hear. They will get bored, and start talking amongst themselves. I have seen it happen a hundred times.'

'But I must read the words,' he said. I shook my head.

'You shall have to learn them, there's nothing else for it. You shall have to get the piece by heart.'

'What? All this?' He gazed miserably at the pages.

'A day or two's work,' I said. Then I put my hand upon his arm. 'It is either that, Ralph, or we shall have to put you in a funny suit . . .'

And so through the whole of April and half of May – for of course it took considerably longer than one or two days for him to learn even so much as a quarter of the words – Ralph and I laboured together over his little speech, forcing the phrases into his head and finding all sorts of tricks to make them stay there. I would sit like a prompter, the papers in my hand, Ralph declaiming before me in an effortful monotone; I would have him recite to me over breakfast, or as we washed the dishes, or sat together beside the fire; I would stand outside the kitchen door and have him shout the words out to me as he lay in his bath.

'How many times have you heard economists say that England is the richest nation in the world? If you were to ask them what they meant by that, they would answer . . . they would answer . . .'

'Ralph! They would answer: *Look about you*—'

'They would answer: Look about you, at our great palaces and public buildings, our country houses and our . . .'

'Our factories—'

'Our factories and our . . .'

'Our *Empire*, Ralph!'

In time, of course, I learned the whole wretched speech myself, and could leave the sheets aside; but in time, too, Ralph managed more or less to con it, and was able to stumble through from start to finish, without any prompts at all, and sounding almost sensible.

Meanwhile, the day of the rally drew nearer, our hours grew ever fuller and our tasks more rushed; and I – despite my grumbles – could not help but grow a little eager to see the thing take place at last, and was as excited and as fretful, almost, as Florence herself.

'If only it does not rain!' she said, gazing bleakly at the sky from our bedroom window, the night before the appointed Sunday. 'If it rains, we shall have to have the pageant in a tent; and nobody has rehearsed that. Or suppose it thunders? Then no one will hear the speakers.'

'It won't rain,' I said. 'Stop fussing.' But she continued to frown at the sky; and at length I joined her at the window, and gazed at the clouds myself.

'If only it doesn't rain,' she said again; and to distract her I breathed upon the glass and wrote our initials in the mist, with a fingernail: *N.A., F.B., 1895 & Always.* I put a heart around them and, piercing the heart, an arrow.

It did not rain that Sunday; indeed, the skies above Bethnal Green were so blue and clear you might have been forgiven for thinking God Himself a socialist, the brilliant sun a kind of heavenly blessing. At Quilter Street we all rose early, and bathed and washed our hair and dressed – it was like getting ready for a wedding. I very gallantly decided not to risk my trousers on the crowd – socialists having such a poor name already; instead, I wore a suit of navy-blue, with scarlet frogging on the coat, and a matching necktie, and a billycock hat. As ladies' outfits went, it was a smart one; even so, I found myself twitching irritably at my skirts as I paced the parlour waiting for Flo – and was soon joined by Ralph, who was dressed up stiff as a clerk, and kept pulling at his collar where it chafed against his throat.

Florence herself wore the damson-coloured suit I so admired: I bought a flower for her, on the walk from Bethnal Green, and pinned it to her jacket. It was a daisy, big as a fist, and shone when the sun struck it, like a lamp. 'You shall certainly,' she said to me, 'not lose me in that.'

Victoria Park itself we found transformed. Workmen had been busy raising tents and platforms and stalls all through the weekend, and there were strings of flags and banners at every tree, and stall-holders already setting up their tables and displays. Florence had about a dozen lists of duties upon her, and now produced them, then went off to find Mrs Macey of the Guild. Ralph and I picked our way through all the drooping bunting, to find the tent he was to speak in. It turned out to be the biggest of the lot: 'There'll be room for seven hundred people in here, at the least!' the workmen told us cheerfully, as they filled it with chairs. That made it greater than some of the halls I had used to play at; and when Ralph heard it, he turned very pale, and retired to a bench for another reading of his speech.

After that, I took Cyril and wandered about, gazing at whatever caught my eye and stopping to chat with girls I recognised, lending a hand with fluttering tablecloths, splitting boxes, awkward rosettes. There were speakers and exhibitions there, it seemed to me, for every queer or philanthropic society and cause you could imagine – trade unionists and suffragists, Christian Scientists, Christian Socialists, Jewish Socialists, Irish Socialists, anarchists, vegetarians . . . 'Ain't this marvellous?' I heard as I walked, from friends and strangers alike. 'Did you ever see a sight like this?' One woman gave me a sash of satin to pin about my hat; I fastened it to Cyril's frock instead, and when people saw him in the colours of the SDF, they smiled and shook his hand: 'Hallo, comrade!'

'Won't he remember this day, when he's grown!' said a man, as he touched Cyril's head and gave him a penny. Then he straightened, and studied the scene about him with shining eyes. 'We'll all remember this day, all right . . .'

I knew he was right. I had grumbled about it to Annie and Miss Raymond, and I had sat sewing flags and banners, not caring if the stitches were crooked or the satin got stained; but as the park began to fill, and the sun grew ever more brilliant and all the colours more gay, I found myself gazing about me in a kind of wonder. 'If five thousand people come,' Florence had said the night before, 'we shall be happy . . .': but I thought, as I walked about, then moved to a rise of ground to lift Cyril to my shoulders and put my hand to my brow and survey the field, that there must be ten times that number there – all the ordinary people of East London, it seemed to be, all jumbled together in Victoria Park, goodnatured and careless and dressed in their best. They came, I suppose, as much for the sun as for the socialism. They spread blankets between the stalls and tents, and ate their lunches there, and lay with their sweethearts and babies, and threw sticks for their dogs. But I saw them listening, too, to the speakers at the stalls – sometimes nodding, sometimes arguing, sometimes frowning over a pamphlet, or placing their name upon a list, or fishing pennies from their pockets, to give to some cause.

As I stood and looked, I saw a woman pass by with children at her skirts – it was Mrs Fryer, the poor needlewoman whom Florence and I had visited in the autumn. When I called to her, she came smiling up to me. 'I got my place in the union, after all,' she said. 'Your pal persuaded me to it . . .' We stood chatting for a moment – her children had toffee-apples, and held one up for Cyril to lick. Then there came a blast of music, and people shuffled and murmured and craned their necks, and we stood together, lifting the children high, and watched the Workers' Pageant – a procession of men and women dressed in all the costumes of all the trades, carrying union banners and flags and flowers. It took quite half an hour for the pageant to pass; and when it had done so the people put their fingers to their lips, and whistled and cheered and clapped. Mrs Fryer wept, because her neighbour's eldest daughter was walking in the line, dressed as a match-girl.

I wished that Florence were with me, and kept looking for her damson-coloured suit and her daisy, but – though I saw just about every other unionist who had ever passed through our parlour – I did not see her once. When I found her at last, she was in the speakers' tent: she had spent all afternoon there, listening to the lectures. 'Have you heard?' she said when she saw me. 'There's a rumour that Eleanor Marx is coming: I daren't leave the tent, for fear of missing her address!' It turned out she had eaten nothing since breakfast: I went off to buy her a packet of whelks from a stall, and a cup of ginger ale. When I returned I found Ralph beside her, sweating, still pulling at his collar, and paler than ever. Every seat in the tent was taken, and there were people standing, besides. It was stiflingly hot, and the heat was making everyone restless and cross. One speaker had recently made an unpopular point, and been booed from the platform.

'They won't boo you, Ralph,' I said; but when I saw that he was really miserable, I took his arm, left the baby with

Florence, and led him from his seat into the cooler air outside. 'Come on, come and have a fag with me. You mustn't let the crowd see you are nervous.'

We stood just beyond a flap of the tent – a couple of men from Ralph's factory went by, and raised their hands to us – and I lit us two cigarettes. Ralph's fingers shook as he held his, and he almost dropped it, then smiled apologetically: 'What a fool you must think me.'

'Not at all! I remember how frightened I was on my first night; I thought I would be sick.'

'I thought *I* would be sick, a moment ago.'

'Everybody thinks it, and no one is.' This wasn't quite true: I had often seen nervous artistes bent over bowls and fire-buckets at the side of the stage; but I did not, of course, tell Ralph this.

'Did you ever play before a crowd that was rather rough, Nance?' he asked me now.

'What?' I said. 'At one hall – Deacon's, in Islington – there was a poor comedian on before us and some fellows jumped on to the stage and held him upside-down over the footlights, trying to set his hair on fire.' Ralph blinked two or three times on hearing that, then looked hastily back into the tent, as if to make sure there were no naked flames about, over which an unfriendly audience might take it into their heads to try and tip him. Then he looked queasily at his cigarette, and threw it down.

'I think, if it's all the same to you,' he said, 'I shall just go off and have another run through my address.' And before I could open my mouth to persuade him otherwise he had slipped away, and left me smoking on my own.

I did not mind: it was still pleasanter outside the tent than in it. I put the cigarette between my lips and folded my arms, and leaned back a little against the canvas. Then I closed my eyes, and let the sun fall full upon my face; then I took the fag away, and gave a yawn.

And as I did so, there came a woman's voice at my shoulder, that made me jump.

'Well! Of all the gals to see at a working people's rally, I should've said that Nancy King would be about the last of 'em.'

I opened my eyes, let my cigarette fall, and turned to the woman and gave a cry.

'Zena! Oh! And is it really you?'

It was indeed Zena: she stood beside me plumper and even handsomer than when I had seen her last, and clad in a scarlet coat and a bracelet with charms on. 'Zena!' I said again. 'Oh! How good it is to see you.' I took her hand and pressed it, and she laughed.

'I've met just about every gal I ever knew here, today,' she said. 'And then I saw this other one, standing up against a tent flap with a fag at her lip and I thought, Lord, but don't she look like old Nan King? What a lark, if it should be her, after all this time – and here, of all places! And I stepped up a bit closer, and then I saw that your hair was all clipped, and I knew it was you, for sure.'

'Oh, Zena! I was certain I should never hear from you again.' She looked a little sheepish at that; and then, remembering, I pressed her hand even harder and said in quite a different tone: 'What a nerve you've got, though! After leaving me in such a state, that time in Kilburn! I thought I should die.'

Now she made a show of tossing her head. 'Well! You done me very brown, you know, over that money.'

'I do know it. What a little beast I was! I suppose, you never did get to the colonies . . .'

She wrinkled her nose. 'My friend who went to Australia came back. She said the place was full of great rough fellows, and they don't want landladies; what they want is wives. I changed my mind about it after that. I'm happy enough, after all, in Stepney.'

'You're in Stepney now? But then we're almost neighbours! I live in Bethnal Green. With my sweetheart. Look, she's over there.' I put my hand on her shoulder and pointed into the crowded tent. 'The one near the stage, with the baby on her arm.'

'What,' she said, 'not Flo Banner, that works at the gals' home!'

'You don't mean, you know her?'

'I have a couple of pals what've lived at Freemantle House, and they are always talking about how marvellous Flo Banner is! You know, I suppose, that half the gals there are mad in love with her . . .'

'With Florence? Are you sure?'

'I'll say!' We looked into the tent together again. Florence was on her feet now, and waving a paper at the speaker at the stage. Zena laughed. 'Fancy you and Flo Banner!' she said. 'I'm sure, *she* don't take no nonsense from you.'

'You're right,' I answered, still gazing at Florence, still marvelling at what Zena had told me. 'She don't.'

We moved into the sunshine again. 'And how about you?' I asked her then. 'I bet you have a girl, don't you?'

'I do,' she said shyly. 'The fact is, indeed, I have a couple of 'em, and can't quite decide between the two . . .'

'Two! My God!' I imagined having two sweethearts like Florence: the thought made me ache and start yawning.

'One of them is about here, somewhere,' Zena was saying. 'She is part of a union and— There she is! *Maud!*' At her cry, a girl in a blue-and-brown checked coat looked round, and wandered over. Zena took her arm, and the girl smiled.

'This is Miss Skinner,' said Zena to me; then, to her sweetheart: 'Maud, this is Nan King, the singer from the halls.' Miss Skinner – who was about nineteen or so, and would still have been in short skirts on the night I took my last bow at the Brit – gazed politely at me, and offered me her hand. Zena went on then, 'Miss King lives with Flo Banner –' and at once, Miss Skinner's grip tightened, and her eyes grew wide.

'Flo Banner?' she said, in just the tone that Zena had. 'Flo Banner, of the Guild? Oh! I wonder – I've got the programme of the day about me somewhere – do you think, Miss King, you might get her to sign it for me?'

'Sign it!' I said. She had produced a paper giving the

running-order of the speeches and the layout of the stalls, and held it to me, trembling. Florence's name, I now saw, was printed, along with one or two others, amongst the list of organisers. 'Well,' I said. 'Well. You might ask her yourself, you know: she's only over there—'

'Oh, I couldn't!' answered Miss Skinner. 'I should be too shy . . .'

In the end I took the paper, and said I would do what I could; and Miss Skinner looked desperately grateful, then went off to tell her friends that she had met me.

'She's a bit romantic, ain't she?' said Zena, wrinkling her nose again. 'I might throw her over for the other one, yet . . .' I shook my head, looked at the paper another time, then placed it in the pocket of my skirt.

We chatted for another few moments; and then Zena said, 'And so, you're quite happy, are you, in Bethnal Green? It ain't quite what you was used to in the old days . . .'

I pulled a face. 'I hate to think of those days, Zena. I'm all changed now.'

'I dare say. That Diana Lethaby, though – well! You've seen her, of course?'

'Diana?' I shook my head. 'Not likely! Did you think I'd go back to Felicity Place, after that dam' party . . . ?'

Zena stared at me. 'But, don't tell me you didn't know it? Diana is here!'

'Here? She can't be!'

'She is! I tell you, all the world is here this afternoon – and her amongst 'em. She is over at the table of some paper or magazine. I saw her, and nearly fainted dead away!'

'My God.' Diana, here! The thought was awful – and yet . . . Well, they do say that old dogs never forget the tricks their mistresses beat into them: I had felt myself stir, faintly, at the first mention of her hateful name. I looked once into the tent, and saw Florence, on her feet again and still shaking her arm at the platform; then I turned to Zena. 'Will you show me,' I asked, 'where?'

She gave me one swift warning sort of look; then she took my arm and led me through the crowd, towards the bathing lake, and came to a halt behind a bush.

'Look, there,' she said in a low voice. 'Near that table. D'you see her?' I nodded. She was standing beside a display – it was for the women's journal *Shafts*, that she sometimes helped with the running of – and was talking with another lady, a lady I thought might be one of the ones who had come dressed as Sappho to the fancy-dress ball. The lady had a Suffrage sash across her bosom. Diana was clad in grey, and her hat had a veil to it – though this was, at the moment, turned up. She was as haughty and as handsome as ever. I gazed at her and had a very vivid memory – of myself, sprawled beside her with pearls about my hips; of the bed seeming to tilt; of the chafing of the leather as she straddled me and rocked . . .

'What do you think she would do,' I said to Zena, 'if I went over?'

'You ain't going to try it!'

'Why not? I'm quite, you know, out of her power now.' But even as I said it, I looked at her and felt that doggishness come over me again – or doggishness, perhaps, is not the term for it. It was like she was some music-hall mesmerist, and I a blinking girl, all ready to make a mockery of myself, before the crowd, at her request . . .

Zena said, 'Well, I ain't going nowhere near her . . .'; but I didn't listen. I glanced quickly again at the speakers' tent, then I stepped out from behind the bush and made my way towards the stall – straightening the knot in my necktie, as I did so. I was within about twenty yards of her, and had lifted a hand to remove my hat, when she turned, and seemed to raise her eyes to mine. Her gaze grew hard, sardonic and lustful all at once, just as I remembered it; and my heart twitched in my breast – in fright, I think! – as if a hook had caught it.

But then she opened her mouth to speak; and what she said was: 'Reggie! Reggie, here!'

That made me stumble. From somewhere close behind me came a gruffer answering cry – 'All right' – and I turned, and saw a boy picking his way across the grass, his eyes in a scowl and fixed on Diana's, his hand bearing a sugared ice, which he held before him and sucked at very gingerly, for fear it would drip and spoil his trousers. The trousers were handsome, and bulged at the fork. The boy himself was tall and slight; his hair was dark, and cut very short. His face was a pretty one, his lips pink as a girl's . . .

When he reached Diana she leaned and drew the handkerchief from his pocket, and began to dab with it at his thigh – it seemed, he had spilt his ice-cream after all. The other lady at the stall looked on, and smiled; then murmured something that made the pretty boy blush.

I had stood and watched all this, in a kind of astonishment; but now I took a slow step backwards, and then another. Diana may have raised her face again, I cannot say: I didn't stop to see it. Reggie had lifted his hand to lick at his ice, his cuff had moved back, and I had caught the flash of a wrist-watch beneath it . . . I blinked my eyes, and shook my head, and ran back to the bush where Zena still stood peeping, and put my face against her shoulder.

When I looked again at Diana, through the leaves, she had her arm in Reggie's and their heads were close, and they were laughing. I turned to Zena, and she bit her lip.

'It is only the devils what prosper in this world, I swear,' she said. But then she bit her lip again; and then she tittered.

I laughed, too, for a moment. Then I cast another bitter look towards the stall, and said: 'Well, I hope she gets all she deserves!'

Zena cocked her head. 'Who?' she asked. 'Diana, or . . . ?'

I pulled a face, and would not answer her.

We wandered back to the speakers' tent, then, and Zena said she had better try to find her Maud.

'We'll be friends, won't we?' I said as we shook hands.

She nodded. 'You must be sure to introduce me to Miss Banner, anyway; I should like that.'

'Yes, well – you must at least come round some time and tell her you've forgiven me: she thinks me a regular brute, over you.'

She smiled – then something caught her eye, and she turned her head. 'There's my other sweetheart,' she said quickly – she gestured to a wide-shouldered, tommish-looking woman, who was studying us as we chatted, and frowning. Zena pulled a face. 'She likes to come the uncle, that one . . .'

'She *does* look a bit fierce. You'd better go to her: I don't want to end up with another blacked eye.'

She smiled, and pressed my hand; and I saw her step over to the woman and kiss her cheek, then disappear with her into the crush of people between the stalls. I ducked back into the tent. It was fuller and hotter than ever in there, the air thick with smoke, the people's faces sweating and jaundiced-looking where they were struck, through the canvas, by the afternoon sun. On the platform a woman was stumbling hoarsely through some speech or other, and a dozen people in the audience were on their feet, arguing with her. Florence was back in her chair before the dais, with Cyril kicking in her lap. Annie and Miss Raymond were beside her, with a pretty fair-haired girl I did not know. Ralph was nearby, his forehead gleaming and his face stiff with fright.

There was an empty seat next to Florence, and when I had made my way across the grass I sat in it and took the baby from her.

'Where have you been?' she asked above the shouting. 'It has been terrible in here. A load of boys have come in, intent on causing a stir. Poor Ralph is to speak next: he is so feverish you could fry an egg on him.'

I bounced Cyril upon my knee. 'Flo,' I said, 'you will never believe who I have just seen!'

'Who? she asked. Then her eyes grew wide. 'Not Eleanor Marx?'

'No, no – nobody like that! It was Zena, that girl I knew at Diana Lethaby's. And not only her, but Diana herself! The both of them here at once, can you imagine? My heart, when I saw Diana again – I thought I should die!' I jiggled Cyril until he began to squeal. Florence's face, however, had hardened.

'My God!' she said; and her tone made me flinch. 'Can we not enjoy even a socialist rally without your wretched past turning up to haunt us? You have not sat and listened to one speech here today; I suppose you have not so much as glanced at one of the stalls. All you have eyes and thoughts for is yourself; yourself, and the women you have . . . the women you have . . .'

'The women I have fucked, I suppose you mean,' I said in a low voice. I leaned away from her, really shocked and hurt; then I grew angry. 'Well, at least I *got* a fuck out of my old sweethearts. Which is more than you got out of Lilian.'

At that, her mouth fell open, and her eyes began to gleam with tears.

'You little cat,' she said. 'How can you say such things to me?'

'Because I am sick to death of hearing about Lilian, and how bloody marvellous she was!'

'She *was* marvellous,' she said. 'She *was*. *She* should have been here to see all this, not you! She would have understood it all, whereas you—'

'You wish she was here, I suppose,' I spat out rashly, 'instead of me?'

She gazed at me, the tears upon her lashes. I felt my own eyes prickle, and my throat grow thick. 'Nance,' she said, in a gentler tone – but I raised my hand, and turned my face away.

'We agreed it, didn't we?' I said, trying to keep the bitterness from my voice. And then, when she wouldn't answer: 'God knows, there are places I'd sooner be, than here!'

I said it to spite her; but when she rose and moved away from me with her fingers before her eyes, I felt desperately sorry. I put my hand to my pocket for a handkerchief: what I drew out was the programme that Miss Skinner had given me,

drew out was the programme that Miss Skinner had given me, for Flo to sign; I found myself gazing at it, quite bewildered by the sudden turns the afternoon had taken. And all the time, the woman on the platform talked hoarsely on, arguing with the hecklers in the audience – the air seemed clotted with shouts and smoke and bad feeling.

I looked up. Florence was standing near the wall of canvas, beside Annie and Miss Raymond: she was shaking her head, as they leaned to put their hands upon her arm. When Annie drew back I caught her eye, and she walked over and gave me a wary smile.

'You should have learned better than to argue with Florrie,' she said, taking the seat beside me. 'She is about as sharp-tongued as anyone I know.'

'She tells the truth,' I said miserably. 'Which is sharper than anything.' I sighed; then, to change the subject, I asked: 'Have you had a good day, Annie?'

'I have,' she said. 'It has all been rather wonderful.'

'And who is that girl with your Emma?' I nodded to the fair-haired woman at Miss Raymond's side.

'That's Mrs Costello,' she said, 'Emma's widowed sister.'

'Oh!' I had heard of her before, but never expected her to be so young and pretty. 'How handsome she is. What a shame she ain't – like us. Is there no hope of it?'

'None at all, I'm afraid. But she is a lovely girl. Her husband was the kindest man, and Emma says she is just about despairing that she will ever find another to match him. The only men who want to court her turn out to be boxers . . .'

I smiled dully; I was not much bothered about Mrs Costello, really. While Annie talked I kept glancing over to Florence. She now stood at the far side of the tent, a handkerchief gripped between her fingers but her cheeks dry and white. However long and hard I looked at her, she would not meet my gaze.

I had almost decided to make my way over to her, when there came a sudden clamour: the lady on the platform had finished her speech, and the crowd was reluctantly clapping. This meant, of course, that it was time for Ralph's address; Annie and I turned to see him hover uncertainly at the side of the little stage, then stumble up the steps as his name was announced, and take up his place at the front of the platform.

I looked at Annie and grimaced, and she bit her lip. The tent had quietened a little, but not much. Most of the afternoon's serious listeners seemed to have grown tired and left: their seats had been taken by idlers, by yawning women and by more rowdy boys.

Before this careless crowd Ralph now stood and cleared his throat. He had his speech, I saw, in his hand – to refer to, I guessed, if he forgot his lines. His forehead was streaming with sweat; his neck was stiff. I knew he would never be able to project his voice to the back of the tent, with his throat so stiff and tense.

With another cough, he began.

'"Why Socialism?" That is the question I have been invited to discuss with you this afternoon.' Annie and I were sitting in the third row from the front, and even we could hardly hear him; from the mass of men and women behind us there came a cry – 'Speak up!' – and a ripple of laughter. Ralph coughed yet again, and when he next spoke his voice was louder, but also rather hoarse.

'"Why Socialism?" I shall keep my answer rather brief.'

'Thank God for something, then!' called a man at that – as I knew somebody would – and Ralph gazed wildly around the tent for a second, quite distracted. I saw with dismay that he had lost his place, and was forced to glance at the sheets in his hand. There was a horrible silence while he found the spot; when he next spoke, of course, it was into the paper, just as he had used to do in our Quilter Street parlour.

'How many times,' he was saying, 'have you heard economists say that England is the richest nation in the world . . . ?' I found myself reciting it with him, urging him on; but he stumbled, and muttered, and once or twice was forced to tilt his

paper to the light, to read it. By now the crowd had begun to
groan and sigh and shuffle. I saw the chairman, seated at the
back of the platform, making up his mind to step over to him
and tell him to speak up or to stop; I saw Florence, pale and agitated to see her brother so awkward – her own griefs, for the
moment, quite forgotten. Ralph started on a passage of statistics.
'Two hundred years ago,' he read, 'Britain's land and capital
was worth five hundred million pounds; today it is worth . . . it
is worth . . .' He tilted the paper again; but while he did so, a
fellow stood up to shout: 'What are you, man? A socialist or a
schoolmaster?' And at that, Ralph sagged as if he had been
winded. Annie whispered: 'Oh, no! Poor Ralph! I can't bear it!'

'Neither can I,' I said. I jumped to my feet, thrust Cyril at
her, then hurried to the steps at the side of the platform and
ran up them, two at a time. The chairman saw me and half-rose
to block my path, but I waved him back and stepped purposefully over to the sweating, sagging Ralph.

'Oh, Nance,' he said, as close to tears as I had ever seen
him. I took his arm and gripped it tight, and held him in his
place before the crowd. They had grown momentarily silent –
through sheer delight, I think, at seeing me leap, so dramatically, to Ralph's side. Now I took advantage of their hush to
send my voice across their heads in a kind of roar.

'So you don't care for mathematics?' I cried, picking up the
speech where Ralph had let it falter. 'Perhaps it's hard to think
in millions; well, then, let us think in thousands. Let us think
of three hundred thousand. What do you think I am referring
to? The Lord Mayor's salary?' There were titters at that: there
had been a bit of a scandal, a couple of years before, about the
Lord Mayor's wages. Now I gratefully singled out the titterers
and addressed myself to them. 'No, missus,' I said, 'I'm not
talking of pounds, nor even of shillings. I am talking of persons. I am talking of the amount of men, women and children
who are living in the workhouses of London – of London! the
richest city, in the richest country, in the richest empire, in all
the world! at this very moment, as I speak now.'

I went on like this; and the titters grew less. I spoke of all the paupers in the nation; and of all the people who would die in Bethnal Green, that year, in a workhouse bed. 'Shall it be *you* that dies in the poorhouse, sir?' I cried – I found myself adding a few little rhetorical flourishes to the speech, as I went along. 'Shall it be *you*, miss? Or *your* old mother? Or this little boy?' The little boy began to cry.

Then: 'How old are we likely to be, when we die?' I asked. I turned to Ralph – he was gazing at me in undisguised wonder – and called, loudly enough for the crowd to hear, 'What is the average age of death, Mr Banner, amongst the men and women of Bethnal Green?'

He stared at me dumbfounded for a second, then, when I pinched the flesh of his arm, sang out: 'Twenty-nine!' I did not think it was loud enough. 'How old?' I cried – for all the world as if I were a pantomime dame, and Ralph my cross-chat partner – and he called the figure out again, louder than before: '*Twenty-nine!*'

'Nine-and-twenty' I said to the audience. 'What if I were a lady, Mr Banner? What if I lived in Hampstead or – or St John's Wood; lived very comfortably, on my shares in Bryant and May? What is the average age of death amongst such ladies?'

'It is fifty-five,' he said at once. 'Fifty-five! Almost twice as long.' He had remembered the speech and now, at my silent urging, kept on with it, in a voice that was soon almost as strong as my own. 'Because for every one person that dies in the smart parts of the city, four will die in the East End. They will die, many of 'em, of diseases which their smart neighbours know perfectly well how to treat or prevent. Or they will be killed by machines, in their workshops. Or perhaps they will simply die of hunger. Indeed, one or two people will die in London this very night, of pure starvation . . .

'And all this, after two hundred years in which – as all the economists will tell you – Great Britain's wealth has increased twenty times over! All this in the richest city on earth!'

There were some shouts at that, but I waited for them to die

before taking up the speech where he had left it; and when I
did speak at last, I did it quietly, so that people had to lean,
and frown, to hear me. 'Why is this so?' I said. 'Is it because
working people are spendthrifts? Because we would rather
use our money to buy gin and porter, and trips to the music
hall, and tobacco, and on betting, than on meat for our children and bread for ourselves? You will see all these things
written, and hear them said, by rich men. Does that make them
true? Truth is a queer thing, when it comes to rich men talking
about the poor. Only think: if we broke into a rich man's house,
he would call us thieves, and send us to prison. If we set a foot
on his estate, we would be trespassers – he would set his dogs
upon us! If we took some of his gold, we would be pickpock-
ets; if we made him pay us money to get the gold back, we
would be swindlers and con-men!

'But what is the rich man's wealth but robbery, called by
another title? The rich man steals from his competitors; he
steals the land, and puts a wall about it; he steals our health,
our liberty; he steals the fruits of our labour, and obliges us to
buy them back from him! Does he call these things robbery,
and slave-holding, and swindling? No: they are termed *enter-
prise*; and *business skill*; and *capitalism*. They are termed
nature.

'But is it natural, that babies should die for want of milk? Is
it natural, that women should sew skirts and coats long into
the night, in cramped and suffocating workshops? That men
and boys should be killed or crippled to provide the coal upon
your fires? That bakers should be choked, baking your bread?'

My voice had risen as I spoke; and now I bellowed.

'Do you think that's natural? Do you think that's just?'

'No!' came a hundred voices at once. 'No! No!'

'Neither do socialists!' cried Ralph: he had crushed his
speech between his fingers, and now shook it at the crowd.
'We are sick of seeing wealth and property going straight into
the pockets of the idle and the rich! We don't want a *portion* of
that wealth – the bit that the rich man cares, from time to time,

to chuck at us. We want to see society quite transformed! We want to see money put to use, not kept for profit! We want to see working women's babies thriving – and workhouses pulled to the ground, 'cause no one needs 'em!'

There were cheers at that, and he raised his hands. 'You are cheering now,' he said; 'it is rather easy to cheer, perhaps, when the weather is so gay. But you must do more than cheer. You must *act*. Those of you that work – men and women alike – join unions! Those of you that have votes – use 'em! Use 'em to put your own people into parliament. And campaign for your womenfolk – for your sisters and daughters and wives – that they might have votes of their own, to help you!'

'Go home tonight,' I went on, moving forward again, 'and ask yourselves the question that Mr Banner has asked you today: *Why Socialism?* And you will find yourselves obliged to answer it as we have. "Because Britain's people," you will say, "have laboured under the capitalist and the landlord system and grown only poorer and sicker and more miserable and afraid. Because it is not by charity and paltry reforms that we shall improve conditions for the weakest classes – not by taxes, not by electing one capitalist government over another, not even by abolishing the House of Lords! – but by turning over the land, and industry, to the people who work it. Because socialism is the only system for a fair society: a society in which the good things of the world are shared, not amongst the idlers of the world, but amongst the *workers*" – amongst yourselves: you, who have made the rich man rich, and been kept, for your labours, only ill and half-starved!'

There was a second's silence, then a burst of thunderous applause. I looked at Ralph – his cheeks were red, now, and his lashes wet with tears – then seized his hand, and raised it. And then, as the cheers at last died down, I looked at Florence, who had moved to join Annie and Cyril, and was watching me with her fingers at her lips.

Behind us, the chairman approached to shake our hands; and when this was done we made our way off the platform, and were surrounded at once by smiles and congratulations and more applause.

'What a triumph!' Annie called, stepping forward to greet us first. 'Ralph, you were magnificent!'

Ralph blushed. 'It was all Nancy's doing,' he said self-consciously.

Annie smirked, and turned to me. 'Bravo!' she said. 'What a performance! If I had had a flower, I would have thrown it!' She could not say any more, however, for behind her had come an elderly lady, who now pushed forward to catch my eye. It was Mrs Macey, of the Women's Cooperative Guild.

'My dear,' she said, 'I must congratulate you! What a really splendid address! They tell me you were an actress, once . . . ?'

'Do they?' I said. 'Yes, I was.'

'Well, we cannot afford to have such talents in our ranks, you know, and let them lie unused. Do say that you will speak for us another time. One really charismatic speaker can work wonders with an indecisive crowd.'

'I'll gladly speak for you,' I said. 'But you, you know, must write the speech . . .'

'Of course! Of course!' She clasped her hands together and raised her eyes. 'Oh! I foresee rallies and debates, even – who knows? – a lecture tour!' At that, I gazed at her for a second in real alarm; then I felt my attention sought by a figure at my side, and turned to find Emma Raymond's sister, Mrs Costello, looking flushed and excited.

'What a wonderful address!' she said shyly. 'I felt moved almost to tears by it.' Her lovely face was indeed pale and grave, her eyes large and blue and lustrous. I thought again what I had thought before – what a shame it was that she was not a tom . . . But then I remembered what Annie had said about her: how she had lost her gentle husband, and sought another.

'How kind you are,' I said earnestly. 'But, you know, it's really Mr Banner who deserves your praises, for he composed the entire speech himself.' As I said it I reached for Ralph, and pulled him over. 'Ralph,' I said, 'this is Mrs Costello, Miss Raymond's widowed sister. She very much enjoyed your address.'

'I did,' said Mrs Costello. She held out her hand, and Ralph took it, then gazed blinking into her face. 'I have always found the world to be so terribly unjust,' she went on, 'but felt only powerless, before today, to change it . . .'

They still held hands, but had not noticed. I left them to it, and rejoined Annie and Miss Raymond, and Florence. Annie put her hand upon my shoulder.

'A lecture tour, eh?' she said. 'My word!' Then she turned to Flo: 'And how should you like that?'

Florence had not smiled at me since I had stepped from the stage; and she did not smile now. When she spoke at last, her expression was sad and grave and almost bewildered – as if astonished at her own bitterness.

'I should like it very much,' she said, 'if I thought that Nancy really meant her speeches, and wasn't just repeating them like a – like a dam' parrot!'

Annie looked uneasily at Miss Raymond, then said, 'Oh Florrie, for shame . . .' I did not say anything, but gazed hard at Florence for a second, then looked away – my pleasure at the speech, at the shouts of the crowd, all dimmed, and my heart all heavy.

The tent, now, was quiet: there was no speaker on the platform, and people had taken advantage of the break to drift outside into the sunlight and the bustle of the field. Miss Raymond said brightly, 'Let us all sit down, shall we?' As we moved to occupy a row of empty seats, however, a little girl came trotting up, and caught my eye.

'Excuse me, miss,' she said. 'Are you the gal what give the lecture?' I nodded. 'There is a lady just outside the tent, then, says will you please step up and have a word?'

Annie laughed, and raised her eyebrows. 'Another lecture tour offer, perhaps?' she said.

I looked at the girl, and hesitated.

'A lady, you say?'

'Yes, miss,' she said firmly. 'A lady. Dressed real smart, with her eyes all hid behind a hat with a veil on it.'

I gave a start, and looked quickly at Florence. A lady in a veil: there was only one person that could be. Diana must have seen me after all, and watched me give my speech, and now sought me out for – who knew what queer purpose? The idea made me tremble. When the girl stepped away I turned to gaze after her, and Florence shifted in her seat, and stared with me. In the corner of the tent there was a square of sunlight, where the canvas had been tied back to form a doorway – it was so bright I had to narrow my eyes to look at it, and blink. At one edge of the square of light stood a woman, her face concealed, as the girl had said, by a broad hat and a width of net. As I studied her, she lifted her arms to her veil, and raised it. And then I saw her face.

'Why don't you go to her?' I heard Florence say coldly. 'I dare say she has come to ask you back to St John's Wood. You shall never have to think of socialism again, there . . .'

I turned to her; and when she saw how pale my cheeks were, her expression changed.

'It's not Diana,' I whispered. 'Oh, Flo! It's not Diana . . .'

It was Kitty.

I stood for a moment quite dumbfounded. I had seen two old lovers already today; and here was the third of them – or, rather, the first of them: my original love; my one true love – my real love, my best love – the love who had so broken my heart, it seemed never to have fired quite properly again . . .

I went to her, without another glance at Florence, and stood before her and rubbed my eyes against the sun – so that, when I looked at her again, she seemed surrounded by a thousand dancing points of light.

'Nan,' she said, and she smiled, rather nervously. 'You have not forgotten me, I hope?' Her voice shook a little, as it had used to do, sometimes, in passion. Her accent was rather purer, with slightly less colour to it, than I remembered.

'Forgotten you?' I said then, finding my own voice at last. 'No. I'm only so very surprised, to see you.' I gazed at her, and swallowed. Her eyes were as brown as ever, her lashes as dark, her lip as pink . . . But she had changed, I had seen it at once. There were one or two creases beside her mouth and at her brow, that told of the years that had passed since we were sweethearts; and she had let her hair grow, so that it curved above her ears in a great, glossy pompadour. With the creases and the hair she did not look, any more, like the prettiest of boys: she looked, as the girl she had sent to me had said, like a lady.

As I studied her, so she gazed at me. At last she said, 'You seem very different, to when I saw you last . . .'

I shrugged. 'Of course. I was nineteen then. I'm twenty-five, now.'

'Twenty-five in two weeks' time,' she answered; and her lip trembled a little. 'I remembered that, you see.'

I felt myself blush, and could not answer her. She gazed past me, into the tent. 'You can imagine my surprise,' she said then, 'when I looked in there just now, and saw you lecturing from the stage. I never thought you'd end up on a platform in a tent, speaking on workers' rights!'

'Neither did I,' I said. Then I smiled, and so did she. 'Why are you here, at all?' I asked her then.

'I'm in rooms at Bow. Everyone has been saying all week, that I must come to the park on Sunday, since there was to be such a marvellous thing in it.'

'Have they?'

'Oh, yes!'

'And – are you here quite alone, then?'

She glanced quickly away. 'Yes. Walter's in Liverpool just now. He has gone back to managing: he has shares in a hall up there, and has rented a house for us. I'm to join him when the house is ready.'

'And you're still working the halls?'

'Not so much. We . . . we had an act together.'

'I know,' I said. 'I saw you. At the Middlesex.'

Her eyes widened. 'The time that you met Billy-Boy? Oh, Nan, if I had only known that you were watching! When Bill came back and said he'd seen you—'

'I couldn't look at you for long,' I said.

'Were we so bad as that, then?' She smiled, but I shook my head: 'It wasn't that . . .' Her smile grew fainter.

I said, after a moment: 'So you don't work so much? How's that?'

'Well, Walter is kept busy with the managing now. And then – well, we kept it quiet, but I was rather ill.' She hesitated. 'I was to have a child . . .'

The thought was horrible to me, in every way. 'I'm sorry,' I said.

She shrugged. 'Walter was disappointed. We have quite forgotten it now, however. It only means that I am not quite so strong as I once was . . .'

We fell silent. I looked for a second into the crowd, then back at Kitty. She had coloured. Now she said: 'Nan, Bill told me, when he met you that time, that you were dressed – well, as a boy.'

'That's right. I was. Quite as a boy.' She laughed and frowned at once, not understanding.

'He said, too, that you were living with a . . . with a . . .'

'With a lady. I was.'

She blushed still harder. 'And – are you with her still?'

'No, I – I live with a girl now, in Bethnal Green.'

'Oh!'

I hesitated – but then I did what I had done with Zena, two hours before. I moved slightly into the shadow of the tent, and Kitty followed. 'That's her over there,' I said, nodding towards the seats before the platform. 'The girl with the little boy.'

Annie and Miss Raymond had moved away, and Florence sat alone now. As I gestured to her she looked over at me, then gazed gravely at Kitty. Kitty herself gave another little 'Oh,' and then a nervous smile. 'It's Flo,' I said, 'who's the socialist, and who has got me into all this . . .' As I spoke, Florence took off her hat: immediately, Cyril began pulling at the pins that fixed her hair, and twisting the curls about his fingers. His tugs made her redden. I watched her for a little longer, then saw her look again at Kitty; and when I turned to Kitty herself I found that her eyes were upon me and her expression was rather strange.

'I cannot stop myself from gazing at you,' she said, with an uncertain smile. 'When you ran off, I was sure, at first, that you'd be back. Where did you go? What did you do? We tried so hard to find you. And then, when there was no word of you, I was sure that I would never see you again. I thought – oh Nan, I thought that you had harmed yourself.'

I swallowed. '*You* harmed me, Kitty. It was *you* that harmed me.'

'I know it, now. Do you think I don't know it? I feel ashamed to even talk to you. I am so sorry for what happened.'

'You needn't be sorry now,' I said awkwardly. But she went on as if she had not heard me: that she was so very sorry; that what she had done had been so very wrong. That she was sorry, so sorry . . .

At last, I shook my head. 'Oh!' I said. 'What does all that matter now? It matters nothing!'

'Doesn't it?' she said. I felt my heart begin to hammer. When I did not answer, only continued to stare at her, she took a step towards me and began to talk, very fast and low. 'Oh, Nan, so many times I thought about finding you, and planned what I would say when I did. I cannot leave you now without saying it!'

'I don't want to hear it,' I said in sudden terror; I believe I even put my hands to my ears, to try to block out the sound of her murmurs. But she caught at my arm and talked on, into my face.

'You must hear it! You must know. You mustn't think that I did what I did easily, or thoughtlessly. You mustn't think it did not – break my heart.'

'Why did you do it, then?'

'Because I was a fool! Because I thought my life upon the stage was dearer to me than anything. Because I thought that I would be a star. Because, of course, I did not ever think that I would really, really lose you . . .' She hesitated. Outside the tent the bustle of the day went on: children ran shrieking; stall-holders called and argued; flags and pamphlets fluttered in the May breezes. She took a breath. She said: 'Nan, come back to me.'

Come back to me . . . One part of me reached out to her at once, leapt to her like a pin to a magnet; I believe the very same part of me would leap to her again – would go on leaping to her, if she went on asking me, for ever.

Then another part of me remembered, and remembers still.

'Come back to you?' I said. 'With you still Walter's wife?'

'All that means nothing,' she said quickly. 'There's nothing – like that – between him and me now. If we were only a little careful . . .'

'Careful!' I said: the word had made me flinch. 'Careful! Careful! That's all I ever had from you. We were so careful, we might as well have been dead!' I shook myself free of her. 'I have a new girl now, who's not ashamed to be my sweetheart.'

But Kitty came close, and seized my arm again. 'That girl with the baby?' she said, nodding back into the tent. 'You don't love her, I can see it in your face. Not as you loved me. Don't you remember how it was? You were mine, before anyone's; you belong with me. You don't belong with her and her sort, talking all this foolish political stuff. Look at your clothes, how plain and cheap they are! Look at these people all about us: you left Whitstable to get away from people such as this!'

I gazed at her for a second in a kind of stupor; then I did as she urged me, and glanced about the tent – at Annie and Miss Raymond; at Ralph, who was still blinking and blushing into Mrs Costello's face; at Nora and Ruth, who stood beside the platform with some other girls I recognised from the Boy in the Boat. In a chair at the far side of the tent – I had not noticed her before – sat

Zena, her arm looped through that of her broad-shouldered sweetheart; close to them stood a couple of Ralph's union friends – they nodded when they saw me looking, and raised a glass. And in the midst of them all, sat Florence. Her head was still bent to where Cyril clutched at it: he had tugged her hair down to her shoulder, and she had raised her hands to pull his fingers free. She was flushed and smiling; but even as she smiled, she lifted her eyes to mine, and I saw tears in them – perhaps, only from Cyril's grasping – and, behind the tears, a kind of bleakness, that I did not think I'd ever seen in them before.

I could not meet her smile with one of my own. But when I turned again to Kitty, my gaze was level; and my voice, when I spoke, was perfectly steady.

'You're wrong,' I said. 'I belong here, now: these are my people. And as for Florence, my sweetheart, I love her more than I can say; and I never realised it, until this moment.'

She let go of my arm and stepped away as if she had been struck. 'You are saying these things to spite me,' she said breathlessly, 'because you are still hurt.'

I shook my head. 'I'm saying these things because they're true. Good-bye, Kitty.'

'Nan!' she cried, as I made to move away from her. I turned back.

'Don't call me that,' I said pettishly. 'No one calls me that now. It ain't my name, and never was.'

She swallowed, then stepped towards me again and said in a lower, chastened tone: 'Nancy, then. Listen to me: I still have all your things. All the things you left at Stamford Hill.'

'I don't want them,' I said at once. 'Keep them, or throw 'em away: I don't care.'

'There are letters, from your family! Your father came to London, looking for you. Even now, they send me letters, asking if I have heard . . .'

My father! I had had a vision, on seeing Diana, of myself upon a silken bed. Now, more vividly, I saw my father, in the apron that fell to his boots; I saw my mother, and my brother, and Alice. I saw the sea. My eyes began to smart, as if there was salt in them.

'You can send me the letters,' I said thickly: I thought, I'll write, and tell them of Florence. And if they don't care for it – well, at least they'll know that I'm safe, and happy . . .

Now Kitty came nearer, and lowered her voice still further. 'There's the money, too,' she said. 'We have kept it all. Nan, there's almost seven hundred pounds of yours!'

I shook my head: I had forgotten about the money. 'I have nothing to spend it on,' I said simply. But even as I said it, I remembered Zena, whom I had robbed; and I thought again of Florence – I imagined her dropping seven hundred pounds into the charity boxes of East London, coin by coin.

Would that make her love me, more than Lilian?

'You can send me the money, too,' I said to Kitty at last; and I told her my address, and she nodded, and said she'd remember.

We gazed at one another then. Her lips were damp and slightly parted; and she had paled, so that her freckles showed. Involuntarily I thought back to that night at the Canterbury Palace, when I had met her first and learned I loved her, and she had kissed my hand, and called me 'Mermaid', and thought of me as she should not have. Perhaps the same memory had occurred to her, for now she said, 'Is this how it's to end up, then? Won't you let me see you again; you might come and visit . . .'

I shook my head. 'Look at me,' I said. 'Look at my hair. What would your neighbours say, if I came visiting you? You'd be too afraid to walk upon the street with me, in case some feller called out!'

She blushed, and her lashes fluttered. 'You have changed,' she said again; and I answered, simply: 'Yes, Kitty, I have.'

She raised her hands to lower her veil. 'Good-bye,' she said.

I nodded. She turned away; and as I stood and watched her, I found that I was aching slightly, as from a thousand fading bruises . . .

I cannot let you go, I thought, *so easily as that!* While she was still quite near I took a step into the sunshine, and looked about me. Upon the grass beside the tent there was a kind of wreath or bower – part of some display that had come loose and been discarded. There were roses on it: I bent and plucked one, and called to a boy who was standing idly by, handed the flower to him and gave him a penny, and told him what I wanted. Then I moved back into the shadows of the tent, behind the wall of sloping canvas, and watched. The boy ran up to Kitty; I saw her turn at his cry, then stoop to hear his message. He held the rose to her, and pointed back to where I stood, concealed. She turned her face towards me, then took the flower; he raced off at once to spend his coin, but she stood quite still, the rose held before her in her clasped, gloved fingers, her veiled head weaving a little as she tried to pick me out. I don't believe she saw me, but she must have guessed that I was watching, for after a minute she gave a kind of nod in my direction – the slightest, saddest, ghostliest of footlight bows. Then she turned; and soon I lost her to the crowd.

I turned then, too, and headed back into the tent. I saw Zena first, making her way out into the sunshine, and then Ralph and Mrs Costello, walking very slowly side by side. I didn't stop to speak to them; I only smiled, and stepped purposefully towards the row of chairs in which I had left Florence.

But when I reached it, Florence was not there. And when I looked around, I could not see her anywhere.

'Annie,' I called – for she and Miss Raymond had drifted over to join the group of toms beside the platform – 'Annie, where's Flo?'

Annie gazed about the tent, then shrugged. 'She was here a minute ago,' she said. 'I didn't see her leave.' There was only one exit from the tent; she must have passed me while I was gazing after Kitty, too preoccupied to notice her . . .

I felt my heart give a lurch: it seemed to me suddenly that if I didn't find Florence at once, I would lose her for ever. I ran from the tent into the field, and gazed wildly about me. I recognised Mrs Macey in the crowd, and stepped up to her. Had she seen Florence? She had not. I saw Mrs Fryer again: had *she* seen Florence? She thought perhaps she had spotted her a moment before, heading off, with the little boy, towards Bethnal Green . . .

I didn't stop to thank her, but hurried away – shouldering my way through the crush of people, stumbling and cursing and sweating with panic and haste. I passed the *Shafts* stall again – did not turn my head, this time, to see whether Diana was still at it, with her new boy – but only walked steadily onwards, searching for a glimpse of Florence's jacket or glittering hair, or Cyril's sash.

At last I left the thickest crowd behind, and found myself in the western half of the park, near the boating-lake. Here, heedless of the speeches and the debates that were taking place within the tents and around the stalls, boys and girls sat in boats, or swam, shrieking and splashing and larking about. Here, too, there were a number of benches; and on one of them – I almost cried out to see it! – sat Florence, with Cyril a little way before her, dipping his hands and the frill of his skirt into the water of the lake. I stood for a moment to get my breath back, to pull off my hat and wipe at my damp brow and temples; then I walked slowly over.

Cyril saw me first, and waved and shouted. At his cry Florence looked up and met my gaze, and gave a gulp. She had taken the daisy from her lapel, and was turning it between her fingers. I sat beside her, and placed my arm along the back of the bench so that my hand just brushed her shoulder.

'I thought,' I said breathlessly, 'that I had lost you . . .'

She gazed at Cyril. 'I watched you talking with Kitty.'

'Yes.'

'You said – you said she would never come back.' She looked desperately sad.

'I'm sorry, Flo. I'm so sorry! I know it ain't fair, that she did, and Lilian will never . . .'

She turned her head. 'She really came to – ask you back to her?'

I nodded. Then, 'Would you care,' I asked quietly, 'if I went?'

'If you went?' She swallowed. 'I thought you'd gone already. I saw a look upon your face . . .'

'And did you care?' I said again. She gazed at the flower between her fingers.

'I made up my mind to leave the park and go home. There seemed nothing to stay for – not even Eleanor Marx! Then I got as far as here and thought, What would I do at home, with you not there . . . ?' She gave the daisy another twist, and two or three of its petals fell and clung to the wool of her skirt. I looked once about the field, then turned to face her again, and began to speak to her, low and earnestly, as if I were arguing for my life.

'Flo,' I said, 'you were right, what you said before, about that address I gave with Ralph. It wasn't mine, I didn't mean the words – at least, not then, when I said them.' I came to a halt, then put a hand to my head. 'Oh! I feel like I've been repeating other people's speeches all my life. Now, when I want to make a speech of my own, I find I hardly know how.'

'If you are fretting over how to tell me you are leaving—'

'I am fretting,' I said, 'over how to tell you that I love you; over how to say that you are all the world to me; that you and Ralph and Cyril are my family, that I could never leave – even though I was so careless with my own kin.' My voice grew thick; she gazed at me but didn't answer, so I stumbled on. 'Kitty broke my heart – I used to think she'd killed it! I used to think that only she could mend it; and so, for five years I've been wishing she'd come back. For five years I have scarcely let myself think of her, for fear that the thought would drive me mad with grief. Now she has turned up, saying all the things I dreamed she'd say; and I find my heart is mended already, by you. She made me know it. *That* was the look you saw on my face.' I raised a hand to stop a tickling at my cheek, and found tears there. 'Oh, Flo!' I said then. 'Only say – only say you'll let me love you, and be with you; that you'll let me be your sweetheart, and your comrade. I know I'm not Lily—'

'No, you're not Lily,' she said. 'I thought I knew what that meant – but I never did, till I saw you gazing at Kitty and thought I should lose you. I've been missing Lily for so long, it's come to seem that wanting anything must be only another way of wanting her; but oh, how different wanting seemed, when I knew it was you I wanted, only you, only you . . .'

I shifted closer towards her: the paper in my pocket gave a rustle, and I remembered romantic Miss Skinner, and all the friendless girls who Zena had said were mad in love with Flo, at Freemantle House. I opened my mouth to tell her; then thought I wouldn't, just yet – in case she hadn't noticed. Instead, I gazed again about the park, at the crush of gay-faced people, at the tents and stalls, the ribbons and flags and banners: it seemed to me then that it was Florence's passion, and hers alone, that had set the whole park fluttering. I turned back to her, took her hand in mine, crushed the daisy between our fingers and – careless of whether anybody watched or not – I leaned and kissed her.

Cyril still squatted with his frills in the lake. The afternoon sun cast long shadows over the bruised and trampled grass. From the speakers' tent there came a muffled cheer, and a rising ripple of applause.

Acknowledgements

Thanks to everyone who read and commented on the various drafts of *Tipping the Velvet*, in particular Sally O-J, but also Margaretta Jolly, Richard Shimell and Sarah Hopkins. Thanks to Caroline Halliday, Monica Forty, Judith Skinner and Nicole Pohl, all of whom offered encouragement, advice and enthusiasm while I was writing, and afterwards; thanks to Sally Abbey, my editor at Virago, and to Judith Murray, my agent. Thanks, finally, to Laura Gowing, who has taught me many marvellous things about history, and about love. This book is for her.